M000291092

HELL'S HORIZON

RICHARD FOX

&

JONATHAN BRAZEE

Copyright © 2020 Richard Fox & Jonathan Brazee

All rights reserved.

ISBN: 978-0-9914429-5-9

For Craig Martelle, USMC
An officer and a gentleman

Prologue

This war's getting to me. Shouldn't, right? I fought on Hansen's World and managed to get out of that one. Lost a bit of myself there, but I made it. Plenty of boys went home feet first. Why didn't I join them? Just enough luck to make it to the next battlefield. My luck's still holding out.

Fighting on Ayutthaya's nothing like the tundra of Keppler-22 from my last deployment. The jungle . . . we don't have this back home. We'll patrol into the deep canopy, and it'll get dark as night. Yeah, we have optics, but they're made by the lowest bidder and maybe they work, maybe they don't. We'll be in that dark, the smell of rot and mud all around us. Every step and sound we make gives us away to the enemy.

Then there's the big cats. Imagine a tiger and a bear had a bad-tempered cub. Locals call them chayseux, and hunting them used to be big business on the planet before the war. They'll hide up in the branches, drop down, and take a man in full gear. At least, that's what we tell the new recruits. That way they keep an eye to the sky for traps that've been left behind. Couple years of the front line's changing and the smart mines don't act so smart. The attack drones' targeting gets real wonky.

At least there's no orbital bombardment. The navies are up there above this godforsaken planet, but so far, it's just us ground pounders.

But the enemy's bad enough, and he's out there. Always. Most fights are blind shots at wherever we think they are. Sometimes we'll rip the jungle up and find not a damn trace of them. Sometimes we'll find them lying there, waiting for us as they bleed.

I've seen the dead before. I worked the mass graves after the Battle of Bellis when some officer deep in a bunker decided to send a battalion's worth of green recruits against an armor advance. You'd think he wanted those boys to throw themselves into the tracks to slow them down.

But those few times we see proof that we're fighting someone real, that the brass don't have us chasing ghosts in the jungle . . . it's almost worse than when we have to bag up our own.

When a man dies of violence, he don't lay right. Arms and legs at bad angles. Uncomfortable just to look at. It's how the wrist bends that gets me. Like they were reaching to touch God's face at the end, but they lost strength a moment too soon. No one would choose to die like that, but they wouldn't have chosen to go anyway.

We'll find them. Half in, half out of a bush. Maybe on a path with a mess of first aid stuff around them. Guess everyone quit when the kid gave up the ghost or they heard us coming and thought we'd finish them all off in one go.

We don't do that. And don't you believe what the vids tell you either. The war here's bad, but we still got our dignity. Other side will kill us just as quick as we'll kill them, but they don't fight like godless barbarians. Don't let their looks fool you.

After so long in the shit, you'd think my boys and I would start to slip. Nah. We'll go home with our heads high.

When we find them . . . they look just like us. Same nothing in their eyes as our dead. The dead kid at my feet's no different than the new guy just assigned to my squad. Just dressed different. The officers keep telling us they're the enemy, and I guess they are, but when they're dead, I don't see much difference. Just another body whose mother or wife is going to cry over.

That's what it comes down to out here. Kill the other. But every time I find them bled out, or I hear their wounded crying out there in the jungle . . . there's no other. It's me that's dying. Only person I kill in this war is myself.

Like I said. This war's getting to me. Got to prep for the next patrol.

Be—

--Partial document recovered during routine intercept. Belligerent party unknown.

Supreme Union Humanitarian Mission. Ayutthaya Civil War. Day 1,733

Chapter 1

Marines

"Don't get bunched up, Trace. I want to see dispersion."

Captain Mateo Alcazar, Alliance of Democratic Peoples' Marines and Kilo Company commander, ran down the beaten path as he followed the movements of Third Platoon on his CCD, his Command Combat Display. He knew he should hold back, but he was an enlisted grunt before his battlefield commission, and that hands-on approach to combat was too deeply ingrained into his very DNA to lead from the rear. He'd probably get his ass chewed by the battalion CO, but so be it. He wasn't going to stand back and let Third get bunched up where a single Hegemony mortar round could wreak havoc upon them.

He watched as First Lieutenant Trace Okanjo took charge and spread his platoon out. The lieutenant was an Academy grad and a rising star, destined to go far in the Corps, but that didn't mean he didn't need supervision.

At least, that was what Teo told himself as an excuse to get closer to the fight.

Up ahead, he could hear the sounds of combat as First Platoon opened up their base of fire on tiny, abandoned Rawai, hoping to fix the Hegemony infantry in place. Up until a day ago, the destroyed village no longer had any tactical or strategic value, but with the crabs nosing around, Teo couldn't let them get a foothold so close to his company's lines. He had to slap them hard to remind them that even with the peace talks on Phoenix, the war wasn't over yet.

"*Skipper, where're you heading?*" First Sergeant Oak Lippmaa asked over the Person-to-Person.

Teo winced. The first sergeant was his minder—part nanny, part teacher—tasked by the battalion commanding officer and sergeant major to keep the junior officer acting as a commander, not as a sergeant. Teo outranked his first sergeant, but he understood the dynamics involved.

"*Just had to get better positioning,*" he said as he ran forward.

"*And Rios? Why isn't he with you?*"

Because I didn't want him in the line of fire. Or to keep me out of the action.

Big, goofy Rios, married just before the deployment and someone with whom Teo had formed a deep connection in the short time he'd been company commander. Just because Teo was being stupid didn't mean he wanted to put Rios needlessly at risk.

"*He's securing my six,*" Teo said of the sergeant assigned as the one-man security force to keep him safe.

The first sergeant didn't respond, but Teo could picture him reporting up to the CO. He'd been angry when he first realized the first sergeant's real job, but that had long faded. The first sergeant was a good man, and he was just following orders. To Teo he was simply part of the landscape now.

He turned his attention back to his CCD and the battle forming just 200 meters ahead of him. This should be a cakewalk—"should" being the operative word. Marine drones, in a moment of clarity, had spotted a four-man crab team setting up in what was left of the Sawadi Friend Hotel. The drones were lost soon thereafter, but Teo had already sprung into action, using one of his hip-pocket contingency plans in sending First and Third forward, leaving Second and Weapons back at camp. Only this time, there was a difference. The CO had been pushing him to engage the tank section that had just been assigned to Kilo Company. The three MT-49 Badger tanks were waiting just down Provincial Route 3 a klick out, ready to move in as soon as First secured the village.

Staff Sergeant Horatio, the tank section leader, had protested that wasn't the best use of his tanks, and maybe he was right, but Teo didn't think Krabi, with its heavy jungle vegetation and limited roads, was good armor country. He'd decided to keep a tight lid on the armor boys, using them just enough to get the CO off his back.

The lead squad of Third Platoon was approaching their Final Coordination Line, the FCL. It was almost go-time. Out of habit from too many battles, he went through his almost superstitious routine for the third time today. First, he checked the charge on his VP-51, then visually sighted down the barrel and the mag rings. A bent mag ring could render the dart-thrower ineffective. Next, he seated his VW-9 Jonas in its holster. Not many of his Marines carried the crossbow handgun, only those who'd served on anti-pirate patrol. Then, he patted the ornate Eagle Warrior handle of his tecpatl, the modern version of the Aztec knife that his ancient ancestors used to cut the hearts out of their enemies. Next, a quick glance at his Command Combat Display gave him all greens for both his Individual Fighting Uniform and internal nanos. Finally, he punched himself hard in the chest, feeling his IFU's Protective Outer Layer stiffen up, the shear-thickening armor in action.

The five steps weren't just superstition. He was checking his equipment—but he realized there was that superstitious element to it. No matter. Everything was green. He was ready for bear.

Teo pulled up Sergeant Gauta's Individual Combat Display feed and switched to meshed view. It took a moment for Teo's AI to coordinate the sergeant's feed with that of the Marines around him, but after a brief flicker, Teo was looking ahead as if he were there. He could turn his head, and the viewpoint would shift, the view synched by his AI. As long as someone in the squad had visuals, Teo could see what he wanted.

Teo adjusted the feed to 75% opacity, leaving 25% for the real world in front of him. Alone, without Sergeant Rios watching his back, that was bordering on dangerous, but Teo had lots of experience with overlaid displays. He slowed to a walk, putting his personal tactical view on mental autopilot as he focused on what was facing his Marines.

Maybe not enough experience. He grimaced as his shin slammed into a chunk of cerrocrete—his POL's armor needed a stronger, quicker impact to thicken. For a moment, he contemplated adjusting the feed to 66% opacity, but he left it there. He could take bruised shins.

The shell of what had once been a restaurant, pock-marked by battles past, stood just to his left, the jungle already taking it over. This was the visual reference for the FCL and for First Platoon to shift its base of fire. Third Squad, led by Sergeant Gauta, would clear the mostly destroyed buildings on the west side of the main drag while First Squad, led by Sergeant Adoud, would clear the east side. Then both squads would provide security around the objective for Sergeant Win's Second Squad to clear the hotel itself.

Speed was of the essence. Teo had considered an envelopment, but with only four crabs, they probably had orders to withdraw in the face of a Marine reaction, and he didn't want to give them time to escape. Using one squad from First Platoon as a blocking force on the other side of the village was his security blanket to ensure they killed or captured the crabs. Most likely killed. The crabs weren't in the habit of surrendering, much like his own Marines.

The lead team reached the restaurant and crossed the FCL, and Teo had to bite his tongue as First Platoon kept up the base. He was just about to break in when Trace ordered the shift fire.

Almost immediately, the two lead squads rushed forward. It made Teo's heart sing as he watched the choreographed ballet that was MOUT, Military Operations in an Urban Terrain. To call Rawai "urban" might be a stretch, but the techniques were the same had this been an archology holding tens of millions on Lancaster or Nouveau Niue.

The Alliance Marines might lack all the newest military equipment, but no one could deny their training and discipline. This could have been a training demonstration back at The Infantry Warrior School at Camp Woramo, not actual combat, and Teo was filled with pride as two teams from the squad rushed into the first husk of a building, clearing it in seconds before crossing the alley to the rubble of the next.

With the squad breaking into teams, Teo's feed became somewhat more disjointed. He hungered for the thrill of the fight, but duty took over. He couldn't indulge himself. He backed out of the meshed feed, then relegated it to the upper left corner of his CCD. Real life snapped in front of him. He'd been advancing on autopilot and hadn't realized he'd moved as far as he had. Right in front of him was Lieutenant Okanjo and Second Squad. Sergeant Win, the squad leader, swiveled and nodded at Teo before turning back to the front.

Teo held up. He needed to let Okanjo fight this battle.

That didn't mean he wasn't going to listen in, however. His Combat AI was monitoring all comms, ready to alert him based on any of a thousand messages being sent.

That also didn't mean he was going to hang back and out of the fight. If he wanted to do that, he'd have stuck with Rios. So, as Okanjo led his platoon across the FCL, Teo followed in trace.

Teo almost chuckled as he realized what he was doing: following *Trace* in *trace*.

Come on, Mateo! No time for stupid jokes.

Razor Fuentes reported taking fire from the crabs at the objective, which was the plan. Hopefully, that would give Lieutenant Okanjo and his platoon time to get close before the crabs knew he was there.

Probably not. The crabs weren't stupid. But hopefully, there wouldn't be much they could do.

Most of the buildings were shells or rubble, so as Teo watched though the feed, Third Platoon was quickly able to clear them, reaching the objective within six minutes. First and Third Squads surrounded the old hotel's main building while Second moved in for the assault.

Teo stopped short of the objective despite an almost overwhelming desire to be in on the assault. With his back against a chunk of rubble, he switched back to meshed view on his CCD as Second Squad was given the order to kick off the final assault. He couldn't help it. He needed the rush of combat. His display flickered, and he was *inside* the hotel lobby. A blood trail led across the floor to the far wall where a crab sat, his head lolled slackly onto his chest. His weapon at the ready, one of the Marines kicked the crab hard in the chest, knocking him over, but this crab was gone.

Teo's heart pounded as if he were a sergeant again, back in combat instead of merely hitching a ride. He didn't even realize when he drew his tecpatl, so deeply was he immersed in the fight.

Sergeant Win led his Marines across the lobby and to the stairwell. A string of fire reached down, peppering the stairs and sending splinters flying. PFC Ramirez yelped and jumped back out of the line of fire, holding his chest. His avatar didn't pop up light blue on Teo's CCD, so, if he'd been hit, his armor had held.

"Use a Gryphon, Win!" Staff Sergeant Weiss yelled from somewhere behind the squad.

The Gryphon was a small, fire-and-forget anti-armor missile. Made on the independent planet Waterson, they weren't part of the Marine standard issue, but they were available through a parallel supply chain if the Marines paid for the missiles themselves.

Teo started to protest, then held his tongue. He didn't want to waste a Gryphon on clearing a hotel, but then again, he wasn't the one taking fire.

Sergeant Win motioned to Lance Corporal White Horse, who pulled the small tube out of his assault pack and extended it, arming the impeller.

"Impact plus two," Win told White Horse.

Teo nodded. The impact on the ceiling above would start the fuze, and the missile's warhead would detonate two meters after that. The Gryphon wasn't designed as an anti-personnel weapon, but it could sure mess up someone's day.

Sergeant Win pointed to a spot on the ceiling, some ten meters above the deck. White Horse nodded and got ready while the rest of the squad moved closer to the stairwell. The Gryphon was powered by ram-impellers, so there wasn't a backblast to worry about, but there would probably be debris raining down.

"On three," Sergeant Win said. "One . . . two . . . three!"

With a whuff, the little missile shot out of the tube, its fins snapping into place, followed a micro-instant later by a boom as it detonated.

The Marines were already moving, bounding up the wide stairs, peppering the area with fire. Teo's mind was with them, leading the charge, just like in the old days before he was yanked out and commissioned. His body, sitting in the rubble 60 meters away from the hotel, subconsciously swung his 51 around with one hand as if he had a target, his other gripping the handle of his tecpatl.

The lead Marines charged over the top of the stairs. One stumbled and fell, cut down by a crab flanker ten meters away in what looked to have once been a ballroom or conference room, now filled with smoke. The crab was on his knees, looking stunned, but not stunned enough to keep him from fighting.

"*Get him!*" Teo instinctively shouted over the platoon battle net.

His Marines didn't need him for that. Four Marines converged their fire on the crab. A dart hit his hand, making him drop his weapon, and he tried to get up, screaming in defiance before he fell under the Marine's combined onslaught.

Teo shifted his view. The smoke was clearing. Chairs were flung around, and a curtain was flickering with fire as the breeze from outside fed the flame. Another crab body lay still on the deck, one hand pointed up to nothing as if beseeching Valhalla.

A grey avatar blinked on Teo's CCD. He didn't want to look, as if he didn't acknowledge it, it wouldn't be true. But he couldn't ignore facts. Lance Corporal Carl Mooney was dead. He'd just gotten married before the deployment, and Teo had attended the wedding. One more Marine killed under Teo's command, one of the ghosts he'd have to answer to for the rest of his life.

"*All clear,*" Sergeant Win passed. "*Three crabs down. One friendly KIA.*"

"*Roger that,*" Lieutenant Okanjo passed. "*Hold fast, Second. Third, go in and clear the rest of the hotel.*"

Not quite what Teo would have ordered, but it was Okanjo's platoon. Now all that was left was to clear the rest of the village. He wasn't going to attempt to hold it, but maybe this would be a message to the crab commander that he shouldn't try and make inroads like this again.

Sergeant Win walked over to the smoldering curtain and yanked it off the rod. He stomped out the flames, then took a moment to look out what must have once been a huge picture window.

Teo lowered his 51, just now sheepishly aware that he'd been ready to blast away at the bad guys. He was about to switch back to general command mode when Sergeant Win's head and upper chest exploded into a pink mist. Before the rest of the sergeant's body had time to fall, the sound of heavy fire reverberated down the main street.

"*Horatio! Bring your Badgers forward now,*" he ordered even before he'd consciously realized what was happening.

Teo recognized the reports. He switched off of mesh mode and stood, poking his head out from around the chunk of cerrocrete behind which he'd taken cover. From beyond the edge of the village, crabs in their jacks were moving forward and had engaged the blocking force.

"*Staff Sergeant Horatio, respond,*" he ordered again before the flashing yellow triangle on the edge of his CCD caught his attention. Comms were down, jammed. His AI would be frequency hopping to try and break through, but when and if it would be successful was anyone's guess. He had the Quantum Communicators, so he could communicate with the XO, the battalion S-3, and the four platoon commanders, but he didn't have a repeater for the tank section commander. All he could do was hope his initial message got through, or if not, that Staff Sergeant Horatio would realize that the situation had just gone to shit.

Teo ducked his head and ran forward, taking cover behind the burnt-out husk of a car, poking his head up to try and spot the crabs. Bits of a wall 150 meters up the road exploded as it was hit by one of the crabs' cyclers, their 8mm heavy machine gun. The unique *tot-tot-tot* of the nasty weapon was something once heard, never forgotten.

"*Razor, what do you have there?*" Teo asked First Lieutenant Razor Fuentes, his First Platoon commander, over the QC company net.

Costing more than any other piece of company equipment, the quantum-matched sets were essentially jam-proof . . . when they worked. They were notoriously finicky.

"I've lost comms with Sergeant Roy, but we're moving to support him now," the lieutenant passed. *"Are we getting the Badgers?"*

Teo turned around to look down the road. Nothing. He swore under his breath. As a grunt, he didn't completely trust armor, but he wanted them now. One shot from a Badger's 90mm smoothbore, much less the 70mm anti-armor round, and the crabs' vaunted jacks were just so much mangled metal.

He was just about to order Trace to send a runner back when the first Badger coalesced from out of the light rain as it bolted into the village, followed by the next two.

"We've got the Badgers," Teo passed. *"Keep your heads up."*

The fighting from up ahead intensified as Teo crouched behind the wreck. He waited until the first tank almost reached him before he jumped up, waving at it to stop . . . and then had to dive out of the way before the beast ran him over. He ate a faceful of muddy water and came up sputtering.

"Stop!"

But the Badger kept going, firing its first round.

"Son-of-a-bitch!"

The Badger was an adequate chunk of armor, but it was hardly invincible. Made in Waterson as the MT-23, it was a medium tank, light and maneuverable, with the ADP Marines' model being amphibious for up to twenty minutes. The cost of being light was that it could be knocked out, and with their muscles augmented by their jacks, the crabs could carry heavy-enough weapons to do the job.

The second two tanks rushed past, surprisingly quiet with their fuel-cell powerplants, but still making the ground tremble.

Teo stared at them for a moment, then passed, "*Razor, the Badgers are going cowboy. Get Sergeant Roy and his squad out of the Badgers' line of fire.*"

"*Roger that.*"

Up ahead, barely visible in the rain, a crab appeared as he awkwardly ran between two ruined buildings. Almost immediately, the lead tank opened fire, and Teo almost shouted out in excitement. The round hit with a flash, but when the debris settled, Teo couldn't see if the crab had been taken out or not.

Flashes sparkled off of the second tank—it was taking fire. Teo half-expected to see that followed with something more powerful, but the three tanks split up in a smooth move, getting off the road.

"At least they're well-trained," he mumbled to himself.

His CCD flashed for a moment as a free frequency was found, and the frozen forces display jumped ahead before freezing again. Two Marines from Sergeant Roy's squad were the light blue of WIA, but their vitals weren't in the critical range.

Roy had started a bounding overwatch to rejoin the rest of First Platoon, engaging at least a squad of crabs to the north of them.

At least. Maybe more.

Without working drones, Teo didn't have a full picture of what faced him. All he could see was a compilation of what any of his Marines could detect. Unis to doughnuts, if he had eleven of them on his CCD, then there were more out there.

How many more? Do I engage or withdraw?

As a private, and up through sergeant, Teo didn't have to make decisions like this. His job had been to close with and kill the enemy. Period.

He needed to know what he faced, and he couldn't get that sitting on his ass. It was time to move forward. But he hesitated. His VP-51 was in dart mode—which was fine for the crab flankers, but not the best weapon for a jacked crab. There weren't many places where one of the 2mm hypervelocity darts could penetrate. He had the grenade module in his assault pack, which packed a bigger punch, but it had a minimum arming distance, and in among the buildings, he probably would be too close.

No, darts it is.

Teo looked down the road then sprinted across and inside a half-standing shop of some sort—whatever had been in it had either been long destroyed or long looted.

His CCD flashed again as the system momentarily defeated the jamming.

Shit!

From his display, he could see that crabs had bypassed Sergeant Roy and his squad and were now intermixed within his Marines, two of whom were down hard. Lieutenant Fuentes was consolidating the rest of his platoon. The three tanks were separated on the ground, and Teo didn't have a clue if they were coordinated with each other or they were fighting independently.

Okanjo and Third were moving forward, but another twenty-three crabs had now appeared on his CCD.

This wasn't a mere squad.

Teo had to act. His ancient Aztec ancestors didn't have modern comms, yet they conquered Mesoamerica. He didn't need comms to fight, either. It took him a second to create an image of the battle area in his mind, and he knew what he wanted to do.

"*Trace, set up a hasty defense across PL Juniper. Deploy the Switchblades across your frontage, but leave First a way back in. Hold that line. Razor, I'm going to get you some covering fire. Use it to get Roy, then move back and consolidate on Third's left flank. Make the crabs come to you, then take them down.*

"*Harris, fire mission. I want three anti-armor rounds each on . . . targets Robin, Osprey, and Vulture,*" he passed to his Weapons Platoon commander, who he knew had been anxiously waiting for a mission. Rawai no longer had any civilians, so it was weapons free, no need to go up the chain for permission to use their supporting arms.

"*Roger that. Three rounds each on Robin, Osprey, and Vulture. Time of impact . . . forty-three seconds.*"

Teo hoped the nine rockets would be enough to slow down the crabs. The seeker heads on the anti-armor rockets gave them limited smart capability, and a direct hit would take down a jacked trooper. Even near misses, however, should catch their attention, and the rounds would convince the enemy to back off First Platoon's flank, giving them room to maneuver or find better cover.

The rockets swooped in, hitting in rapid succession, and lighting up the village and surrounding jungle. Teo wished he could tie into Roy and his squad, but for the moment, he had to trust his Marines' training.

Hoping to be able to spot the tanks, he moved forward another twenty meters before he realized that with his orders to the two rifle platoons, he was now isolated on the wrong side of the main road. As if listening to his thoughts, one of the Badgers crossed the road fifty meters ahead and disappeared into the buildings. He considered crossing back, but with the tank up ahead, he thought he was secure, at least for the moment. And he was going to take advantage of that.

He bounded forward, dashing from one bit of cover to another, straining to make out what was happening. The intense, continual firing had died out, changing to sporadic bursts of fire from both sides. His CCD flickered again, giving him a new snapshot. First Platoon had retrieved their blocking force and was falling back to link with Third. Two more Marines

19

were WIA. The defense was coming together . . . except for the damned tanks. Two were pushing forward and were well beyond PL Juniper and were approaching PL Pine, which had been their limit of advance. With them back in the fold, Teo was confident that he could withstand anything the crab commander would be willing to throw at them.

The tank on his side of the road, *Blue Ice* stenciled on the bore extractor, a metal hump halfway down the barrel, kept firing. Sergeant Bean, as the tank commander, was hanging back, sending measured round after measured round downrange. If Teo could reach him, maybe Bean could get a hold of Staff Sergeant Horatio.

Teo knew he was exposed, and as the commander, he needed to be with the Marines he was commanding. He had to rejoin them instead of cowboying it like a fool. The CO would be able to track what he did, and the man would be livid. But the *Blue Ice* was just ahead of him, and the colonel was going to go off on him no matter what now. He might as well make the ass-chewing worth it.

He crouched and ran along the back alley. At one time, it might have given him cover, but with most of the buildings destroyed, he felt like the turkey in a turkey shoot. With enough time, he'd low-crawl, making full use of every bit of cover. But, as was often the case, he had no time.

He turned in when he reached the tank . . . but it wasn't there. His CCD disposition of troops display was still frozen, not showing the here and now.

Teo hesitated. He couldn't afford to go wandering around in bad-guy territory, looking for a Badger. He needed to get back to his Marines and lead the defense.

But the Badgers would sure help. If I could only get eyes on . . .

He had to go forward and see if Sergeant Bean could contact Horatio. That hadn't changed.

He pulled up the map of the village, trying to envision where a tanker might move his Badger. There weren't many choices, but right at the village's main intersection might be a good choice. He could move forward another 70 meters or so. If Bean was gone, then he'd abandon the effort and rejoin the rest of the company.

Teo kept low, running around the back of the building, jumping what was a surprisingly intact pig pen, the former resident now a bloated mass of putrefying flesh rising out of the mud. Luckily, his IFU, his Individual Fighting Unit, filtered the air, and he didn't experience the stench that thing must be putting out.

Back against the next wall, he gave the carcass one more look before he started around the next corner . . . and jerked back. A crab was slowly edging toward the main street, using what was left of what the sign said was the best Indian food in Krabi for cover. Even jacked, Teo had read the body language of a soldier moving forward to engage.

He had to act.

Teo didn't trust his 51 against the crab. Killing a jacked crab with the darts was more chance than skill, and at maybe ten meters away, he was too close to switch to grenade mode. For a moment he considered his blade. Within the Marines, there were kills, and then there were *kills*. Long-range kills didn't count as much within Marine culture as those with personal weapons, and those didn't count as much as killing hand-to-hand. Teo had sent many an enemy to his grave, but never with his tecpatl, and the temptation was strong.

He fingered the ornate handle for a brief moment. It might be patterned after the ceremonial knife made of flint, the blade itself was high-tech, made by Okinawan bladesmiths back on Earth itself. He didn't doubt that it could pierce the crab's Cataphract armor.

Stop chasing glory, Mateo! Just kill the son-of-a-bitch.

He knew he had to use his Jonas anti-pirate gun. Normally carried by spaceborne Marines, it was essentially a crossbow without the cross, firing two different bolts: one with an expanding head that would keep it from puncturing the skin of a spacecraft, and another that would pierce through almost anything, to include body armor. The range was short in an atmosphere, but at ten meters, it was deadly.

He gave the indicator a quick check—using the expanding head would only piss the crab off—but he had the armor-piercing bolt in the slot.

His CCD flickered again, and his battleview updated before freezing in place once more.

Hell!

The crab was now on his display, but so was another just around the corner of the restaurant. That made things a little more dicey. He had to take out the crab without alerting the next one. The Jonas was silent, but dying soldiers rarely went quietly into the night. He had to get a quick kill.

He never considered withdrawing. His mental targeting was locked on, and the only acceptable outcome was a dead crab.

The sound of a shod foot knocking rubble away was the trigger. He had to move now before the two crabs hooked up and engaged his Marines with enfilade fire. With one smooth movement, Teo swung around the corner, bringing his anti-pirate gun to bear. His target was the back of the crab's helmet, and at this range, it was impossible to miss. With a click, the bolt flew forward, hitting the back of the helmet, almost tearing it off, and sending the crab to his knees. Teo was already rushing forward as his Jonas cycled the next bolt and the retention spring returned to the ready position, something that took a long second-and-a-half.

The bolt had destroyed the crab's helmet, and blood splattered from his head, but he wasn't dead. The helmet must have been able to deflect the bolt, a miraculous escape from the crab's point of view.

But a short-lived miracle.

The crab started to raise one hand to his head when Teo kicked him in the ass and knocked him down, brought the muzzle of his Jonas up to the back of the crab's head, and fired. The bolt passed through his skull as the crab collapsed.

Teo didn't stop to admire his kill. There was still the other crab indicated on his frozen display. Back against the restaurant wall, he edged forward until he reached the corner, then spun around, Jonas at the ready . . . but there was no one there, and now he was exposed. Teo jumped back.

His CCD might have picked up a ghost, but more likely, there was another crab nearby, and he was pretty vulnerable on his own. Across the main road and just behind was the rest of the company, where he should be.

But he still needed the tanks. That hadn't changed. And that last update showed that Sergeant Bean was just two alleys over.

He might still be there, he might not, but Teo had to find out. If he could only get a better picture of what was happening around him. Looking at his display, he had an idea . . . if it was still standing. With one last look at the dead soldier, his kill, he sidled to the back of the restaurant, then peeked around the corner.

Just ahead, visible over the next ruined shop, the sat tower still stood, canted, but surprisingly upright. If he could climb that, he might be able to get a better picture of the Area of Operations, where the crabs were, and what they were doing. And what his wayward tanks were doing.

That excuse wasn't going to hold up with the CO, but Teo let it be enough for him. The tower was wide enough to protect a single person from fire from the front, and it would only take a few moments of time.

He holstered his Jonas, brought up his 51, and poked his head around the edge of the building before darting across the small alley to the next one. He hit it with his back and froze for a second, waiting to see if he'd been spotted. The sounds of battle filled the village, but nothing seemed directed at him. He gave a quick glance around the next corner. It was clear. Teo took a moment to check his 51, wondering if he should switch to grenade mode, but nothing had changed about minimum arming range, and he was more likely to run into a flanker than a jacked crab.

Time to go, Mateo!

He bolted around the corner . . . and a crab was right in front of him, 15 meters away. Teo fired on instinct, darts blasting around the crab as the enemy jumped forward and out of the line of fire. Teo jerked back out of sight, behind the building.

Shit!

If the crab had been looking in his direction, he'd have been a dead man.

What now?

Teo could hear the creak of road wheels. The *Blue Ice* was near, but so was the crab. He could withdraw and rejoin the rest of the company, and that was the text-book answer. But Marine infantry were embedded with the need to protect armor.

He knew what he was going to do and a smile spread across his face. He drew his knife and moved into the attack.

Chapter 2

Paladins

Major Richter of the Hegemony Army flinched as a bullet burst through the wall right next to his head. Cerrocrete fragments spattered his face shield, and dust caked against the rain-wet lenses. He ducked and spun into the wall as the Alliance Marine kept firing, punching more holes in the wall, each another stab at Richter.

He ran in a crouch toward a metal door on the alley side of a small building, his optics sputtering as they vibrated to dislodge the dust coating. A round cracked past his head as he lowered the armored pauldron on one shoulder and bashed through the door, losing his footing. He fell forward, twisting to land on his armor and spare the cycler rifle held by the augmented frame in his other hand.

A puddle exploded as he landed and slid forward. He rolled to his back and fired a burst through the broken doorway. The jack frames down his back around the outside of his legs stiffened up, programmed to brace his body every time he used the heavy-caliber weapon—vital for accurate fire when he was on his feet. On his back, he felt like a turtle with broken legs.

"Briem? Kontos? Report, damn you," Richter sent over the infrared broadcasting system built into his helmet. He rolled hard to his left and used the frame down his gun arm to push off against the floor to shift the forward weight of his armor up and over. The ballistic plates bolted to his frame gave him the look of a medieval knight, but the protection cost him maneuverability.

The company net holo on the inside of his optics blinked several times; the IR had no connection through the rain and humidity.

Richter grabbed a moldy reception desk and shoved it at the doorway. Putting a boot to the edge, he used his frame to augment his strength and kicked it into the opening, where it buckled. Not much of an obstacle, but it would slow down any Marine trying to charge in after him.

His IR crackled and he tapped the receiver built into the side of his helmet, just as a squeal rose in the air, the squeak of treads over wet asphalt roads. He looked through a broken window and saw an Alliance Badger come around a corner, the double-barreled turret scanning from side to side.

"Ah ... shit." Richter gripped the ammo belt connected to his cycler, a band around his wrist pulsed, and the breach released the feed. Slotting the lead round into a port on his forearm, he reached back to a drum on his left hip and slapped a magazine loaded with armor-piercing rounds into the weapon. A tremor went up his arm as a round locked into the breach.

The Badger's turret froze then traversed to point straight at him.

Richter dove forward as a main gun shell blew through the building. The blast wave slapped him into the wall as it collapsed, and he exploded through in a shower of mortar and dust. He landed hard, the armor plating knocking the air out of his lungs before his frame could compensate for the landing.

He kept rolling with the momentum and thrust out a foot to dig into a wet, overgrown yard, stopping him. The Badger was a dozen yards ahead of him, the turret still trained on the building from which he'd been ejected. Richter laid his aiming reticle on the vision blocks on the driver's hatch and opened fire.

The antitank rounds were self-contained sabot shell, designed to impart a tungsten bolt with tremendous velocity. Even with his jack's frame to compensate, each shot kicked like a mule.

His rounds sparked off the Badger's hull, but two struck the vision blocks, sending spider-web cracks through the thick ballistics glass. He shifted his fire up and blew a small sensor dome mounted on top of the turret into fragments. He didn't have the firepower to destroy the tank, but at least he could make the crew's job harder.

If he had a Spike antitank grenade, this fight would already be over, but the expensive, rare hand-thrown weapons with their explosively formed tungsten lances were all with his flanker troops, none of whom were near enough to help him.

The tank's barrels slewed toward him and Richter lurched to one side, lowering his aim. Firing from the hip, he ran for a low, blown-out wall. He emptied the rest of the magazine into the forward tread, breaking the links between the flat sections. The tread dropped off the road wheel like a drawbridge.

A bullet struck the back of his pauldron and knocked him off-balance. Instead of bounding over the low wall like he planned, his shin struck hard, and he went head over heels forward. He got a brief glimpse of the deep shell hole on the other side before he went tumbling down the side. Mud smeared across his visor and filled his mouth as he splashed into water and sank.

Richter felt panic at the back of his mind as he thrashed around. The Hegemony's Cataphract armor was an advanced, lethal battlefield weapon system, but a jacked trooper could not swim. Grasping a rock with one hand, he pulled his head and shoulders out of the water.

A bloated corpse of a dead pig floated right in front of him, pus and maggots seeping through torn skin. Richter had to swallow the water in the back of his mouth, and he got to his feet, the dark, fetid pool coming up just over his knees. Shaking his cycler hard to dislodge mud and water, he felt a sticky warmth drain down the body glove within his jack.

The empty magazine fell out of his rifle with a chop from his hand, and he reloaded the weapon with the antipersonnel ammo belt feeding into another magazine on his back.

"Any Paladin element, this is Richter." He looked up the slope of the crater to the gray sky as the *chunk-chunk-chunk* sound of the enemy tank rolling off its broken tread sounded through the pouring rain. "Requesting backup."

The sound of the tank grew louder, and its forward edge poked over the lip, the soil buckling slightly beneath the weight, sending twin falls of mud and water down into the pool. Richter looked around the shell hole. The walls were steep and slick—no way he could get out quick or easy.

The dead pig bumped against his leg.

"Paladins, fall back to rally point alpha," he said as he cranked his IR up to maximum power, having no faith the signal could reach anyone. He switched to radio, knowing that any broadcast would be traced within seconds.

The Badger sank a bit deeper into the mud, almost aiming the turret level with him. He had to give credit to the crew's tenacity.

Richter repeated his message through radio frequencies and brought his cycler up to his shoulder, firing single shots at the auxiliary sensor nodes. Between rounds, he heard the tank load a shell into the breach.

This is how it ends, he thought. *What a grave.*

A rocket slammed into the back of the tank, and it tipped forward, smoke billowing out of the back as it slid down the crater straight toward Richter. He sloughed through the water as the twin turrets struck the bottom and bent like plastic straws. The ammo compartments on the back of the tank began cooking off, sending brief showers of sparks and dull thuds as warheads exploded.

Richter used the side of the tank to haul himself up and out of the crater as explosions grew faster. The top hatch clanged against the hull as the crew tried to escape, and Richter reached up and grabbed a hunk of concrete still firm in the foundation of nearby building. He pulled his chest up and over the edge as screaming began behind him.

The tank crew was burning alive.

The major swung his legs up and out as the last of the shells went off. Fire and metal fragments shotgunned out of the crater, and another blast wave slapped against his body, pushing him into a roll. He came to a stop against a wall, chest heaving as he tried to regain his bearings.

The turret slammed into the ground a few yards away, licks of flame dancing as they died in the rain.

Pressing his back to the wall, Richter used it as a brace to stand back up. He checked his cycler for damage and the comms overlay on his visor blinked. Another of his troopers had connected to his IR.

A shadow cast across the edge of a wall between him and the burning turret.

"Park," said Richter, giving his company's battlefield challenge. If the other man didn't respond with "dog" in the next heartbeat, he'd know it was an enemy.

He swung his cycler up as a Marine vaulted over the top of the wall. The Marine's active camo swirled with grays of the wall and green of the nearby jungle as he dropped onto Richter and knocked his weapon aside.

Richter bashed his shoulder into the Marine, and the other man thudded into the wall. The metal on the back of his close-fitting helmet whacked against the bricks, the padding absorbing most of the impact. The Marine came right back at Richter, slashing an almost ornate knife up and cutting through Richter's beard, nicking his jawline.

When the Marine reversed his grip on the knife, Richter saw an eagle warrior carved into the base of the hilt. That he was almost killed by a blade modeled off something so primitive almost struck him as absurd. A Hegemony officer in a full jack frame killed by some savage with an obsidian knife?

Ignoring the sharp pain, Richter opened fire, shooting into the ground and wall as he brought the muzzle up to his enemy with his jack's help. The Marine jumped forward and into the sweep of the cycler before it could hit him, stabbing his knife into Richter's breastplate. The armor turned the blade, and the Marine's arm shot around Richter's side.

Richter pinned the Marine's arm to his body and held him as he hauled them both backwards, twisting as they fell. He landed on top of the Marine with his entire weight—enough force to crack the bones of a normal man. The Marine's body armor stiffened against the impact and Richter slid off.

Grasping the ammo belt, the Marine ripped the links apart as Richter struggled to get space between the two of them. Richter raised his cycler up and fired, but the Marine kicked the weapon to one side as the last two bullets shot out, missing him.

Richter grabbed the barrel with his other hand and shoved the cycler at the Marine's chest. The enemy took the hit on the outside of one arm, then stabbed at Richter's face with his knife. The blade hit above the vision slit, gouging the metal.

Richter grabbed the front of the Marine's uniform and jerked him close as he slammed his head forward. His helmet connected with the Marine's faceplate, making his knees give out.

Richter kicked forward and missed. The Marine swept one hand across the ground and flung a handful of mud up at Richter's head.

The trooper backpedaled, sputtering and cursing, as he brought a hand up and hit the emergency release. The helmet popped off and he saw the Marine draw from a thigh holster a long-barreled pistol, one of their specialist weapons, a bolt-thrower that packed enough of a punch to defeat his jack's plates.

Richter ducked his exposed head behind his armored pauldron as a bolt struck the plate and punched through, stopping inches from his face. Dropping his cycler, Richter drew his own pistol. He swung the pauldron up to one side, keeping half his face protected . . . but the Marine was gone.

Cycler fire sounded nearby, and a squad of Cataphracts raced toward him.

"Sir!" Lieutenant Briem called out, firing a burst past Richter and shuffling against the wall. "Got your radio signal."

"'Bout God damn time." Richter swiped a hand across his cut chin, noting a little blood, and slapped his helmet back on. The holo overlays within came alive with a map showing all his nearby troopers.

"Think that pattie got away." The lieutenant turned his head to one side and mumbled orders to his platoon. "Tank didn't. There's that."

"There's that." Richter glanced into the crater at the smoking hull. One Alliance soldier had made it out, and his charred body bobbed up and down in the water. "Who got the hit?"

"Ozol," Briem said. "I don't think he'll ever shut up about it either."

"He's earned his spurs. Finally." Richter paused as a coded message hit his system. "Squadron commander's ordering us back to our lines. No air support available."

"Figures." Briem glanced at the sky. "Can't expect them to fly through anything but perfect weather, can we?"

"Tanks," Richter said. "The patties commit tanks to a fight and you'd think the pilots would be all over the chance to do some plinking. Paladins!" he said as he reached to his back and removed a mud-caked cylinder. "Active seeking, three minutes!"

He twisted the base of the cylinder and two lights lit up on the side. He pulled the base out until it clicked three times, then tossed it toward the direction the Marine had retreated. Cataphract troopers repeated the order up and down the line and threw out their own cylinders.

The Benedict-37 Smart Mines hit the ground and the shells broke apart and reformed into tiny legs for the weapons. They crawled like crabs over broken walls, each communicating with each other to identify likely dismounted avenues of approach and then burrow into rubble or dig into mud.

An icon pinged inside Richter's HUD. The minefield would lock on to and swarm any enemy that tried to follow them. The smart mines would stay active for hours, then self-destruct. At least, that was how they were designed. The 37s used across Ayutthaya had a reputation for being buggy.

"Emplaced, fall back." Richter slapped Briem on the shoulder and ran down a sidewalk, his jack's servos stiff with mud and grit, a dull pain rising along his jawline.

A red-cross holo hovered over a nearby building and he went inside. Flankers, Hegemony troopers who fought in lighter armor with no jack support and carried smaller carbines, guarded a perimeter around the roofless building with a mortar tube at the center. A robot stood against a wall where a medic knelt over a pair of downed Cataphracts.

Richter went to the medic, who had his helmet off and carbine slung over his back. His kit was open, but Richter noted that the contents were undisturbed.

Both Cataphracts' armor were facedown, but the troopers within had been flipped over. One—dead eyes staring at the sky, unmoved by the patter of rain—had a scruffy beard and small triangles tattooed over one brow. The other didn't have much face left.

"Parn. Cengic." The medic flopped the back of his hand against his knee. "Both flatlined before I could reach them. I pulled their chips. Winnie's got their gear."

"Unit at eighty-seven percent load capacity," the robot chimed.

"Fucking patties," the medic said, shaking his head. "You get some, sir?"

"Kill tally's still on our side, Shala." Richter put a hand to the man's shoulder. "Let's get them back for the deacon."

Shala stood and canted his head to one side, examining the cut on the major's chin.

"It's nothing." Richter crossed himself then beat a knuckle against his chest twice, the metal ringing, as the faint chime of other Cataphracts doing the same echoed through the space. He grabbed a carry handle on one of the dead trooper's armor as Briem grabbed the man's feet, and they lifted the body up.

"Flankers out," Richter said. "Armor close. Orders are to return to base. Heads on swivels. I don't want to carry anyone else."

He waited a moment as another pair of Cataphracts picked up their comrade, then began the trek back. His jack carried most of the weight, but his mind was heavy with nearly dying in that shell hole and the fight with the Marine.

Death had taken notice of him before, but today was not his day to die.

More time to kill Alliance, he thought. *That one with the eagle warrior knife is still out there. I'll find him again.*

Chapter 3

Marines

"What in the hell were you thinking, Captain?" Lieutenant Colonel Nicholas Khan III shouted loud enough over the vidcomms so that the rest of Teo's small command group could hear. *"You think Badgers are expendable?"*

Teo took two deep breaths, trying to control his breathing. Around him, the XO, gunny, and console operator were studiously looking at anywhere else but at him.

"Staff Sergeant Horatio took it upon himself to move beyond the LOD against my orde—"

"You're blaming Horatio? From what I see, his actions were all that kept you from being overrun, Captain. Christ-on-a-stick, you'd blame your grandmother for your fuck-ups, wouldn't you?"

Teo closed his eyes and counted to five, tuning out the battalion CO for a moment. It was Horatio's direct disobedience of orders that cost him and Lance Corporal Glynn their lives, trying to be the hero and wiping out the retreating crabs. The company's mission had already been a success as far as his commander's intent. They'd ejected the crabs from Rawai and beat back the counterattack. Chasing them served no tactical purpose.

" . . . your fault for not controlling your tanks," the CO continued.

That hit closer to home. Yes, Horatio didn't follow the operations order, but as the commander on the ground, everything that happened, for good or bad, fell on Teo's shoulders. He'd quickly realized what kind of Marine Horatio was, and he'd feared the acting section leader would cowboy it chasing glory, but he'd still given the Marine too much leash.

"*We were without comms—*"

"*We're always without comms. It's up to you to adapt. God, you're useless. If it wasn't for . . .*" the CO started before trailing off, realizing he was treading on dangerous ground.

Teo wasn't going to let him off, however. He wasn't completely powerless in their dynamic, their respective ranks notwithstanding.

"*. . . the fact that the Secretary Prime herself placed the People's Order of the Alliance around my neck, in front of all the media and the entire Alliance? Is that what you were going to say, sir?*" he snapped.

Teo was out of line, and he knew it. But at the moment, he didn't care. He'd been uncomfortable with his fifteen minutes of fame, and he felt like a fraud wearing the POA, but it did give him ammunition—and a good Marine never wastes ammo.

There was dead silence over the net, and for a moment, Teo wondered if the crabs had managed to find a way to jam QM comms.

"*You're out of line, Captain. Way out of line,*" the CO said quietly, but with venom dripping from his voice. "*I don't care what the fuck medal you wear, I'm still your commanding officer, and I own you. I own your entire company, and I'm not going to let some jumped-up captain get my Marines killed. You can call the Secretary Prime and tell her I said that, but I am still your commanding officer. Got that, Captain?*"

Teo stood there. Across the tiny CP, built into what was once the Tradewinds Resort's main swimming pool, Gunny Walters risked a quick glance at him before riveting his eyes back to his pad.

The CO was right—both on Teo being out-of-line and the fact that his medal meant jack-shit out here in the field. He just didn't want to admit it.

"*I said, got that, Captain?*" the colonel repeated.

"*Yes, sir,*" Teo said through gritted teeth.

The pause stretched out into eternity, but finally, sensing victory, the CO said, "*You've used up all your mulligans, Captain. You screw up again and you're relieved, no matter what the brass says.*

"*I'm going to leave Corporal Tennyson with you for now, but try not to get him killed.*"

Great. One Badger. What the hell am I going to do with that?

A tank platoon was two sections of two tanks each. With one tank deadlined and the platoon commander pulled for some battalion staff job, only three had arrived, and now two of them were destroyed. Tanks didn't like to work alone without their mutual support, and now he had only one.

He was just going to have to figure out how to use a lone Badger with a corporal as the tank commander.

"*Aye-aye, sir.*"

"*Six, out,*" the CO said, cutting the connection.

Teo could feel the eyes burning into him, but he refused to meet them. He should have climbed out of the CP and sought some privacy, but what was done was done.

"Screw him," he muttered under his breath.

His medal and subsequent promotion had been fodder for the masses, to show them that even a barrio bum from Safe Harbor could make it. As one of only nineteen living POA awardees, he'd been feted, promoted, then left for the wolves when his usefulness was over. The colonel had been afraid of the Secretary Prime? Ha! She'd long ago forgotten him, a tool used and discarded. Sure, the brass wanted him, if not to succeed, then to simply survive. No bad press coming after the fact.

Down in the trenches, it was another story. Most of the other officers respected him for what he'd achieved on Rather's World, where the then Sergeant Alcazar had saved what was left of his recon company and beaten back the Royalist assault. But he wasn't part of the officer brotherhood. He didn't have a uni degree, and his tastes tended more to grubby, back-alley bars than the Officers' Club.

As a butterbar, Teo had been a bright and shiny new toy, with the press following his first officer assignment, but that had gotten stale quickly, and by the time he'd made captain, he was old news. Now he knew he was considered a token commander by many of his peers. Probably a couple of his lieutenants as well.

Why the hell did I ever accept the commission? he asked himself for the thousandth time.

He could have stayed in recon, made gunny, and ignored politics, then retired to drink beer and tell war stories at the local VGW with all the other liars and drunks.

He looked at the empty holster on his field desk, and that got him even angrier. He'd lost his Jonas bolt-pistol after the *Blue Ice* had exploded and sometime during the fight with the crab. He wasn't going to be able to get that replaced unless he was on anti-pirate patrol again, something unlikely once he got promoted. If he got promoted. And the crab had gotten away, to boot.

A rush of water interrupted his pity party, crashing to the ground and making Gunny Walters swear and jump as he was drenched.

"Fuck! Wainsett! Go tack down the tarp!" he yelled.

"No! I've got it," Teo said.

He needed to get out of the CP, and maybe the rain would cool him down.

"You sure, Skipper? Corporal Wainsett can take care of it."

"I'm sure. Just start bailing."

Teo crossed to the shallow end of the pool and pushed up the door, emerging into the rain. Putting his CP in the old pool had seemed like a good idea at the time. Build some overhead cover, and being below ground level, it rendered the CP as one of the safest places in the company area. But as if drawn by some supernatural power, the empty pool seemed to suck in all the water in the vicinity, and without a working pump, it all settled in the pool's deep end. The first few weeks were great, but with the arrival of the rainy season, he felt more amphibian than human.

The tarp stretched out over the beams that provided the cover from indirect fire provided camouflage (not that he doubted that the crabs knew where the CP was) and was waterproof, but it had a habit of breaking free of the tacks, dropping water into the CP.

And yes, as he walked to the other side, he could see a portion of the tarp had ripped free. Without the weight of water, however, he was able to stretch it back out, then jam it down on top of the stake pounded into the ground.

"It's probably not going to hold. I need something more," he pondered. "Maybe try a Q-rod?"

But that wasn't his job. As a commander, he had to . . . well, command, not use his time to construct the camp.

He looked back to the horizontal door that led down into the CP. At the moment, though, he had no desire to sit there, watching nothing.

"Screw it," he said. "I might as well do something useful instead."

Whistling a tune, he headed through the rain for the supply shed to grab some tools and a Q-rod. He was going to fix that damned tarp.

Chapter 4

Paladins

Landing struts smacked against tarmac, and hot air seeped into the shuttle's hold. Dozens within caught their breath at their first taste of Ayutthayan atmosphere which sent them sweating as the heavy, wet air enveloped them.

Four rows of soldiers inside a cramped shuttle struggled out of their seats at the crew member's command. Overstuffed bags rustled against each other as Private First Class Szabo double-checked the name tag on the duffle between his knees. Not that his gear had been out of arm's reach since the shuttle'd come in from orbit, but his heart raced as the mugginess grew even worse.

The crewman kicked a release rod, and the ramp cracked open, letting in a gust of humid air that smelled of burnt tires. Szabo blinked hard as more light broke into the shuttle. Whispers rose from the rest of the cohort around him as they made their way down to the spaceport. Several layers of tall fencing cut off the surrounding jungle, security drones formed dotted lines in the air, and a chain gun with a massive drum was cocked and aimed to the sky. Quonset huts and larger hangars bordered the landing pads.

"Get your shit and form an orderly line off my shuttle!" The crewman waved an arm up and down then pointed at a robot at the bottom with yellow bands around its head, limbs, and torso. "Stay with the guide bot and do *not* go near the fences! None of you are strapped, and if you set off a Bennie because you're stupid, the Hegemony *will* dock your pay. Welcome to hell."

He kicked the duffle of the nearest soldier and swore at her until she started down the ramp, practically waddling under the weight of the bag on her back and another clutched in her arms.

"It supposed to be this hot?" asked a man in front of Szabo as they shuffled forward.

"Least it's not a dry heat," another said with a smirk. "Humidity cuts down on the chaffing, doesn't it?"

"You do not need your mouth to walk!" the crewman shouted. "My big, beautiful shuttle is a prime target for pattie Switchblades while you cherries are on it. Fucking. Move!"

At the bottom of the ramp, Szabo glanced back at the cargo bay to see how many more were still behind him. One of the pilots, her vac suit unzipped at the shoulder and neural bridge helmet tucked under an arm, looked up at a gash along the fuselage. Tiny silver pockmarks scarred the aft section, damage Szabo didn't remember seeing when he'd loaded up less than two hours ago.

When fresh sweat broke across his bow, he slapped a thigh pocket where his cap was, but no one else on the flight line was wearing theirs.

A Hornet jump jet idled a few dozen yards away as robots fixed rocket pods to the undercarriage, the VTOL engines rotating as they went through pre-flight checks. Crudely painted, white tick marks gave a tally just beneath the cockpit.

"Knew I should've done better in school," said the soldier in front of him. "Could be flying one of those. Nope. Infantry."

One engine on the jump jet twisted perpendicular to the flight line, and a blast of hot wind almost sent Szabo tumbling.

"Fucker did that on purpose," someone said.

"Shut up and follow the damn robot," came from behind.

Szabo's mouth went dry and his stomach roiled. How could there be a war in someplace so miserable? His drill sergeant had constantly harped on how different the "real army" would be from the training base, but the jungle and the shock of Port Tarl were leagues apart from the mountains of Essach where he'd finished basic training.

The robot led them into a hangar devoid of aircraft or heavy machinery. Several desks were set up with numbered stations, each manned by a bored-looking soldier.

"Fall in, mind your gear," a Navy petty officer hollered as they filed into the room, each soldier moving to a painted square on the ground and dropping their kit.

A holo formed in the air overhead, and the soldiers went to attention and saluted as the Hegemony crest appeared. A static-laden video of a female colonel played.

"Welcome to Port Tarl and Ayutthaya," she said, giving a very un-colonel-like smile. "Your duty to the Hegemony continues as we fight to protect the human rights and sovereignty of the true Ayutthayan Kingdom. This marks the—" the holo scrambled as new dialogue overplayed what had been originally recorded "—third—year of Hegemony support, and our victory is both assured and very close. You will now be in-processed and given follow-on duty assignments. And remember, we are all greater together."

"We are all greater together," the soldiers intoned.

"Wait for your name and station to be called!" the petty officer said, wiping a cloth over his brow. "Have your ID pip ready. Longer we're out here, the longer we're a target."

Szabo touched his left forearm and pulled his sleeve up to the elbow. A ruby-red dot the size of a fingernail twinkled.

"Move, move," said a tall soldier in faded fatigues as he pushed his way through the formation. His face was hard, his eyes flecks of granite, and swaths of gray cut through short, dark hair and a beard that almost touched the base of his neck. He bore a first sergeant's rank cuff on one arm and carried a sheet of paper with a picture and tight text on it. His name tape read MOLENAAR.

The first sergeant did a double take at Szabo, then glanced at the paper.

"This you?" he held up Szabo's year-old Indoctrination Day picture, when he still had a fair amount of baby fat on him.

"Yes, Drill—I mean First Sergeant," Szabo almost squeaked with the error.

"Get your shit. Follow me." Molenaar tipped his head to one side.

"But don't I—"

The older soldier gave him a steely glance, and Szabo shut up. He picked his gear up by the handles and waddled after Molenaar out of the formation and around a small partition covered with announcement and motivational posters tacked to it.

A warrant officer stood beside a desk, sipping coffee in the too-hot and humid air. He wore a bio-monocle, and rings of text moved along the edge.

"This one," Molenaar handed over the paperwork. "Don't dick around with me, Torgerson."

"The dash-charlie?" Torgerson frowned. "He's already got a by-name request on file."

"Then *un*-file it," Molenaar said, touching a bulge within a thigh pocket.

"Sorry, sir, First Sergeant, should I wait—"

Torgerson shushed Szabo and adjusted his monocle.

"This is a bit above and beyond," the warrant officer said, "even for me."

"You want more, then?" Molenaar reached into a pocket and set a bottle wrapped in a threadbare towel on the desk. "Because I can get you more."

"Two." Torgerson removed a stylus from a small sheath on his sleeve and touched the tip to Szabo's ID pip, then he raised the pen and tapped at a holo interface only he could see. "I know you're good for it, and let Richter know we're even."

"The major will tell you when the scales are balanced," Molenaar said. "You got this one in the system yet?" He pulled a beat-up slate out of a deltoid pocket. "OK, he's on my books. Pleasure."

Torgerson unwrapped the towel from a glass bottle of amber liquid with a label Szabo couldn't read.

"Pleasure as always. Now I suggest you *kung tao* before someone else wants to make a bargain," the warrant officer said as he placed the bottle in his desk.

"I'm confused," Szabo said.

"Get your shit and follow me, trooper. I'm your new first sergeant, and I'll explain on the way." Molenaar picked up one of the bags and hurried out a side door, Szabo following quickly after him.

Outside was an alley between hangars and a cargo truck with the rear gate down. Two bare-chested troopers—their uniform tops draped over the gate—perked up as Molenaar heaved the bag up and into the mostly full bed.

"This the cherry?" one of them asked, tired-looking and bald with a poor attempt at growing a beard.

"He's the cherry. You're his battle buddy until we get him strapped." Molenaar pointed at Szabo with a knife hand then at the back of the truck. "Get comfortable," he said as he went to the cab.

The other trooper, with a bad sunburn and a pale-blond beard so faint it was almost translucent, jumped off the truck and threw Szabo's other bag up.

"So much for having enough room to sleep," he said. "Get in, cherry. It'll be pumpkin time soon and we don't want to be on the road when that happens."

"I'm . . . " he began, gesturing back at the hangar. "Don't I need to check in or . . . something?"

"Get in the fucking truck!" the driver yelled from the cabin.

Szabo shrugged, put a foot in a handle on the gate, and climbed into the bed. Cases of supplies were locked down, and a robot was folded into a recharge station.

"Be careful with Winnie." The blond pulled the gate up and locked it in place. He slapped the back twice and the truck lurched forward. "He bites."

"Don't mind, Spiteri," the other trooper said. "If he was any more full of shit, his eyes would be brown." He pulled a patrol cap from a pocket and slapped it against his thigh. "I'm Nemec."

"Hey! Hey!" someone shouted from the side door of the hangar. A pair of NCOs ran after the truck, shouting for it to stop.

Nemec mimed hearing difficulty and shrugged his shoulders as the truck pulled away.

"Lantar Rifles," Nemec said as he sat and put his uniform top back on. "Bunch of useless assholes. You're better off with us Paladins. We've got it pretty good in our sector."

"Yeah? Tell that to Parn and Cengic, rest their souls," Spiteri said. "Fucking patties got competent all of a sudden these last few weeks. You want to tell him about the last dash- charlie?" he asked Nemec.

"The major can do that, if he wants." Nemec picked up a carbine and slapped in a magazine. The truck slowed as it drove through serpentine turns of concrete barriers and passed guard posts bristling with machine guns and anti-drone emplacements. Red triangle signs with a skull and crossbones flapped against fencing.

"Minefield? Wait, I don't have a-a-a," Szabo said as he tried to retreat deeper into the truck, but Nemec pushed him away with his boot.

"Relax." Spiteri held up his left hand and pointed to a black band around his wrist. "I'm strapped. Nemec's strapped. We're all strapped here. The mines won't target anything within ten meters of a strap. Just don't go wondering off if you've got to take a piss or something."

"But at basic training, the DIs said—"

"Cherry," Nemec said, rolling his eyes, "you think we'd take you outside the wire if you were a Bennie magnet? The blast radius on those things is something else. If you pull a Bennie, it'll whack us too. You think I want my old lady to miss out on my death benefit because I died stupid?"

"Name of the game out here," Spiteri said, loading his carbine. "Don't die stupid. Don't die at all if you can manage it."

Szabo sat down and moved his other bag behind his back and against the side of the truck bed. "What was that about pumpkin time?" he asked.

"Patties like to float balloons with Switchblade kill drones on them after dark. Sensors don't always pick them up. We're good on the post or if you're patrolling in your jack, but you don't want to be naked and afraid when the sun goes down."

"We don't even have an EMP puff on this rig," Nemec said. "Hopes and prayers don't stop the kill drones."

"Oh." Szabo swallowed hard as sweat stains grew in his armpits and collar. "Good thing we left when we did."

"Food's shit in the mess hall anyway. We eat good at the post. Don't cost too much," Spiteri said. "Where you from, cherry? You don't sound Syddan."

"Essach," Szabo said. "The *Highest* was just there. I got to see her with my own eyes on the jump out."

"Essach . . . never heard of it. How was your shuttle down?" Nemec asked.

"The pilot burned us in. Lot worse than any other descent I've done."

"The orbitals are still fucked." Spiteri shook his head. "They're going to extend our asses. Again."

"They do and it won't be a line assignment," Nemec said, shrugging. "Public works shit or a QRF gig. They won't send us to repple-depple, not with the major on us."

"I don't follow," Szabo said.

"You notice some damage to your bird when it landed?" Spiteri asked. "Yeah, I see those wheels turning. This planet used to have a starlink net around it. Full-on modern comms and data speeds as good as anything in the Hegemony. Then the patties showed up to support the rebels, and they took out a couple satellites in their first strike. Well, somebody forgot to tell the patties that when you blow up something in orbit, it don't just all magically go away. Shrapnel took out more of the net, which took out more of the net, etc. etc., until the entire low orbit of Ayutthaya became a fucking blender."

"Why doesn't the Navy drop a friction cloud to clean out the orbitals? Slow the debris down so it burns up in atmo?" Szabo asked.

"Ooo . . . we've got a smart one over here," Nemec said. "You go to college or something?"

"No. Just like to read a lot."

"A friction cloud would be a good idea," Spiteri said, "but then the patties will float up their fucking Sabers. Make the Switchblade kill drones look like Nemec's tiny dick in comparison."

"Stop thinking about my dick all the time." Nemec flashed his middle finger.

"And the patties won't blow a cloud because our Navy will see them do it and declare them hostile within the Freesome exclusion zone, and then the planet will get smashed in the fighting."

"So, the rebels don't let the patties do it," Nemec said. "So, the low orbitals stay hazardous, and it takes a supercomputer to figure out the windows to get stuff on and off world without it getting killed in the process. And guess where the priority for transferring units at the end of their deployments falls? Way below moving wounded and returning empty cargo birds."

"And the local economy's gone straight to shit," Spiteri said. "Not that war was good for a tourist economy, but now they can't get anything on or off world."

"Used to be grunts like us could never afford to stay someplace like that Tradewinds resort the patties are holed up in. Now we've got the run of the whole planet. Welcome to paradise," Nemec snorted.

"Blue line." Spiteri racked a bullet into his chamber as the truck passed a group of blue-painted rocks along the side of the road.

"Fun's over." Nemec turned around and put his weapon to his shoulder. "Shouldn't be any Alliance this far south, but you never know."

"How can they get through the mines?" Szabo looked around for a weapon and found nothing. His hands opened and closed out of reflex.

"They can if they're ghosts," Spiteri said. "There are ghosts out here. Some of them are real motherfuckers."

The cargo truck pulled into a small garage whose walls were reinforced with concrete T-barriers and sandbags. A double stack of bags made the metal roof bow ever so slightly. Szabo jumped off the back and looked to the horizon as the small green sun set on the horizon.

"Shit, we had like eight more minutes," Nemec said, going to a clearing barrel and unloading his weapon.

Shadows grew longer through the post, between wooden bungalows with concrete slabs tracing the walls and a main building with raised roof corners and shattered roof tiles blown out of scorched holes.

"Welcome to the Great Khorngalore Lodge," Nemec said. "Should reopen any day now."

"Cherry." Molenaar walked over and tapped him on the shoulder. "Come with me. Spiteri, secure his gear. He'll be in your section."

"New guy's already getting preferential treatment." Spiteri threw his hands up. "I get it. Us cannon fodder's easy to replace."

"Stow that shit—or do you want a detail washing Mama-san's pots? Again?" Molenaar asked.

"Yeah, I'll get him tucked right in, Top," Spiteri mumbled.

"Stay close," Molenaar said. "We've got smart mines all around the perimeter."

"Roger, First Sergeant." Szabo fell in behind the taller man, matching the pace of his stride like a cadence was being called out. "I'm really excited to be here. To fight for the Hegemony and the Ayutthayan people. It's been a dream of mine to—"

"You even seen a Yuttie yet?"

"Well . . . I don't think so."

"You're still pissing off-world water. I appreciate your enthusiasm, but we're going to slam you with everything we can to get you ready for your first trip outside the wire. Put all that happy energy you've got into a pocket and pull it out when you need it. I'm taking you to the major, and your primary duty as a dash-charlie's to him, you understand that?"

"Roger, First Sergeant. We did field exercises with the officer basic school on Essach, and I got top marks from the lieutenants," Szabo said as he followed the first sergeant into the main building.

The walls bore pictures of hunters standing over bodies of large reptilian creatures, some with a blue-and-white-dappled feline with a silver mane. Cots lined the walls with boxes and duffels stuffed underneath. Most bore sleeping troopers. The room smelled of body odor and mildew—more than one bucket was placed under leaks in the ceiling.

In the center of the room was a massive brick fireplace extending up to the ceiling. A stuffed alien great cat stood on its hind legs, teeth bared, claws extended. It looked like an amalgam of bear and tiger, the wild colors of the fur inspired by someone on a psychedelic trip. It would have been more intimidating if it wasn't wearing a Hegemony Army patrol cap, rank band around an arm, and spent bullet casings plugged into each claw tip.

"That's a *chayseux* cat. Name's Mickey. Don't touch him, or its bad luck the next time you leave the wire," Molenaar said as he led Szabo up to an office door and knocked four times.

"Come," Major Richter called out from the other side.

"Stay here. Remember how to report to an officer. Should be second nature to you, as you're so new, you squeak." The first sergeant went inside and closed the door behind him.

Szabo glanced around. The place must have been a hunting lodge at some point. Signs in several languages pointed around the main room. The smell of cooking drifted over him, and he heard the clang of pots and pans from around a corner.

Light strips had been bolted to the walls, and simple
announcement boards bearing a calendar and notices in moving text like
he'd seen at basic training were placed next to the gap between all the cots.

The door opened, and Molenaar held it for Szabo. The young
trooper straightened his uniform and marched into the office.

Richter sat at a large wooden desk, the legs of which were several
different colors of wood and carved into the shape of the larger cat-bear
animals Szabo'd seen in the main room. The major had a blank piece of
egg-shell white paper set out in front of him, metal seal press with the
Hegemony Army crest embossed at the top. He didn't look up as Szabo
approached the desk, stopped the requisite two steps away, and stomped
one foot hard against the floor. The trooper hinged a flat-handed salute up
to his temple.

"Sir, Private First Class Croll Szabo reports as ordered, sir!"

Richter leaned back in his seat and tossed the pen onto the desk, a
hint of annoyance behind his eyes.

"Top said you were fresh off the boat, and he's right as always."
Richter stood and returned the salute. "You're a dash-charlie."

Behind Richter were several photos, simple printouts placed into
frames that fit the lodge's interior decorating: Richter with more hair and a
bald chin in a new uniform and second lieutenant bars on his collar, an
older man in the crimson of the High Guard to his left, an attractive young
woman with a familial resemblance to his right. Another photo of an even
younger Richter in spacer utilities standing in the middle of a grand
ballroom, the intricate tile floor behind him forming the Hegemony crest, a
wooden balcony of polished oak stretching across the background,
overlooking the space.

Szabo did a double take. That picture was taken aboard the *Highest*, the void ship capital of the Hegemony, and it was in the Pronouncement, where the Most High gathered to give direction to the state and to issue state proclamations. The holy of holies for the Hegemony, and Richter was there as a crewman?

"Sir, yes, sir."

"One 'sir' at a time is fine, Szabo. If you're a dash-charlie, then what's the standard IR bandwidth for Hegemony close-combat communications?"

"Sir, standard frequencies are from 800 nanometers to 899 with time-based frequency modulation. Photon energy quantums provide sender identification and—"

"We don't go below 850 on Ayutthaya. Relative humidity cuts the range too far. What did the schoolhouse tell you about non-IR coms in combat?" Richter scratched a fresh scar on one side of his face.

"If you emit a high-powered message, then you give your position away to the enemy, sir," Szabo said.

"You emit, you die, Szabo. Radio. Microwave. Anything that can be detected will be detected, and then the Alliance will fire off a Switchblade, vector in a gunship or hit the area with rockets. Nothing will get you—and the rest of us—killed faster than poor comms discipline. Is that clear?"

"Yes, sir."

"IR bleeds out to nothing in the air, so that's why we rely on it instead of bugles and whistles. You're certified on Cataphract armor Mark III?"

"Yes, sir."

"My troopers are almost all from Syddan. I'm not. You're not with that accent, but this is a cohort unit, so we adhere to their customs as the Hegemony requires. No issues."

"No, sir."

"I need a dash-charlie to weave all our field comms together, Szabo. I've been without someone trained for weeks, and it's getting us killed out there. You're a key part of the battlefield, and your fellow troopers know this. As such, they know your skills and abilities are valuable. It makes you a target. If I or someone else is telling you to do something, it's to save your life—and by extension, other lives—so react first, question and understand later. Is that clear?"

"Crystal, sir."

"Now to keep you from blowing up." He spun around in his chair and opened a cupboard. Inside was a safe with a spinning dial, which he opened with a few quick twists. Several embossed envelopes were stacked to one side, and Szabo swallowed hard. Death letters. The day that one arrived for his cousin was etched in his mind. Also in the safe were thin black bands bound together by silver tape. Richter plucked a band out and shut the safe.

"Left."

Szabo held his hand out, Richter slapped the band against Szabo's wrist, and it snapped around. The major squeezed the band ends together, and there was a flash of heat. A light traveled around the band twice.

"There, now the Bennies won't read your body heat and decide you're a target. The crypto's good for the next couple months. If you're going to be taken prisoner, snip the band, or the patties will take your hand off to get it."

"They . . . will? I mean, no issue, sir. They won't take me alive."

"Good plan. Now, your hair. It's a problem."

"Sir?"

"Syddans have a number of quirks. Old man Ceban will get you squared away with that. Then there's Mama-san and her boy, Mang. Don't give them any shit. Don't run a debt with her. They're cleared to be here by Planet Command so don't question anything they do."

"Yes . . . sir?"

"It's a lot to take in," Richter said. "See the armorer for your kit. We patrol at daylight and you'll be with me. Understand?"

"Sir, yes, sir."

"Direct and to the point. Maybe some of that will wear off on the Syddans, but I doubt it. Dismissed."

Szabo saluted, stomped loudly, executed a parade-ground-perfect about-face, and left the office.

"He didn't rip your face off," Nemec said from where he leaned against the wall. "The major either likes you or really needs a dash-charlie to run our comms. Maybe both. Come on, if we don't get your filthy scalp bare, some of the boys in Red Platoon will start getting the wrong idea about you."

"Wrong idea?" He followed Nemec outside and into another reinforced building, this one surrounded by several stacked strands of razor wire. Szabo squinted at trip wires leading to flash-bang grenades mounted on the walls.

Nemec shoved a door open, and the whine of a grinder hit Szabo. Inside were weapon cages, stacked ammo crates, and several Cataphract armor suits with their arms locked out into a T-pose.

The robot Szabo'd shared the truck ride with paced back and forth, juggling ammo drums and suit battery packs.

A man hunched over a suit laid out on a worktable and braced a tool against a pauldron, sparks fanning out and into the air like an Alignment Day celebration.

"Ceban!" Nemec shouted, but the other man didn't respond. Nemec shouted again, then reached for a tool on the table. The grinder snapped to one side, almost striking the trooper's wrist.

Ceban turned around slowly, wisps of smoke rising from burning embers in a beard that stretched down to the center of his chest. A pair of black goggles reflected the spinning wheel on the grinder before he turned it off with a snap.

"I knew you heard me," Nemec said.

"I'm working. There's nothing important you can tell me, buck." He lifted the goggles onto his forehead. "What's this? The Hegemony sending girls to the front line now?"

"Dash-charlie," Nemec said, jerking a thumb at Szabo. "Major wants him suited up for the next patrol."

Ceban set the drill down and crossed meaty arms over a slight paunch. "Major's just going to throw her out there so soon? Least pop her cherry as a flanker before she gets the metal."

"I'm not..." Szabo said, looking between the two men, "I'm not a girl."

"Then why do you have hair? And where's your beard if you're a man?" Ceban shook his head. "Should've had him say something. Least then I'd know he's from some bumpkin of a planet. Sit down."

Nemec brought a folding chair off the wall and snapped it open behind Szabo. He pushed the young trooper down and tousled his hair.

"You serve with men of Syddan, and you keep your scalp clean." Ceban took a pair of shears from a drawer and a water bottle. He sprayed mist over Szabo's hair and gave his scalp a vigorous massage. "Relaaaax."

He set the bottle down and began chopping away at Szabo's hair.

Szabo closed his eyes as the blades snapped shut around his head, a stray cut setting an ear on fire.

"You shave your head each day with your bayonet—shows your officers you're alert. Ready. But no blade will touch your face until you leave this planet in victory. That's our way." Ceban tapped the scissors against Szabo's shoulder. "How's he look, buck?"

"Awful. Rest of the boys won't think he's here just for morale." Nemec clicked his tongue twice and Winnie stopped juggling. "Winnie. Bayonet."

"Unauthorized request," the robot said, dashed lights lighting up across its "mouth."

"Thought you fixed that?" Nemec asked as he rummaged around the drawers.

"Software update unfixed it. Some cheese-dick lawyer decided all blades are weapons, so now Winnie won't toss." Ceban knelt level with Szabo's face, frowned, and went back to cutting.

"Winnie. Bullets." Nemec held a hand out to one side and the robot tossed a magazine into his outstretched hand. It landed perfectly flat against his palm.

"Winnie. Battery." A black brick hit Nemec's other hand. "Bullshit. The robots can give us packs to run our armor and rounds to kill patties, but not a knife?"

"Take it up with the cheese-dicks. I just keep the suits running." Ceban picked up a tuft of Szabo's hair and tucked it into his palm. "Send that back to your family. It's luck." He shooed Nemec away from his workbench and bent down to open a cupboard.

On the table, a glint of silver metal embedded in the pauldron caught Szabo's eye. Part of a bolt lay next to the armor plate, the rest of it still where it had hit.

"What did that?" Szabo asked.

"Pattie designation is the VW-9. A Jonas," Ceban said. "Bolt-thrower. Cataphract armor's tough, but the bastards have figured out a couple different ways to get at the weakest part of the suit," he said as he came back with a straight razor in hand and tapped Szabo in the chest with the handle.

"Don't let them get close," Nemec said. "You've got flankers to keep an eye out, but the patties are bastards."

"The Alliance are the patties, I assume," Szabo said as Ceban took a small squeeze bottle out of his apron and dabbed the contents on Szabo's scalp. The smell of gun oil almost overwhelmed him as Ceban went to work with the razor.

"They eat these shit pucks made of dog meat and roots they dig out of cemeteries," Nemec said.

"They're made from ground pork with loads of onion, garlic, and fennel—that last one is the stuff they make licorice from. Not really that bad, except for the fennel." Ceban wiped the blade against his apron. "You'll always know a pattie by their breath. Not that you're going to get any of them confused with the Yutties."

"Still smell like shit," Nemec snorted. "And the Alliance Marines season their patties with crayon shavings."

"Passable." Ceban folded up the razor and turned Szabo's now-bald head from side to side as he examined the shave, then jerked a thumb to a Cataphract with its arms held to its sides in a T-pose. "You're certified?"

"Yes, sir." Szabo ran a hand over his head, the sting of razor burn growing stronger.

"Don't 'sir' me. I'm a civilian. Hegemony can't keep proper armorers like me in uniform, so they just hire us out of the heavy-gravity worlds where the Cataphracts were invented. Step in. Let me see you run your start-ups," Ceban said, moving to one side.

Szabo went to the back of the armor, stuck a thumb into a slot, and lifted up a small panel. Armor plates opened off the rear, and Szabo stepped into the suit. He pressed his forehead against a plate and the suit closed around him, pinching and shifting against his body until it molded to his shape.

The optics turned on, and a screen lit up inside the visor. Most of the HUD remained offline except for power readings. Szabo lifted the thicker weapon-support arm and rolled it backwards and forwards.

Ceban looked down at a greasy data slate as the test went on.

"Haptic feedback slow in the number two gun-support hinge." Szabo bent his right arm several times, pushing hard against the internal sensors, but the thicker frame of the jack stuttered.

"Try now." Ceban tapped a knuckle on the screen and Szabo's gun arm reared back.

"In line." Szabo tapped the back of his head with both hands, then swept his arms across his chest several times. "Still getting a bit of jerk with the radial pneumatics."

"That's rust. You need to lube up before and after every time you leave the wire. Digits." Ceban picked up a wrench and tossed it at Szabo, who missed and took the tool to the breastplate.

"Tracking assist had some lag." Szabo tried to bend forward, but the spine plates didn't stretch far enough. He went to one leg and picked up the wrench. "This software's out-of-date."

"You mean you didn't bring the new patch with you off your transport?" Nemec chuckled. "Play catch with Winnie. Get used to the almost-to-standard gear we've got on the front lines."

Szabo lobbed the wrench at the robot, who plucked it out of the air and fastened it to a magnetic holster on one leg.

"Winnie. Number seven wrench." Szabo missed the catch again.

"You got a problem with your gear, buck?" Ceban asked Nemec. "You're free to do your own maintenance if you can do any better."

"Nah, nah, you're so valuable, we can't even let you out of your workshop," Nemec said with a smile.

"Not that I could with the workload you shell-heads lay on me." Ceban caught the wrench as it flew between Szabo and the robot. He lifted Richter's pauldron and beat the tool against the silver dart embedded in the metal. It flopped out and rolled across the floor to stop at Szabo's feet.

"It'll take another two hours before his targeting systems are lined up, and then I have to run him through recovery drills," Ceban said. "Why don't you piss off so we can work in peace?"

"I think Mama-san's got tom yum tonight," Nemec shrugged. "Have fun, cherry."

Szabo lifted one foot off the ground, feeling his weight shift slightly as internal gyros stabilized his jack.

"Go to a T." Ceban tapped a spanner against the trooper's gun arm and went to his back as Szabo lifted both arms to his sides. "Every Cataphract in this company started off as a flanker. You know why? Because flankers have dilatant-3 treated combat fatigues that can stop shrapnel on a good day and not much else. Takes a single firefight to appreciate you're not invincible. Just because you're a Cataphract doesn't mean you can tank a pattie's darts. Don't tempt fate, you understand?"

Ceban tilted Szabo's head back so he could see where the walls and ceiling met. Broken and battered pieces of Cataphract armor were hung like hunting trophies.

"I thought . . . I thought these suits were stronger than that." Szabo's mouth went dry.

"Oh, they're plenty tough, then the patties paid those fuckheads on Waterson for weapons that'll crack us. Switchblade drones. Gryphon launchers. The bolt pistols. Hell, they've got pretty adept at aiming for the seams with their darts." Ceban ran the edge of his tool around the base of

Szabo's neck and then where the breastplate met the abdominal guards. "Don't expect to march through their fire without a scratch. All those propaganda vids you grew up on before you got to basic are bullshit, buck. Your metal can only do so much. You need the other Cataphracts and your flanker—especially your flankers!—to keep you alive. Get it?"

"Got it. I'm the dash-charlie radioman. So long as I keep the commo nets together, we can all fight better."

"There you go. Don't piss off the major, or he'll have you bolt on an AT-99." He rapped his tool against the back of Szabo's left shoulder.

"What's wrong with that?"

"Slight manufacturer's defect. The warhead takes a bullet and it explodes. Patties love aiming for them. That happens, you won't have a chance to realize something went wrong. Won't have an open-casket funeral either. Let's get your net package installed. I love me some tom yum and Mama-san might not have any left soon."

****

Richter shrugged off his fatigue top. The ever-present dampness of this part of Ayutthaya in the middle of the rainy season had left a mustiness in the fabric that never seemed to leave, no matter how many times he had Mindy run it through the lodge cleaner units they had jury-rigged back into service.

He sniffed at the clothing, then hung it up on a hook bolted to the wood paneling of his office. Jamming his fists against his lower back, he stretched. The grip settings on his jack tended to slip after so many hours in the field and put a crimp in his back. There was a joke about jack troopers getting shorter as their career progressed, one he found less and less funny the older he got.

Richter walked past the map board to his desk and stopped a few steps short of his chair. The Army-issued tablet buzzed with a new message, another in the litany of never-ending ankle biters from squadron headquarters.

Next to the tablet was a single sheet of white paper. He could feel the grain of the pulp against his fingers as he thought through the ugly task ahead of him. He had to know the message before he began. There was no margin of error there.

"Damn it." He turned back to the map board and held up his palm for the biometric reader. The board snapped to life. A field with all his unread e-mail traffic came up on top of everything else, the edges blinking red. When he didn't see a message from Colonel Toman, he swiped it aside.

Richter dragged the map to Rawai, the town where he and his troop had just been in a scrap, and added in data layers. The Cataphract recorded everything their optics saw, as did the visors the flankers used, and the onboard computers kept precise positioning and ballistics data. The information was normally bounced back to squadron once a day, but too many relay satellites had been lost, and now it all went up the chain of command on crystals every time he sent a supply convoy back to Port Tarl.

Supposedly, the data was crunched to find improvements for ground systems, but Richter suspected it was just stored until someone in a chain of command—or above—needed a reason to cashier an officer ... and there was always a mistake to be found somewhere in the records.

He dialed back the time on the data to the battle. Blue unit icons for his troopers down to the squad level moved in and out of the city as casualty alerts came and went, the fight playing out in reverse. He stopped the replay just as his troopers first pressed into the town and set the speed to 5x.

Red diamonds for the Alliance troops appeared and disappeared over the map as the jack's systems tagged sightings. White lines of cycler fire stabbed from building to building and across streets. Richter rubbed his chin, fighting to remember just what he ordered his troopers to do when the first Badger tank was detected.

Combat was a special beast. The body flooded with adrenaline and stress, heightening awareness and bringing much more than usual into focus. But after the fighting ended…parts became difficult to recall as the brain did what it could to shunt the trauma away from memory.

Recalling a fight took work, even for seasoned warriors. More than once, he'd been in an after-action review and had to be reminded of an order he'd given before total recall came back. The Academy taught that this was a normal neurological response to an event that put too much stress on the mind, but he still felt like he was failing as a commander for not remembering every life-and-death order he gave.

There. He stopped the replay as a firefight broke out around a ground-car battery depot. The Alliance fought from buildings overlooking the depot, striking at his men from cover and then falling back as cyclers came to bear and leaving Switchblades in their place. Then new contact on the flanks. Rocket strikes against pockets of his troopers. The Marines hadn't rushed into a slugging match with his Cataphracts; they'd baited come-on attacks, trying to draw his platoons away from each other.

"He had an ambush waiting." Richter frowned and shifted the replay back and forth around a bombed-out sporting-goods store. Several Marine squads appeared seemingly out of nowhere and withdrew to their lines.

A KIA icon popped up to the south end of the town, and Richter's heart went to ice, remembering the edge-of-panic transmission from Cengic about Parn going down. Richter watched his own blue square move to assist.

Then the enemy Badgers attacked. With hindsight and a bird's-eye view, it became obvious to him that the tanks had run ahead of their infantry support. There was a fine line between aggressive and foolhardy, and the Alliance crews had paid the price to learn it.

"But the Marine commander's not the one that made that mistake," Richter muttered. "He had situation awareness…I never caught his men in the open. Never managed to get the upper hand. I hate it when they're competent."

Richter touched the fresh scar on his jawline, remembering the hilt of the knife that did it … was that some sort of Marine affectation or a symbol of rank? The Alliance drew from so many neo-barbarian systems, it was hard to tell.

He went to his desk and tapped a code into his secure phone. The speaker clicked as the connection established itself. He gently picked up the blank white sheet of paper from two sides and set it on top of his safe.

"Toman," came from the phone.

"Sir, Richter." He glanced at his tablet and double-tapped an icon. "I have a request for forces: the sniper team detailed down from regiment."

"The Alliance are acting up across the squadron front, Richter. Ops and I have plans for that asset. What do you want to do with them?"

"Ambush, Colonel. There's a Marine commander in my sector that needs to eat a bullet."

"Tell me more…"

Richter smiled and hurried back to the map board.

Chapter 5

Marines

Teo trudged through the ever-present rain, which had somehow made it past the neck seal of his long johns and was trickling down his back. Thirty-nine days without a let-up, and he was sick of the gray skies and constant rainfall.

How the hell was this ever a resort world? he wondered for the thousandth time.

Sure, he could see through the ruins that the Tradewinds might have been a luxury resort at one time, but at the moment, the rain, gloom, and mildew were overpowering. The sunlight of their arrival and the deep turquoise seas that gently lapped over coral reefs were long-lost memories by now.

His boots squelched in the mud as he moved through the dusk to the next position. One more line-check, then sticking his head in at Third in their berthing, and he could retreat back to his CP in the old pool, or better yet, get back to his BOQ room (a rather tongue-in-cheek nickname for the empty and damaged room he'd commandeered) for a few minutes and get into a dry set of long johns. Not that it would do any good. The insidious rain always found a way in.

It wasn't just the rainwater. He could feel sweat building up. The R&D types swore that the micro-climate cooling and heating system embedded into his long johns, his IFU's (Individual Fighting Uniform) inner, life-critical layer was waterproof, but all he knew was that it wasn't cooling him. The cooling gel was not circulating through the microtubing in the fabric, and he was overheating, even in the rain. And he didn't have on the PCL, the Power Central Layer, nor the POL, the Protective Outer Layer, just a set of rain slicks and his battle rattle. When the Marines went out beyond the wire, they had on all three layers, and overheating had become a real problem.

No matter how many times he brought the issue up with battalion, however, he received the same response: there was nothing they could do about it until a Breyers-Manuel tech rep arrived on planet and to just suck it up until then.

Teo hadn't helmeted up to check the positions—he wanted the Marines to see his face, not his visor display, so he glanced down on the mobile CCD in his hand to pinpoint the next position. Momentarily distracted, his right foot slipped, and Teo fell hard on his ass with a whump.

"Son-of-a-bitch!" he muttered, wincing at the pain in his hip.

Then he remembered where he was. He quickly looked around, hoping against hope that no one had seen him. It looked clear. He gingerly stood up and tried to wipe as much of the mud off of his ass and legs as he could. It didn't do much good, so he gave up. The rain would take care of it soon enough.

Standing still this time, he checked his CCD again. The final position should be just ahead of him and to his right. Teo had his Marines displacing every eight hours, a habit he'd learned from his first company commander when he was a boot private on Ryestone. He'd grumbled along with the rest of the Marines, but a Royalist missile demolishing his previous day's fighting position was a valuable lesson-learned.

He knew his Marines thought he was being too cautious and hated the extra work, but he made the orders, not them.

Teo heard the position before he saw it, and his anger started to bubble up. Pushing through the undergrowth, he spotted the position . . . covered by a tarp. What he'd heard was the tap, tap, tap of drops falling off the leaves above the position.

The tarp was made with the same octofabric tech as their POL's outer covering, so there could be something said about it providing camo from drones or orbiting surveillance, but the position was already under the cover of the forest. No, they were using the tarp to stay dry, and by doing so, they were putting themselves at risk.

The Marines under the tarp never heard him approach. He grasped the edge of the tarp and yanked it back, exposing a very surprised Private Arroyo, who was facing the front, and Corporal Twinning, Lance Corporal Singh, and another private, one of the new joins, whose name escaped Teo for the moment. Twinning, Singh, and the new join were scrunched together at the bottom of the fighting hole, playing cards.

Teo was seething. There was nothing technically wrong that only one Marine was facing out, the fire team's sensors in front of him. Poor judgment on the corporal's part, but within his prerogative. But to have only one Marine so the other three could play cards, even old-fashioned physical cards, which didn't emit a signature? They were on the front lines, not back in the rear.

And then there was the tarp itself. Teo had passed that while on the lines, the tarps were not to be used. The fabric of their POLs was woven with sound-deadening technology—the tarps were not. The sound of the drops hitting the tarp was like a neon arrow pointing out their position.

Corporal Twinning scrambled to his feet, his mouth gaping open.

"Sir, I —"

"Save it, Twinning," Teo snapped, his eyes shooting fire, the tarp still grasped in his hand.

"But—"

"I said, save it, or do you intend to disobey that order too?"

The corporal looked down at his feet for a moment as if he'd find the magic answer that would get him out of trouble.

It wasn't there.

"You, Private Arroyo, you don't need to be looking back at me," Teo said. "Back to your sensors."

He felt a little guilty at the anger that bubbled through at Arroyo. The private had been the only one doing his job.

"The rest of you, I think you'd better put those cards down and start doing what you're here to do. Corporal Twinning, I want to see you and Sergeant Roy as soon as you're relieved.

"Aye-aye, sir," a miserable-sounding Twinning said.

The corporal knew he was in deep shit.

Without another word, Teo rolled up the tarp, then turned and stepped back into the gathering darkness, striving to control his anger. Erupting would do no one any good.

He paused as he passed through the undergrowth, trying to regain his equilibrium. Teo had always had a hair-trigger temper, something that had gotten him into trouble before, and it had been the inner demon he'd had to battle ever since becoming an NCO.

He took a moment and started to tap out a message on his CCD for Sergeant Roy to see him, then wiped it clean. That wasn't his job, something that still was difficult for him to grasp sometimes. He wasn't a sergeant anymore.

See me in the CP as soon as you're relieved, he passed to Razor Fuentes, the First Platoon commander.

He didn't need to pass anything else. If Twinning had an ounce of sense, he'd be passing up his chain what had happened. If he didn't, well, that was on Razor, so let him be surprised when Teo took a chunk out of his ass.

Teo glanced at the tarp in his hand.

Am I being too much of an asshole? he wondered for a brief second.

No! Getting wet isn't going to kill them, but a crab scout sure could.

Teo's job was to close with and destroy the enemy, all while keeping as many of his Marines alive to return to Momma as he could. He was not there to be everyone's buddy.

He was just about to step off when a quiet voice reached him from the fighting position. "I swear, Corporal, I was awake. I just never heard him come up."

"No, but if the water wasn't dropping on the tarp, you might have," Teo muttered.

"My bust, Arroyo. It's on me. I should have known better. Been nice, though, if Sergeant Roy'd given us a fucking warning that the skipper was on the prowl."

"How'd he do that? I mean, sneak up on us like that?" another voice asked. Probably the new join.

Teo did a quick check on his T/O readout: Private John West.

"Recon," Corporal Twinning said. "He was in recon when he was a sergeant. When he got his POA."

"Oh," someone else said, as if that answered it all.

Despite his lingering anger, Teo had almost laughed out loud. Being a former recon Marine had nothing to do with it. They'd just screwed up with the damned tarp.

No one else better have pulled the same stunt.

Chances were, though, that Twinning would warn the others.

Teo flipped his CCD back to map mode, noted the next position, and stepped off. Two more positions to check, and he could get out of this infernal rain.

Chapter 6

Paladins

Richter stirred a ceramic spoon into a yellow soup, mixing thin noodles and bits of pork together.

"Look, if the Most High demand current lines, the patties will give it to us," Lieutenant Kontos said from the other side of the table. The major and his three other officers sat at one end of several card tables pushed together, each covered by a thin plastic tarp for a tablecloth. Local music warbled out of a nearby kitchen. A wok banged against a stove as an Ayutthayan woman in a dirty apron gathered a handful of ingredients from several small bowls and flung them into the mix. Steam flared up and a string of expletives carried through the small restaurant.

A screen on the wall played a data chip loaded with Hegemony-approved media. Several troopers argued over whether to watch a football match or the latest episode of a series set during the Alignment War.

"If we go with current lines, we lose Estalla." Briem leaned back, a toothpick working in his mouth. "And then there's the fronts on Tiberon. Naptha. Here."

"None of those worlds have petitioned to join the Hegemony. We'd gain—"

"Estalla is part of the Hegemony," Richter said. "We paid blood to liberate it from the Zaibatsu. The Most High won't surrender it to the Alliance just because they have temporary possession of the planet."

A lieutenant with three cybernetic fingers poked at a dirty bowl of rice and processed pork cubes, and said, "You lived aboard the *Highest* for so long. Maybe you've heard something about the cease-fire rumors?"

"Nothing, Kontos. The rumors are just that, rumors. Don't give them power by discussing them around the men. If they think the war might end next week, they'll get sloppy. Patties won't cut us any slack out in the jungle. You all know that," Richter said.

"Historically … fighting gets worse before a cease-fire," Briem said with a shrug. "Last hours of World War I killed thousands, even though the commanders knew what time the guns would stop firing. Then there's the 'forever truce' between the Zaibatsu and the United Planets. Couple million went up in nuclear fire as the 'Batsus drew back to their territory."

"Which pissed the Unis off enough for generations," Richter said. "Turned out to be a boon for Hegemony."

"Praise be to their 'volunteer' fleet," Frakes said, raising a can of soda in toast.

"Praise be," Kontos said. "Major, there's your buck. He finally looks decent."

"Szabo! Over here." Nemec waved the radioman to the group arguing over the screen. "Come vote to watch *Blood and Iron*. No one gives a shit about pansy-ass soccer."

Szabo hurried over, but Richter stopped him with a glance.

"Sit." Richter pointed at the newly vacant seat as Frakes bid farewell with a knock on the table.

"Sir?" Szabo sat, back straight, feet planted on the floor, a fist perched on each knee.

"Who's breaking him in? Molenaar?" Briem asked.

"I've got him," Richter said. "The first sergeant's got other things to worry about. Your fitting went well?"

"Sir, yes, sir," Szabo said. "IR package integrated and cycler zeroed."

"Where'd they find this one? He a Uni world import?" Kontos said, the toothpick bobbing like a metronome as he spoke. "So damn serious."

"The Syddan ease takes some learning, don't you think?" Richter asked. "What would you think of our new radioman if he was as relaxed as the rest of our troopers?"

"He's got bad habits to unlearn," Kontos said. "Hope he does better than the last man."

"Don't—I'm still eating." Briem leaned forward and went to work on his rice.

"Ohhh, who's this?" An Ayutthayan woman came over, her apron dirty and moist from steam. She had short hair run through with gray and plump features, despite her thin, gnarled hands. Following behind her was a young man in his teens, his head shaved and with a dull look to him.

"Szabo, this is Mindy Qwan, post Mama-san," Richter said. "New trooper, fresh off the loggie ship. Go easy on him with the spicy."

"This one looks so young, so strong," Mindy pressed her hands together and bowed slightly. "Ayuttayan spicy or Syddan spicy. He knows how to pay?"

"Ayuttayan spicy, please," Szabo said, nodding quickly.

Kontos fought back a smile.

"First one's on me." She smiled with a quick bob of her head and went back to the kitchen. High in the corner was a small shelf on which an alabaster statue of an elegant woman overlooked her workspace. Small ceramic cups with dead incense sticks, a clear glass with a bright red liquid, and a small stack of coins stood as offerings before the statue.

"Sir," Szabo said, raising a finger, "she is not a Hegemony citizen or soldier."

"Damn, Major, you sure you can't spare him as a flanker?" Briem asked. "I could use a scout with those powers of observation."

"Mindy's our Mama-san," Richter said. "She's value-added to our supply situation. By which I mean she cooks for us. Runs the laundry machines. Procures local items as she can to make our post a bit more livable."

"But . . . sir . . . " Szabo leaned over the table and spoke at a whisper, "what if she's a spy?"

Briem stifled a laugh.

"She's with the Ayutthayan Kingdom. So's the rest of her clan," Richter said. When Szabo responded with a dumb look, he kept going. "The monarchists petitioned the Hegemony for aid to fight the revolutionaries. The king's people have no love for the revolutionaries…there were a number of atrocities carried out by the rebels before we came to help."

"So, she's a good Yuttie," Briem said. "Same with her boy, Mang. Not to be confused with the only way a pattie can be good."

"Mang's got some learning issues. He's not to be bothered," Richter said.

Mindy set a chipped bowl of soup in front of Szabo, a spoon and pair of chopsticks jutting out over the edge.

"Not too spicy." She gave the young trooper a pat on the head and left.

"Is this the tom yum, sir?" Szabo sniffed at it.

"Nah, looks like you've got the special," Kontos said. "You got to be quick to get the tom yum; the boys love it."

Szabo picked up the chopsticks, frowned at them, then spooned some of the broth into his mouth. "Huh, that's got some kick to it." He slurped down some noodles and glanced at a red pepper before chewing on it.

Briem smacked Kontos on the shoulder and pointed at the young trooper.

Szabo swallowed hard and his face went red.

Richter sighed. "The Ayutthayans are a very hospitable people. This planet was known for the beach resorts, hunting…other things. The civil war wrecked the economy and sent millions into refugee camps. The income Mama-san makes off us helps support her whole clan. She's got no reason to help the enemy."

"And it's not like we have a lot of choice to have her around," Briem said. "You OK there, buck? Looking a little sweaty."

Szabo nodded and reached for a water bottle in the middle of the table. He took a long swig and then wiped his hand over his mouth and then his eyes.

"Rookie mistake," Kontos said.

"Be aware, Szabo—you listening to me?" Richter asked.

The radioman nodded quickly and drank more water.

"Be aware that the Hegemony Army learned fairly quickly that having a local national on each post to provide logistics support solved a number of other problems, namely theft from the more austere locations like this one," he said.

"Slinky boy comes a callin'," Briem said. "You don't have a Mama-san? Shit goes missing until you hire one. Nothing mission critical at first— uniforms, personal items—then unattended rifles get lost. We hire a local matriarch and suddenly all our stuff magically reappears and nothing else vanishes. So, we have a Mama-san on post. Sure beats eating the same freeze-dried shit that comes out of ration packs over and over again."

"The beef stew ain't so bad," Kontos said, "and anything tastes great when you're hungry."

Szabo opened his mouth and began breathing very slowly.

"Mama-san will keep a ledger of what you order from her," Richter said. "The special's about three Hegemony shillings. Cheaper than any meal you'd get back home. Finance comes out once a month. Draw the cash you need and settle accounts right away."

"Or slinky boy," Briem said. "No one wants slinky boy."

"You think our perimeter's secure, but slinky boy always finds a way in," Kontos said.

Sweat poured off Szabo's brow.

"He's taking it like a champ, not gonna lie," Briem said. "Mercy?"

Szabo opened an eye.

Richter leaned to one side and moved a small bowl of cucumber slices next to Szabo's bowl. Szabo looked from the slices to Richter and back.

"They'll kill the heat," Richter said, shaking his head slowly as Szabo wolfed down the entire bowl. "Just so you know, the murder-peppers at the bottom of the bowl aren't supposed to be eaten. They're to season the broth."

"He eat it?" Mindy yelled from the kitchen.

"Think he swallowed it too," Briem called out.

"Oh...that bad," Mindy said.

"What? Why?" Szabo asked.

"Take a shit before we suit up in the morning," Briem said, standing up. "Sir."

"My apologies," Szabo said to Richter. "I've messed up already."

"Don't worry about it. Everyone eats the pepper the first time. You did better than the last new troopers. Even Nemec had to get an IV after he almost passed out." Richter checked his watch. "No moon tonight...you won't have watch until you're off ship time and on local sunrise/sunset. On

73

Ayutthaya we fight during the day, but night doesn't mean we're safe. Get some sleep and finish your food. It's an insult to the locals if you don't."

Szabo looked at his bowl and laughed weakly.

"Skip the peppers," Richter said and patted Szabo's shoulder.

****

Richter sank into his office chair, which had once belonged to the head of the hunting lodge where he and his troop had established their base. It had an oversized, padded back, with cracks through the leather finish patched over by green tape. The smell of sweat and cloves came through when it rained, which was more often than not on this part of Ayuttha.

He'd found a stash of local cigarettes called Kretek with the same scent. Given the prevalence of the smell throughout the office and the cartons hidden in the ceiling panels, Richter suspected the previous lodge master feared shortages when the civil war began. Just why they'd been left behind remained a mystery.

The desk where he'd laid his carbine out for cleaning was hand-carved wood from the jungle. On one side's corner posts were reliefs of the chayseux cats, and rather exaggerated figures of a local woman on the other side's posts, better suited for the prow of an ancient sailing ship than receiving guests and employees, in his opinion.

Richter removed his boots, dropped small packets of baking soda wrapped in gauze into the toes, and rubbed his sore, water-softened feet.

He glanced at his Army-issued tablet blinking with messages from squadron headquarters, demanding updates on supply levels and paperwork he would have hoisted onto his executive officer, if he'd had one.

Lieutenant Jardan was evaced weeks ago after losing an arm to an Alliance explosive. The Adjutant promised a replacement was in the works, and Richter had pushed off addressing ankle biters like the percentage of his troopers that had finished their annual security-system training or local culture-appreciation classes. Whenever the squadron staff bleated at him for the delays, he sent back a picture of his company organization with the XO position highlighted.

With a sigh he brushed the tablet away. A different tablet came out of the desk, sleeker and with a glossy black finish. He swiped a thumb down a reader and waited until a microphone appeared on the screen.

"Hello, Eliseabeta, I hope this finds you well. I hope it finds you at all. Haven't heard from you in the past few months. I assume you're in transit to somewhere else in the Union. You can move faster than Net packets, after all.

"Ayutthaya remains…remains here. Still the same green hell of humidity and mold and bastard Alliance hiding behind every plant. The chain of command doesn't seem especially interested in forcing the issue against the patties. Nothing but local actions at the squadron level or below. Nothing to stoke the Alliance into a large-scale reaction. It irks me, Sis. Irks me that we're not fighting this war to win it here.

"So, all we do is bleed. Our patrols run into theirs through the great No Man's Land between their rebel Yuttie city and our government Yuttie cities. Our Bennies sting them. Their Switchblade drones get us. Every so often, we'll catch a bigger dustup as we try and seize some once-prosperous location.

"My troop and I are in a hunting lodge—pretty famous one too. The Great Khorngalore Lodge. Bet you can find travel videos for it somewhere on the Net. Five-star place…once upon a time. We pushed the Alliance off a month before the lines stabilized. Now we've been here so long, we've almost developed into a routine.

"Growing up aboard the *Highest*, routine was everything, you remember. Time for meals. Time for the refreshers. Everything in its place and at its time. Whenever anyone learns I come from a High Guard family, they ask why the hell I'm in the Army and not the Navy.

"Decent question…you remember when the *Highest* arrived on Gudrun and Father took us planet side? Of course, you do. It was the first time we'd seen a waterfall. I remember standing under that constant rain with you, laughing forever at something so novel and so strange. There was nothing like that aboard the ship. Nor would there ever be. So, I joined the Army to see the rest of the galaxy. The view of the void through a porthole? Star fields are star fields.

"Ayuttha has all sorts of novelties. Monsoons. Insects. Mud. So much goddamn mud. There are times when I do miss the steady state of life aboard starships, but every time it rains, I think of you.

"What are you doing in the Union, Eliseabeta? The Intelligence types have stopped asking me about you. Now it's the gavel, the Justice Department, that keeps tracking me down to ask if I know anything about Freedom Synthetics. The only thing I do know about that company is that they were blacklisted by the Hegemony…right around the time you went on an extended vacation to the Union.

"Father will not speak of you. He's still aboard the *Highest*, but reassigned from the High Guard. He won't speak of that either. The Guard is his life; you know that. It became everything to him after we lost Mom. My colonel's hinted that some senior officers—flag rank—want me out of command for reasons they won't give.

"Why can't you tell me what happened? We use gene-locked messaging. I use cutouts to send and receive letters from you. If you'd just…give me something to work with. Let me do what I can to help you, work out a deal with the gavel or whoever else in the Hegemony is angry with you…let me help. I've got a little bit of rank and a full ribbon rack to shield me if I learn something that might embarrass certain people in the Hegemony.

"In the meantime…I've also got a war to fight. My Syddans are…good troopers. Tough. Fierce. But I swear the incorporation treaty was more of a suggestion to them. They speak Standard well enough, but the amount of cultural drift between them and the Hegemony's norm is pretty plain.

"Remember my hair? Gone. The Syddan soldiers won't be led by women, and if you've got a head of hair—too feminine. A beard, though, that's a must. Damn thing itches. Requires brushing. Treated with special conditioners. It's like a pet! Are you rolling your eyes? Women don't have a good deal of empathy when I mention all this.

"But the Syddans…they'll tolerate troopers from other worlds, but if you want their respect, you have to respect their ways. They're not afraid to fight and seem to enjoy finding new and explicit ways to complain about their situation. I swear, if they're not complaining, they're not happy.

"There I was—no kidding—a few days ago walking the perimeter in the middle during the small hours of the morning and I hear this grunting coming from in between some of the buildings on the FOB. This isn't *that* kind of story. Don't worry. One of my troopers was doing physical training with his cycler. Squat thrusts with his twenty-five-pound weapon. Damn heavy things and he wasn't taking a break.

"I stopped him out of curiosity. Turns out, he'd lost a bet to another trooper over…not taking part in a certain guilty pleasure. First one to give up owed the other five hundred reps. I thought he'd be relieved to be so…relieved, but no. He was angry with himself for lack of discipline.

"Cengic, he's like that and…Parn. That reminds me. I've been remiss in another duty of mine. Please, Eliseabeta, tell me what's happened. I can't do anything for you if I'm in the dark.

"Be well. Love, Emil."

Richter clicked a button on the tablet and a small, thin crystal popped out of the side. He pressed the edge against his thumb to draw a sliver of blood, and the crystal pulsed with light. The message went into a pocket for delivery to Qwan for her to pass on to her network of Ayutthayans who would eventually upload it into the Net to find its way to his sister.

He brought out a sheaf of blank paper with a matte-black leather cover and a small pen pouch on the side. Almost half the pages were removed from where they were glued to the top spine. He peeled a sheet away and set it gently over the cover.

The pen came out and he held up the antique-designed brass tip. This duty was as old as the Hegemony, and the ink allowed for no mistakes; any blemish or mis-stroke could not be fixed. A tradition that forced the writer to confront whatever fault had led to this duty being performed.

He hated writing death letters, but this was his duty and his responsibility. He was the commander.

Chapter 7

Marines

Teo stuck his fork into the mess that was supposed to be Pasta St. Ermile, which was just a fancy name for plain old noodles in lemon sauce, and tossed it onto his field desk in disgust.

"When was this shit made? During the Branstonite Rebellion?"

"Come on, Skipper. You don't like this good Marine Corps chow?" Gunny Walters said with a laugh as he sat on the other side of the desk, stuffing his own rats into his mouth. "This is great! And all for free."

"Free? They take it out of my pay. Three forty-five a meal."

"Well, it sucks to be an officer, I guess," the gunny said, laughing so hard that a chunk of half-masticated pasta flew out of his mouth to land on Teo's desk.

The gunny made a show of scooping it back up with his forefinger, then popping it into his mouth. He licked his finger clean and then smacked his lips.

"Can't waste my free chow."

Teo just rolled his eyes. Marine Corps L-Rations were guaranteed to provide a fighting Marine all the calories and nutrients he needed to fight in a temperate climate. And they weren't really horrible-tasting—not good, but not horrible—but after four months without a break, the six different meals were mind-numbingly boring.

"What I wouldn't give for a steak right now. A ribeye. No, a Lexington Strip. Medium rare, juices running into garlic mashed, Jelly's steak sauce."

Sergeant Rios overheard him and turned around. "Medium well, sir. And ketchup, not Jelly's."

"Ketchup? Barbarian, Sergeant! It has to be Jelly's."

"Fried chicken. Extra-crispy, with crawdad grits and honeyburst apple slaw," Doc Sanaa added.

"Now look what you've done, Skipper," the gunny said. "You've got them all salivating and shit."

Teo ignored him. "Teresa's Most Excellent Patties," he said. "Best on Safe Harbor. So light, they'd almost float away. But at the original shop, in Freetown. I'd give ten unis for a pattie right now."

Doc, Gunny, and Rios gave each other guilty looks, then quickly broke away, refusing to meet Teo's eyes.

"What? What's going on?" Teo asked, his something-is-up-detector pegged.

"Nothing, sir," the gunny said.

"Bullshit, Gunny. Tell me."

Teo looked at the others, but Rios was now buried in his inventory sheets, and Doc was suddenly interested in his fingernails.

"What am I missing here, Gunny?"

"Uh . . . I'd rather not say, sir."

"And I'd rather you tell me, *Gunny*."

Teo had no idea why they were all acting weird, but he knew they were hiding something.

The gunny took a last bite of his pasta, then crumbled up the dish and stuffed it into his mouth.

"You're wasting time."

The gunny held up a finger and swallowed the dish, which was infused with needed minerals and nano-boost, but tasted like rice cakes.

"Uh . . . how should I put this . . . ?"

"You should put this by just telling me and stop beating around the bush. Is this something I need to know?"

Gunny Walters shrugged, took a deep breath, and as Rios and Sanaa turned back to listen, said, "There may be a way to have a pattie."

"What? We're not getting any chowhall food delivered out here."

It wasn't out of the bounds of imagination to think that a crewchief or supply tech might bring out a chowhall pattie on a run to the company, but nothing had come in for the last two weeks.

"Nothing delivered, sir."

"Then what?" Teo asked, confused. "The Yutties?"

The locals thought that patties were disgusting, from what he'd heard, but they were used to tourists from across the galaxy, so it wasn't crazy to think they would sell them to Marines if they had the means to make them. But from what he knew of the town and the refugee camp, they didn't.

So, what is the gunny talking about?

"Lance Corporal James," the gunny said, almost in a whisper.

"James? Which James?"

"Second Platoon James. Mortimer James."

Teo was confused. "What about James?"

"Well, he makes them. Three times a week."

Teo was stunned, his mind refusing to grasp what the gunny had said. James. Lance Corporal James was making patties? Teo had seen fellow Marines make hootch before. Hell, he'd helped do it more times than he could remember back in the day, donating his dessert to the cause. And there was an underground market for weapons, battle gear, and all the other things that enabled a rifle company to function when the supply chain couldn't deliver. But patties?

It was taken as gospel that the Alliance ran on patties—hell, that was why the crabs and others called Alliance Marines "patties." There were several kinds, depending on which planet created them, but all were fried dough filled with meat, sometimes veggies, and spices, notably garlic and fennel. The one thing in common was that they were not particularly easy to make—or at least make right.

"And how does he do that?" Teo asked.

"He rigged a little Kingston Oven, over in the back pumphouse."

Teo shook his head. A pattie could be fried in anything, but to be a real pattie, it had to be pressure-fried in a Kingston Oven, which were expensive and not on the Marine Corps Table of Equipment, or T/E. Even the patties served back at the Force chow hall were prepared in corporate fabricators and only reheated in the galley.

"Where does he get the ingredients?"

Force Supply checked all rations going out to the Marines for contagions, either natural or of the bio-weapon-type, and as far as he knew, they didn't pass out pattie-making ingredients.

"I didn't ask, sir. You know how it is sometimes."

Yes, Teo "knew how it was." He tried to avoid asking Sergeant Rios or the gunny where they scrounged up the things they did. But this was beyond the pale.

"And when does he do this? You said three times a week?"

"Yes, sir. When his squad is off the lines, so no duty time is lost. I heard he's firing up the oven today."

Teo stared at the gunny, who looked miserable. Without saying a word, he stood up and went to the ladder to climb out of the CP.

"Wait, sir!" the gunny shouted as he reached the top of the ladder.

Teo stopped, the ever-present rain falling lightly around him. The gunny climbed up after him.

"Yes?" Teo asked.

"Sir, I'm sorry I never told you. But sometimes . . . well, you know how it goes. You were enlisted."

Teo didn't know what to say. This was his company, and he needed to know what was going on at all times. He was embarrassed, more than anything else, that he'd been completely in the dark.

"If you're going to blame someone, blame me. I knew from the beginning."

"Does the first sergeant know?"

The gunny hesitated, then nodded.

"And the XO?"

"Oh, no, sir, no officers."

"No officers. Hmm."

He turned and strode off to the pumphouse that kept the water flowing and clean for the resort's rear series of pools, leaving the gunny behind. It ran on solar power, which was efficient enough to run the filters even during the rainy season, so it made sense. That, and it was isolated.

As Teo passed the diamond pool, a slight whiff of heaven reached him through the rain, making his mouth water. He swallowed hard and reached the pumphouse, which was disguised as a jungle rock with plants hanging from it. PFC Seymore was standing outside the door, sucking on a spike. He spotted Teo, put out the spike, and came to a sloppy position of attention, reaching back to knock on the door into the pumphouse itself.

"Seymore," Teo said, nothing more, as he pushed open the door.

Inside, Lance Corporal James, in his IFU bottoms and a white t-shirt, was watching gauges of what had to be the most convoluted Kingston Oven in the galaxy, looking like it used half of the pumphouse parts to make it work. Lance Corporal Sung, his battle buddy, was cleaning out a tub at the sink.

"Sir!"

Teo stepped forward, examining the setup, which looked surprisingly . . . *professional* . . . for a Marine jury-rigged operation.

The room was filled with the aroma of patties. They smelled right, at least. That didn't mean that James wasn't poisoning half the company.

"Do you know what you're doing?" he finally asked.

"My mother owns Wonder Patties on Wayfarer, best on the planet. I've helped her since I was six."

Teo swept his gaze around again, relieved. At least food poisoning didn't seem likely.

"Where are you getting your ingredients?" he asked.

James shifted his feet as he realized he might be in big trouble. "All sorts of places, sir. Mostly Sergeant R— . . . I mean, I just get it."

"And the pork?"

James shook his head slightly and said, "We wanted to get it from the Yutties, sir, but they ain't got none. So, I had to use P-21 flakes."

Teo raised his eyes. "P-21 flakes?"

"Yes, sir."

That threw Teo. P-21 flakes were textured vegetable protein. They weren't real meat, but they had a vague semblance to pork.

"I know it ain't the real deal, sir, but . . ."

But when they're without, Marines make do.

Teo couldn't imagine that P-21 flakes would make a decent pattie, but the aroma of garlic and fennel that permeated the pumphouse sure smelled good.

"What are you charging for the patties?" he asked.

"Charging? Nothing, sir. I mean, we all gotta chip in for the ingredients, but this is just a taste of home. You know, for all of us."

Teo ran through what he'd been told, checking off each one. Was what James was doing illegal? Almost assuredly. But the big regulations, court martial-worthy regs? He wasn't breaking them all.

"When will they be done?" Teo asked, pointing at the oven.

"Close enough to now, sir."

"Let me see them."

With a sigh of someone who knew the gig was up, James opened the release valve, and a wave of succulent goodness spread through the pumphouse. He cracked the oven and pulled a tray out of the fry sprayers, placing it on a table he'd dragged in from somewhere.

Teo leaned over and sniffed them. They smelled OK. He picked one up, blowing on his fingers and bouncing it back and forth in either hand, to keep them from burning. Sung smirked, but Teo ignored it.

"Are these safe?" he asked.

James pulled himself up in righteous indignation, and with the bravado of someone on death row, said, "I gauran-fucking-tee it . . . sir."

What James was doing was illegal, and if the CO found out, he'd have Teo's ass in a sling. But from his perspective, this was a no harm, no foul. No money-making, no dealings with the locals. Still . . .

"No more all the Marines chipping in to buy the ingredients, James. That's over."

The lance corporal-cum-chef's shoulders slumped in defeat, but he didn't argue.

"From now on, you come to me. I'll get you the money from the officers."

James looked up, hope dawning in his eyes.

"You mean . . . ?"

"Only in your downtime, when you're not on the line. And make sure you get your sleep. Deal?"

"Deal, sir!"

"And next time, don't leave the officers out."

"You got it, sir! Yes, sir!"

It was still illegal, but as officers had to pay for their food anyway, he thought he might be able to argue it easier if—no, when—this came out. And if he caught shit from the CO, well, sometimes a commander has to take a hit for the morale of his Marines.

He raised the still hot pattie to his mouth and took a bite . . . and almost moaned. It wasn't a Teresa's Most Excellent Pattie by any stretch of the imagination, but it was still a damned sight better than Pasta St. Ermile!

"*Sir, Battalion's on the hook. The S3 wants to speak to you. They've got a reading of a downed Saber drone in our AO,*" Corporal Wainsett passed through his collarbud.

Teo sighed. "I'm on my way."

He took another bite of the pattie. Duty called, but he was going to enjoy the damned thing first.

Chapter 8

Paladins

Sea air blew over Richter as he switched off his optics filters to appreciate the true view of his surroundings. Dawn was in full swing over a small cove, and storm clouds dumped dark sheets of rain over the ocean. On the beach was a wrecked wooden boat with a pronounced bow, and where the sand met the jungle, the remains of an elephant rotted.

Was there a whiff of decay from the ruddy bones and scraps of skin on the dead beast? Unlikely. War had come to this planet years ago. There weren't any pachyderm analogs on Ayutthaya. The elephant must have been imported from off-world or flash-cloned in a lab somewhere. Still expensive. Had it been killed in the initial fighting between the rebels and the royalists, or left to fend for itself when its caretakers were forced to flee?

He imagined the beach before the war, rich off-worlders soaking up the sun, paying extra for a ride on the elephant up and down the white sands, lounging with a drink served in a coconut shell with paper umbrellas. All that was gone.

He chided himself for losing focus. His troopers needed him on point, not imagining some tragedy of the early days of the war.

Only the war remained.

"Humidity's degrading our direct connection to the far flank of White Platoon," Szabo whispered. The radioman was doing fairly well for his first time outside the wire in his jack; he'd only needed to be pulled out the muck twice after missteps. His ballistics plates were streaked with mud, but the active camouflage blended him into the dark earth at the base of a rocky promontory where they'd set up their rally point.

"Friendlies coming in," a voice said from up the slope. The jungle had a firm grip on the hill, with tall trees and fronds overhead. Richter couldn't see where the sniper team had set up their nest, but he knew they were up there. They had top-of-the-line active camo and blended into their surroundings far faster than the camo liners on his jack's ballistics plates.

He'd positioned himself within earshot of the team to keep them from using their IR transmitters. Even this far from the enemy, he didn't want to risk them being detected.

"About time," Richter said, shifting his stance. His heavy jack had sunk a few more inches into the mud while they'd waited. He couldn't see a disturbance in the undergrowth as the team of flankers approached, so he cycled through optic filters, checking for heat plumes.

The flanker team had been under strict instructions to take the scenic route back to the overwatch position. If the enemy picked up their trail, Richter and his troopers would have time to set up another ambush. If they came straight back while under enemy observation, the flankers could have spoiled the snipers' nest.

"Grish and Tobias, on approach," came over the IR.

"Challenge and password," Lieutenant Kontos said.

"God damn it, don't shoot me. I mean . . . 'skipper,'" Grish said.

"Buddy," Kontos said. *"You drop the beacon?"*

"Never happier to dump expensive shit in my life. You think I wanted a pattie 'kick me' sign on my back?"

"And they dropped it right where I told them to," said Bradford, the sniper team observer. He was beneath an active camo cloak, a slight shimmer against the sunlight the only indication there was anyone else on the hill with Richter besides Szabo. "Beacon's been going for nineteen minutes . . . should pull in some targets soon."

"Are the patties really that desperate to recover one of their Sabers?" Richter asked.

"The guidance system on those bastards are expensive and mostly hardened against EMPs," Bradford said. "One goes down out in the bush, it's worth the risk to make a recovery. Someone at HQ must like you, sir. Using a captured Saber nose cone like this might not work in this A-O again. Fool me once . . ."

"Priority target pattie officers," Richter said. "Let's make this trip worth it."

They'd stepped off from base during the small hours of the morning, pushing dangerously close to Alliance lines to drop the bait. Now all they had to do was wait...

"How do they know if they're shooting an officer?" Szabo asked. "Don't think they walk around with their rank on their helmets, do they?"

"Body language," said Piotrowski, the sniper. "You see how the major's keeping his attention on all around? You're focused on him. The jack down-slope from us is checking on other jacks—there's a lieutenant. Flanker roving from fire team to fire team? Sergeant. I'm waiting for the pattie that everyone keeps looking to for instruction. They ain't dumb enough to salute each other in the field."

"Not that we haven't seen that happen." Bradford chuckled.

"Did you . . . shoot the one that saluted?" Szabo asked.

"Hell no. Shot the light colonel he was talking to right through the grill at seven hundred meters. You don't take the dumb ones off the field, kiddo," Piotrowski said.

"Thank God for the dumb ones." Bradford shifted beneath his camo tarp. "Aaaand time for us to move up into position. Cover us while we move. Be so kind as to not shoot us by accident."

"Guidons, guidons," Richter said into the IR. "Specialists stepping off from my location. Maintain sectors of fire. Weapons amber until I order otherwise."

"Think I can get two in one shot again?" Piotrowski asked as he climbed up the back of the promontory.

"You ain't got a hair on your ass if you don't," the spotter said.

Richter considered reminding them of the mission to kill Alliance leadership, but sniping was their call. He was the security element.

"Pass me video of your kills," Richter said.

Chapter 9

Marines

"It should be down there, sir, on the beach," Sergeant Wymer said, looking at one of his instruments. "Two-hundred and thirty-five meters."

"Rather curious that a Saber just happens to show up here," Gunny Walters said.

Teo brought up his binos, set the range, and scanned. What looked to be the nose cone of a Saber was lying on the shore. Successive waves rocked it, and if they got any bigger, they might reclaim it, taking it back out to sea.

"*XO, any word yet from battalion on our piece of flotsam?*" Teo asked over the secure command net.

Lieutenant Wooster, still sounding a little groggy for being woken in the middle of his sleep to take over the CP, passed, "*No records of a missing Saber in this area. But . . .*"

But the spooks above and beyond Force don't always keep us Marines on the ground informed of what they were doing, I know.

"*What does battalion want?*"

"*No change, sir. They want it recovered.*"

Teo glassed the Saber again. It looked legit, and it was passing out the right codes. He slowly scanned the rock-strewn beach. A creek fed into the ocean another thirty meters past the cone, and the sand was unmarked by tracks—it was clean all the way to the promontory another klick-and-a-half farther down the beach.

"Well, battalion says recover the damned thing," Teo told the gunny.

"Then recover it we shall."

"Sergeant Ling, helmets sealed, and move out your section. Keep on the alert, though. This isn't a walk in the park," he told the Second Rocket Section leader.

"You heard the skipper," Ling shouted to his men. "Move out, but keep your head on a swivel."

The twelve Marines, along with Teo, Gunny Walters, Wymer, and Sergeant Rios moved down onto the beach, a mule trundling behind its minder, Lance Corporal Wumara. Teo could have taken a rifle squad, but Lieutenant Verdun had been complaining that his Weapons Platoon Marines were getting bored and wanted some action. Plus, they had the company's mules, and one of those sure beat a couple of Marines struggling to carry a Saber, even just the cone, back to the company area.

"We're approaching the objective. Stand by," he passed back to Verdun. There might be no sign of the enemy, but that didn't mean Teo was going to just march down to pick up the cone. He had targets plotted along the treeline along the beach as well as on the promontory at the far curve of the beach.

Mules were powerful little machines, but they were not quick, so the patrol moved slowly into position. Teo felt an itch between his shoulder blades but shrugged it off as his imagination. That or the sweat that was building up inside his IFUs. He made a note to complain once more to battalion about the cooling systems acting up again, not that his previous complaints had resulted in anything.

The rocket section Marines might not have gotten to patrol much, but they were still Marines, and they flowed around the cone and set up security, looking professional.

The cone itself had seen better days. That was to be expected, Teo guessed. Something had happened to the complete drone, probably getting shot down, and then being washed around the ocean couldn't have done it any good. Teo doubted it could be salvaged, even if the beacon had activated, but no one wanted any part of a Saber to fall into crab hands.

Sergeant Ling looked around, waiting for an order. Out of habit, Teo started to take charge, but flashes of Officer Training School flashed before his mind. On the first day, they'd been given an exercise. They had a list of materials such as cerrocrete, a flag pole, tools, parts, and personnel consisting of three rifle squads and a platoon sergeant. The exercise asked the fledgling lieutenants how to erect the flagpole. The answers turned in were varied, with some impressive calculation with regard to center of mass, kilos of cerrocrete, angles, and such. Teo didn't have the same schooling, so his answer wasn't as exact, but it was in the same vein.

They were all wrong. The correct answer was to order, "Staff Sergeant, erect the flagpole." And as an officer, that had proven to be one of the most difficult things for him to remember.

He looked at the gunny, then shook his head. Not him.

"Sergeant Rios, you're the police sergeant. Take over."

"Really, sir? Roger that!"

He strode forward and immediately started giving orders to the section.

"Thanks, Skipper," the gunny said quietly. "He's been a great police sergeant, but you know, getting pulled from his squad was hard, and he's been feeling kinda useless."

Teo did know. He lost his own squad back in the day, but that was to go to Recon. Yet it had still been hard. Rios had been pulled to be the police sergeant, essentially the gunny's assistant, responsible for the mundane supplies and maintenance that it took to keep a rifle company functioning.

"Hey, let's pitch in," he told the gunny.

If Rios was surprised when the two senior Marines moved forward to help horse the cone onto the mule, he never let on. He was living for the moment.

Do your time, Rios, and I'll make sure you pick up staff. Your next job will be platoon sergeant.

They had just managed to get the cone up, and the mule was centering it, when there was a dull thunk that Teo had hoped he'd never again hear. He turned as Sergeant Rios collapsed backward to the sand, his helmet visor shattered into pieces just as the far-off report of the shot reached him.

Teo had seen too many people killed in his career to need his CCD display to know Rios was dead. He immediately reacted to keep the rest of his Marines alive.

"Off the beach!" Teo yelled out, darting to the nearest vegetation, only fifteen meters away, but seemingly much farther. Another shot echoed out in the few seconds it took the Marines to scramble for cover.

Teo hit the deck just inside the cover of the vegetation as his CCD chimed again, this time with Corporal Quinlan's avatar turning light blue. Teo spun around, risking raising his head. Rios' body was on its back, his faceshield shattered. Bright red blood was staining the sand under his head, only to be washed away with each wave of seawater. Closer, but still ten meters away, Quinlan was on his face, one arm ineffectively pulling at the sand.

"Stay still, Quinlan!" he shouted as he tried to make sense of the situation.

He looked down the beach, his brain making calculations based on how Rios had fallen. The round had to have come from farther down the beach. He looked in that direction, and within five seconds, he knew where the crab sniper was: on the promontory. At least that was where he'd be. It offered excellent fields of fire over the beach and good cover to conceal the exact location of the sniper.

"Fire mission. Immediate. Four rounds on Bourbon, I repeat, four rounds on Bourbon, and two smoke at . . ." He focused on a spot in the sand, twenty meters away from Quinlan, and blinked up the coordinates. "At three-six-six-two-five, eight-six-one-zero-five."

"Anybody else hit?" Gunny Walters shouted out, but Teo pushed that concern out of his mind for the moment. He brought up his binos and scanned the rocky, tree-covered outcrop.

"Rounds away. HE impact in twenty-three seconds, smoke thirty-one."

Shit. Too far apart.

"I've got smoke in thirty seconds. I need someone to pick up Quinlan," he passed the net.

Several voices responded, but he cut them off, switching to the P2P. "Hang in there, Corporal Quinlan. We've got smoke incoming, and we'll get you back."

"Roger, that," the corporal managed to get out, sounding scared.

Teo pulled up Quinlan's bios. The corporal wasn't doing well, with diminished lung capacity. Probably took a lung shot. But his readings weren't into the imminent danger range. Doc Tessera should be able to stabilize him.

Teo couldn't focus on Quinlan, however. He counted the seconds down. At his count of twenty-two, the top of the promontory erupted in explosions, sending vegetation and rocks flying. Teo didn't care about that. He wanted to spot the sniper. He saw nothing, however. Either he was wrong on the enemy hide or the sniper was very-well disciplined.

Teo wasn't wrong, though, he was sure. He'd gone through the meatgrinder that was Marine Sniper School as a Recon Marine, and he knew where he'd set up his hide: right on the sea side of the promontory, partway down, where the Marine rockets couldn't hit him. Them. The crabs deployed a sniper and spotter, just as the Marines did.

Six seconds after the rounds hit the hill, two rounds slammed into the sand, sending billowing smoke into the air.

"Open fire on the hill!" Teo shouted as Doc Tessera got to his feet and darted to Quinlan. He grabbed the Marine by the "dead man's handle," a bar where the back of the helmet connected to the rest of the IFU, and started dragging him to cover.

"Come on, Doc!" someone shouted.

Just as Doc reached the edge of the vegetation, another round hit Quinlan in the chest, tearing it open. Blood misted around the corporal's body as Doc pulled him in.

Quinlan's avatar shifted to gray, and anger boiled from Teo's core.

Fuck! Who the hell shoots a wounded man?

Shouts of anger rose from the Marines as well.

Teo looked back to the promontory, wanting to unleash Hell's own fury on the sniper, ready to charge, before he caught himself.

The bastard wants to get us angry, to react.

Why else would he shoot a wounded man and not the corpsman rescuing him?

"*Calm down, calm down,*" he passed. "*Be smart.*"

Acting in a rash manner was a sure way to get more Marines killed. He took three deep breaths, then got back to what he had to do next. First of all, he needed to find out exactly where the sniper was. He ordered four more rounds, evenly spaced around the hill, hoping to make the sniper flinch. Once again, however, he caught nothing. He could keep on, but it would be a waste of ammo.

"Skipper, we can't pull back. There's a huge-ass open area behind us." the gunny said.

Teo turned around and took a quick glance. The creek that fed into the ocean was a wide lagoon with a sandy beach. The Marines were now trapped on what was a spit of land covered with low vegetation. Trying to get off the spit would expose them.

Teo looked back up to the promontory with grudging respect. The sniper could not have picked a better spot for the ambush.

"I want everyone to keep down as low as they can and freeze. No movement."

That means me too!

He shuffled back until he couldn't see the hill.

"*What do you want me to do?*" the XO asked.

Teo thought about it. He could send Third Platoon around to flank the promontory, then assault across it. That would take time, cost Marine lives, and possibly lead Third into a bigger ambush. It was an option, however, maybe the textbook solution that some commanders would order.

Not him. Teo knew what he wanted to do. He was sniper-trained, and he knew the best weapon against a sniper was a better sniper.

"Send up Yelsik and Juarez. Tell Yelsik to bring an extra M-209." He pulled up his map display, picked a spot, and highlighted it. "I want them to get here fast, but hold up. I'm going to have to create a diversion to get them over."

Corporal "Snake" Yelsik was the battalion scout sniper attached to the company, Lance Corporal J.T. Juarez his A-gunner/spotter. Yelsik was school-trained, and a certified HOG, "Hunter of Gunman," with twelve confirmed kills. He wore a .3007 round on a parachute cord around his neck that they called a Hog's Tooth—the theory being that every sniper has a round with his name on it. If he wore that round around his neck, the enemy couldn't use it to kill him.

Juarez had gone through the regimental sniper course and was still a PIG, a "Professionally Instructed Gunman." As Yelsik's spotter, it was his job to watch the trace of the 295-grain, .3007 round, and then call for corrections.

With all the modern weaponry available, almost all snipers in militaries across the galaxy still used old-fashioned chemical rounds, not much different from those used on 20th Century Earth. The bells and whistles might be different, and the ranges might have increased, but the act of getting a small hunk of metal to take out an enemy was essentially the same.

And now, Teo and the rest waited. Until the sniper either left or was killed, any attempt to move would be suicide.

Even staying put could be, too. After almost nineteen minutes, another round reached them, and a Marine yelled out in pain.

PFC St. George's avatar turned light blue. He'd been hit in the shoulder, and his nanos were activated.

"The skipper told you to freeze, Rabbit!" Sergeant Ng shouted out, using St. George's nickname.

"Ants were biting me," St. George managed to get out as he moaned in pain.

"Yeah, and look what moving did to you, dipshit. Fuck! All of you, freeze your sorry asses. I don't care if ants are biting your dicks! Just freeze!"

Teo watched St. George's readouts, and his bios started to settle in as the nanos did their work. He didn't know how badly the PFC was hurt, but his readout didn't list him as a Priority 1 medivac. He could afford to wait.

Teo had second thoughts and ordered Third Platoon to saddle up and move to the crossroads of the Beach Highway and Route 22, which would place them about 400 meters from the promontory, to be ready if needed. He was still going to use Yelsik as his first line of attack, though.

Twenty-four minutes after the attack, the scout-sniper team reached their designated spot.

"We're going to give you cover. When I tell you, haul ass to get to me."

"Can we engage from this position?" Yelsik asked.

"That's a negative. I think you're too far back. You need to be here to get a decent line of fire."

"Roger that. We're ready."

"Fire Mission, Immediate, Bourbon, four rounds," Teo passed to Weapons Platoon.

"Rounds away, impact twenty-three seconds," came the almost instantaneous reply.

"Get ready!" Teo called out. "As soon as the rounds hit, light up the hill.

"You've got fifteen seconds," he passed directly to Yelsik.

He counted it down in his mind, and as the rockets hit the promontory, thirteen Marines and a Navy corpsman rose up en masse and fired. The snipers were probably 1700 meters away, technically within the max effective range of a 51 whether in dart or grenade mode, but in reality, without even knowing where the sniper was, the chances of hitting him were remote. Teo wasn't expecting to hit him, however. He just wanted to give Yelsik and Juarez covering fire.

The scout-sniper team tore across the sandy banks of the lagoon and dove for cover in the little islet of vegetation where the Marines were positioned.

"Cease fire!" Teo shouted out as he turned to Yelsik.

"You got the extra 209?" he asked.

Yelsik couldn't quite suppress a slight frown as Juarez handed it over. Teo knew what he was doing was irregular, and he wasn't going to take the mission from Yelsik, but the fact of the matter was that he was the only other HOG in the company. Juarez was a good marksman, but shooting on a range was different from in the field, and if it came to that, Teo trusted himself more than he trusted Juarez.

Besides, he had the inklings of a plan.

Teo took the 209 and entered his numbers. While the barrel and firing mechanism were not much different from early sniper rifles, the sights and stock were lightyears apart from them. The stock and grip started warping, the sight adjusting. Within twenty seconds, the rifle was custom-fitted to him. He raised it to the shoulder, letting the sight run a fitting to his retina. It felt good to get locked in, just as it was when he was a sergeant.

Of course, it would take rounds on a range to completely snap in, but even as it was, Teo was pretty confident that he could hit a target with it, especially at only 1700 meters.

He detached the Firing Scanner from the sling and shot the promontory, just where a rock on the seaward side jutted out. "Seventeen-hundred, thirty-eight meters," he said aloud as he checked it. "Temperature: thirty-one degrees. Humidity: sixty-seven percent."

Teo didn't have to read them aloud. Yelsik had the twin AI. But he'd made it a habit of repeating everything, and old habits died hard.

He checked the planetary input. Ayutthaya was .98 Earth Gravity and had a slightly faster rotation, and that had to be inputted. More than a few Marines had been killed over the years for relying on his Firing AI when another planet's data being used. This one was set correctly.

A sniper was not just a steady hand and smooth trigger pull. He had to be a mathematician. Even with an AI taking into account spindrift, temperature, humidity, planetary rotation, gravity, wind, elevation, and air density, among the major factors, to calculate the precise aiming point, a sniper had to have a feel for shifts and changes. As he looked out past the beach, over the water, and to the promontory, he could see three different wind directions in the intervening space, all of which had to be taken into account.

"What's the plan, sir?" Yelsik asked, clearly not happy with Teo horning in on what he considered his mission.

Teo didn't care . . . much. He was still the commander.

"Here's what we're going to do . . .

****

Teo lay on his belly, the muzzle of his 209 aimed at the promontory as he scoped the hillside. It had taken him forty-five minutes to edge forward, millimeter by millimeter until he had a direct line of fire. Fifteen meters to his right, Yelsik and Juarez were emplaced in their . . . "hide" wasn't the right term. There wasn't any preparation, so he and Yelsik were just lying on spots on the ground, no different than the rest of the Marines. Teo's position wasn't even that good. Several broad-leaf plants were just forward of his muzzle, and they would be blown about by his muzzle flash when he fired.

Teo didn't have to scope the promontory. Juarez had his XKE-50, the mass of technology that fed Yelsik's firing AI, and all that data were now being uploaded to Teo's as well. But he felt better watching the hill, even if that put him more at risk. If he could see the crab sniper, the crab could see him.

101

Not that the crab didn't know where they all were. His spotter would be scanning their position, looking for heat and CO_2 signatures. Helmeted up, there would be no CO_2 signatures, and their IFU Outer Protective Layers diffused the heat. Those might be enough to muddy the waters, but enough traces were there that would tell the crabs that Marines were still huddled in the bushes.

And conversely, once Juarez got his XKE working, there were traces that two crabs were on the hill somewhere. There were probably a couple of others, at least initially, but it looked like they might have bugged out.

"Take a potshot, hoping to get lucky, asshole," Teo muttered, and not for the first time.

But the enemy sniper was not that stupid. He wasn't going to risk revealing his position unless he had a sure shot.

"Harris, how's the displacement looking?" he asked Lieutenant Verdun, checking again if the rest of Weapons Platoon could move into a position where they could target the seaward side of the promontory.

"Not great, sir. If he's where you think he is, I'd need a barge to get into position."

"And battalion?"

"Still a no go. They aren't going to waste assets on a single sniper."

Teo had assumed as much, but he wanted to check one last time.

It's up to us.

"You ready, Wumara?" he asked the lance corporal.

"Ooh-rah, sir! I'm ready!"

"I'm sending Wumara," he passed to Yelsik. "Counting down. Five . . . four . . . three . . . two . . . one . . . GO!"

Lance Corporal Wumara jumped up and ran back to where the bank dropped a foot and dived to the ground.

And there it was. The tiniest motion of a fern-like plant, moving against the sea breeze. No shot, though, as Teo had expected (and hoped). Teo didn't know who the sniper was targeting, but he expected it was an officer or SNCO, not a Marine trying to retreat. And that meant, by letting Rios take charge of the recovery, Teo had painted a target on his back that got him killed. He'd anguish over that later, but he had to compartmentalize for now.

"I've got motion at three-six-five—"

"I've got it, too," Yelsik interrupted.

Teo watched through the scope, trying to pick up something, anything else.

"Who do you think it is?" he asked.

There was a pause, then "Spotter."

Teo agreed, but he'd been hoping Yelsik would say something different.

"Roger that. Aiming in now."

Using the edge of the sand as a brace, Teo slowly, ever-so-slowly, traversed the muzzle of his 209 and brought the crosshairs onto the spot on the side of the promontory. The vegetation was thick, and volcanic outcroppings gave the spot more protection, but that was where the movement had been.

This was almost Kentucky Windage. The Firing AI had given its verdict: 26.5 Minutes of Angle right, 17 Minutes of Angle up. The AI solution. But Teo had no DOPE, or Data on Previous Engagements, on this weapon, so he didn't know how his own personal quirks in firing would impact the AI firing solution.

All there was to do now was to find out.

With the weapon set, Teo slowly moved away from the rifle half a meter to the side and reached back, to the trigger release, the small button that had long ago replaced the old-fashioned pull triggers.

"Firing now."

He pressed the trigger, hoping his movement hadn't shifted the weapon off target. There was a crack as the Thienny .3007 round—coincidentally, the same round the crab snipers used—shot downrange. Teo counted out four seconds, then three back . . . but he was still surprised when the enemy .3007 slammed into the forward handguard of his 209, sending shards into his hand.

An instant later, Yelsik fired. Clutching his hand, Teo rolled on his side, watching Juarez.

"Hit," the spotter said as calmly as if he was saying what he had for lunch.

"Is he dead?" Teo asked.

"No movement. Head pretty messed up. Uh . . . yes, sir. Dead."

"What about the spotter?"

"Can't see. You hit right where the movement was, though, sir."

"Did you get the bastard?" the gunny asked over the P2P.

"Yelsik got the sniper. We don't know about the spotter. Get one of the drones back and see if they can see anything now."

"Hey, are you hit, sir? I'm getting some readings on your bios."

"No. Not by a round. Took some splinters, though."

Teo brought the bloody hand up to look at it. A fairly large chunk of his 209's handguard was lodged in the meaty part of his thumb.

Pretty stupid leaving my hand there.

He felt a little light-headed, but his nanos kicked in. He took off his helmet, pulled out two of the smaller splinters, and gave the larger one a tug, but it wouldn't come. He'd have to let Doc take that one out.

"Good shooting, Yelsik," he called out.

"You, too, sir. You've still got it."

He might have gotten lucky with his shot, but having the real kill shot go to Yelsik was the right choice, and not just because it was his job. Yelsik was a proven commodity, he was using his personal weapon, and he'd been firing recently. Teo had a weapon that was not completely snapped in to him, and he hadn't fired a 209 in six years.

Teo was qualified to be the bait, but not the actual sniper.

He settled in, his mind a little loopy as the nanos did their work. He drifted off a bit, his mind wandering, when the gunny appeared in front of him and said, "We've got images, sir. One confirmed kill."

Teo slid his helmet back on and ran the feed. The sniper was almost completely exposed. Yelsik's round had taken off the back of his head, and that must have knocked off his camo tarp.

The other body wasn't in direct view, but it was obvious that Teo's round had hit the spotter's firing solution AI, destroying it. Whether the round had passed through to hit the spotter, or the pieces of AI-turned-shrapnel had killed him didn't matter. Something vaguely human-shaped was covered by a tarp, and it was probably the spotter's body, but he couldn't be sure.

"What are your orders, sir?" the gunny asked.

Teo stood and looked at the promontory. No round reached out to smack him down. He wanted to climb up there and see his kill, but he had St. George and the two dead Marines here, and Okanjo was in position.

He brought up the Third Platoon commander, keying in the gunny and Yelsik as well.

"Trace, I need you to clear the promontory and confirm the kills. I'll have Weapons and Corporal Yelsik in direct support. Be ready for more crabs. They tend to send out security with their snipers."

There was a snort, then "Pussies" from Yelsik.

Teo rolled his eyes. Marine snipers had pretty high opinions of themselves and pretty low of any other snipers. Not that Teo had been any different.

"I want you to hit the hill hard with the rockets before you move onto it."

"Roger that, sir. We're ready."

He looked over to the east, where Third Platoon was, tempted to run over and catch up to them. With a sigh, he pushed that thought back down.

"Gunny, let's recover Rios and Quinlan and get St. George treated. We still need to take back the Saber. It was obviously a plant, but the mission still stands. If the mule's still working, use it to get it, Rios, Quinlan and St. George back. If not, get another out here."

"What about you, sir? You're bleeding like a stuck pig."

As if reminding him turned a switch, his hand started to ache. He looked at the chunk of handguard still sticking out of his hand, slowly flexing the fingers. It hurt, and there was grating that shouldn't be there, but it worked, and the nanos were swarming to the site, doing their magic. Even now, there was very little new blood seeping around the edges of where the shard punctured his flesh.

"Take care of the others. I'll let Doc Sanaa take a look when we get back."

He picked up the 209 as the Marines got ready to move out. The enemy sniper's round had hit the front handguard right at the barrel, shattering it. If Teo had been firing it in earnest, looking through the scope, he would have eaten the round. The crab sniper had been that good.

Not good enough, though. You're dead.

Teo slung the 209 over his shoulder and shifted back to his 51. It was going to make a good addition to his I Love Me wall when this shit was over.

"*Skipper, we're in position, and we've got movement to our front. What are your orders?*" Trace Okanjo passed.

"*Engage . . . wait, identify, and if they're crabs, engage! I don't want . . .*"

He thought for a moment. Third Platoon was only 450 meters away. He looked at his hand. He knew he needed to let Doc take the shard out of it, but the nanos had stopped all the bleeding.

Screw it.

"Gunny, take over here."

Teo switched back to the command net to Third. "*If they're crabs, kill them. Call for rocket support as needed. But a head's up. I'm on my way to your pos, so don't drop a rocket on my ass.*"

Chapter 10

Paladins

Another rocket exploded in the treetops, and branches and burning leaves fell around Richter. Small pings of shrapnel and wood fragments falling against his ballistics plates felt like hail smacking against a thick jacket.

A blanket of smoke filled the air overhead. He fixed his air filter over his mouth as the crackle of flames and the whoosh of rising air filled the jungle.

Richter ordered a withdrawal as soon as the first Alliance rockets found their range, but Piotrowski and Bradford hadn't acknowledged the instructions or found their way back to the rally point.

More artillery smashed into the promontory where he'd abandoned the sniper team.

"I've got nothing on the IR, sir!" Szabo shouted from a few feet behind him. "Flankers have pulled back, jack section's still with us."

Fire wrapped around tree trunks, and a tree fell into the growing blaze, knocking up a cloud of sparks that drifted through the air and past the major.

"We can't get through that," he said.

"The beach? We can cut around and—"

"And be exposed to direct fire from the patties," Richter said. "We can't take the smoke, even in our jacks."

"We can't just leave them up there!" Kontos shouted, trying to move past Richter, but the major grabbed him by the carry handle on the back of his jack.

"No!" Richter pulled him back. "They're dead. We try and recover them and we'll bleed for nothing."

Kontos turned and broke Richter's hold on him. "You're an outlander. You don't—"

A burst of rifle fire flashed to one side and bullets stitched up Richter's leg. His knee brace buckled and he stumbled against Kontos.

"Action left!" Szabo leveled his cycler and unloaded, sweeping the muzzle back and forth as his bullets chewed up the undergrowth and sent whirls through the smoke.

Kontos stepped between Richter and the enemy as a rocket launcher on his back snapped up next to his head, and he fired into the jungle. The recoil forced him back and his thigh slapped against Richter's helmet.

"Up, sir!" Kontos joined Szabo in laying down suppressing fire.

Richter kicked his bum leg out and the servos locked.

"I'm lame, damn it." The major pushed himself up with his working jack leg and hobbled backwards.

A patch of jungle erupted with rifle fire, and bullets sprang off his breastplate, punching Richter into a tree. The back of his head hit the bark, dazing him for a brief moment.

More gunfire broke out. Flankers charged out, coughing as they fired carbines at the unseen Marines.

"Fall back!" Richter shouted and joined the shooting, each burst sending his cycler wide as his jack failed to compensate.

A gust of wind off the cove carried a blanket of smoke with it, throwing the entire fight into a choking haze.

"Buddy teams! Call out by sections!" Kontos shouted.

Szabo slapped Richter on the back twice as they moved away.

Richter strained to hear every pair of troopers calling out that they were together, praying that more men weren't lost in the fire. Praying that he wouldn't leave more behind.

Chapter 11

Marines

"We need to close the gap, Trace," Teo passed. *"They're flankers, not jacks. Push."*

"We're on it," Okanjo almost snapped into his mic.

Teo felt a twinge of guilt, but Okanjo was being too cautious. He needed to keep up the pressure on the fleeing crabs, not giving them time to react.

"No, you're not on it!" Teo snapped back. *"They're increasing the gap between us."*

Teo knew his anger was not aimed solely at his lieutenant. The crabs had laid a trap, a good one, and one into which battalion had ordered him. That had cost him Rios and Quinlan.

But the crabs were going to pay. There were the two dead snipers, and at least two more flankers in this running firefight, but that wasn't enough. He wanted them all, and Okanjo wasn't reacting quick enough. The crabs had gotten around Third Platoon's blocking position and were now in running mode.

A string of carbine fire cut leaves and branches five meters from Teo's head, but he didn't flinch. He could tell it wasn't aimed fire. Probably a rear guard, randomly firing to slow the pursuit.

He raised his own VP-51 to return fire, wincing as he hit the forestock shard still stuck in his hand.

This is getting ridiculous.

Marine Corps training was to never take something foreign out of yourself or another Marine. Only corpsmen were authorized to do that. He could take his medkit and bandage it in place, but it was interfering with functioning.

He rolled over on his back and took a closer look. The shard was about two centimeters across, and four centimeters was sticking out of the meaty portion of his hand. He didn't know how deep it ran. His hand and glove were covered in drying blood, but it looked like the bleeding had stopped.

Fuck it.

With his left hand, he grabbed the hunk of forestock and ripped it free.

Shit, that hurts!

The nanos had deadened the pain, but they couldn't block this.

He pressed on the hand as the bleeding recommenced and looked up to catch Sergeant Gauta's eyes.

"Hardcore, Skipper," the big, broad-shouldered sergeant said, having watched him do his own extraction.

Teo shrugged and rolled back over to his belly and fired a burst into the jungle. More rockets slammed up ahead, tearing up the jungle.

"I need more eyes," he passed back to Sergeant Wymer.

"I'm almost at the CP. I'll have them up in five."

"Make it three."

Teo needed those drones. He had to know what he faced and where they were.

Okanjo ordered Third Squad to try and flank the retreating crabs. Sergeant Gauta stood up to get his Marines moving, and Teo jumped up to join them. If Wymer didn't have eyes up yet, then he'd have to get closer.

So far, Teo hadn't heard the *tot-tot-tot* of a jacked crab's cycler, but that didn't mean they only faced flankers, or that jacked crabs weren't hiding in wait ahead. As much as Teo wanted Okanjo to push it, he didn't want to walk into another trap.

Gauta led his platoon at a jog—dangerous and exposed, but necessary. If Okanjo and Second Squad could fix the crabs in place, Gauta and Third could run right up their flank.

Teo slipped in the formation, using them as security. Firing was off to their left flank, and close. No cycler fire yet, only the sharp crack of crab carbines with the snap of 51s in counterpoint.

A burst of fire reached out from the jungle, hitting Lance Corporal Anand. Teo joined the rest in returning a withering fire, and they either hit the crab or drove him off. Anand got back shakily to his feet, giving the rest of the squad a thumbs-up.

Within another minute, the squad reached the rice fields bordering Kallaprapruek Road, the small road running up the west side of the peninsula to Patong Beach. Sergeant Gauta brought the squad to a halt at the edge. Some two hundred meters to the north, four crab flankers jumped up from a drainage ditch and darted across the road, and at least twenty rifles opened up, but the four were too quick and melted into the jungle on the other side.

"Wymer, I need that—"

"On station in one mike. Channel 104."

Teo switched to the channel, and the road came into view. Teo blinked a ref-point, just where the crabs had crossed the road, and the drone flew into position.

"Channel 104, Trace," Teo passed to the platoon commander.

Sergeant Gauta shifted over beside him, without saying a word. Teo got the hint, though, and patched him into the drone feed.

"Lyle, I want everyone in the CP watching this." Wainsett had the comms suite, and he could manipulate the feed a thousand ways so they could analyze what the drone picked up.

The drone followed the crabs' trail. Within twenty seconds, it had acquired them hurrying down a well-worn trail.

"I'm sending over Second Squad," Okanjo passed to Teo.

The rice field, coupled with the road, was a big danger area. The crabs could be setting up an ambush. But if they stopped, the rest of the crabs would get away.

"Stand by for targets," Teo passed back to Weapons.

If it was an ambush, the crabs would pay.

To his right, Teo could see motion as Second Squad, led by Sergeant Cheung, started to move forward, covered by First and Third. It was a good choice. The sergeant was an old hand. He knew the drill.

With a snap, the drone's feed went dark.

Damned crab EMPs!

Wymer would get more in the air, but Teo needed eyes now. He switched his CCD to the sergeant's view. The squad reached the edge of the road where the three teams went to their bellies and scanned across.

Sergeant Cheung's feed fluttered on Teo's display.

"Gunny, let's check those helmets when they get back. They're getting more and more out of kilter," Teo passed on the P2P.

"Aye-aye, sir. I'm on it," the gunny said.

Kilo Company had only been out beyond the wire this time for 2 1/2 months, but the relentless rainy season and the accompanying mold was wreaking havoc upon the Marines' equipment. Gunny Walters and Sergeant Rios spent most of their time managing the upkeep of the company gear.

Teo felt a lump in his throat. Sergeant Rios wouldn't be doing that any longer.

He made a mental note that he had to replace Rios, then focused on the feed knowing that the gunny would get on it. At least the feed was still coming through. That was never a sure thing anymore. Between the elements and the active jamming by the crabs, it was a rare day when the system worked even this well.

Sergeant Cheung sent across his First Fire Team. Their dispersion was good as they moved, and the Marines stopped just short of the treeline on the other side, taking a knee. One of the Marines—Teo had to look on his command pad to see that it was Lance Corporal Richardson—swept his P-30 scanner to their front, checking for the crabs. A moment later, Corporal Wes Tiolette, the fire team leader, turned to signal the rest of the squad to move forward.

There was a time when Teo knew every Marine in the company and could pick them out from behind if necessary. But with the rash of new joins sent to replace losses, to include Lieutenant Popovitch, too many of the Marines were new to him. Richardson was just a name on his command pad. He'd never even talked to the kid yet. He made another mental note to get out tomorrow morning and make the rounds. It had been easier as a platoon commander, and much easier as a squad leader, to know the Marines under his command, but that was no excuse. Even with only 156 Marines in the company and attached in direct support, he needed to know every one of them, and not just as a billet.

Corporal Tiolette got his Marines up and led them forward toward the trail the crabs had taken where they would provide cover for the rest of the squad moving over the open area. Teo kept expecting to hear the sound of fire, but the jungle was silent.

"Time is fleeting, Trace," Teo passed.

"I'm on it."

Almost immediately, Sergeant Cheung stood up, and covered by his First Fire Team, the rest of the squad hurried across, taking cover on either side of the trail. The sergeant turned to wave at the rest of the platoon, then signaled Tiolette to move forward.

Teo was just about to cut the lead and tell Gauta to cross, when Tiloette's point man, PFC Rose-Wilcox, suddenly looked down to his left into the jungle foliage, and there was the slightest sign of movement before a blast momentarily whitened the feed while compensators struggled to adjust.

Teo leaped to his feet.

"What was it? Did we have incoming?" he shouted as the feed cleared.

Not that he could see much. Sergeant Cheung had hit the deck and was only now looking up as he yelled out orders to his Marines.

"Give me eyes, Wymer!"

"Launching U-20 now."

The U-20 was a very basic, non-stealthy drone. Controlled by Sergeant Wymer but carried at the fire team level, one came online, and Teo switched over his feed. Vampiring off the comms net, it was more difficult to jam. The drone rose into the air, giving Teo a birds-eye view.

At the trail head, four bodies lay jumbled, a sight that made Teo's stomach churn. PFC Rose-Wilcox, "RW," had been torn apart by the blast.

He looked at his command pad. RW's avatar was grayed out. KIA. The other three were light blue of being wounded, but still alive.

"Was that incoming?" he shouted again, this time over the net, forcing himself back to what he had to do.

"Negative, sir. No incoming," Wainsett passed.

But Teo already knew that. This was just confirmation. He'd seen too much in his career. There was no crater, and the foliage had been shredded "up," something that was hard to explain, but he knew it when he saw it. An air blast shredded "down."

"It was a mine," he said, more to himself than to his small CP. "Right there."

He blinked twice as he stared at the spot, marking it on the feed.

"But the crabs just walked past there," Sergeant Gauta, who'd been watching it all said.

"*Gunny, you see that?*" Teo asked over the P2P.

Teo and Gunny Walters had never before served together, but he'd come to heavily rely upon the fellow recon Marine as his sounding board since taking over the company. He'd had more combat experience than Teo, and he'd know what that was.

"*Had to be Bennies,*" the gunny said.

That was what Teo had thought, but he wanted confirmation.

Teo turned his head, flipped up the edge of his helmet, and spat on the ground, bile rising in his throat. The four crabs they'd seen had been bait, and with the Bennies, the stakes had just gotten higher.

First the ambush on the beach, and now this. The crabs were upping the ante.

Intel hadn't put the Benedicts on the crab T/E, but Intel had been wrong before. The damned things were deadly, taking out anyone who came near without a special transponder wristband worn by every crab soldier. Bennies could be detected with Marine gear at close range . . . but the evil things had limited mobility on long spider legs that could rush their targets and detonate before they could be detected. If the crabs had them in any numbers, then Kilo Company was hemmed in just as much as if there was an entire regiment surrounding them.

Teo switched back to Cheung's feed, and he could see Doc Zuma, the squad corpsman, rushing forward to Tiolette and his team. Lieutenant Okanjo was yammering on, demanding updates from Cheung as the sergeant tried to manage the scene.

"*Lieutenant, back off,*" Teo said on the person-to-person, the P2P. "*Let him do his job. He doesn't need to be giving you a second-by-second tally of what's going on. I want you to take the rest of your platoon and get over there. Secure the area, and I'm sending out a mule for a medivac, coordinates to follow.*"

Teo winced at his last words. He hoped it would be a medivac, and not simply a recovery. RW was KIA, he knew, but he didn't know how bad the others were yet. Hopefully, Doc Zuma could keep them alive long enough to get back to the battalion aid station.

"*And run a sniffer at the blast site. Take samples, too, from the dirt and the foliage.*"

It was one thing for the gunny and him to think it was a Bennie, but the Intel folks would want to make sure.

"*You got that?*" he asked.

Whatever the lieutenant said was cut off when the battalion CO's voice cut in, overriding everything else. "*What the hell is going on out there, Captain Mateo?*"

Teo waved his hand to catch the Sergeant Gauta's attention, then mouthed, "Call in a medivac," using the twirling finger that was the hand-and-arm signal for the medivac jet-hover. The sergeant gave him a thumbs up.

"Third Platoon hit a landmine. I've got one KIA and three WIA—"

"*I can see what the hell you've got, Captain. I've been vampiring off your feeds. What are you doing about it?*" the man screamed over the net.

Teo looked at the feed. Sergeant Cheung had his Marines in a defensive position around the dead and wounded while Doc tended them. He'd stay there until the rest of the platoon crossed the road. Other than calling in a medivac, there wasn't much he personally could do, and there certainly wasn't anything the battalion CO could do.

He had to let Sergeant Cheung, and then Lieutenant Okanjo do their jobs without having to worry about higher headquarters. He gave a mental sigh. The best thing he could do would be to keep the colonel out of everyone's hair until the wounded were taken care of.

"Well, sir, we've formed a hasty perimeter around our WIA until we can reinforce it with . . ."

****

"So, what are we going to do?" the first sergeant asked. "It's gonna be a bitch to try and find each and every one of those friggin' things."

Teo shook his head. He didn't have a ready answer. Five minutes ago, Regiment had confirmed that the mine that had killed Rose-Wilcox and wounded the other three Marines was a Bennie.

Small and with no metallic parts, they were almost impossible to detect from any distance, and getting closer resulted in the mines going mobile, rushing them, and detonating . . . unless, of course, you had one of the personal transponders which blocked the detonator, and the crabs weren't about to pass them out.

"No help from the engineers, sir?" the XO asked.

"They're on higher priority missions," Teo said, biting back the anger.

Those hadn't been the CO's exact words. His were more in the line for Teo to just effing take care of it and not wait for someone else to bail him out.

"I don't suppose you've got anything in your bag of tricks, Sergeant Wymer," Teo asked without much hope.

The sergeant looked down at the ground and murmured, "No, sir. Nothing. Sorry."

Teo looked around at the others: the XO, first sergeant, gunny, all four platoon commanders, and Wymer. All were good Marines, but the Bennie mines were tech they weren't equipped to address. But his command staff was all he had, and they had to come up with something.

He gave a glance at the Tac Board. He'd had the company in Condition Alpha since the ambush—and it had been an ambush, pure and simple, one into which he'd allowed his Marines to blunder. Nothing showed beyond the company lines, but that didn't mean the crabs weren't out there. They knew the company was trapped, and his opposing crab commander wasn't going to pass up on that advantage. It wasn't a matter of "if" but of "when."

"We can use our Badger to clear paths, sir," Popovich said.

Gunny Walters snorted in derision.

Teo ignored the gunny. It was a stupid idea, but he had to cut the lieutenant some slack. Sam's butterbars hadn't even begun to tarnish in Ayutthaya's rainy season, he was so new. He was as eager as a puppy to ingratiate himself with the rest.

"We can't send it forward without infantry support. It'd be a sitting duck to one of the crabs' hunter-killer teams," he said.

The lieutenant turned red and stammered out an apology.

"Don't ever apologize for offering an idea, Sam," Teo said. "The worst idea is the one that's never brought up."

Except that was a really bad idea. What are they teaching the boot lieutenants at Officer Basic School?

First Lieutenant Trace Okanjo cleared his throat. "Sir, we've still got Sergeant Gauta."

Teo rolled his eyes. Trace was a good young lieutenant, one with all the degrees and schooling that he lacked, but with a practical head on his shoulders . . . except as it pertained to Sergeant Gauta.

Sergeant Gauta G. Gauta was a broad-shouldered, barrel-chested, mountain of a Marine who made Teo look skinny. A native of Nouveau Niue in the Pasifiki Federation, he was a mass of muscle. Like many Pasifikis, he followed—almost worshipped—ancient traditions. While Kilo Company was acting as the aggressors for deployment workups, and before Teo took over the company, the sergeant had stripped down to a loincloth one night (or grass skirt, depending on who you believed), snuck into the battalion lines, and "killed" the CO and his Alpha Command.

The CO was royally pissed, and he would have brought the sergeant up on charges if the sergeant major hadn't intervened. It might have been bad for morale had Sergeant Gauta been demoted, but the CO wasn't going to let his embarrassment go without taking action. Jeremy Thaeder, the former Golf Company Commander, was transferred to regiment, and Teo was transferred in with direct orders to "get rid of the fucking cowboys and bring the company into line."

When the first rains slowed operations to a standstill almost a month ago, Trace had asked Teo for permission to let Gauta recon the crabs. Teo had given that idea an immediate and resounding "NO!" And that wasn't just because of the CO's orders. Yes, it might have been funny for a mostly naked island warrior to sneak into the battalion CP, but this wasn't a war game. This was the real deal, and not back in the South Pacific on Mother Earth a couple of millennia ago. This was a modern battlefield where a Marine's body armor and battle kit kept him alive.

"We've gone over this, Lieutenant," Teo said, end of subject.

But it wasn't.

"I think he can get in and steal some of the transponders. He says he can, at least."

Gunny Walters laughed out loud, a short bark before he could stop himself. "What, Lieutenant, he's just going to go to their supply chief and ask to check out a couple of dozen Bennie bands?"

A flash of annoyance crossed the lieutenant's eyes before he turned back to Teo. "Me and Sergeant Gauta have gone over this, Skipper. The crabs keep them attached to their harnesses, and we think he can snatch some when they're sleeping. I mean, they're not going to be on alert, right? And if he can't get close, he can abort."

"The Bennie bands are on their wrists, Lieutenant," the gunny said.

"Well, they also keep the spares somewhere, right?" he replied, not willing to let the idea go. "We send up an RFI to find out where that is."

"And S2 is going to tell you where to stick that Request for Information . . . with all due respect, sir," the gunny said.

Teo opened his mouth to shut the lieutenant down, but something wouldn't let him. What Trace was saying was ridiculous. Everything he was taught told him not even to consider it. But . . .

Teo wasn't an Academy grad. He wasn't from any of the First Planets across the Alliance. He was a sergeant at heart, and something about the audacious idea resonated with him. His own brush with fame hadn't been thought out, after all—a sane man would never have attempted it, and yet, he'd come out unscathed, his platoon saved.

Worst case scenario, Gauta was captured to be held until the bigwigs finally brought this "un-war" to a close.

The worst that could happen? Are you really considering this, Mateo Alcazar? The CO said get rid of the cowboys, not to give them free rein.

He also said to take care of this problem yourself, the devil on his other shoulder whispered in his ear.

He looked around to the rest of his staff. All were staring at him, waiting to hear him render judgment. No one was offering another idea.

This is stupid, he thought, knowing what he should say.

"All of you. Get out of here. Come back in an hour with an idea.

Any idea."

And I hope at least one of them is good. Until then . . .

Lieutenant Okanjo tried to keep the scowl off of his face, almost succeeding.

"Not you, Lieutenant. Go get Sergeant Gauta and bring him here. I'm not saying I'm going to go along with your plan, if what you said even rates the term. But I'm willing to listen, at least."

Lieutenant Okanjo's eyes lit up, a broad smile creasing his face.

"Aye-aye, sir. I'll get him right away!"

He bounded out of the makeshift conference room, full of the enthusiasm of youth.

Teo hesitated, then swiveled his head to catch the first sergeant's eyes, afraid that he might see disapproval. To his surprise the first sergeant gave him a nod and a crooked grin.

You, too? What the hell's wrong with us? I just hope that whatever Trace and Gauta have cooked up is so ridiculous that I have no choice but to say no.

But no matter how hard he tried to convince himself of that, Teo knew that was a lie.

Chapter 12

Paladins

Richter stepped into a pair of foot holsters on a low stool outside the armory. His boots snapped into place, and the haptic sensors pressing against his body went slack. He unloaded the ammo line from his cycler and the belt drew back into the magazine beneath his plates. Winnie took the rifle from him and a thumbs-up appeared on the robot's face.

The jack released off him with a pneumatic whine, and as he stepped back, he pulled off his helmet and turned around. The platform with his jack rolled into the armory.

The three lieutenants were there: Briem and Kontos in the same body glove as Richter, Frakes in flanker fatigues and his flak armor vest. First Sergeant Molenaar was there in simple fatigues, a dire expression on his face.

None would look him in the eyes.

"Alright," Richter said, running the back of his forearm across the upper edge of his beard, "alright, we've had better days than this."

Thunder boomed in the distance as the sun set.

"It's bad luck to leave dead on the battlefield, sir," Briem said. "Their ghosts come back with us."

"The snipers weren't Syddans." Kontos shrugged. "May not be the same."

"They're Hegemony," Briem snapped. "Souls are souls. The men will be skittish for a fortnight until the snipers can find their rest."

"And how many more would I have lost if we'd tried to recover the bodies?" Richter asked, holding up a hand to stop Szabo from coming over, a linked squad radio on his hip and a hand raised with a mic in it. No doubt it was the squadron commander demanding an update.

"We're a superstitious lot, sir," Frakes said, "but we're no fools."

"Remember when Yriel ate it back at Hill 137? What was Ceban's idea?" Richter's body felt like a wet blanket over his bones as his system recovered from the sustained adrenaline dump during the mission. Thirst hit him and a headache grew behind his eyes.

"We offer a *brennifórn*. Slaughter and cook an animal, then leave it on the spit overnight to burn. The spirit feasts on it and our hunger is penance for the insult," Briem said.

"One of my flankers accidentally killed a *cackla* on the way back to the wire," Frakes said. "Tripped and fell on a bayonet a couple of times. Tragic."

"Does it have to be Ceban for this bren-if . . . bren. The fucking pig?" Richter watched as more Cataphract troopers stepped out of their jacks and gave them over to the armorer and Winnie for servicing.

"Vukovic's got the shaman blood, doesn't he?" Briem asked Kontos.

"He does, but he's on the verge of a calm-me-down shot from the medic after taking too many hits to his jack . . . I'll get him on the *brennifórn*. Should get his mind in a better place," Kontos said, shifting the weight of his flak vest on his shoulders.

"Do it," Richter said and waved Szabo over. "Quick turn on cleaning gear and then—"

"Souls are hungry, sir," Molenaar said. "Perimeter's set. May I suggest, for the welfare of the troopers, that we follow protocol a little bit later. The men will know we're not cutting them slack."

"Fair enough, Top. As you will," Richter said.

"Sir." Molenaar sniffed and turned away.

"Squadron." Szabo lifted his handset ever so slightly as the three Syddan officers went with Molenaar. "The Actual's on the line, sir. He doesn't . . . sound patient."

Richter took the handset and gave a brief summary as to the loss of the sniper team. He kept the receiver to his ear, his eyes closed and his chin bobbing slightly as a one-sided conversation ensued. After a few minutes, he handed it back to Szabo.

Richter let out a slow breath and wiped his face down.

"Everything . . . good, sir?" Szabo asked.

"Follow me." He went up a short staircase to a raised platform around the main lodge and stopped at the corner of the building. A small fire burned next to a gazebo beside the landing pad. A trooper wearing nothing but a loincloth, blue swirls of tattoos down his arms and across his shoulders, held a bayonet over his head. Two men carried a spit to the fire, a hairy pig impaled from tail to snout on the bar.

Vukovic thrust the bayonet up and down, then shouted, "*Aman uu rama!*"

Troopers, most of them in the same bodyglove as Richter and Szabo, others still in flanker fatigues, congregated on the landing pad. Each held something in one hand.

Richter fought the urge to shout out a warning about being so close in the open. They were a perfect target for any Alliance Switchblade that might be lingering overhead.

Szabo leaned over the railing to look up at the lodge roof.

"Yes, we've got anti-drone systems in place," Richter said. "The Syddans believe their ancestors will protect them while they're giving their respects. We can observe. Not participate."

126

The spit bar went down over the fire, and Vukovic slapped the flat of his blade against the metal, the clang carrying through the base.

"I am so lost," Szabo said.

"Abandoning the dead—which is what we did—is a sin for them." Richter leaned on the handrail and his chin drooped to his chest. "They believe the soul hungers once it moves into the spirit realm. If one of their faith isn't at the body to pray and comfort the soul, then it will find those that abandoned the dead and eat at the spirit of the living before carrying that essence to the afterlife."

"And that brings death, the Reaper, back to the living?" Szabo asked.

"You've been studying?" Richter raised an eyebrow at him.

"Essach isn't that different—for the cities out on the plains. Faith in the cities where I'm from is more . . . standard, sir."

Vukovic picked up a small bottle and drank deep. He spat onto the pit and a fireball burst up, singeing the pig's fur. It smoldered for a few moments before dancing flames grew on the offering.

"Aman uu rama!"

A trooper walked past and dropped something at the edge of the pit. One by one, Syddans left offerings.

"Ration packs," Richter said. "They're supposed to leave their favorite then skip their next meal. Stay hungry so the spirit knows they're contrite."

"Can I . . . participate? Leave something? I've got some hemp bars from home that I—"

"You're not Syddan," Richter smirked. "Your soul's too sour."

"But the sniper team wasn't Syddan . . ."

"I respect their ways. I don't try to rationalize them." He stood up and pinched the bridge of his nose. "You know what happened to my last dash-charlie?"

"No, sir. I assume I inherited his bunk."

"Bokan. Good trooper. Always ready to step off before anyone else. He could keep a network linked in the middle of the worst shit storm the patties could throw at us. Always had his head screwed on tight when we were outside the wire. Then one day we were recovering Benedict mines before their crypto expired. He was worried our bands had expired and suggested he drop a message to squadron before we moved into the minefield. I agreed, and he broke seal on his jack. He climbed up a tree to place a satellite dish. Bold move. Most jack troopers are of the death-before-dismount breed.

"You wouldn't think there'd be a Bennie in a treetop, but the engineers that dropped that minefield seeded a couple in shrike configuration. They forgot to annotate that on the obstacle plan I was sent before the mission. Bennies will switch to a disturbance trigger once they lose their crypto or their batteries get too low. That's why the *chayseux* are extinct around here. They're big enough to trigger the Bennies. Bokan was almost to the top when he set off a shrike.

"He landed right next to me. Hands were gone . . . face was . . ." Richter waved fingers over his mouth and nose. "He lived for an hour. Died before an evac bird could reach us back here. Couldn't get a pickup where he was injured, more shrikes in the area, obviously. Squadron had us hold the body overnight for regular pickup. Bokan was my dash-charlie since the first day I was assigned to Ayutthaya. Good kid.

"Despite he and I working so close to each other for so long, I was discouraged from sitting with his body overnight as is Syddan custom. The Hegemony . . . we've got a lot of work to do to become one people, Szabo, despite the war against the Integration Corp that cemented the need for Hegemony. This years-long fight against the Alliance . . . too many of us are foreign to each other."

"Roger, sir." Szabo nodded. "I'll make sure the Syddans know we're all on the same side."

"They don't need to be told that. They know. You, on the other hand, need to understand that you are not one of them. We can play at it," Richter said, tugging at his beard, "but we'll never be of their kind. So long as we're fighting the Alliance, it isn't much of an issue. They hate the patties more than anyone else."

"Me against my brother," Szabo said. "My brother and I against our uncle. My uncle and I against the stranger."

"Pretty much. Don't eat dinner in front of anyone tonight."

"But you said—"

"And now I'm telling you not to poke the bear. Good talk, trooper. Though I admit I'm goldbricking just a bit. Time to write up a lengthy report to squadron explaining how this cock-up happened. In excruciating detail. Enjoy the rest of your night."

Richter gave Szabo a slap on the shoulder and left the radioman to watch the rest of the ceremony in silence.

Chapter 13

Marines

Teo adjusted his battle harness, then jumped up and down a few times. He tapped Okanjo's shoulder and pointed at the harness. The lieutenant gave it a few jerks, then nodded.

He knew he shouldn't be going out on the raid, but with this so far out of the ordinary, Teo couldn't sit back and let things play out. He had to take an active part. And while both the lieutenant and sergeant didn't know it yet, he was ready to pull the plug at any moment.

It wasn't that he didn't trust Okanjo . . . well, maybe it was. The lieutenant was the son of a major general, and he'd been at the top of his Academy and Basic Officer School classes. That kind of background tended to create a sense of superiority and purpose in a young man. Teo wouldn't put it past him to "suddenly" find that his comms had gone down if he was ordered to cancel the mission.

Despite his nervousness as to what Gauta was about to do, Teo was still excited. He hadn't gone out on a small night patrol like this since he was a lieutenant. His warrior spirit was taking over.

Not that Teo expected to get into contact. The focus of the patrol was Sergeant Gauta. The rest of the Marines, Teo included, were just there as security to make sure he made it to the Hegemony camp at the hunting lodge in one piece.

Teo checked his M-88 Wilder, which replaced the VW-9 he'd lost at Rawai, then holstered it before looking over to where Sergeant Gauta was inspecting Private Hikok, one of the new joins.

"You don't look like a crab, Sergeant," Hikok said, his eyebrows scrunched together in confusion. "How are you going to keep from getting spotted?"

"Going at night," the sergeant rumbled in his deep bass as if it was intuitively obvious.

The other Marines laughed, and Hikok said, "Oh," obviously not convinced, but astute enough to drop it.

But the private was right. Sergeant Gauta G. Gauta was a huge slab of a man, dark-complected, with hair, if short, on his head, and without the beard the crabs favored. He wasn't going to pass as a crab if he was spotted, and his outrageous plan seemed doomed to failure. Still, it might be so outrageous that it could work.

The little voice in the back of his head kept telling Teo that was a stupid rationalization, but he was able to squeeze that voice out. The reality was that he wanted this work.

"No sign of activity along the track?" he asked the XO, who was hovering around the back of the makeshift briefing room.

"Nothing, sir. I think we're clear out to 800 meters."

Teo grunted. "I think" was not what he wanted to hear.

They still didn't know how many Bennies might have been planted in their sector, so Teo had improvised. He'd sent out their lone tank, along with a squad of infantry in trace, to clear a way through the jungle as a jury-rigged minesweeper, a Marine perched on its prow, sweeping the way ahead for anti-tank mines. The Marine couldn't pick up Bennies like that, but they posed little threat to the Badger.

One mine had detonated as the tank made multiple paths through the undergrowth, and sensors had been deployed along them. If the crabs were monitoring the process, there were now seven "cleared" paths out of the area.

He hoped his minesweeping had worked, that is. If it had, they had 800 meters of cleared space. If not . . .

Then there was the long hump to the crabs' camp. They'd have to take their chances with that, but Teo wasn't leaving it entirely to chance.

He walked up to Lance Corporal Lester "Tow" Uribe, a former corporal—twice—whose love of the nightlife had gotten him busted back for his third try at lance corporal. A shitbird in the rear, he was nevertheless one of the company's best field Marines.

"You ready, Uribe?"

"Locked and loaded, Skipper," Uribe said, laughing and slapping the barrel of his VP-51 with the EMP module attached. "No damned Bennie's going to get past me."

"This is serious. Once we break away, we could be in seeded ground. If one of them detects us, you'll have maybe a second before the Bennie detonates. You've got to spot it and take it out."

"Like I said, sir. No damned Bennie's going to get past me."

"OK, then," Teo said, slapping him hard on the shoulder. "I'm counting on that."

He could see the smile of pride almost split the Marine's face in two. His mission bordered on suicidal, but he never hesitated to accept it.

Hell, bar fights or not, I'd take a squad of you in a heartbeat, Uribe.

"*Five minutes,*" his earpiece intoned.

"Lieutenant Okanjo, you get that? Five minutes."

"Roger. We'll be ready to move out. Staff Sergeant Weiss, let's get 'em ready!"

"Going dark, Lieutenant," Teo said.

The QCs were completely secure, but powered up, they did have a tiny but unmistakable signature which could be detected, if the crabs had the right surveillance measures in place and were looking at the right location. Not *what* was being passed, but that *something* was being passed. Okanjo was going to keep his powered up, sending messages back to the XO. When they split, Okanjo would stay with the platoon and patrol back to the company while he, Gauta, Uribe, and the company's scout/sniper team would break away and head for the crabs' position.

Teo felt naked with his Command Control Display turned off, and he was back in snuffy mode. But he'd spent five years as a snuffy and only four as an officer, so in a way, it was like coming back home.

Still, he felt out-of-place as the lieutenant reluctantly took over— he'd wanted to be the one to lead Gauta to his release point—as the platoon passed through the company lines and out into bad-guy territory. When the patrol started to bunch up, he wanted to tell him to get his Marines dispersed, but other than running up and slapping Okanjo's helmet, he was out of luck. He just bit his tongue and carried on.

Every two hundred meters, a Marine swept the air above them with his EMP module. That should clear any unseen drones for twenty or twenty-five meters, which with the dense jungle and darkness, might be enough.

On the fourth time, at 800 meters and in a small jungle creek bed, Teo, Gauta, and the other three Marines kicked out of the patrol and hunkered down, weapons outboard, for a few moments until they were alone. Teo listened, trying to hear anything out of the ordinary.

Satisfied, he signaled Uribe, who nodded and took the point. Teo let him get a good fifteen meters away before he started the rest of the small raid force, and they disappeared into the bush.

The raid was now truly on.

Chapter 14

Marines

"Remember, you can cancel the raid anytime you want, Sergeant Gauta. Don't push the envelope."

"Roger that, sir," Gauta said, but instantly dismissed the notion. He hadn't come this far to back out now.

The skipper was basically a good guy, he knew. He'd proven himself a warrior as a recon Marine on Rather's World, but becoming an officer was like catching some sort of disease, with caution being the prime symptom.

Not all officers, of course. The real assholes were the medal-chasers, and they got Marines killed. But still, the good ones thought too much for Gauta's tastes, weighing the pros and cons of every tiny thing and spending too much time trying to figure out what could go wrong. Sometimes, the best course of action was to simply act, to go with the gut and take the big chances.

Back at boot camp, the civvie history and traditions instructor had quoted an ancient Earth wet-water Navy officer who said, "He who will not risk, cannot win." Private Gauta "Trunks" Gauta had made that his mantra ever since.

I can do this, he thought with certainty . . . and not without cause. He'd been confident in his abilities ever since he was a child, earning his black belt in limalama at the age of eight. But he really blossomed on the rugby pitch, being selected for the All-Nouveau Niue 12-17 B-Side as a second-row. He'd bounced up a few times as an A-Side on the 18-23 planetary team, where his wide frame and tree-trunk-like legs (which earned him the nickname "Trunks") caught the attention of the Premier League.

But Gauta lacked patience, and he didn't want to bounce around the C-leagues while waiting for his chance, so he enlisted in the Corps, taking it by storm. In just three years, he was a sergeant squad leader with a bright future ahead of him.

And this little mission was going to make him a legend.

All I've got to do is steal some Bennie-bands from an armed enemy camp. Easy-fucking-peasy.

At least Intel had come through. Somehow, they'd located a concentration of the Bennie bands in one of the VIP cabins adjacent to the main hunting lodge—how they'd done that, he had no idea. Maybe high-tech spook-stuff, maybe the Mama-san who cleaned the rooms. But the intel was welcomed.

He should be more than a little concerned about the mission, he knew. Gauta was nervous, but the kind of adrenaline-fueled nervousness before a match. Fear wasn't even in the equation.

Not like Uribe. Gauta could still smell the fear on the man. He stunk of it. Not that he was blaming him. The lance corporal had every reason to sit there, his heart still racing.

Gauta had protested to the lieutenant when he was told that the skipper and the other three Marines were going with him, but it turned out to save his ass. Twice, Uribe had spotted Bennies darting at them and zapped the bastards with EMP blasts before they could detonate.

Gauta was good, but not that good, at least with his VP-51. Without the alert and deadly-quick lance corporal, Gauta would have been dead meat.

A squealing reached them from across the darkness, and Gauta almost jumped to his feet.

"That's it," the skipper said as he attached two ends of a long lead to the crabs' perimeter wire, then cut the wire itself.

The scout/sniper team of Corporal "Snake" Yelsik and Lance Corporal J.T. Juarez were good, Gauta had to admit as they all moved silently through the night jungle, but the key was the *cackla* Juarez had trussed up and in his assault pack. The little pig-like animal had just been set free and forced across the wire about 150 meters from their position. The lead the skipper had attached to the wire in front of them should keep an alarm from going off, but there would be a small spike in the continuity that an astute crab could catch. Hopefully, the crab on duty would react to the *cackla* first and miss them.

"Kick some ass," Uribe said as Gauta stepped through the breach. No automatic weapons reached out to knock him down, no mortar round came down out of the rain, and he let out a breath he hadn't realized he was holding.

OK, Gauta-boy, make your momma proud.

He turned, gave a half-salute to the skipper, and stepped off.

Taking off his boots was only partially for show. As a boy, barefoot was a way of life, and he felt far more comfortable that way than in the heavy boots of a combat Marine. More sensitive, too. He could feel every leaf, every pebble, every disturbance on the ground . . . and hopefully, any tripwires or other nasty surprises before they could do whatever they were designed to do.

Thirty meters from the wire, Gauta turned around. He was hidden from the skipper. It was time for his final prep, something he hadn't told anyone except for the lieutenant he was going to do.

First, he had to ditch his 51. Nothing like a Marine weapon to let the crabs know who he was.

136

Next came his combat harness and assault pack, which he dropped at his feet for the moment. Now it was time for his IFUs, the Marines' three-layered combat uniform. The POL, the protective outer layer, was his body armor and camouflage. He stripped it off, folded the top and bottom neatly, then placed them on top of his 51. He moved on to the PCL, the power central layer, which provided the power to the system. That left the LCL, the life-critical layer, what the Marines called their longjohns.

He stripped off the top, and rain was almost welcoming as it hit his bare chest and back. Gauta had considered going full native, but in the end, he decided to keep the skin-tight underwear.

Gauta pulled his pahoa la'au and sheath from the harness now lying at his feet and ran his thumb over the cutting edge before he attached it to his right thigh. He was leaving the 51 behind, but he wasn't going to go in weaponless.

Like all Marines, Gauta spent hundreds of hours a year in the sawdust pits training in the Marine Corps Individual Combat System—or, as the Marines referred to it, "Mc-kicks"— and coupled with his limalama black belt, he knew he was a deadly son-of-a-bitch. And a good part of MCICS was blade fighting.

And also like most Marines, he'd chosen his own blade. The current fad was to choose a blade from history, from ethnic backgrounds or interests, but with modern tech to bring them into modern times. Lieutenant Okanjo had his iklwa, the skipper famously had his tecpatl, which he'd used to earn his POA, and Staff Sergeant Chowdhury had his glorious kukri.

Gauta had chosen a pahoa la'au for his blade. The originals were made of koa wood, as metal was unknown to the Pacific islanders of old Earth, but with his molymarage-blade copy, he knew if he could get close enough, not even the crab body armor could withstand his attack.

Now I'm ready, he thought as he picked up his assault pack and stepped off again.

Gauta slid through the jungle like a ghost, despite his bulk. The local version of tree frogs kept up their mating songs, unperturbed as he passed beneath them.

This is how it should be. Man against man, survival of the fittest, without tech to protect the weak.

The rain intensified, all the better for Gauta. Soldiers tended to withdraw into themselves in the rain, and the drops themselves muffled any sounds he might make.

Intel had given him a path in, saying that it was used by the locals who serviced the crab facilities. Hopefully, that meant it wasn't mined. Still, he didn't want to be observed.

He pushed forward, thankful, for once, of the regulations both sides had about destroying the planet's habitat. In most conflicts the area around a camp would be cleared to have open fields of fire and observation. But here, while some of the trees had suffered during the fighting, most were still upright, and that gave him cover as he approached the crabs.

Twenty minutes later, Gauta lay on his belly at the edge of the crab camp. The rain was heavy now, and that limited his vision, but nothing seemed to be moving around. He searched the area around him, trying to spot a guard outpost, but there was nothing.

Maybe not here in sight, but they've got guards somewhere, he reminded himself.

Gauta was a confident Marine, but that didn't mean he was a foolish one. What he was doing was crazy-risky, but that didn't mean he shouldn't take precautions to lessen the risk, even if only a little.

The night was half over, though, and he had to get a move on. His mind drifted to the out the skipper had given him. He could slink back into the jungle, tell the skipper that the crabs were out and about, and no one would blame him.

But I would.

Gauta pulled the assault pack off his back and pulled out two towels, a rolled-up poster, a commercial mini-flashlight, and two small SR-88 timed mines. He strapped the poster, flashlight, and mines to his left thigh, took one towel and wrapped it around his waist, and put the other over his head. Hikok had been right about that. His unshaven head would be a dead give-away among the shaved crabs.

Let's do it.

Gauta stood up and sauntered into the camp as if he hadn't a care in the world, just another crab going about his business. The skipper probably, and the SJA for sure, would have an eruption if they could see him now. In uniform, he would simply be a combatant. Out of uniform? A spy?

But the lieutenant said these are Marine towels. And my underwear is part of the C-3, he told himself as he reached the first cabin, more to try and convince himself than because he believed it.

He paused, back up against the wall. A muffled laugh broke through the rat-a-tat-tat of raindrops hitting the roof. He edged around to look in a window, and four crabs were sitting at a table playing some sort of game. One of them casually looked up, and Trunk jerked his head back.

There were no shouts, and no one came bursting out of the door, but his heart was pounding.

"Don't look guilty, Gauta," he whispered to himself. "Act like you fucking belong."

He took two deep breaths, pushed himself away from the cabin, then started hurrying down the paved path, both hands holding the towel on his head out as if to ward off the rain, but allowing him to see while keeping his head hidden.

If he had his bearings, then his target was up ahead and to the left, with the shower tent to the right. But seeing both on the overhead holo and finding it in the rain and dark, with the towel on his head getting soaked, were two different things, and Gauta was suddenly afraid of wandering around the camp forever, never finding his objective.

A shape materialized out of the rain on the path ahead, and Gauta tensed, ready to go for his knife, but the poncho-covered crab stood aside as he rushed by.

"Stupid shit," the crab said. "Just soap down in the rain and get back inside."

Gauta's heart pounded with excitement, adrenaline rushing through his body. He'd never been this close to the enemy before, and he had a sudden urge to take the soldier on. But he wasn't here to fight. He was here for the Bennie-bands. With regret, he pushed on.

He kept up, searching for a landmark. He was sure he'd gone too far, so he stopped, trying to picture the map of the hunting lodge compound. For all his back-to-basics talk, he could sure use his ICD at the moment. Maybe he was more used to his Marine Corps gear than he thought.

On a hunch, he turned left between two cabins, a dull light emanating from one window proof that more crabs were still awake. As he emerged between the two, the dark shape of a pavilion rose, fifteen meters ahead.

"Hell, yeah."

The pavilion was in the center of the camp, and his objective was on the other side of it. He sped up, crossed the garden, and started to pass through when a shape sitting inside stirred.

"What the fuck you doing out in this shit?" the crab asked.

"Shower," Gauta grunted, trying to mimic a Heg accent.

The crab laughed and said, "Who the hell wants to get even wetter in this place. But you got turned around. The shower tent's that way."

Which wasn't where Gauta wanted to go. But he made a show of turning and looking in the direction to where the crab was pointing, still holding the towel over his head. He'd have to head off in that direction, then double back for the Bennie-bands.

"Hey, who are you?" the crab suddenly asked. "I don't—"

Gauta was already moving, instinct and muscle memory from thousands of hours in the pits taking over. With his hands over his head, his knife was too far away, so he fell on the crab, grabbing the arm that was reaching to pull out a sidearm. Limalama focuses on holds and smashing joints, so as the crab struggled to raise his arm, Gauta assisted the motion, pushing it around and in back while using his chin and right arm to come down on the point of the shoulder, his left lifting and shoving on the forearm.

One hundred and twenty kilos of rock-hard Marine were more than the crab's shoulder joint could bear, and it snapped. The crab yelled out in pain and anger, his left arm hitting Gauta in the back of his head with powerful blows, but Gauta hunched his shoulder and swept the crab's feet from under him, riding the soldier to the ground as he gained the man's back. He snaked his left hand across the crab's mouth, getting bitten in the process, then pulled out his blade with his right.

It was quick. The tip went in, skittering across the vertebrae, and with a shove, he cut out and away. The crab screamed through Gauta's hand over his mouth, gave three huge bucks, and then he collapsed.

Gauta held the body close, listening for an alert. Only the pounding of the rain on the pavilion roof broke through the darkness.

Slowly, Gauta released the body. In the darkness and blood, he couldn't really see the man's face, and for some reason, he thought he should. This was the first human Gauta had killed, at least like this. He'd killed a thousand simulacrums over the years, and that training had paid off. But putting a knife into the neck of the Corps' best training dummies was not the same as spilling real blood.

"Shit," he said quietly, trying to gauge his emotions. "I fucking did it."

He slowly stood up and gave one last look at the body. If he'd been in his full IFUs, the kill would have been recorded, and he'd have it forever. But maybe it was better this way. Maybe his first kill should be private between his victim and himself.

"Don't stand here admiring your work. Get the job done."

He turned away, the dead crab forgotten. A short dash through the rain, and he was at his objective. It was different from most of the other cabins; a bit taller and with lacquered tiles on the roof. The door was wider, meant to be left open and welcoming to guests. As the former manager's office, it was connected to the main lodge itself, but with an outside entrance as well. If Intel was right, this was now the crab commander's quarters.

His pahoa la'au was still in his hand. He brought it up close and ran his finger over the side of the blade. Whatever blood had been on it had already been washed away in the rain.

Maybe you'll drink again tonight.

And now, he had to get inside. There could be an officer sleeping there or a group of crabs, and he had to be ready.

The SR-88 on his side would be enough to blow out a wall of the cabin if not take the whole thing down. But that would alert the camp. He'd have to find the Bennie-bands in the rubble and move before the crabs could react.

Not good.

He started sliding around the cabin, quietly testing the windows, seeing if any were unsecure. No such luck. They were sealed shut. He could break through, waking whoever was inside, but that was not a great option.

When you want to get in someplace, try the door.

The front door was a basic faux-wooden door, too strong to break. And, of course, it was locked. That meant it was back to the windows. "Not a great option" was better than "no option."

Gauta tried to score the front window with the tip of his blade. It barely made a mark. As he'd expected, the window was some sort of crystal silicate, and that meant it wasn't going to be as easy as smashing it with a rock.

If not the pane, then the frame.

Gauta ran his finger around the edge of the window, feeling a soft, almost pliable putty, as if the window had been taken out and replaced some time, and that gave him hope. Again using the tip of his knife, he ran it through the putty, cutting as deep as he could. He considered cutting into the wooden frame, but if there were crabs asleep inside, they wouldn't sleep through that.

Voices reached him, and he froze, hugging the wall. Two shapes barely materialized across the path and continued on.

The longer I fart around, the bigger the chance I'm going to get spotted again.

It was now or never. He waited an agonizing long minute to let the two crabs get farther away, then stepped back five or six steps. With his blade in hand, he gave a mental count to three, then ran forward, launching himself at the low window, turning to hit it with his shoulder with all the force of a premier rugby tackle.

The window blew out of the frame, shooting across the inside of the cabin, and Gauta rolled on the ground, struggling to get to his feet to meet any threat. But no shouts of alarm greeted him. The place was empty.

He ran back to the opening where the window had been, expecting a hue and cry, but once again, all he heard was the rain. Somehow, gods be praised, he'd managed to get inside without the crabs catching him.

"Now if only the Intel weenies are right."

He pulled out his flashlight and turned it on, using his fingers to shade the light. The cabin was a made-for-holo hunting cabin with heavy faux-wood paneling and the stuffed head of a *chayseux* over the small fireplace. It was clean, an overstuffed couch in front of the fireplace, a cot with neatly folded blankets at foot along one wall. A plastic card table, incongruous and almost ugly compared to the rest of the room, had cardboard boxes full of weapon cleaning kits and packs of vacuum-sealed socks and undershirts. Gauta spied a nice-looking civilian eReader and considered swiping it, but he wasn't here as a common thief.

What he didn't see were Bennie-bands.

Gauta checked the head. Just a tub and shower unit. He tried the switch, but it didn't activate, which was probably why the crabs had set up a shower tent.

I guess their camp's just as bad as ours.

His Marines would want to know that. They'd been convinced that the crabs were living in luxury while they were in the piece of crap that was the Tradewinds Resort.

He went back to the desk and rifled through the drawers. Most were empty. Same with the chest of drawers. Only the top shelf had neatly folded underwear and clothing.

That left one place: the closet.

He pulled open the door. Several pieces of clothing and military gear hung on hangers. A security box along the wall made his heart

144

momentarily jump, but if it was still working, someone would have already responded. The shelves were empty except for a lone weapons cleaning kit. And in a cubbyhole in the shelf was a typical hotel safe.

Gauta was about to close the door when it hit him—a safe. Why not?

He crouched down and looked at it. There had to be a millions of them throughout the galaxy. Small, they were generally foolproof, and they gave a feeling of security to the masses of people who used them.

He knocked on it, as if that would give him x-ray vision and he could see inside. He had no way of knowing if the Bennie-bands were inside, but it made sense. Two hundred of the bands would fit. Gauta jiggled the handle, hoping against hope that it had been left unlocked.

It hadn't.

The more he looked at the safe, however, the more he was sure the Bennie-bands were inside, but he had no way to break into it. A professional thief, yeah. A good mechanic with the right tools, yeah. But not a Marine sergeant standing in his underwear.

He slowly waved the miniflash around, checking to see it he was missing anything, but no. The Bennie-bands had to be in the safe. And if he couldn't break in, there was only one other option.

Gauta put the tip of his knife at the bottom of the safe where it met the shelf. With five solid hits on the butt of the handle, he drove the tip in, creating a little space. Then he pried it up, hoping to pull it free.

It wiggled but held fast.

He moved the knife a few centimeters to the right and drove it in again.

Sorry about that. This is a letdown for you after drawing blood, he apologized to his knife.

Some Marines treated their blades as holy relics, but they were nothing more than tools, after all.

Gauta made four more gouges, but he couldn't pry it loose. What he did have, however, were small gouges in the shelf. He tried to slip the tips of his fingers in, and they just fit. He needed more. It took a few more minutes of worrying the holes with his knife, but finally, he had a couple of slots. He stepped into the closet and slipped his fingers in. He squatted, set his feet better, and heaved with all his might.

It wasn't the bolts that gave, but the entire shelf, which broke with a snap, sending Gauta back on his ass, still holding the safe, but with three-quarters of the shelf still attached.

"I guess that works," he said with a laugh before he realized the noise he'd made. He froze, listening for a cry of alarm. None came.

But that reminded him that he was in the middle of the enemy camp, and the night was waning. He had to get out of here before the dead crab was discovered, before he was discovered.

But first, he had a message to send. Not even the lieutenant knew about this. The poster was still rolled up on his thigh. He took it off, unrolled it, and used the miniflash to read it one last time.

He couldn't help it. He laughed out loud, a deep guffaw as he placed in on the table, right where it couldn't be missed.

Feeling pleased with himself, he picked up the safe and walked over to the window. He couldn't see any sign of movement in the rain, but he knew there were crabs on duty out there. Getting the Bennie-bands was one thing—getting out with them was another altogether.

Now to get out of here.

He picked up the window, trying to put it back in place after he stepped through. It wouldn't pass muster in the light, but maybe it could buy him some time in the darkness. He picked up the towel he'd dropped there while busting in and put it back around his waist. It would be a little harder pretending he was just on his way to the shower while holding the safe, but it was better than nothing.

He still was not confident in his bearings, but the pavilion was still right in front of him. He crossed and passed through, the body of the dead soldier still lying on the ground, the blood now pooled across the deck, the roof keeping the rain from washing it away. Gauta carefully stepped over the blood and back out into the rain, which was now beginning to taper off.

Which makes me more visible. Now, did I come in between these cabins or . . .

Anywhere out was good for him. Gauta chose the first path and took it.

Unless he was mistaken, there were a few more lights showing through the windows now as he passed. The crabs were stirring, and his handiwork would be discovered sooner rather than later. He needed to move.

But that last mine was itching on his thigh, begging to be used. Gauta started looking for a target on which to leave his going-away present.

This is stupid, he told himself, but his perverse sense of humor would not let the idea go.

And then, there it was: a low, squat building with three jack frames in front. An armory, if he'd ever seen one. He couldn't imagine his luck. Taking it out would be a huge blow to the crabs. Without their jacks, they'd just be flankers, and there wasn't a crab flanker alive who was a match for a Marine

He pulled open the door and gave it a quick survey. Equipment and jacks were barely visible in the dark. The mine he had on him wasn't the most powerful in the Marine inventory, but it was big enough to do a number on this place.

With an evil grin, he set the mine up on the door to the armory, giving it ten minutes. Once again, stupid. They'd react to the explosion, and an alert camp would make it that much harder for him to get away.

Then again, it might just focus attention off of him if it came to that.

Satisfied with his reasoning, Gauta picked up the safe and took one step before he heard shouting behind him, in the direction of the pavilion.

"There we go," he muttered, and broke into a jog.

More lights came on, both from the cabins and from the main lodge, which was just becoming visible in the slackening rain and dawn light. Gauta had to get out of the camp. Once in the jungle, he felt he could avoid the crabs, but inside the camp, he was extremely vulnerable.

The safe was making running awkward, but it was the reason for the mission, and he wasn't going to give it up. He managed to get to the edge of the cabins, and he thought he'd made it when the chatter of a machine gun opened up, and the cabin wall beside him disintegrated into splinters.

Gauta juked to the side, getting the bulk of the cabin between him and whoever was firing at him. He stood there a moment, back against the wall as he tried to place the weapon in his mind.

It didn't really matter. The crabs would be on him in a moment. He had to move. Hopefully, this cabin would give him cover until he disappeared into the jungle. He wasn't at the same point where he'd come in, so the area in front of him might be mined, but hopefully, the Bennie-bands in the safe—if they were really in there—would keep him safe.

Only one way to find out.

With a last prayer, Gauta broke out into a run.

Chapter 15

Paladins

The cycler bucked as Richter fired on full auto, fighting to control the weapon as the recoil lifted the barrel with each yellow flash from the muzzle. The heavy machine gun was meant to be fired from a jack, and he wore only fatigue pants and boots. Adrenaline and hatred fueled his muscles as he swept the weapon across the perimeter wire, the rounds ripping through the jungle, severing fronds into shadows pinwheeling through the night, moments of discordance captured in each brief burst from his weapon.

The weighty *chunk* of his shots grew less and less as the sound deadened his ears. The drum went empty, and his cycler dipped down. Richter hinged the barrel up before it could hit the mud, the heat from the metal full against his face as he backed away from the perimeter.

Floodlights snapped on, and a pair of Cataphracts ran out from between the TOC and the armory.

"Sir, he made it out," said one, pointing to the other side of the camp.

"No, he didn't." Richter grabbed him by the side of the helmet and pressed his thumb to a reader. A green light blinked twice.

"This is Paladin Actual. Shelter in place. Full sniffer drone sweep over the entire post. Assume that son-of-a-bitch left something behind. Once you find one explosive, find the next and the next. Ceban?" Richter's arms quivered as the adrenaline wore off, and a sense of dread filled his stomach as he waited—prayed—for the armorer to answer him. If the ghost had taken him out too...

"Ceban. Go."

Richter wanted to sigh in relief, but he couldn't in front of his men. This was a time for complete authority. There could be no crack in the mask of command.

"Armory status?"

"Fucker rigged my door with a grenade. Kontos is doing remote EOD through Winnie, but I'm starting to think that ghost did it just for shits and giggles. I'm just fine, by the way."

"Prep Red Platoon's gear. We're going after him." Richter waited a moment for a response and heard two clicks of Ceban's tongue. The delay was enough for him to know Ceban didn't approve, but this was his company. His decision. He dropped his hand as Szabo ran over, radio on his back and headset on.

Panting under the weight of the radio that was meant to be bolted into a jack, Szabo handed Richter his helmet. Richter snapped the earpiece out of the side and slipped it on, then snapped the helmet onto his belt. He listened to the command frequency as his lieutenants called out orders.

A cluster of drones rose above the roofline of the main lodge, then fanned out over the post. He clicked his earpiece.

"Briem, give me a situation report soon as the sweep's done. Szabo, stay behind me. I didn't blow up on my way out. I'm taking the same way back in," he said.

"Oh," the trooper said, looking back over his shoulder, "oh, crap, I didn't think of that."

"The ghost might've left a couple other souvenirs." Richter made for the lodge. "We're walking on eggshells right now, and this is not a good thing, you understand that, RTO?"

"Sir, yes—need the battalion net?"

"Toman doesn't want partial updates unless I'm in need of

immediate support," Richter said, shouldering his way into the lodge. The living area was a riot of troopers getting dressed, eyes wide at their shirtless, sweaty, and very angry commander as he marched between the rows of cots, his cycler perched in a bent arm.

Richter made for the medics' station and handed off his weapon to Szabo. The room had once been a tour-guide station, and pictures of local waterfalls, *chayseux* cats in the wild, and scenic views available to hunters for an extra fee still clung to the walls. Triage lists and a med holo showing the outline of a trooper lying on a gurney were new additions. The holo had a red highlight down one side of the neck and flatlines for all biometric readings.

The body was draped with a black bag, but one arm hung off the side, blood dripping down and into a tarp with raised sides.

Sergeant Iliev, the troop medic, sat on a chair against the wall, his head back, a lit cigarette in his mouth. His hands were clean, but blood stained his forearms and the front of his uniform.

"Who?" Richter asked.

"Consanio." Iliev took a long drag. "Gone before I could even get to him. Torchev got some minor lacerations from razor wire. Spritz of quick-seal and maunaka fixed him right up."

Richter lifted the edge of the body bag. The dead trooper's eyes were closed with medical tape, and a blood-soaked compression bandage lay on the front of his neck. The skin had gone so sallow he was nearly blue, his mouth open just enough that Richter thought the corpse was still trying to shout out a warning.

"We are less without you. May angels guide you to your rest." He touched the dead man's face. Cold and dry. The major put the bag back in place.

"Give time for respects once the lockdown's over," he said to the

151

medic, "then ice him up. Don't know when we can get a bird in for him."

"Soul guard will stay with him," Iliev said.

"Fair enough." Richter gave him a pat on the shoulder and went toward the TOC.

A step past the door to his office, he froze. The door was ajar. He donned his helmet and activated the sensor band. No explosives or trip wires on the other side, but the pulse showed his desk wasn't how he'd left it.

With the toe of his boot, Richter pushed the door open. Papers were strewn across the room, his chair knocked over. On the desk, a single piece of paper lay surrounded by a ring of blank space, then the contents of the drawers. The ghost meant for him to find it.

The item was a wanted poster for a known Alliance commander, Captain Mateo Alcazar, that had been spread all across the front and airdropped by balloons over rebel towns. The royalist government had placed a bounty on him for a long list of crimes. Richter didn't know or care if the allegations were true. He fought to kill the patties, not bring them to justice. The bounty price on Captain Alcazar had been scribbled out and a much larger price tag written in.

He looked over his desk to where his safe should have been. Gone.

A distant explosion sounded, not loud enough to carry a blast wave with it.

Richter took a step around his desk and beat a fist against the top.

"Maybe the bastard hit a Bennie," Szabo said.

"Wasn't that." Richter stared at his open space where his safe used to be and the broken window—just large enough for a determined man to crawl through. "He got our IFF bands . . . and some important papers."

Szabo looked down at the device on his wrist.

"Oh . . . then that means—"

"The targeting and detection systems on the mines will be useless until the next hot swap." Richter broke into a string of expletives. "Radio squadron HQ. The colonel has to know about this. The ghost got away with enough bands to cover an entire pattie company."

"Roger, sir." Szabo ran a finger down a small tablet and frowned. "Problem. Seems our antenna is off-line. The ghost must've fouled the power lines somewhere."

"Son of a . . . get our comms back online. Make sure wherever you go's been looked over by the sniffer drones."

"Sir," Szabo said and hurried away.

Richter stared where his safe used to be. The ghost was toying with him, flaunting that he'd snuck right into the heart of his command and taken one of the most valuable items Richter had. Once the ghost got the bands back to his side of the lines, the Alliance would have a distinct advantage over him and his men. More troopers would die because of this, and Richter had no one to blame but himself.

He ripped up the wanted poster and tossed the pieces aside as he stormed out of the office and into the operations center, where three men were in their flanker armor, carbines, and helmets in hand. A trio of screens sat atop the troop computer box, a crate with thick data and power lines plugged into it. Red alert icons flashed along the edges of the screens. Several data feeds were off-line.

One young man, his chin supporting the barest of a beard, began trembling.

"Who was on camera watch?" Richter asked, already knowing the answer.

"Sir," said Private First Class Shala, raising a hand. "There was a wire hit on the north sector. I brought all the cameras to see it, but it was another one of those stupid *cackla* trying to get at the burn pit."

One of the other troopers tapped on a keyboard and a night-vision video of a small porcine animal nosing around stacks of barbed wire came up.

"Everyone was sleeping and it was just an animal, so I didn't . . . didn't hit the alarms." Shala swallowed hard.

"We don't have video of the ghost getting in," said the sergeant on duty. "Just you shooting at him on the way out, sir."

"What's the standard for any wire disturbance?" Richter asked, his eyes hard.

"Alert red section," the three murmured. "Hit the floodlights."

Richter glanced at a poster outlining the alert procedures the TOC was to follow—the same ones the troopers had just repeated.

"Consanio is dead," Richter said, ripping the rank insignia off all three of them. "Shala. Go to green section and have them send over their TOC crew. Then the three of you report to Iliev for soul guard. Get out of my sight."

Demoting the three of them was almost merciful by Hegemony standards. Officers had full summary execution authority, an option Richter had never wanted or needed to utilize. Shala and the others had fallen for the ghost's bait, a simple misdirection that took their attention away from wherever he'd infiltrated through the wire. He knew what would happen come daylight and a better inspection was performed: a section of the alarm wires had been disabled, allowing the ghost to get through.

He'd have his troop reset the entire perimeter. It would mean uniforms and skin torn up by razor wire and they'd be vulnerable during the work, but it was a task that should've been done days ago.

A task he should've ordered done days ago.

An invisible weight pressed against his shoulders and his head dipped forward. He was in command. This was his responsibility. All of it.

Chapter 16

Marines

"Hell, sir, I thought you said you have a safe," Private First Class Cesar Xicale said as he stood, in the CP, hands on his hips, looking at Sergeant Gauta's prize with disdain.

"But it *is* a safe," Lieutenant Popovitch said, confused. "And Staff Sergeant O'Neil said you were . . . uh . . . that you can open it."

The Second Platoon sergeant had said more than that. Xicale had, by all accounts, lived a life of crime before he chose the Marines instead of prison, and safe-cracking was only one of his many skills.

"This piece of crap?" Xicale said, slapping it on the top. "Come-on, El-tee. Hotels don't give a shit if a room safe is really secure. They just want something to give the tourists a sense of security. I'm almost ashamed to waste my efforts on something so easy."

"I don't care if you think it's beneath your capabilities, Xicale," Teo interrupted. "We just need it open."

"Oh, no problem, Skip. Just like back in the barrio, huh? A bandito's gotta do what a bandito's gotta do, right?"

Teo chose to ignore the insolence that bordered right at the limit. Too many times, Xicale went over the limit, and that was why this was his third time at PFC, never keeping his lance corporal's crossed rifles for more than a month before being busted back down.

And, of course, when they needed a criminal, it had to be a fellow Safe Harbor Marine. Teo didn't care about that . . . much. What was

155

important was what the safe held. Without the Bennie-bands, then Gauta's mission would be a bust.

With a swagger Xicale took a step closer to the safe sitting on XO's field desk and squatted. He made a show of closing one eye, then another, as if studying it.

"Just get to it, Xicale," the first sergeant growled.

"Ah, a guy's gotta have some fun," he said before his demeanor changed into something more serious. He pulled out a small instrument from his pocket that looked decidedly un-Marine, and held it to the safe's thumbscanner.

Teo made a mental note to find out what the instrument was. He doubted it had a place in a Marine rifle company.

The PFC read the display, then frowned.

"Problems, Xicale?" the first sergeant asked.

"Didn't think they'd have an XC-5102 interface," the PFC muttered. "That's pretty high-tech for a resort."

"But you can open it, right?" Sergeant Gauta asked as he crowded forward.

"Give him space," Lieutenant Okanjo said, pulling his sergeant back.

"Yeah, yeah. Just give me a moment," Xicale said, his swagger gone.

Teo was on edge. He wanted—no, he had to—see what was inside. They needed the Bennie-bands, and if he droned the entire safe to battalion, who knew if they'd ever get any back . . . and that was if there were any inside in the first place. Intel had been wrong before, and they'd only put a 65% chance that the crab commander would bother to lock them up. For all Teo knew, the Bennie-bands could be in the crab armory.

"Hey, Corporal Wainsett, you got a TK-30? Or a 32?" he asked the comms NCO.

Wainsett went back to his console and pulled out a piece of gear. Teo had no idea if it was a "TK-30" or "32," or what either of them did, for that matter. He tossed it across the CP, and Xicale snatched it out of the air with one hand.

The CP was crowded with each of the officers, most of the Staff NCOs, and Sergeant Gauta, and all sets of eyes were focused on the PFC as he took two leads, ran them across the thumbscan, and powered it up. He adjusted the TK-30-or-32, then studied the readout again.

"Skipper, you need this fast?"

"As quickly as possible," Teo said.

"I can get this open, but it might take a while. I've got to connect to my ICD and run the algorithms."

Teo didn't want to ask how he'd be using his Marine helmet to crack a safe. He'd worry about that later.

"How long will that take?"

"No way to know. Maybe thirty minutes. Maybe hours."

Teo looked at the XO, who said, "Battalion's not going to wait hours. They're already asking for one of the Bennie-bands to send up to Force."

"I need it quicker than that, Xicale," Teo said.

"OK, it's not going to be pretty, though."

"Just open the fucking thing," the first sergeant exploded.

Xicale ignored the outburst, keeping his eyes locked on Teo's, who finally nodded.

The PFC reached into his assault pack on the deck, pulled out a shiny hammer and what looked like a cross between a chisel and a pogo stick.

"Anything breakable in here?" he asked.

"Just do it," the first sergeant said.

Xicale shrugged, twisted the collar of the chisel, and turned the safe around. He applied the cutting edge of the chisel to the back corner of the safe and tapped it with the hammer.

The tap itself wasn't hard, but the impact chisel augmented the force, and the cutting edge bit in, creasing the safe's corner. Two more taps, and he was through. He turned the safe on its side and began expanding the cut.

"If you knew you could cut through the damned thing, why didn't you do that first?" the gunny asked as Xicale methodically started separating the back of the wall of the safe.

"Not very sophisticated, Gunny. Any fool can cut open one of these things. It takes an artist to go through the lock. Especially an XC-5102. But they always make the same mistake. Spend a thousand unis on the lock, but still use the same crap bodies.

"Besides, sometimes they've got these things boobytrapped. Cut into one, and you get a nasty how-do-you-do. Does a number on whatever's inside, too."

"And you didn't think to tell us that before you started cutting?" the first sergeant asked.

"The skipper said he wanted fast. This is fast."

It still took a good five minutes, but finally, Xicale was able to pry down the back far enough for someone to stick in his arm.

Xicale stopped and looked questioningly to Teo, but this was Gauta's prize.

"Sergeant, if you'll do the honors."

Sergeant Gauta beamed as he stepped forward and stuck his meaty hand inside the small safe. He withdrew a folder and handed it to Teo, who ignored it for the moment.

Are the Bennie-bands inside?

Next came two crystals. They might be routine, or they might be something important, but Teo wouldn't be able to read the data inside. That was for the crypto boys in G7.

"I've got something," Sergeant Gauta said. "But I need more room to get it out."

He withdrew his hand, and PFC Xicale gave his impact chisel a few more taps. Then, together with Sergeant Gauta, the two pulled on the back, bending it farther. Gauta reached in and pulled out a bundle of bands, held together with silver foil.

"Holy shit, that's them!" the first sergeant said almost reverently before the CP erupted into cheers and mutual back-slapping.

"You did it!" Okanjo yelled at Gauta as he almost mauled the sergeant, who was grinning ear to ear.

The XO nudged Teo with his elbow. "Those Intel pukes finally got something right, thank God. These are going to help out a lot. Congrats, sir."

Teo let out a huge sigh of relief, first that they had the bands to counter the Bennies, and second, for something more personal. He'd taken a huge chance in letting Gauta go on the mission, and that could have gotten him into hot water with the CO. But nothing was a better shield than success.

He hoped.

"It wasn't me, Lyle. Sergeant Gauta did all the heavy lifting. But let's give battalion the update, and send them one of the bands and the crystals," he told the XO.

"And the folder?"

Teo opened the folder and saw several white envelopes embossed with the Hegemony seal. They looked like letters. He hesitated a moment.

Per SOP, they should go up the chain, but he didn't even know what they were.

"I'll keep them for now until I have a chance to take a look and see if there's anything to them."

He placed the folder back down and looked around the CP. There were some pretty happy Marines there. This semi-war, or semi-truce, depending on your perspective, didn't offer many clear-cut victories, but this sure counted as one. He leaned back against the XO's desk, feeling quite good.

"So, Captain Alcazar, was this good enough to get back my skeeter wings?" PFC Xicale asked, suddenly not as brash as he was a few minutes ago.

It had only been four months ago that Teo had taken Xicale's "skeeter wings," the crossed rifles beneath the single chevron that signified a lance corporal. Xicale had hooked up with a local during the battalion's final 96-hour pass before deploying, and he had either been so drunk or so infatuated with the young lady that he unilaterally tried to extend the 96 to a 108.

"All you did was cut open the safe," Teo said. "And you said that any fool could do that."

Xicale's eyes fell.

"I know, sir. But I kinda thought, I mean, I haven't gotten into any more shit—"

"Relax, Xicale. Come back to the CP this afternoon. I'll make sure the paperwork's done."

"Really? Wow! Thank you, sir. You won't regret it."

"Just make sure you keep them this time."

"Aye-aye, sir. I will."

Teo held back the smile as he turned back to the bundle of Bennie-bands that the gunny was laying out on the ops table. There looked to be at least thirty of them. A nice haul.

Teo picked up the nearest one. It didn't look like much, no more than a hospital band. But these meant life, both to his Marines and maybe his career as well. He gave it a kiss before giving it back to the gunny.

Yes, sometimes things worked out, and it was better to enjoy it when you could. Who knew how things would work out next time?

Chapter 17

Marines

"So Fausten goes to Second Squad, then?" Teo asked First Sergeant Lippmaa the next day.

Teo was waiting for a response from battalion about Gauta's raid, but routine admin never stopped.

"That makes sense. That still leaves Win short one, but Corporal Nyoki's strong."

"Where's he at on promotion points for sergeant? Nyoki, I mean."

"Short by eight points."

"Hell. That's gotta hurt. Keep an eye on him. Battalion's still got this quarters' two field promotions to sergeant," Teo said.

Every Marine amassed points while serving in each grade, and until he reached the designated number of points for the next rank, he could not be promoted . . . except for a meritorious field promotion.

"We're going to have to fight tooth and nail for one of those. Corporal Smith's got the first one of them locked up."

Teo shrugged. "Well deserved, taking on three crabs like that. I heard he's—"

"Skipper, we've got company," the XO said, puffing as he stuck his head in Teo's small room.

"Who?"

"The CO. He just came ashore on a go-fast."

"Shit! When?"

"Sergeant Orion just passed it up."

Teo gave a quick glance at the first sergeant. Did he know about this?

No time for wondering now. Just like the bastard to come on without warning.

And the go-fast was a logical choice for him. The multi-mode watercraft were used by smugglers throughout the quadrant, where their high speed in foil mode, coupled with their semi-submersible mode for in-close navigation, made them difficult to track and catch. Getting the CO into the resort wasn't any different than bringing in smuggled goods from remote landings into the population centers.

"Let's go," he said, jumping to his feet and heading out the door.

Down on the beach, he could see the pointed prow of the go-fast with a local standing next to it. He was much more concerned with the lean Marine lieutenant colonel striding up the beach, Sergeant Orion and Lance Corporal Haffstetter struggling to keep up.

Teo wasn't going to rush up to meet the man. He stopped at the entrance to the lobby, at the base of one of the few still mostly-intact palm trees, and waited. The first sergeant and XO took positions on either side of him and one step back.

"Sir, welcome," Teo said as the CO reached him.

Teo didn't like the man . . . no, that was too weak a term. He despised the man. Teo had despised more than a few of his commanders and leaders during his career, but in each case, he had at least a degree of grudging respect for them. He had none for Lieutenant Colonel Nicholas Khan III. Most of that was personal. The CO was probably competent enough on a tactical level, although Teo hadn't seen enough of that to overturn his opinions of him. Where he failed was as a leader of Marines . . . not the least of them being Teo himself.

Teo might not be an Academy grad, he might not have a uni

degree. He didn't play ultra-squash, he didn't play golf, and he didn't stay past the minimum time at battalion officer calls, kissing the CO's ass, but he was a damned good Marine. He'd proven that in the field of battle.

And if there were any slight doubts as to his abilities as an officer instead of a dirt-and-fists-type warrior, he wanted a commanding officer who would mentor him, not dismiss him out of hand. The enemy on Ayutthaya were the crabs, not fellow-Marines.

The CO nodded at both the first sergeant and XO, then crooked his finger in a follow-me motion before striding down the path that fronted the lobby. Teo followed silently, trying to tell from the man's posture what was coming down the pike.

The CO stopped where the path turned to go around the lobby and stood there a moment, just staring out over the beach and gray waves coming ashore.

Just get it over with and don't play these bullshit games.

"So, Captain," the colonel finally broke the silence as he continued to look out over the beach. "Sergeant Gauta went into the Hegemony camp barefoot, unarmed, and wrapped in a towel?"

Oh, here it is. I should have expected this.

Teo had sent up the full report last night, then followed through by having the XO send a carrier drone with one of the Bennie-bands and the crystal drives—everything except for the folder of what looked to be a personal letter and a few letters to fallen crabs. He'd been riding high on the success of the mission, but now reality was setting in. He'd probably broken about every regulation in the books.

But the mission worked!

One thing was for sure. He wasn't going to let anyone else take the blame. It may have been Trace Okanjo's idea, but he'd OK'd it, and it was on his shoulders. No one else's.

This is going to suck, he thought. The colonel had given him his last "mulligan," as he'd told Teo. *Am I getting relieved?*

Doesn't matter. Do what you have to do.

"Yes, sir. He did. And that decision falls on my shoulders. I take full responsibility."

The CO slowly turned to look Teo in the eyes, his face impenetrable.

"You really are a piece of work, Captain, aren't you?"

He'd spoken in a quiet voice that failed to hide his disdain.

"Sir?"

The corner of the CO's lip raised in a sneer.

"Of course, you would be trying to take credit."

"I made the decision . . ."

What? He's thinking I'm trying to take CREDIT?

"Sure, you signed off on it, but this was Lieutenant Okanjo's plan. I know that he and Sergeant Gauta came up with it and put it into motion. You did jack shit, Captain, and now you want credit for Kilo finally doing something right?"

Teo's mouth dropped open in shock.

"I—"

"I don't want to hear it, Captain," the CO said, waving a dismissive hand to cut him off. "I came to you first as a courtesy, nothing more. I want to talk to Lieutenant Okanjo and Sergeant Gauta. I want to discuss with them how real Marines think outside the box."

"Sir—" Teo started in protest before he was cut off again.

"I said can it. You're on thin ice, so I'd shut up if I were you in the hope that I can forget that you just tried to hog the credit and not relieve you on the spot."

Teo was in shock, and he didn't know what to say.

"So, let's just walk over to First Sergeant Lippmaa and have someone round up the two Marines, then I want you out of my sight. Understood?"

"Uh . . . yes, sir," Teo managed to stumble out.

Teo followed the CO back down the path to the XO and first sergeant, his mind whirling in confusion.

What just happened?

"First Sergeant," the CO said as he slapped the Marine hard on the back. "Why don't you send someone to round up Lieutenant Okanjo and Sergeant Gauta. I'd like to congratulate them both."

Behind the first sergeant, the XO gave Teo a questioning look, but Teo just shook his head. He still wasn't sure what was going on. But as he followed the CO into the lobby where the man made a point of examining the old real wood reception counter, Teo's anger began to build.

Teo hadn't been trying to take credit himself but rather to shield the others from what he expected to be the CO's wrath. And it was hardly Okanjo's plan. The Third Platoon commander had suggested the basics, but the "plan" had come together in the normal fashion with Teo and the XO, who then ran it by Sergeant Gauta to make sure it worked.

Not that Teo was begrudging Okanjo credit for bringing up the idea, but he'd hardly come up with the operations order itself.

More importantly, how had the CO "known" that Trace Okanjo had come up with the initial idea, even if he hadn't done much about the actual planning for the operation? Who was on the hook with the CO? Who had briefed the man outside of normal channels?

Too quickly to be simple coincidence, the first sergeant, Okanjo, and Gauta came jogging into the lobby.

"There's the hero of the day," the CO said, clapping the beaming Gauta on his shoulder. "And you," he directed to Okanjo. "Your father already knows what happened, and I can tell you, he's mighty proud of you."

Teo struggled to keep his face neutral. Of course, the CO would get word to Major General Okanjo, the Third Marine Division commanding general on Nouveau Niue.

"I want to know everything that happened," the CO continued. "Let's take a walk."

Teo started to follow, but the CO waved him back. He was being dismissed.

"Sir . . . ?" the XO asked as the three Marines headed off down the beach.

"He just wants a first-hand account," Teo said, not wanting to say anything more in front of the first sergeant. "And, First Sergeant, go get a fire team to dog them. They should be safe, but still . . ."

Teo watched as the CO put his arm around Gauta's broad shoulders and laughed at something the sergeant said.

I've got a spy, and I'm going to find out who it is.

But what could he do about it? Taking any sort of action would be deemed retribution, and that could get him relieved as well.

Still, better to know your enemy than get surprised, he thought as he kicked the sand and walked away.

Chapter 18

Paladins

"Rest halt." Richter raised his left arm, drew a circle in the air with his hand, and pointed at a massive downed tree. A wedge of Cataphract troopers pushed through the jungle to a small clearing bisected by the tree and formed a perimeter. Their armor plates shifted color as they stopped amidst bushes and tall trees, blending them into the foliage within a few tens of seconds.

The major made his way up to the fallen tree. The moss-and-vine-wrapped trunk was taller on its side than Richter in his jack. He whacked the bark with the butt of his cycler, and a hunk of rot fell off, exposing alabaster wood beneath.

"Mortars," he said and waved at Szabo and another Cataphract with a base plate and tube on his back. A pair of flankers followed and went to work emplacing the mortar system after the heavy metal plate fell off the back of the Cataphract.

"Cycle men through for chow and dry socks," Richter said into the IR. He put a hand on Szabo's shoulder, and the radioman went to one knee. Antennae popped out of his comms module as the equipment began a scan.

A pair of flankers shrugged packs off their backs and flopped against the trunk. One pulled a boot off with a wet *schlurp* and shook mud and water out of it. His foot was ghastly pale, the skin puckered with faint blisters at friction points.

"This fucking planet have a dry season?" the trooper asked, wincing as he massaged his foot.

"Spectrum's clean, sir." Szabo looked up at Richter. "Maybe the patties decided to stay home? Too wet out here for them?"

"Don't ever think that," Richter said. "Pigs love their mud. Eat something. Hydrate."

"Roger that." Szabo's breastplate hissed as it popped a few inches off its frame. He slipped one hand inside and pulled out a shrink-wrapped package. "Heard all about the shelf-stable peanut butter and jelly sandwiches back in basic. Never had them in any of our rations. Drill sergeants said they were meant for the front lines and we would never get them back on Essach."

"Did he?" Richter stifled a smile.

The flanker changing his socks slapped his battle buddy's shoulder and pointed at Szabo.

"I was real surprised when other troopers wanted to trade their PB&J to me for my field packs." The young trooper wagged the small package in front of his face. "Got three of these for one tuna with noodles, which are the best, based on my experience."

"Your experience. Yes." Richter made a mental note to have a talk with the first sergeant once they returned to the lodge.

Szabo ripped a side off the package and sniffed the sandwich within. His nose crinkled and he sniffed again, then looked at text printed on the side.

"That's funny." He pulled a corner off and crumbs sprinkled out, leaving a hunk of a congealed purple and orange substance pinched between his fingers. "The expiration date's not for another six months . . ."

He took a bite and promptly spat it back out.

The two flankers chuckled.

"What the hell?" Szabo took out the rest of the desiccated meal, which crumbled like an ancient mummy suddenly unwrapped.

"Hegemony food science has yet to crack the code on a shelf-stable peanut butter and jelly sandwich," Richter said. "Whatever they used to stabilize the fats in the butter reacted badly with a preservative in the jelly. Supply still sends them to us."

"New guy," said a flanker, waving at Szabo, "it's only the grape ones that have that problem. I got some strawberry if you still want to trade."

"No." Szabo shook his head quickly. "No, thank you."

The two broke out laughing.

"I was hungry too," Szabo grumbled as he slipped what remained of his sandwich into the pouch and put it back in his breastplate. "Man . . . I've got like a dozen of them in my footlocker. Sir, do you think the supply sergeant would let me—"

"The supply sergeant called in all his favors to get the loggies to stop sending us egg loaf for every hot meal. He's been a bit surly since then. What do you think he'd do if you show up at his section with an armful of dog turds?"

"'Dog turds'? Oh, that's what they were talking about . . ." Szabo frowned. "Supply would probably want me to get headlight fluid for him. Again."

The flankers laughed even harder but stopped after a hard look from Richter.

"Chili mac." Richter tossed a packet to the radioman. "Get with Mama-san for pogey bait until the next supply drop of new field rations."

"Thank you, sir." Szabo kneaded the meal to loosen up the contents and activate a heater built into the packaging. "You think the Alliance eats this good?"

"We searched a good pattie a couple weeks ago," a flanker said. "He had locally-processed stuff on him. Guess they like eating ramen noodles raw when they're out in the field. Alliance is too cheap to give them anything, so they forage."

"Or their supply situation's just as shitty as ours," the other said.

"Hold up." Szabo canted his head slightly to one side. "Got a data squirt . . . weird frequency."

"Send it to me." Richter waited a moment for a blip to come up on a map within his HUD. "It's on old Highway 37. Not even a kilometer from here. Odd."

The two flankers hurried to put on new socks and their boots.

"My module's decrypting it . . . it's Yuttie. Don't know what it says, though." Szabo double-tapped a screen.

"Rotig-klon. Choi song krai ma choi noi!" played in Richter's helmet.

"Patrol, get ready to step off." He zoomed in on the map and prepped a movement order to send through the network running through Szabo's jack.

A pulsating dot appeared on the HUD close to the source of the transmission, and Richter swore softly.

The *whoomph* of an explosion carried through the jungle.

"Was that a good boom or a bad boom?" Szabo wolfed down his lunch.

"Bennie mine went off, and this day just got worse." Richter issued curt orders and marched toward the highway, his troopers forming a screen ahead of him with flankers bounding forward. He left a section behind to cover their rear while the mortar team readied shells dropped off by other flankers as they ran through the clearing.

It didn't take long before the forward scouts sent back pictures of a half-dozen civilian cargo trucks stopped on a partially overgrown double-lane road. One truck was half on the shoulder, wheels sunk in mud, a crowd of Ayutthayans—a mixture of men, women, and children—at the back of the convoy.

"What the . . . what are civilians doing out here?" Szabo asked.

"Good question. Ready a satellite bounce back to squadron and keep a link to the mortar section in case we need a fire mission," Richter said.

"Fire mission? But they're civilians . . ." Szabo looked up at the jungle canopy and found a gap in the branches.

"We'll see. Briem, put an element on comms and send three jacks with me. Flankers on overwatch. Hostile intent before anyone fires, that clear?"

"Crystal, sir," the lieutenant said through the IR. *"Jacks from first squad with you."*

Richter stopped when he made out the convoy through the jungle. Ayuttayan voices, loud and laced with panic, were in the air.

Three Cataphracts came too close to the major for his comfort. Too many troopers too close together would be a tempting target for any Marine with a 51 grenade or Gryphon rocket—civilians on the battlefield or not.

"You asked for muscle," said Sergeant Woad, whose breastplate had several kill tallies scratched on it.

"Look menacing, but not too menacing," Richter said. "Women and children are in there . . . probably not a rebel force. Heads on swivels, troopers."

"Roger, sir. They fuck around and they'll find out how we treat rebels," Woad said.

Richter snapped off the ammo line to his cycler and grabbed the weapon at the base of the barrel. Holding it overhead, he came out of the jungle and onto the road well behind the convoy. He walked toward the trucks, his other arm held out to the side with his hand open.

The Ayutthayans noticed him and started yelling at each other.

They milled about like they wanted to bolt but were afraid to leave the highway. The back of one truck, the cargo bed covered by canvas, shifted from side to side.

"Union-sanctioned transport!" A sunburnt man, taller than the locals, pushed through the crowd and held both hands high over his head. His shaggy blond hair and blue trousers marked him as an off-worlder.

"Fuck," Woad said from behind Richter as the major lowered the weapon and held it low across his chest, the barrel pointing toward the jungle.

The blond man skidded to a stop, his hands still high.

"Union-sanctioned transport," he said. The man's white undershirt was soaked through with sweat, boots caked in mud, his hands filthy. "I'm Jerome Niedermeyer, Supreme Union representative for our humanitarian efforts on—"

"Drop your hands. You look like a complete idiot," Richter said. "What the hell are you doing in this sector?"

"Yes," Niedermeyer said, flopping his arms down. "Please tell your men that not all of the refugees speak Standard. I'm evacuating them from an area that didn't receive many tourists. I'm fluent, so no worries there. Yes, there was a bit of confusion, as the GPS system seems to have failed."

"Satellite navigation hasn't been a thing on Ayutthaya for years," Richter said.

"There was supposed to be, for a little while." The Union man pulled a dirty map out of his back pocket. "The civil conflict between Royalists and—" he glanced over his shoulder to the crowd of civilians who were inching closer to him—"non-Royalists got much worse near Sekong. The Union decided to evacuate Refuges numbers—"

"The satellites you floated were destroyed by orbital debris, and you took a wrong turn because you don't know how to read a map,"

Richter said.

Niedermeyer opened his mouth wide, then shut it and nodded quickly.

"Then our lead vehicle went off the road, and one man we sent into the jungle to get some branches to help get it unstuck . . . he . . ."

Richter grabbed Niedermeyer by the arm and held it up to see the Hegemony-issued band on his wrist.

"I'm so used to having it," the Union man said. "I didn't think that the area was mined. Can your men check on him?"

Richter let him go and spoke into the IR.

"You ever have one of those days that just goes from bad to worse?" Niedermeyer tried to smile, and Richter felt a stab of empathy for the man.

"Any weapons in the convoy? Rebel fighters?" Richter asked.

"What? No! This is a sanctioned Union convoy. We would never allow our flag of truce to be used to move combatants or lethal aide. That would violate so many of our policies, our remit to operate on this planet would be in jeopardy."

"So you inspected everything in the trucks," Richter deadpanned.

"Well . . . we left in such a rush that I—"

"My brother!" An Ayutthayan woman pushed through the crowd, a toddler on her hip. "My brother went out in the woods and he hasn't come back."

"I'll send my men to look for him," Richter said and pointed a knife hand at Niedermeyer's sternum. "Move everyone to the north side of the highway away from the trucks while we search for contraband."

"That won't be necessary." Niedermeyer became flustered. "There's nothing to find."

"So you won't mind if we look." Richter's knife hand raised slightly to the base of the Union rep's neck. "We'll run facial recognition scans of everyone to make sure they aren't wanted for crimes against the Ayutthayan King."

"Ridiculous! Just get—"

The knife hand rose to point directly between the man's eyes and he backed down.

"Can you get the truck out of the mud?" he asked, raising his palms.

"Yes. Soon as I'm satisfied this convoy is clean." Richter spotted Lieutenant Briem at the edge of the jungle and canted his head toward the trucks. Two squads of flankers emerged and hurried toward the vehicles.

"My brother?" the woman asked as the child, a little girl, squirmed against her, one thumb in her mouth and fear in her eyes as she stared at Richter.

"Give me some time, ma'am." Richter removed his helmet so the girl could see his full face.

"Crab," she said.

Her mother's eyes widened and she turned her body to one side to shield the girl.

"I've been called worse," Richter said. "Move your people." He glanced at Niedermeyer, who shouted commands in Ayutthayan. The people hesitated, then obeyed.

Richter marched past four of the trucks to the one he'd seen moving around. He put his helmet back on and reloaded his cycler. The trucks were old Ayutthayan military issue, ubiquitous to both sides of the civil war and used to carry anything and everything that would fit in the back. The tailgate had a Union seal on the back, and blue paint had faded on the plastic sideboards. The canvas covering snapped in the breeze.

"Woad, lift the back flap on my signal." Richter lifted his cycler up

175

to his shoulder, the servos in his gun arm and shoulder whining.

"Wait, wait!" Niedermeyer ran over. "There's no reason for this. You're frightening the people under my protection, and I will put all of this in my report!"

"Send me all the strongly worded letters that you like. Now."

Cataphract soldiers on either side of the truck flung up the back flap. Inside, a skinny Ayutthayan man yelped in shock. Several cargo chests were open around him. He reached into one and froze, his eyes locked on Richter.

"Don't," Richter said firmly, his finger tight on his cycler's trigger, the weapon aimed at center mass. "Whatever you've got isn't worth your life."

"There's nothing there!" Niedermeyer reached for Richter's arm, but a trooper yanked him back.

"He not understand me? Tell him to raise his hands slowly and get out." Richter shook his head at the man, who was breathing hard, his eyes dilated like saucers.

Refugees shouted and Niedermeyer spoke in halting sentences in the local dialect.

The man jerked his hand out of a case, bringing a rifle with it. Richter fired a quick burst that shredded his chest and shot through the windshields. The man went down in a heap, twitching.

Wails went up through the refugees as Richter grabbed Niedermeyer by the scruff of the neck and forced him to look inside. The rifle clicked against the metal floor as the dead man's muscle spasms trailed away.

"What's that on the bed? Huh? What is it?" A cold rush of adrenaline hit Richter's heart, adding fuel to his anger. Even with the immediate danger gone, his body still flooded his system, ready to keep fighting.

"They told me . . . they told me there was nothing!" Niedermeyer began crying as blood dribbled down the tailgate. Richter pushed him toward the refugees.

"This is how the Union always operates." He slapped Niedermeyer's thigh with the side of his barrel to prod him closer to the civilians. "Claim to be perfect while there's nothing but rot and corruption underneath."

"I swear!" Niedermeyer whirled around, trying and failing to control the emotions in his face. "I swear that they told me they were moving nothing but food and medical supplies. And people. These are the victims of this conflict." He gestured to the crowd, who were drawing in on themselves, terrified of Richter and the smoke rising from his barrel.

"Victims," Richter sneered.

"Sir, found the blast seat of the Bennie they set off," Briem sent him. *"You want a video? Ain't pretty. Dude's going home in a bucket. Did find this, though."*

One corner of his HUD flashed with an image of a rifle, a dismembered hand ending partly up the forearm clinging to it in half-burnt undergrowth.

"I can't tell if you're a complete idiot or on the take," Richter said to Niedermeyer. "Why are there so many guns in this refugee convoy?"

"They . . . they said something about chayseux cats." Niedermeyer swallowed hard.

"Send three of your people to pick up the body." Richter pointed toward the front of the convoy. "Yutties are all about proper burials. You know that, don't you?"

Niedermeyer put a hand to his mouth.

"My men are there. No threat from the mines. Go. You're running out of time before the Alliance starts taking an interest in all this. You want

177

to test your luck in between cross fire?"

The Union rep turned to the crowd and spoke softly. The woman with the child on her hip tried to stay strong, but Richter saw her lips quivering.

"Back three trucks are clean," a flanker said through the radio. *"One with the idiot's got some contraband. Booze and some nano packs that don't look like they're street legal."*

"Move all the contraband to the side of the highway. Centralize it for disposal," Richter said.

"Stuck vehicle's cargo bed's empty."

"Heard. Szabo, run facials scans off my optics. See if anyone here's on the blacklist from the Yuttie government."

"Already done, sir. They're clean," the radioman said.

"Criminals. Not rebels." Richter reached beneath his breastplate and took out Captain Alcazar's wanted poster.

He held it up and walked slowly down the line of refugees.

"Anyone know this man?" he asked. They glanced at the photo, then turned their heads away. There was more guilt than anger to them. Some flinched as the crash of cargo containers being thrown off the trucks punctuated the air.

"War criminal," Richter said. "The Alliance is why your people continue to suffer. They leave this planet and the war ends. You see this one—this Alcazar—you tell him the Hegemony knows what he's done. The Hegemony will make him pay for what they've done to you all. *I* will make him pay. Major Richter. Paladin Troop."

He pushed the wanted poster into Niedermeyer's chest.

"See he gets that, yeah?"

Niedermeyer was about to protest, but he flinched at the sound of glass bottles breaking.

"Woad, with me." Richter led his security detail to the stuck truck and they stacked their cyclers into a pyramid. Each Cataphract went to a wheel and grabbed the truck's frame with their heavy frame arm.

"Ready, lift." Richter's jack whined as the servos strained. The truck shifted as the troopers walked it forward and back onto the highway. He kicked mud off the tires, then pointed his knife hand at Niedermeyer and jerked a thumb at the convoy.

The Union man spoke in Ayutthayan, then approached Richter, a sheepish look on his face. "Thank you for . . . the assistance. My report will . . . will be . . ."

"Truthful, I'm sure," Richter huffed. "You stay on this highway and it'll take you to Krabi-Town. Might want to approach the Alliance lines with a bit of caution. Their Marines don't have the same fire discipline as my men."

"We'll leave as soon as . . . oh, here comes the recovery party with Trang's body. Thank your crabs—men, I meant men—for donating a body bag."

"Piss. Off."

Richter retrieved his weapon and waited as the convoy rolled away.

"I've got a satellite bounce lined up," Szabo said through the comms. *"Shall I send a situation report to squadron?"*

"Wait until we've recovered the mortar team and are moving south. Enemy might detect it and then it'll be our turn to have a bad day."

"Roger. Standing by."

Lieutenant Briem stood next to a messy pile of nano packs and bottles of amber liquid. He held a thermite grenade in one hand, a bottle in the other. Two rifles lay on top, one from the man Richter shot, the other recovered from the one killed by the Bennie. Both were of local—and very old—manufacture, the stocks made of wood and had iron sights.

179

"Mekthong brand whiskey," Briem said. "Not the cheap hooch the locals try and sell back at the spaceport. I've heard. Would be a shame to just—"

"Burn it all. We don't have time to pick through this garbage."

"I don't consider one dipshit Yuttie getting ventilated a tragedy, but this should be a goddamn war crime," Briem said as he tossed the bottle onto the pile then twisted the top of the grenade. "Five-minute timer. Should give us time to get some distance before the patties pick up the heat signature."

He held the grenade in his fist and pushed it deep into the mound of contraband.

"Let's go. Return to base," Richter said.

He waited as the platoon filed across the highway and into the jungle. A flanker trotted past him and Richter heard a faint clink of glass. He stopped the trooper and looked him dead in the face.

"Sir! I . . . I . . . there may be some souvenirs in my pack." The trooper smiled faintly. "Must've fallen in there during all the confusion."

"How many?"

"Four? Seven. I mean seven. Just the liquid kind of souvenirs."

"See that all seven are delivered to the first sergeant soon as we're back inside the wire. He may need them for 'collectors' the next time he makes a supply run."

"All . . . seven, sir? I mean, yes, of course, all seven. That's what I was going to do anyway. For sure."

"Move out. Draw fire."

Richter let him go.

****

180

Richter felt sweat dribble down his back. Even in his jack, the jungle heat and humidity still drained him after a long patrol. A battery amber warning popped up on his visor. He'd pushed his men hard as they moved away from the refugee convoy. If there'd been any rebels in the mix, they would surely have sent word to their confederates that a Hegemony patrol had just left their position.

Especially after one of their own had been killed by a mine. That Richter had personally shot and killed one made the target on his troopers' backs even bigger.

"Patrol, send flankers ahead to scout out that clearing," he relayed through the IR and went to a knee next to a thick tree. Szabo fell in close by and more of Frakes' platoon formed a perimeter around him, jack sections at compass points and flanker teams filling in the gaps. "We're going to risk crossing that in the open. Need more distance between us and the Yutties."

Szabo took a long drag on his water line, panting between sips.

"You good, radio?" Richter asked.

"I . . . I set my haptics to low to conserve battery life," Szabo said.

"So, you're using muscle power to augment the hydraulics." Richter rolled his eyes beneath his visor. "You came up with this idea on your own?"

"Negative, sir. Nemec suggested I adjust my levels. Switch them back to normal if we're in contact. Less strain on logistics . . . man, didn't think this would gas me like this." Szabo went back to his water line.

"I have vis on every battery level in the patrol, Szabo. You know what your level's at?"

"Twenty-one percent," the radioman said, sounding almost proud, "after six hours on patrol. Must be a record?"

"I kept my haptic levels normal and am at twenty," Richter

deadpanned, waiting as the gears turned inside Szabo's head.

"Nemec . . . that fucker."

"Reset to default. Give yourself a break." Richter moved away, bumping the top of Szabo's head with the butt of his fist. He raised his cycler barrel as he sidestepped through a gap in the bushes.

He came to the edge of a small clearing and spotted a pair of his flankers on the other side. Both had their necks craned back, staring up. One held out a hand and extended his thumb and pinky, then wagged the digits up and down.

Drone sign.

He followed their gaze to a treetop. A dead balloon flapped in the breeze, light catching against the silver material.

"Ah . . . shit." Richter searched the skies and saw faint black shapes circling overhead. He grabbed a small cord on his chest plate and tugged hard. His visor lit up with warnings as the IR links across the patrol severed.

"Sir?" The tap-tap-tap of Szabo knocking against his helmet sounded through the forest.

Richter's jaw clenched. He prayed the young trooper would know what to do.

"Sir, did you just trip the kill switch? I can't even access my spider overlay." Undergrowth rustled as the radioman moved toward the major.

A low wail began overhead, the sound growing louder as Richter turned and ran. He shoulder-charged Szabo, knocking the radioman back with a clang of steel on steel.

A Switchblade drone smashed into a tree trunk a foot over where Szabo's head had been a moment earlier and exploded. Splinters and smithereens bounced off Richter's armor and the smell of burning hair filled his nose.

He coughed and rolled over, glimpsing the falling trunk coming right for him. He stopped on his back and thrust his cycler up to catch the blow.

The trunk smashed into the ground next to him, branches slapping against his cycler as a flock of black birds struggled out of the mess, their squawking drowning out everything.

"EMPs! Load and fire!" Richter tried to get up, but the branches had him pinned down like a net. He couldn't gain any leverage to roll over or even sit up.

A flanker appeared over him and began hacking away with a small axe. The blade nicked Richter's arm plates but caused no real damage.

"Get out of here!" Richter shouted.

"Birds. Screwing with the drone tra—" An explosion overhead sent Spiteri into a deep flinch. "No more birds!"

Richter ripped a branch off and threw it aside. He got to his feet, the stink of sap and smoke from his burning beard all around him. Explosions rippled through the jungle and shouts rose up from his troopers.

"Cover, sir, cover!" Spiteri ran off, arms over his head as if that would protect him from the Alliance drones.

Richter raised his cycler and planted his feet against the ground. He opened fire at shadows circling overhead, knowing full well that he just put a giant bull's-eye on himself. Drones shot up and arched toward him. His bullets struck one, and the ensuing explosion knocked out two more.

He yelled, the sound lost to the cycler as he swung his aim from group to group of oncoming drones.

A ring of blue light flashed overhead and his armor suddenly became very heavy and his visor cut out. He froze in place, but the cycler kept firing, the barrel jerking higher and higher, wasting ammo.

Whoever had fired off the EMP had done so far too close to him, and it knocked his jack's systems off-line. The cycler ran empty and he saw a drone corkscrewing straight at him against the clear blue sky.

The drone struck between his feet, the dead rocket engine sputtering. Richter looked down at it, the servos in his neck straining against the effort.

"Sir! Sir are you—"

"Back," Richter commanded. Lieutenant Frakes was in the corner of his eye. "Everyone stay back."

On the drone fuselage, an orange light blinked. The EMP had knocked it off-line for a moment, but its system was rebooting. It wouldn't fly again, but the warhead was still live.

Richter bent his non-augmented arm up, the frame over that limb stiff as he brought the inner strap up to his mouth. He bit hard and pulled the arm down, releasing it from the frame with a snap. Then bringing his arm around to his lower back, he slipped a thumb into a small loop and jerked it up, releasing the pads over his body.

Richter slipped his head out of the helmet and wiggled free from his jack, like a butterfly emerging from its cocoon. He stumbled back over cut branches, his eyes still on the now-beeping drone between his abandoned jack's feet.

He stepped away lightly, unsure if even the slightest disturbance from his footfalls would set off the warhead.

Sweat broke out almost instantly, bright light stinging his eyes as he made his way over to a group of his troopers. Two jacks were on either side of a tree, flankers deeper in the undergrowth.

"Recovery?" Frakes asked as Richter ducked behind him. Jacks pressed together, forming a wall of armor around him.

"Safer to pop the drone from here," a flanker said. "Easy shot."

"Then the major has to patrol back in his skivvies," Frakes said.

"I'll dismount for him," the other jack said. "Could use the exercise."

"No one's dismounting for me. Keep your jack," Richter said, slapping embers out of his beard. "Any casualties?"

"Dormer took some lacerations. Doc got him stable," Frakes said.

"Could've been worse. We need to get out of here before another balloon drops on us," Richter said. "We got a recovery set?"

"Sure do, sir." Spiteri held a hand through the gap between the Cataphracts, a corded line with a flat magnet dangling from the end. "L-T's gonna drag for us?"

"No," Richter said. "Too much risk of setting off the warhead if the jacks are moving around. Flanker line haul. I've got point."

"Heard." Spiteri withdrew his arm and set his carbine against a jack's leg. He stepped out into the open and flipped a switch on the side of the magnet before swinging it overhead like a bola. The recovery line arced through the air and shifted midflight to clamp down onto the statuesque Cataphract's shoulder.

Spiteri held the back end of the line in both hands and laughed nervously.

"Stop being such a pussy," Frakes said.

"Well, my pussy ass isn't behind ballistics plate, now is it . . . sir?" Spiteri gripped the line hard.

"I'm calling him 'pussy-ass' from now on," the other jack muttered.

Spiteri ran back, the line went taut, and the jack teetered back. Spiteri let go of the line and kept running as the suit crashed down on the fallen treetop.

No explosion.

"See, pussy-ass? All that sand in your vagina for nothing," Frakes said.

Richter went to the end of the line and laid it over his shoulder. More flankers gripped the line behind him.

"Ready? Heave!" Richter took a step forward and the downed jack shifted forward as he and the other troopers pulled. "Heave!" The next step was harder as the jack caught branches.

"Heave!"

The process continued until the jack was brought to the rest of the patrol, well away from the unexploded drone. Frakes lifted the mud-caked jack back up and brushed dirt off its shoulder.

"Ceban won't like this." Frakes flicked a finger against a muddy servo. "But he's a civilian, gets paid double when he's working overtime, right?"

The ground shook as the drone exploded, sending a shower of wet earth into the air. Shrapnel hissed around them and there was a *whack* behind Richter as he threw himself to the ground.

"God damn it," Frakes said as the last of the explosion's boom roiled through the jungle.

Richter rolled onto his back. A hunk of jagged metal the length of his hand was embedded in the lieutenant's chest. He gripped it with his crab hand and yanked the sizzling metal out.

"Now I gotta buff that out," Frakes said, holding the shrapnel up. "I'm keeping this fucker."

"Lieutenant," Richter said as he flopped back to the ground, "ready patrol formation. We'll step off soon as I can mount back up. Szabo!"

"Sir?" the radioman piped up from off to the side.

"We're going over react-to-drone drills again when we return to base. You and me. Over and over until you can teach from the manual without having to read it!"

"Sir, yes, sir."

Chapter 19

Marines

Teo leaned back in his field chair and rubbed his burning eyes.

"Skipper, why don't you catch a few Z's?" Lieutenant Wooster asked. "I've got it for a while."

Teo shook his head in an attempt to clear it—an attempt that failed. He was running on fumes, and he knew it.

But the damned reports were calling his name, and the CO wanted them by morning. Just more of his piddly-ass BS. He hadn't relieved Teo for supposedly trying to take credit for Gauta's mission, but he was punishing Teo in other ways.

But reports were a way of life for junior officers. If he'd known he'd spend so much of his time as a glorified clerk, he might have turned down his commission.

He pulled up the pad and looked at the I-203, the Ordnance Expenditure Report. The only change was in a few Switchblade detonations since the one sent in on Sunday, but the console would not let him simply copy and paste that report. The powers that be designed them so that every number in the reports had to be individually entered.

A "You have been inactive for five minutes. This session will cut off in twenty seconds" warning flashed on the screen.

Hell, did I zone out?

He quickly entered the next number, forestalling having to go back to the beginning and starting over.

"Have you done an I-203?" he asked his XO.

"Not on the company level, but yes, sir, on the platoon level."

Teo handed the pad to the lieutenant and said, "OK, then. You've got the con. There're four more reports. Get what you can done, and then have someone wake me at zero-four-thirty."

Six hours of sleep? I'm getting six hours? Yeah, baby!

He saved the I-203, signed out, and handed the command pad to the XO. He started to walk to the back of the CP where he'd had a cot set up, looking forward to shutting his eyes.

"Skip? Maybe you'd better go to your quarters?" the gunny asked. "You're not going to get much rest in here."

Teo turned to the gunny to argue, but he realized that the man was only doing his job—in this case, training his officers.

And he was right. If he stretched out on the cot, he'd be half-asleep, his mind on what might be happening, starting at each word or message coming in.

"Point taken, Gunny. I guess I'll go back to the BOQ, but if anything—"

"If anything needs your attention, the XO will let you know. Straight to bed, captain, or no dessert." He wagged a finger.

He stood there like an idiot for a few moments while the gunny, XO, and Lance Corporal Teigen stared at him. He knew he needed sleep, but were these three ready to run the company?

Screw it. They'd better be. They're the Bravo Command for the company. And it's not like we've got anything going on tonight. If the crabs play ball, then it should be quiet.

"Very well," he said, climbing up the ladder and pushing open the double flaps to the CP and stepping into a light rain.

"Recon sunshine," he muttered automatically as he let his eyes adjust to the darkness. Someone from the TOC watched as he walked away, only retreating back inside once he'd gone a short distance.

Strange that they're suddenly so concerned about me getting shut-eye . . .

The "BOQ" was a rather grandiose name for four almost undamaged rooms in the resort's main building. Teo's room even had a real bed, albeit with no linen or other niceties of civilization. The entire resort, once a jewel of Ayutthaya's tourist industry, had been stripped to the bone early in the war.

Still, even bare of furnishings and without power, it was better than sleeping out in the mud. Teo headed down the promenade.

A Marine came out of the dark, poncho over his head. "The line's too freakin' long," he said before he came to a sudden stop. "Oh. Sir. I didn't see it was you. Nice . . . night for a walk!"

Teo couldn't recognize the Marine in the dark. "The line?"

"Nothing, sir," the Marine blurted nervously. "Uh . . . you're about to turn in? By your leave, sir."

Teo stopped, hands on his hips, as he watched the Marine hurry off toward Second Platoon. He'd been around long enough to know when something dodgy was going on. The question was what.

He slowed his breathing, then simply listened. In the light rain and darkness, his mind took him back to ambushes on Rather's World, his mind on full alert as he listened for sign of the enemy soldiers . . .

These are your Marines, not the enemy, he reminded himself. *Still . . .*

And he heard the quiet murmur of talk past the old resort lobby.

The Tradewinds Resort had stressed the tropical nature of the place, making use of open air and tall ceilings. The resort's reception lobby was open to the front and back, letting the ocean breezes flow through. Teo turned and took the four wide steps into the lobby, crossed it, and emerged on the back side.

The sounds were coming from the left, down toward what had been the maintenance and staff building. He could just make out a line of Marines up against the side of the building.

This doesn't look good.

He walked down the path, joining the end of the line.

"What's up?" he asked the last Marine.

"You gotta wait your turn, man, and it's taking too long," the Marine said, whose Lancaster-drawl immediately identified him.

"What's taking too long, Seibbert?" Teo asked in his best command voice.

"The . . . oh, shit," Lance Corporal Klip Seibbert, from First Platoon, said as he turned and saw who'd asked the question. "I mean, sir. Hello . . . sir." He raised his tone ever so slightly in warning to the rest of the Marines in line.

"I asked you a question, Seibbert."

"Saw a line, thought I'd join it," he said, his voice cracking. "Bad habit from growing up on a prosperity-challenged world. Should be something good at the front. Bread, maybe?"

"You're in line for bread?" Teo dead-panned.

"Klip, who's that?" the Marine in front of Seibbert asked.

Teo could force the lance corporal to answer, but he could just find out himself.

"Get back to your squad, Seibbert. Tell Sergeant Adoud I want him to report to the first sergeant in the morning."

"Uh . . . he's here, sir. Up there." He pointed to the front of the line.

Teo ignored the lance corporal and started up alongside the Marines. He heard a few "Hey, no cuts" and more than a few "Oh, shits" as he passed the dozen or so Marines. One Marine tried to escape into the

190

night, but Teo caught him by the shirt and pushed him back into place. By the time he got to the front, the line of Marines had gone silent, and each man had gone to the position of attention.

"Stay put," Teo rumbled. "You'll all get *exactly* what's coming to you."

He turned into the doorway. Just ahead, lit by an LED tacked to the wall of the hallway, he could see Sergeant Adoud—soon to be ex-Sergeant Adoud and Third Platoon's First Squad leader—talking to PFC Rein Kopek.

"No time for romance. Stick and move, Marine. Stick and move."

"Yes, Sergeant." Kopek rubbed his palms together and adjusted his crotch. "Who said a combat deployment has to be all bad, right?"

Adoud laughed and clapped the big Marine on his shoulder.

Teo took that moment to step into the hallway.

Sergeant Adoud looked up, ready to say something, but the moment Teo stepped into the light, a resigned expression came over his face, and he came to a position of attention, whispering for Kopek to come to attention as well.

"Oh, I'm already at attention," Kopek broke into a little dance and turned around slowly, snapping his fingers. "Bow chicki-bow-wow—oooh hi, Captain!"

Teo poked two fingers into Kopek's chest and pushed his back against the wall with the slightest touch, then stepped up until his face was centimeters from Aboud's. "Where?"

Sergeant Adoud nodded to the hatch over his right shoulder.

"Does this mean I don't get my turn?" Kopek asked as Teo opened the hatch to what had once been an office, lit by another single LED. The room wasn't being used as an office now.

A pile of mattresses had been stacked against the wall, desk and furniture shoved to one side to make room. A Marine stood before the makeshift bed, his pants around his ankles, pale butt cheeks exposed. A woman was on her knees in front of him, one hand at his crotch. She leaned to one side and scowled at Teo.

"One at a time!"

"Yeah, what the fuck? Haven't even started!" The Marine flipped the bird over one shoulder.

"You're done."

The bare ass clenched and the hooker rolled her eyes at the Marine's crotch and tossed her hand up, the short-arm inspection now pointless.

Lance Corporal Cesar Xicale struggled to get his pants back up and whirled around, his eyes wide and face red.

"Sir! I can explain!"

Teo put his hands on his hips.

Xicale, chagrined, kept working on his pants.

"Passageway. Now."

"Damn, sir, I can't even make terminal lance." Xicale fumbled with his belt, the buckle clanking as he left the room in a most undignified fashion.

"You the boss-man?" the woman asked. Upon closer look, she wasn't as young as he'd thought. Crow's feet creased the sides of her eyes, and her brittle-looking hair lacked the vitality of youth.

The smell in the room finally registered . . . and it was something else.

"I'm the company commander, yes."

"You gotta pay just like anyone else," she said, not bothering to pull down her top.

"I'm not paying for anything. Neither are my Marines. You're leaving."

She gave a slight shrug, as if she didn't care what happened, and fished out a spritz bottle from a bag. A silicone marital aid flopped out and rolled across the floor, stopping against his boot.

He stared at it for a moment, then gave it a nudge, sending it back to her. "How much did they pay you?"

"Twenty unis a pop. I already done eleven so far. Then they paid to see the banana show and—"

Teo grimaced. Eleven of his Marines? He was going to have a lot of clean-up to do after this. And only twenty unis? It wasn't much.

"I'm keeping it. We got laws here, boss-man, and you can't take my money," she said with bluster now tinged by fear. She pulled down her top and reached for her buspad, clutching it to her chest.

Technically, she was right. This was a resort world, where laws allowed for almost any activity that serviced the tourists. She was not breaking the local laws, per se, as far as it went. But she was inside the Marine compound, and that gave him wartime powers.

"This is a restricted area," he told the woman. "You're not allowed here, and under the Status of Military Forces Agreement, I am authorized to restrain you and confiscate whatever you have with you."

Her eyes went wide, and she grabbed the pants next to her, struggling to put them on.

"Please, sir, I need the unis. My family does," she pleaded as she pulled the loose trousers up, tying them at the waist. "Since you soldiers got here, you and the Heggies, we've got nothing. Nothing."

"There're camps," he said automatically. "They'll provide for you."

"Prisons," she spat out. "Better to starve out here."

There was truth to her charge, he knew. The refugee camps were, by all accounts, hell. He stared at her as she clutched her pad to her chest,

193

staring at him with hope in her eyes. He had full authority to confiscate the pad and lock her up. She was in the Marine compound without permission, and that was a huge security breach.

Crap, I'm going to have to report this to the CO, he realized. *Is this going to be the thing that gets me relieved? Marines getting laid?*

But that was his problem, not hers. She was just taking desperate measures to try and provide for her family. No matter what he thought of her choices, he was not going to try to take the moral high ground.

"Come with me," he said.

"What are you going to do to me?" she asked, her voice faltering as she stepped up but kept her distance.

He didn't answer but opened the door. His eyes landed on Xicale first.

"Xicale, escort this woman out of the compound."

"Aye-aye, sir."

"And I can keep the unis?" she asked hopefully.

"You're to leave the compound and never come back. I never saw that pad, and I never saw any transactions, so there's no reason for me to look. But I want you to tell everyone out in the town what happened, that you did all of this for nothing. You got nothing. Understand?"

"Yes, sir! I understand. I'll tell them. Thank you, sir!"

There was a rumble from the Marines when they heard Teo tell the women she could keep the unis.

"But, Skipper, we never got to . . . you know!" Seibbert said in protest as the woman hurried past him.

"Atten . . . HUT!" Teo roared.

Thirteen Marines locked to attention.

"Article 9-19, unauthorized fraternization with local nationals." He walked slowly. "Article 2-12, procurement of illicit goods or services." Teo leaned close to Kopeck and sniffed his breath. "Article 4…88, unauthorized adjustment to implanted nanos. I smell them on you."

"Actually, sir, that's article 4-89," Seibbert said.

Teo stopped and slowly turned around. Seibbert snapped his head back.

"I don't give a fuck what article it is, Private First Class."

"Uh . . . I'm a lance corporal, sir," he said with a tremor in his voice.

"NOT FOR FUCKING LONG!"

He stood there, hands on his hips as the Marines wished they were anywhere else but here.

"All of you, get out of my sight. Wait to hear from the first sergeant in the morning. Now! Asses and elbows."

Teo watched them leave, disappointed with Adoud and the others, but mostly with the sergeant. He was going to be busted back to corporal—Teo didn't have much choice in that. The rest? Maybe extra duty would be enough. It wasn't as if Teo hadn't pushed the envelope himself back in the day.

He made a mental note to have each and every Marine checked for STDs, not just the eleven who had actually done anything. And the old-fashioned way, with a long swab, not a simple scan. Old Cotton Eye Joe.

This was trash fire, no doubt, and he'd get his ass chewed by the CO at the least, maybe even finally relieved. Just one more reason for the man to hate on him.

Time to take some action and at least have that done before he reported this up to him. Better to be proactive and have already taken corrective action to keep the CO out of it as much as he could. Maybe Gauta's success would temper the CO's reaction.

He started to ping the first sergeant as a wave of weariness swept over him.

Just get some sleep and let the first sergeant sleep too. All of this can wait until morning. Do those assholes good, too, to wonder all night what's going to happen to them.

With a sigh, he stepped out of the building into the now pouring rain.

Chapter 20

Paladins

Scattered raindrops hissed as they hit ash, the burn pit smelling of burnt meat and iodine. The carbon-based batteries the Hegemony used carried a certain stench that Richter wasn't sure would ever come out of his uniform.

He dumped the contents of a metal mesh wastebasket into the pit, then picked up a long metal rod and stirred the embers, coughing as a gust of smoke hit his face. He looked away, his eyes squeezed shut as they teared up.

Stepping to one side, Richter raised the rod to stab again, but paused. At the edge of the pit was a flyer, the corners blackened and crinkling as the paper burnt slowly.

He tossed the rod aside and went prone. One arm went into the pit, the hair on his knuckles singeing from the heat. He snatched up the flyer and shook it back and forth. When the fire kept burning, he ripped the corner away and tossed it. Blowing on his fingers, he stared at the picture on the flyer.

Captain Alcazar.

"It keeps you warm inside, sir?" First Sergeant Molenaar walked up, a metal jerry can in hand. He swung it forward and clear liquid arced out of a nozzle and onto the pit. Lines of flame sprang up where it landed.

"The pit? It does the job. Not that being cold's a problem here." Richter folded up the picture.

"No, sir. All that hate." Molenaar stuck a toe under the rod and kicked it up into his other hand.

"You don't hate the patties, Top?"

"Kill 'em. Kill 'em all. Let God sort 'em out." Molenaar rustled the ashes. "There's only one kind of a good pattie, and we aim to make 'em that way, don't we, sir?"

"Then I don't understand your issue."

"You've got your eye on that one. The captain. It's not good to fixate. Be an equal-opportunity killer, sir."

Richter caught a glimpse of the ugly remnants of the pig used as the offering to the dead spirits of the lost snipers. True to form, the Syddan troopers hadn't eaten a bite from the animal.

"I'm not picky about my kills, Top."

"There's a story from the old country, sir, of a great warrior named Sigurd. Fought well for his king. Killed when he had to, ruled the lands given to him with honor, and cared for the people. But there was an outlander who refused to be ruled. Named Maelbrig. This Maelbrig raided Sigurd's lands, kept at it even after Sigurd drew blood in return. It went on so long that Sigurd's king began to doubt him. This hurt Sigurd more than anything—he was bound to the king through kinship and battle. But, after a few seasons of fighting, Sigurd managed to bring Maelbrig to talks. A chance to end the feud.

"Maelbrig believed the stories of Sigurd's honor—as he'd conducted himself like a proper man of Syddan—and came to the meeting place with forty men as the peacemakers got them to agree to. Sigurd did not trust Maelbrig and brought twice as many, two to each horse. Sigurd saw an advantage and took it. Killed Maelbrig and all his men.

"Sigurd wanted to show his king that he'd dealt with the thorn in his side once and for all, so he cut off Maelbrig's head and strapped it to his belt to carry back to the king. As is our ways.

"But Sigurd took a wound to his thigh in the fighting, and Maelbrig's tooth scraped against the wound during the march back to the king. The wound became infected, and Sigurd took ill before he could reach the castle. He died of fever two days later in a barn."

Molenaar sniffed and spread more fuel on the fire.

"So, what's the moral there, Top?" Richter asked. "Fight without malice? Your people aren't the detached type."

"Can't tell you, sir. That's not how it works. Evening." He gave the major a curt nod and walked off with the jerry can.

Chapter 21

Marines

"So glad to finally meet you, Captain," Brigadier General Ricardo Mullens, the Task Force G2 said as he stepped off the helo, his hand out, followed by two Mālietoa Cordon bodyguards and four other Marines, probably from his staff by the looks of their ranks.

Teo eyed the two Mālietoas who stood like rabid guard dogs on either side of the Intel officer, looking like they were ready to pounce. But it was the general holding out his hand, so he stepped up and took it.

"I've been following your career ever since you earned your POA. Great story, that. Enlisted out of the slums, now a Marine officer. You should be proud of yourself. Yes, proud."

Teo inwardly winced. He hated the entire barrio-bum storyline, and how he became an officer *despite* his home. Sure, life had been tough, but it bred a tough person, and that was an asset in the Corps. But he detected no rancor in the general's demeanor. The man seemed generally pleased to meet him.

The general looked around the resort and smiled. "Ah, this was worth the trip. You must be thanking your lucky stars that you've got this little neck of Ayutthaya to call home."

Thanking my lucky stars? For this shithole?

This was the first day in over two months that they'd even seen the sun.

"Yes, sir. Happy to serve wherever the Corps wants me."

He looked around, then had to admit to himself that with the sun peeking through the scattered clouds, the water had that deep turquoise hue that had enraptured him when the company had first arrived.

"Of course, you are, of course you are. Well, for me, I'm just damned glad to get out of the head-shed for a few hours. When this came up, I almost begged General Pauapoa to let me take the honors."

"Uh, General? This is Sergeant Gauta Gauta," Lieutenant Colonel Khan said, pushing forward to take the general by the arm as if he didn't want Teo to receive any more attention.

The two Mālietoas bristled, and for a moment, Teo had a wonderful image of the CO face-first in the sand, one of the guard's knee implanted in his back. No such luck, though.

They could do it, though, without breaking a sweat. As a general officer, the G2 was a CS-9-level official, and as such, rated two of the elite bodyguards. One of them, the woman, looked to be of pure Oceania ancestry, but the other, the man, could have come from the same barrios as Teo did.

The Mālietoas had the mystique of their secretive service, and these two looked like death on the prowl, but Teo would just as soon have Marines for his security. He knew Marines, knew how they would react. These civilian bodyguards were an unknown quantity.

"Good to meet you, Captain. I'd like to chat with you sometime, you know, get the real scoop on what happened on Rather's World. Those Intel guys always get it wrong."

Teo joined the general in laughter at his joke. He was the task force G-2, the Intel Officer. His job was to take the information collected by all available assets and turn it into usable intel for the force commander to use. He was "those Intel guys."

Maybe he's one of the good ones, Teo thought as the general shook hands with Sergeant Gauta.

Gauta was beaming. Teo had watched the sergeant closely since the Bennie-band mission, and he came away with his own analysis about the Marine. Sergeant Gauta was a tough son-of-a-bitch, violent and dedicated to the Corps. In other words, a good Marine. Teo didn't think he was the one who'd gone behind the company's back to the battalion CO.

The first sergeant or Okanjo, maybe. But not Gauta. And Teo was happy that the sergeant was getting recognized today. Normally, a Gold Sword took six months to approve, but this one had been pushed through in only three weeks, a miracle of Marine administrative procedures.

Having it awarded in the field was better, as Teo well knew. The only press was a Marine holographer who would record the ceremony for Marine Corps Public Affairs distribution.

Teo glanced at Lieutenant Okanjo, who looked proud as a peacock as the general chatted with his sergeant. Okanjo had received his own award an hour ago, a Bronze Sword presented by the battalion commander. It was a low-level award, approved at the battalion commander level, and normally given to enlisted Marines and junior officers. Teo had two of them back from his Recon days to go along with his POA and his Silver Sword.

Teo didn't think Okanjo rated it for the mission, and he had his suspicions that the CO was kissing up by proxy with Okanjo's father. You never knew in the Corps when a senior officer would be in a position to better your career.

"General, if we can proceed? You have a 1415 holocon with Lieutenant General Patel," a captain who'd followed the general out of the helo said, the light green aiguillette around his right shoulder indicating that he was the flag officer's aide.

The general looked back at Teo, gave him a wink, and said, "I still don't understand why we can have a holocon from halfway across the galaxy, but I still have to be back at the Task Force conference room to do it."

"That's because of the quantum commu—"

"Have a sense of humor, Captain Tilleen," the general said, cutting his aide off. "Did they knock the sense of humor out of you at the Academy?"

"Uh . . . no, sir. I have a sense of humor," the flustered aide said as Teo bit back a laugh.

"Yes, I'm sure you signed for one from supply," he said, before turning to the CO. "Now, Colonel, so I don't give the good captain a conniption, shall we present this young Marine with his award?"

I think I like this general.

The general and his aide let the CO lead them on, with the rest of the general's staff Marines staying back with the helo. As the small group walked, the CO babbled on how well Kilo Company was doing on Krabi, and with just an OK from the commanding general, they could sweep the crabs from the region.

Gunny Walters glanced at Teo, one eyebrow raised. Colonel Khan generally disliked Kilo and thought it the weakest of his companies, but they might as well be walking on water to hear the colonel now, bragging in front of the G2.

Teo just smiled and shook his head. The praise would only last until the general took off to return to headquarters.

They passed through the lobby and into the courtyard. It had seen better days. Only about twenty percent of the tile had survived the war so far, and the statue that made up the fountain consisted of just a pair of feet on the base, the rest broken off. But other than down on the beach, it was the only spot where the Marines could form up.

Third Platoon was standing at parade rest until the group entered the courtyard when Staff Sergeant Weiss called them to attention. The CO had wanted the entire company in formation, but when Teo reminded him that although things had been quiet lately, the crabs were still out there, and without normal security, one of their hunter-killer teams might love taking on a general officer target of opportunity.

The CO quickly agreed that a single platoon was a sufficient show of respect.

Lieutenant Okanjo left them to take over the platoon, and Teo slipped back to join the aide, leaving the CO to stand by the general.

"This is your company, Captain Alcazar, why don't you join me here," the general said before turning to Khan and adding, "If you don't mind, that is, Lieutenant Colonel Khan."

The CO did mind, Teo could see, but he gave a tight smile and said, "Of course, not. As you say, this is Captain Mateo's company."

I'm going to suffer for this. But screw it. General's order, you know . . . you dick.

He refused to meet the CO's eyes as he marched to take his place one step behind and to the general's left. The two bodyguards slid into position behind them, and Teo could feel their presence. He was curious about the man, wondering if he might have even come from Safe Harbor or one of the other heavily LatinX-settled worlds. But the woman fascinated him. Teo was no slouch in hand-to-hand combat, but he had no doubt that the giant of a woman could take him, if it came to that.

"Kilo Company, atten . . . HUT!" the aide yelled out in a powerful baritone, even though Weiss already had them at attention. Teo and the general snapped to, however.

"Marine to be awarded, front and center . . . MARCH!"

Sergeant Gauta had left them to stand to the right of his platoon. On order he marched forward until just shy of the general, then performed a left turn, continuing forward until he was even with the general. He halted, completed a right face, and saluted. The general returned the salute.

"Attention to orders . . .

The Secretary of the People's Military Forces takes great pleasure in presenting the Order of the Palm, First Class, to Sergeant Gauta G. Gauta, Alliance Marines, for service as set forth in the following citation:

While serving with Kilo Company, Second Battalion, Seventh Marines, and attached to Task Force 31 for Operation Renewed Will in support of the Republic of Ayutthaya, Sergeant Gauta displayed exceptional fortitude and innovation in action against the enemy. When the enemy introduced an illegal weapon of terrorism into the area, one that placed the local population at great risk of injury and death, Sergeant Gauta volunteered for a perilous mission into the enemy camp to mitigate the terrorist weapon's threat. Alone and unarmed except for his personal dagger, Sergeant Gauta infiltrated the enemy camp, overcoming and killing an enemy soldier before locating the suppressors that would disarm the weapons. While leaving the camp, Sergeant Gauta created a diversion, destroying the enemy headquarters. As a result of his actions, Sergeant Gauta has significantly decreased the risk to the local population, saving countless lives. His courage and military skill reflect great credit upon himself, on the Marine Corps, and the People's military forces.

Given under my hand on this Fourteenth Day of Mati, Three-Twenty-Three

Alfryd L. Gunga
Secretary of the People's Military

Teo didn't change his expression as the citation was read, taking some of the liberties in it in stride. The Bennies weren't actually illegal—and not much different, at least in deployment, from the Marines' own Switchblades—and the Bennie-bands sure didn't go out to the locals, but the awards were also used as fodder for the masses. Two of his own awards were in a similar vein. The crux of it was that Gauta had gone above and beyond. That fact could not be argued.

The first sergeant marched forward, handing the general the medal.

"I'm proud of you, Sergeant. That took huge cojones, but the payoff was big."

"He who will not risk, cannot win, sir," Gauta said.

The general seemed surprised, then said, "John Paul Jones, 18th Century Earth, American Navy. I don't often hear Marines quoting him."

"That's my mantra, sir."

"And a good one it is, son. A good one it is."

He slipped the base of the gold and black-striped ribbon, the gold crossed swords medal hanging from below, on the connector strip inside Gauta's breast pocket. With a click, it latched into place.

The general stepped back and saluted Sergeant Gauta, who, surprised, nonetheless saluted back, a smile threatening to break his face in two.

"Lieutenant, put your Marines at ease," the general told Okanjo.

The lieutenant gave the order, and the Marines went to parade rest, of course, not that Teo expected anything different. "At ease" in front of a general officer did not mean grab-assing and picking your nose.

He took a step forward and stood next to Gauta.

"Turn around, son," he quietly told the sergeant, "and face your fellow Marines."

The general took a moment to sweep his gaze across Third

Platoon. "Marines of Kilo Company, *Vigilamus pro te!*"

Still at attention, every Marine shouted back, "*Vigilamus pro te!*"

"Damn," the general said, turning to look back at Teo. "That still gives me a hardon every time I hear it."

There was some low laughter escaping from the Marines, hearing a general officer say something so . . . well, "un-general-like."

The general turned back to the platoon. "It's a pleasure to be here with you today as one of your own is honored. We can lose touch up in the head-shed sometimes, as we worry about meetings, reports, the overall bureaucracy. But coming out to the front, where you are the tip of the spear, it reminds me why all of us at the command level are even here. Generals don't win wars. We don't fight them. It is you. You are the ones who bring it to the enemy."

He put his hand on Gauta's shoulder and said, "And it's NCOs like Sergeant Gauta here who are going to lead you to greatness. Not your platoon commander. Not your company commander. And certainly not even the CG himself. It is you, the private. It is you, the team leader. And it is squad leaders like Sergeant Gauta. They will lead you, and then you have to take Lady Opportunity by the throat. And being Marines, you'll probably strangle her, shouting 'Ooh-rah' as you do!"

There were both laughs and "ooh-rahs" erupting from the Marines.

Damn! This guy is good, Teo thought.

Teo was a doer, not a talker, but he wished he had that skill.

"And I know you will. You are the vanguard of the Alliance, protecting the helpless. You are the ones keeping the Ayutthayans free from the crabs' attempt at imperialism."

He took a step back and shouted out the Marine motto once more. "*Vigilamus pro te!*"

Shouting louder, sounding like a full company instead of merely a platoon, the Marines, Teo included, shouted back, "*Vigilamus pro te!*"

The general gave the slightest of nods, and his aide shouted, "Awardee, POST!"

Sergeant Gauta was still facing the platoon, and he hesitated about how to do that, so he improvised, performing an about-face before he saluted the general, did his left-face, and marched off.

The general waited until Sergeant Gauta had reached the edge of the platoon before he turned around and shook Teo's hand.

"You've got yourself some good Marines here. You do them right, you hear?"

"Yes, General! Always."

"I know you will, son."

Lieutenant Colonel Khan took that as being freed from his leash, and he rushed forward. "General Mullens, thank you for coming to present the medal yourself. I really appreciate you taking the time to do it. Sergeant Gauta is one of our best, and that's because I've implemented what I think you'll agree is the most innovative—"

"You've got a good company here, Colonel," the general said, cutting him off. "I applaud your hands-off approach. Good leadership."

Teo stifled a laugh at the CO's expression as the man tried to figure out what that meant.

"Uh, yes, sir. I don't want to micromanage, you know, sir. Give them what they need, then get out of the way."

Oh, give me a fucking break. You? Not micromanaging?

"General?" the aide asked pointedly as he stepped up.

"Yes, Captain Tilleen, I know. Time to go. Captain Alcazar, would you walk me back to the helo?"

The CO stared daggers at him, but a general's invitation was an order.

The aide started talking to the CO, holding him back, and the general and Teo separated a bit.

"How are you doing, Captain?"

What?

"Sir?"

"How are you holding up, out here on your own?"

"I'm . . . the company's fine, sir."

"That's not what I asked."

What the hell am I supposed to say?

"Uh . . . I'm fine. I've got the best job in the Marine Corps, right? Company commander."

"That you do, son," the general said with a laugh. "My best tour, ever."

"You had a rifle company, sir?" Teo asked, surprised.

"Ha! You think I was always a POG? No, son, I was a grunt. Went into Intel as a major. Never looked back, you know," he said wistfully, and Teo wondered how much of that was true. "But leading Marines into combat is the pinnacle of what it means to be a Marine."

"Yes, sir," Teo said with fervor.

The general laughed and said, "I can hear it in your voice. The warrior. You'd love to close in with the crabs, right?"

"Yes, sir!" Teo said, even more fervently before he could catch himself. "But I understand. The peace talks. We're just holding the lines."

"For now. Don't be surprised if things break down and you get your chance to take out your Major Richter." The general paused, then added, "Of course, you didn't hear that from me."

"Major Richter, sir?"

"Your opposing commander."

So, that's his name?

"Quite capable, from all respects. Good reputation. But not as good as you are."

"Good of you to say so, sir," Teo said, but his mind was on the opposing commander. Major Richter.

The general's staff spotted them approaching and started boarding the helo.

"How do you like your CO?" the general asked suddenly.

This was treading on dangerous ground, and Teo had to pick and choose his way carefully.

"He's shown great fortitude and command," Teo said.

"Spoken like a true politician," the general said with a chuckle. He lowered his voice, and in a conspiratorial whisper, said, "Just bear with it. There are eyes on you, and many think you need some tempering, hence . . . Maybe you do, maybe you don't, but that's the way it is. Do your best here, and your future is bright."

What does he mean? Teo wondered, refusing to assume anything.

He wasn't Academy. He didn't have a degree. He wasn't like the other officers. But were there people on high who thought he might have what it takes after all?

Just like that, Teo promised himself to watch what he said, how he reacted. If he understood the general—which was in no way a sure thing— he was being tested, in a way. Maybe someone was pushing him, and punching out the CO would be a sure sign that he wasn't real officer material.

"Of course, if you want out, I wouldn't mind an aide de camp with a sense of humor. It's yours, if you want it."

Teo didn't have to think it over. "No, sir. With all due respect, I'm a company commander, not a secretary."

He froze, wondering if he'd gone too far, but the general smiled

210

and said, "Right choice."

"Thank you for our chat," he said loud enough for the others to hear as he turned and offered his hand. "You've got a good company."

He stepped back to shake the CO's hand, and the colonel's rictus face turned to a smile as he started to tell the general whatever he'd no doubt rehearsed a hundred times.

"Take care of him," Teo told the male bodyguard, out of the blue and even surprising himself.

The guard smiled and said, "On your life."

The accent caught his attention. "You're a Safer."

"From Barrio Blanca," the man said with a smile.

"Almost neighbors," Teo responded.

"No, Colonel. I can't drop you off at your CP. My holocon is waiting, you know. Spend a little time with your company here, then make your way back," the general said, catching Teo's attention.

Not going to make him happy, he noted before turning back to the bodyguard.

Teo would have loved to know more, but the general, at his aide's urging, climbed into the helo, his Mālietoas right behind.

His fellow Safer gave Teo a wink as the crew chief raised the ladder.

Teo and the rest scurried back as the helo rose on its fanjets, quiet for something so big. It slowly rotated until it was pointing north along the shoreline before its nose dipped, and with a whoosh of fans, shot forward.

Teo watched until it disappeared over the trees, feeling both elated and sad. Elated because things might not be as dark as they seemed, and sad that he hadn't had more time with the general.

He turned around . . . into the red-eyed glare of the CO.

I'm not going to let you get to me.

But just as Teo couldn't very well act rashly about the first sergeant or Okanjo, the CO couldn't do much at the moment. Teo had only done what the general asked, after all.

But it was an icy walk back to the company CP, neither Marine talking.

"I need to get back, but you and I, we're going to have a talk, real soon," the CO said, unable to hide the malice in his voice.

None of this was my fault, Teo thought, but said, "I'm free whenever you want, sir."

The colonel started to say something when the XO popped his head out from the CP, waving his arms for their attention.

"The general, sir! He's just been shot down!"

Chapter 22

Paladins

Wind swept through the jungle canopy, each gust sending sheaths of water off high leaves and onto the Hegemony troopers as they sloshed through knee-deep swamp. The afternoon sun, peeking through the clouds, were a welcomed sight after weeks of rain.

Richter pulled a boot from the mud and stepped onto a wide patch of moss. Water squirted out from a small eyelet and the squish of wet socks reminded him to pound proper foot care for his men once they made it back to base.

Moving in flanker gear was a fair deal more difficult than crossing terrain in his jack, but speed was of the essence to reach the downed Alliance aircraft. Any of his lieutenants—all more used to operating as flankers—could've taken this mission, but he would never have delegated an operation just because it meant he'd have to fight outside his jack. To do that would lose face amongst his men.

Szabo struggled to get out of the mud. He stuck one hand down and twisted, keeping his carbine out of the muck. The heavy radio pack tipped him off-balance and he flopped onto the moss patch, trying to sit up and moving like a turtle on its back. Richter grabbed him by the shoulder straps and hauled him up.

"Thank you . . . sir." The radioman's eyes rolled back for a moment, then snapped back to normal.

"Take a knee. Drink some water." Richter took cover against a tree as Lieutenant Briem's flankers swept around to his left. He switched his optics to infrared and a wavering column appeared over the tree line in the false color view. The crash site was close and still smoking.

A map overlay had platoon-leader icons for Briem and Kontos on either side of him. He dialed down to the squad leaders, then to the individual fire teams of three to four troopers. The temptation was always there to micromanage the positioning of each and every one of his men, but he had faith in his officers and troopers to handle basic maneuvers.

"Is . . . is the gravity higher than ship standard down here?" Szabo asked, taking a sip from a water line on his shoulder. "Because it feels higher."

"You're carrying our net gear without your jack and you're still pissing troop carrier water. Now you know how the Void Drop Corps feels. Don't pass out on me."

"Got a structure." Briem's voice came through his earpiece and a grainy picture of a wall overrun with vines came up on one side of his optics along with a ping on the map overlay. It wasn't more than a few dozen yards from the crash site. *"Think the patties are in there or they took off?"*

Richter zoomed out on his visor map.

"Flooded and fast-moving water obstacles to the east. No roads or rebel-occupied towns to the north or west for tens of miles. Our lines to the south. And if they've got wounded, they won't be moving fast. If they're moving at all," Richter said.

"Floater," Kontos said and an alert icon flashed on Richter's HUD as Kontos sent the location of a drone to every trooper linked through the IR network hub that Szabo carried on his back. *"Not a Switchblade or a Saber. Looks like run-of-the-mill surveillance junk. Don't think it's picked us up yet."*

"Remember what happened to Eglan? Remember carrying him back to post after he got run through for making the wrong call?" Richter asked.

"Roger. EMP stick arming."

"Arm but do not fire." Richter rubbed the fresh scar on his chin and looked back at Szabo. The radioman unsnapped a short pole from his pack and drove it into the moss. A satellite dish unfurled and juttered back and forth before locking in place. He held up a hand and looked at a compass built into the back of his glove.

"Need comms with squadron, Szabo," Richter said.

"Yes, sir . . . it's just that the satellite relay seems to be missing. I linked before we stepped off and I've triple-checked my connection azimuth, but . . . nothing," he said.

"Not the first time this has happened. There's a whole different war going on in orbit." Richter tapped a fingertip against the side of his carbine. "If they're burning anti-sat weapons right now, they're doing it to protect whoever was on that transport."

"I can go radio band."

"Do that and the patties will know where we are . . . we're in range of their rocket artillery."

"They won't hit us with rockets, will they?" Szabo asked. "Not when we're so close to their own people."

"Plenty of bad things to say about the Alliance, but they'll avoid friendly fire if at all possible." Richter cocked an ear up as the faint sound of a jet engine rumbled through the jungle.

"Ours or theirs?" Szabo clutched his carbine tighter.

"Can't tell." Richter opened a troop-wide channel. "Paladins. Blue platoon will assault through the structure. Red move to the edge of the clearing and provide overwatch on the crash site. Be prepared to clear on command. Take out the drone once I've linked up with the assault element."

He slipped through the jungle at a crouch, moving toward Briem's icon on his HUD. Szabo followed behind, his ruck catching every frond and leaf as he moved, creating enough of a disturbance that Richter slowed down to give his radioman a chance to move without broadcasting their position to any enemy paying attention to their surroundings.

Richter berated himself for taking Szabo outside the wire in flanker equipment so soon after he arrived. The trooper was trained to fight in a jack, not move stealthily through a jungle in flak armor. The environment was a good deal more punishing to troopers outside their jacks, especially if they had yet to acclimatize. He needed Szabo's comms to coordinate support this far from their lines . . . and the damn re-trans satellites were down.

He found Briem crouched next to the remains of a wooden fence. Water dribbled off the trees and ran down the trooper's back.

"Damn, thought there was a *chayseux* coming for me with all that noise," the lieutenant said, leaning to one side to look at Szabo.

"Put one of yours on him," Richter said, cocking his head at Szabo. "I'm joining your assault."

"Ahern." Briem tapped his chest twice, then pointed at the radioman. A trooper appeared out of the jungle and shook his head at Szabo.

"Sir?" Szabo asked.

"Park yourself here, keep the net linked," Richter said. He did a double take before slipping into the undergrowth. "Stay hydrated."

Richter listed off all the assets he *didn't* have with him: mortars, air support, Cataphracts with their survivability and ability to lay down massive amounts of firepower quick and easy. Tanks. He was out here with what his flankers could carry. Not too different from how soldiers fought for the vast majority of human history, but being in the twenty-ninth century and on a planet so far from Earth, one would anticipate a bit more.

But he did have his men linked through the IR, a simple purpose . . . and a half-dozen Benedict smart mines spread among his troopers.

At least the Alliance that survived the crash would be armed worse than he and his men. Dangerous assumption to make, he knew.

"Kontos. Eyes on the drone?" he asked through the IR.

"Confirm. All friendlies out of radius," the lieutenant said. EMP shots would knock out any and all unshielded electrical systems. Szabo's gear—and the rest of the troopers' comms and optics in their helmets—were rated to survive an EMP hit, but the promises of the manuals and designers didn't always hold up in the field.

Richter glanced at Briem. The man was at a half crouch against a tree, finger on his carbine's trigger guard, his jaw working from side to side. Ready and anxious.

The snap of dying flames from the wreckage sounded through the jungle, and a pale-yellow light warmed one side of the building—a long-abandoned private hunting lodge, its roof sunken into the second floor.

"Engage," Richter said and pressed the stock of his weapon against his shoulder.

The EMP shot went off with a stretched *zap* of sound. A wave of blue light rose up and Richter heard the drone hit the ground. His optics frizzled with static, then snapped back into place.

"Blue, bound forward."

Briem and a squad of flankers moved forward, Richter keeping pace two yards behind the lieutenant.

A silhouette appeared in a bottom-floor window. Richter fired off a burst from his carbine and the glass shattered. The figure within crumpled. Shouts rose from the lodge and Richter leaned into a dead run.

"Covering fire!" he shouted as he fired again, striking the window frame and sending shrapnel of rotting wood flying.

"Squirters!" someone shouted over the IR and Richter heard a door bang open from the left side of the building. Alliance rifles opened fire as a small group of men ran out.

Richter hit the wall with his shoulder, his muzzle on the window as more gunfire erupted from the fleeing Alliance. Their white tracer rounds snapped into the jungle where Briem's overwatch element was emplaced.

A cycler opened up and shredded a rusted-out power cube where the Alliance had taken cover.

Briem slid against the other side of the window, panting hard.

"Peek," Richter ordered and Briem thrust his carbine up so the optics attached to the weapon could see inside. An outline of two adults propped against an inner wall flashed over Richter's HUD.

Briem rolled to one side a split second before bullets punched through the wall right where he'd been. The lieutenant grunted in pain as one shot found its mark.

Richter stood up. Inside, a woman in what looked like Alliance fatigues, but different from the Marines' IFUs, used her upper body to shield someone with his back to the wall, legs splayed out. She saw Richter and swung her pistol at him.

He fired a burst that stitched through her gun arm, and she screamed.

Richter stepped over the window sill—jagged glass tugging at his pants as he kept his aim on the Alliance. An open door behind him swung on the hinges; another to his left was propped up against the frame.

The woman took quick, short breaths through a clenched jaw. One arm was mangled by his bullets, but blood wasn't flowing free like he'd expect from severed arteries. She was dark-skinned, and her blond-dyed hair was a mess around her head. There was no rank on her uniform, but she still used herself to shield the other one. He caught a glimpse of the man behind her; a general by the rank on his uniform.

Richter couldn't make out the man behind her from the waist up, but the crash had chewed up his legs. He had tourniquets over both knees and one foot was mostly gone. Flies buzzed around the bloody stump.

Hatred burned in her eyes and she spat at Richter as she bent her other elbow to hold up a grenade clenched in her fist, the pin gone. The man behind her was unconscious, head lolled to one side.

"Fucking crabs." Blood ran down one side of her mouth as she bit hard on her lips.

Richter thumbed on his laser sight and swept the dot over one of her eyes.

"I've got you dead bang," he said. "They've got the good nanos in you. Strong enough to stop you from going into shock from blood loss and trauma. Enough to keep you alive just long enough to keep fighting . . . you're a Mālietoa, if I'm not mistaken? So I'm inclined to take you—and who you're guarding—prisoner."

"Three enemy down outside the structure," said one of Briem's sergeants through the IR. *"Two more at the crash site."*

That update should've come from the lieutenant, but by Richter's quick math, there could still be more Alliance around and he had to deal with that first.

"Tell the rest to surrender. Now." He took a half step closer to the bodyguard and her charge.

"Think you're bold, don't you?" Her mouth trembled as the nanos in her body pumped her full of adrenaline and painkillers. "Brave. I know what crabs do to prisoners . . . won't-won't let that happen to him."

"Your nanos can't keep you conscious for much longer. Don't set it off and I'll bring my medic—"

219

The bodyguard fixed her eyes on the grenade and started breathing hard.

Richter fired a burst into her forehead, blowing the back of her head out against the wall and over her charge's face. Her body went rigid as her nervous system went haywire, the hand holding the grenade clenching even tighter. Richter lunged for the explosive.

The intelligence officer's eyes popped open. He grabbed the dead woman's arm and pried her fingers off the grenade. It rolled onto the floor, and the spoon flew up with a *sprang*.

"Frag! Frag!" Richter kept moving. His carbine clattered against the floor and he dove forward, both hands stretching toward the grenade. His fingertips touched it, and it spun away, inches from his reach. He landed on his stomach, then hauled himself forward with one arm and grabbed the grenade.

Richter rolled to one side and flung it toward the window next to the door from where the other Alliance had fled. It hit the frame and bounced outside. Richter went flat and wrapped his arms around his helmet.

The grenade exploded with a *whoompf*, the blast wave shattering what remained of the windows, hitting Richter like a giant palm slapping down on him. Even with his helmet, the explosion sent his ears ringing. He snatched his carbine up and aimed it at the Alliance officer.

The other man still lay against the wall, the dead woman's head—what was left of it—on his lap. A black streak of lumpy blood traced an arc from his shoulder down his chest. The bodyguard's eyes were still, her mouth agape.

"Asshole." Richter got to an unsteady knee. "You intelligence types are all the same. Think you're so clever playing dead, don't you? Won't work when I get you back to my people."

"Worked . . . well enough, crab." He smiled.

The other door burst open and an Alliance Marine froze on the threshold. Time slowed down as Richter brought his carbine around, but the Marine had the drop on him.

A weapon fired, and Richter felt the bullets crack as they passed his face.

The Marine crumpled.

Richter looked back and found Szabo standing in the window, his carbine's muzzle smoking, his eyes wide as saucers.

"Medic, status?" Richter asked into the IR as he grabbed the dead bodyguard by the ankle and dragged her off the surviving Alliance officer.

"Briem took a round to the ass. He's mobile, but he'll be slow. Just a flesh wound, but we'll get jokes for miles from it," Iliev said.

"Get in here. POW with tourniquets in place. Litter carry. All elements prepare to exfiltrate." Richter slipped a straight piece of plastic the width of his thumb off the front of his flak vest and slapped it down on the Alliance officer's forearms. The flex cuffs wrapped around his wrists and tightened. The man struggled weakly and swore at him as Richter pushed his bound hands against his bloodstained chest. There was a *click* and bands shot out from the cuffs and snaked around the Alliance's back where they linked together, pinning his arms tight against his body.

Richter pushed him to one side.

"Szabo?" Richter called to the radioman, who was still in the window. The trooper's face was pale, mouth opening and closing.

"I . . . I shot him."

"You did. Give me a glowstick and your fixer tape."

"He's dead . . ."

"Szabo!"

The name hit him like a slap and he looked over at Richter, like he

221

just realized he was there.

"Glowstick and fixer tape," the major repeated, holding out a hand.

"Sir." Szabo shrugged his radio pack off and tossed over a small package the size of a marker and a roll of tape.

Richter shoved the still-wrapped glowstick into the Alliance officer's mouth, then wrapped tape over his lips and around his head.

The man struggled and mumbled what Richter assumed were a stinging series of expletives.

"This is better than the bullet I'll give you if you try and shout out to your pattie buddies," Richter said. He picked up the bodyguard's pistol and shoved it into a small pouch on his belt.

The wheeze of high-pitched breathing came from Szabo as hyperventilation set in. Troopers led by Lieutenant Kontos came through the door and Richter pointed them at the prisoner.

"God damn it," Richter said, stepping through the window and pushing Szabo against the wall. He grabbed the trooper—who was on the edge of panic—by the face and snapped fingers close to his ears. "Look at me. Look at me, son. You just killed a man in battle. You shed blood in war and when you did it, you saved my life, you understand?"

"I shot-I shot-I shot—"

Richter slapped him hard enough to skew his helmet.

"Focus," Richter said, shaking him. "Fast movers. What's the status?"

"Fast . . ." Szabo looked up. "They're . . . oh shit, they're calling me." He righted his helmet and jabbed at a holo screen only he could see.

"We're taking the same route back. Send it to the fighter and tell them to cover us. Don't mention the POW. If the enemy's listening, we don't need to give them a reason to pursue. Kontos?"

"Sir," the lieutenant said as he and his men came around the corner, the prisoner on a stretcher.

"Drop a Bennie in there. Motion trigger. Five-minute delay. Seed the whole crash site."

"Roger, I'm sick of hauling this thing anyway." Kontos spoke orders into his receiver as he unsnapped a thick metal plate from his back and pushed hard on two buttons with his thumb. He kept the trigger down for five seconds, then tossed it through the broken window.

"Take point." Richter slapped the lieutenant on the shoulder and he ran ahead. The rest moved into the jungle, where he found Briem standing against a tree, the seat of his trousers cut out and a bloody bandage fastened to one cheek.

"It's not a million-credit wound," Briem said, "but about five-seventy-three a month."

"You think that much and a Wounded Star medal's worth it?" Richter asked as Briem limped alongside him.

"Should get more. This won't be a scar I can show off to polite company." Briem's face contorted with pain, but he kept moving.

"There's such a thing as 'polite company' on Ayutthaya?"

"Our standards are low and ill-defined, but we have them, sir. Hate to ask this, but keep an eye on my ass. If Iliev botched the patch, I might start bleeding out in a hurry."

"Just keep moving, trooper." Richter stopped and looked back at the thin column of smoke still rising from the crash. How long until the Alliance caught up to them?

A fighter roared overhead, treetops swaying in the jet wash.

Richter smiled. At least the enemy would have to deal with the Hegemony Air Force before they caught up with him.

Chapter 23

Marines

"Keep it moving!" Lieutenant Colonel Khan shouted from the turret of the *Avenger*, the lone surviving Badger.

"Easier said than done," Teo muttered as he ran behind the tank, but he couldn't fault the CO. It had been too long since the general had been shot down.

Brigadier General Mullens was alive, at least according to the last message. Hurt, but alive. Two of his staff had been killed in the crash, but the others and the helo crew had made it to an abandoned building next to the crash site. The Task Force had deployed the reaction team to recover the general, but it was still forty minutes out, and the crabs weren't going to let this opportunity pass them by. Kilo Company had to reach the general first, then hold steady until the Marines could be evacuated.

If not, well, the general was too valuable an asset to let fall into enemy hands. The CG might just give the order to eliminate that possibility with an air-strike. Cold, but necessary, as the CO had confided in him just before they left the camp.

The CO had taken over the rescue mission, and Teo had bristled at first, but no matter what he thought of Colonel Khan, he had to give the man grudging respect at how he'd taken command. Within ten minutes, he had a workable plan in place, and the entire company, minus Weapons, was on the move. Part of Teo had hoped that the CO would prove to be incompetent from a tactical standpoint and he'd have to take over, and that made him feel more than a little guilty, but the man had proven himself.

Not that there was much time nor opportunity for subterfuge—this was an all-out race, and they were less than a klick out. Ten more minutes.

He hoped they were in time. There hadn't been any comms coming from the survivors for seven minutes and counting.

"Get your ass back up there, Cyril," the gunny yelled. "Suck it up!"

With First Platoon leading the movement, Private Cyril had fallen back, unable to keep up the frenetic pace. He wasn't the only one. Marines were straggling, victims of the lack of good PT training in a war zone. Teo shook his head and pushed on. They'd get there with whoever they had and just deal with it.

A muffled explosion sounded from ahead, and immediately, PFC Louis Tentbottom's avatar grayed out. Almost immediately, Sergeant Harris, First Platoon's Third Squad leader, shouted "Bennies" over the net.

"If you don't have a Bennie-band, fall back!" Teo passed on the company net. *"If you have one, push forward. We need to know what's going on."*

Not an elegant order, but it would have to do.

The CO turned to look at Teo from atop the tank, but he didn't cut in.

Teo looked around and shouted, "Those of you here without Bennie-bands, fall in trace of the Badger."

It wasn't foolproof. A Bennie might not be activated by the tank, and then home in on a grunt behind it, but it was all he had.

The fact that there were Bennies in the area was not good news. The most logical conclusion was that the crabs had beat the Marines to the crash site.

"You need to push, Razor," Teo passed on the P2P to the First Platoon commander. *"I think we're too late, but maybe we'll catch them before they*

leave."

"Roger that. We should be there in two mikes."

"No mistakes. We can't afford it."

Teo moved behind the tank, increasing his pace to keep up. His lungs were laboring, and he was heating up, but he could keep it up a lot longer than this.

I just hope the damned Bennie-bands work, he thought as he listened for more explosions.

But it was mercifully silent as he watched on his display as two squads converged on the crash site. Either the crabs hadn't seeded the area or the bands were effective.

Teo was monitoring their movement on his display, but he had to see a real view. He pulled up Sergeant Harris' feed just as the NCO broke out of the low forest and into a wide field. A hundred meters away, the crumpled body of the Marine helo lay as if the pilot had tried to make an emergency landing. A wisp of smoke rose from the tail. Beyond it was an old building.

The Marines spread out and headed for the wreck, but Teo could see from here there were no survivors, just one body in the withered remains of whatever crop had once been planted here. Teo switched to Sergeant Roy's feed as Second Squad moved to secure the building. More bodies were strewn about, and it became painfully obvious that they were too late. The crabs had won the race.

But where was the general? Second Squad entered the old hunting lodge. Two bodies were inside: a major from the G2 staff whose name Teo never caught and the female Mālieto, who was sitting up against the back wall. Shrapnel pockmarked the wall around her, and slow, still-oozing blood showed bright on her face.

That wasn't what killed her, however. The gaping hole in the middle of her forehead had done that.

"Any sign of General Mullens?" the CO asked over the open net.

Teo wanted to snap at the colonel. The crabs did have electronic surveillance, and the open net was not secure. Broadcasting the general's name was a rookie mistake, and one that could have big-time consequences if the crabs didn't know who was on the bird.

"That's a negative," Sergeant Roy passed on the secure net. "No sign of him. But it looks like lots of crabs are heading southeast, and as in not long ago. Maybe minutes."

Teo tried to see what Roy was talking about, but the feed wasn't giving enough fine detail. He trusted the sergeant, however, and didn't question him.

He switched back to the command view, trying to guess where the crabs—and maybe with the general—were heading.

Kilo was on a north heading, with a slight eastward tilt. The crabs were on a southeast heading. If he could only angle off . . .

"Colonel," he broke into the P2P. "I think we might be able to cut them off if we go right now."

Ahead of him, the CO slapped his hand on the commander's cupola, and the *Avenger* slowed to a halt. He looked back at Teo, who used his right arm to point directly east. The CO turned back toward the crash site, then back again at Teo, hesitating.

"I'm still going forward with the assault element," he passed, "but take Third Platoon. If you make contact, hold them in place."

"Roger that."

Using his eyes alone to quickly draw in the coordinating measures on his CCD display took practice, but Teo had done this many times over the course of his ten-year career. Within a few moments, they were in place, and he force-uploaded them to Lieutenant Okanjo.

"Trace, change in plan. Lead with Nyoki, but move it. We need to try and cut them off."

If he was right and the crabs were retrograding with their prisoner, they'd probably be seeding their route with Bennies, and Third Platoon, the support element, only had four of the Bennie-bands, all with Corporal Nyoki's team. That wasn't much, but it was what Teo had, and Nyoki had to lead the movement.

Within moments, Third Platoon started to wheel like a well-oiled machine. Teo felt a surge of pride as he watched on his display.

"Gunny, follow the CO in trace," he passed on the P2P. What he didn't say was, "Keep an eye on him." The gunny would understand the implied order.

The CO hadn't done anything stupid so far—in fact, his orders made tactical sense—but Teo still didn't trust the man, and Kilo was still his company. The CO might have taken command of the mission, but Teo was responsible for his Marines.

Which was why Teo had been keeping close to the CO. But with Teo splitting off, and with the XO and first sergeant back at the camp, the gunny was the only senior Marine in the mission who wasn't actually leading others.

"Roger that, Skipper. I've got it," Gunny Walters said as he started moving over to take Teo's position.

That taken care of, Teo slipped in behind Third Platoon's Second Squad as they double-timed through the forest. Moving at a double-time was risky in the best circumstances, which this wasn't, but they had no choice. Time was of the essence.

Teo switched to Private Fausten's feed, setting the opacity to 75% . . . and within a few steps slammed into a tree trunk with his shoulder, almost knocking him down. He reduced the opacity to 40%, giving him enough of a view of what was in front of him so he could move effectively. He wouldn't be fully combat-ready, but with the squad in front of him, he felt that was a risk worth taking.

Please, let us catch them!

But it was the crabs who struck first. A string of crab carbine fire reached out through the trees. Second Squad immediately started fire and maneuver, never faltering. For once, Teo's combat command AI was working, and by tracing the trajectory, started placing crabs in position on his display. At least four were ahead of Third Platoon. Probably more. Logic would put the bulk of the crabs ready to face Marines coming from the crash site, not coming from out of the woods on their flanks.

"Tra—" he started to order, but Lieutenant Okanjo had already reacted, sending Third Squad to the right and forward to provide a base of fire for Second Squad.

Let him fight his platoon, Teo reminded himself.

Too many commanders just confused things, and that got Marines killed.

"Colonel, we've got contact—" he started to pass up to the CO.

"I see it. We've got nothing here but the dead. Hold the bastards. I'm on my way."

Teo didn't know what "I'm on my way" meant. The CO on foot? On the *Avenger*? With First and Second Platoons?

It didn't matter. And Teo wasn't going to just hold. If the opportunity arose to snatch back the general, he was going to take it.

An explosion burst just over his head, his body armor stiffening up as shrapnel hit him and sending a shower of leaves and woodchips down around him, and Teo belatedly switched his display back to real view, sending the battle display to the upper part of his helmet visor. He wasn't just an observer here. He was in the shit, just like every other Marine, as the crab rifle-launched grenade just reminded him.

His display flashed: two Marines were hit, their ICUs sending up their vitals while turning their avatars light blue. Neither were flashing critical, and Teo forced concern from his mind, leaving Doc Tulagi to take care of them.

He brought up his 51 and fired a burst in the general direction of the known crabs, not expecting to do much good, maybe making them duck at best, but he needed the release. His adrenaline was like fire in his veins, and he needed to get control of himself.

Incoming fire started to increase as more crabs oriented on the Marines, the rounds zipping around Teo like angry hornets. He dove to the ground a few meters from Lance Corporal White Horse, who was pumping out the 30mm grenade rounds from his 51.

"Some shit, huh, Skipper?" White Horse asked, a huge, hungry-looking smile visible through his helmet.

"Yeah, White Horse. Some shit. You get some, now."

"*Vigil tee,*" he said, sending another grenade downrange.

The two Marines were about ten meters from the road. If the crabs were using the road, then it would have made sense for some of them to be on this side as well, but as more and more crabs were identified and popped up on his CCD, they were all on the other side.

What the hell does that mean?

The now unfortunately familiar sound of a Bennie exploding washed over Teo, and his display flashed with a gray avatar: it was Doc Tulagi, the Second Squad corpsman—who, of course, didn't have a Bennie-band.

Teo caught movement on the other side of the road and instinctively fired, sending a dozen of the deadly hypervelocity darts after the crab. He didn't know if he hit anything, but the movement stopped.

"I want all micro-drones launched. We've got to find the general," Teo ordered Okanjo.

He probably should have kept some back. The squad-level drone suite was limited, and the micro-drones didn't have the range nor speed to keep up with the Marines if they were on the move. But Teo had to know if the general was there. For all he knew, resistance could be a ruse while the general was spirited away elsewhere.

More data points started appearing on his CCD, and the ground disposition of troops started to gel. And it looked like they were facing a blocking force, which meant they had to break through if they were going to have any hope of catching up and rescuing the general.

They needed more data. It was Wymer's turn. The CO was in command, but Teo wasn't going to waste time by going through him. He quickly created an overlay.

"Sergeant, I need two of your U-20s on these parallel courses," he passed while uploading the overlay. *"We need to find the package."*

"Aye-aye. Launching in twenty seconds."

The U-20s were larger, faster drones, able to range far and do it quickly.

Another Bennie detonated. Lance Corporal Yarrow's avatar switched to light blue, and then a few moments later to yellow as his nanos shut him down. Teo could pull up the readings to see how bad the Marine was, but that would serve no purpose. Teo couldn't do anything about it. All that mattered was that Yarrow was combat non-effective.

Teo had four Marines hit, two by Bennies, with Doc Tulagi KIA, and still, he didn't know if they were chasing a red herring. But he had no choice.

"Hey, they're running!" Private Hikok shouted from ten meters to Teo's right. "Get the suckers."

"Get the hell down and keep firing," Corporal Bolling, Hikok's fire team leader shouted back.

But it looked like the crabs were withdrawing, giving up their position. That didn't mean they were running, however. The Marines were not putting up that much pressure.

A blast exploded on the other side, a tree shattering and falling to the side. A moment later, another explosion rose from twenty meters farther down.

It was the CO and the *Avenger*, barreling down the road. The CO was still on top, one hand locked on the grip on the commander's cupola, the other waving his 51 like a madman. It was a scene out of the worst war holovid, something only a writer who'd never seen combat could write.

Yet, it was working. The crabs were retreating.

Maybe we can chase them down, Teo thought for a brief second, his hope fanning to life before dual strings of rounds impacted on the road, starting just a few meters from Teo and running right up to the *Avenger*, which sparkled as if adorned with Christmas tree lights for a moment, the CO getting blown off, before the tank slid to the side of the road and stopped.

Teo stood and stared at the tank for a moment, mouth open, when with a whoosh, a crab gunship streaked overhead, pulling up as it passed the tank and sweeping to the right and out of sight.

"Corpsman up!" Teo yelled into the company net as he bolted out of the cover of the trees and started running up the road.

"*You with me?*" he asked the CO on the P2P, but there was no answer.

Teo didn't have much hope. The crab atmospheric craft had twin 20mm canons, and even the best personal armor in the galaxy couldn't stand up to that.

Teo crossed the intervening 150 meters in twenty seconds, vaulting up onto the tank just as the driver's hatch opened, and a stunned PFC Rigby stuck out his head.

"You OK?" Teo shouted as Lance Corporal White Horse jumped up after him.

"Yeah, I think so," Rigby said, not sounding too sure of himself. "But I don't think Corporal Nascient made it."

There was a hole right at the edge of the commander's cupola where the 20mm round had hit and penetrated the *Avenger*'s armor.

He didn't want to look inside, knowing what he'd see.

"White Horse, take care of Rigby," Teo said, looking around for the CO, fearing the worst.

To his surprise, the crumpled body of the CO stirred and struggled to a sitting position. Teo jumped off the tank and ran to him.

"You OK, sir?" he asked.

"I just got shot off a tank, Alcazar. No, I'm not OK. What the hell happened?"

"Crab fast-mover. Looked like a Hornet."

"I feel like I just got hit by a truck," the CO said, raising his arm then wincing and bringing it back down. "Shit, I think it's broken."

With his other arm, he released his helmet and pulled it off. He spit blood out of his mouth, then struggled to his feet.

"I'd better get a corpsman up here to check you out, sir."

"I'm alive. How's the tank?" he asked.

Teo turned back to the *Avenger*. One of the tracks was a twisted mess, and there were two more holes punched into her.

"Don't think it's up. Corporal Nascient's probably KIA too." Teo was in awe that the CO was alive, much less talking. "Where were you hit?"

"What? Oh, I don't know. In my shoulder, maybe."

Teo pulled the CO toward him and ran his hands over his IFU. His outer protective shell was whole, no breaks, but several gouges. He looked into the CO's mouth. He wasn't spitting up blood from his gut. His lip was split.

"I don't think you were hit with a 20mm round. I think you got the shrapnel from the round that got Nascient. And as far as your arm and mouth, probably from hitting the ground."

The CO grunted, then asked, "And the general. Did you see him?"

"Not yet. Let me check."

He just started to ask Okanjo, when another Bennie went off, and just like that, Corporal Utely was KIA.

"*Skipper, we're hitting the fucking Bennies everywhere!*" Lieutenant Okanjo passed on the platoon net, where every swinging dick could hear, his voice tight.

"*Calm down, Trace,*" Teo passed, switching to the P2P. "*Get a hold of yourself.*"

"*What do you want me to do?*"

"*Hold in place. But first, any sign of the general?*"

"*No, sir. Nothing. Not even the crabs. Just the fucking Bennies.*"

Teo turned back to the CO and said, "No sign of the general. And we're getting eaten alive by the Bennies. Third Platoon only has four of the Bennie-bands."

"I can get your Second Platoon here. They've got Bennie-bands . . . oh, fuck me royal. That would make them a target for the Hornet, which sure as shit is just circling on station, waiting to pounce."

He was quiet for a long moment, then plaintively, like a small boy, asked, "We're not going to catch up to them, are we?"

"I don't think so, sir. I wish I had another answer to give you."

The CO stood, looking down the road, then sighed and said, "I'm calling it. Let's get back to the crash site and see what we can do there."

****

"Gently, son," Teo told PFC Jordan as he stepped up to help the struggling Marine.

Teo took one leg of the dead bodyguard, then along with Jordan and Lance Corporal Luna, lifted him to helping hands in the bed of the farm truck someone had confiscated. The fellow Safer's body was limp and heavy as only the dead could be.

Teo had handled too many dead in his life, but he wasn't inured to death. He still felt the losses. He looked into the dull eyes of the Mālietoa, whose name he'd never even caught. They'd come from neighboring barrios, only to meet halfway across the galaxy where the bodyguard had died in a war that was on hold, with peace just around the corner. Maybe they'd met before. He looked of the age. They could have played against each other in school, or maybe met at Landon Mega Mall.

He'd never know now.

One by one, the rest were loaded onto the truck. A major, Captain Kileen, the female Mālietoa. Teo frowned when he first saw her body in the old hunting lodge. A single hole in the middle of her forehead, with the telltale speckling of a close-range shot, was all he needed to see to know she'd probably been executed.

There was no sign of the general, which was about the worst scenario. And if CG had contemplated making sure the G2 wasn't captured, well, that train had passed.

"Sir," Corporal Wainsett said. "The reaction force is being called away. More enemy air in the vicinity."

"Damned cowards," the CO said as he hopped down from the

235

truck where he was helping load the bodies. "At least we tried."

Teo wasn't surprised, however. The best chance to recover the general had been in pursuit of the crabs, but with the arrival of the Hegemony fast-mover, they'd had to break contact. And now, with more incoming aircraft, what was the reaction force going to do? Long before a new plan could be made, the general, if he was still alive, would be whisked out of the area, first for interrogation, then to sit out the war or wait for an exchange of prisoners.

"You, Corporal. Get me Sergeant Gauta and Lieutenant Okanjo." the CO ordered Corporal Nyoki.

The corporal looked up at Teo, who softly nodded. He scurried off to find the two Marines.

"You, Captain, come with me," the CO said before he stalked off.

With a sigh, Teo followed, ready to take whatever came his way. He caught up with the colonel next to the ruined hunting lodge.

"We fucked that up, Captain," the CO finally said, spitting more blood from the gash in his lower lip onto the dirt.

Teo was surprised at the "we."

"We did what we could, sir. The crabs were closer. That's all."

"Doesn't matter. We failed. We let the G2—the fucking G2—fall into enemy hands. How the hell did they let the G2 come out here in the first place?"

Which was a question Teo had been asking himself ever since the helo had been shot down.

"And now they've pulled back the reaction force. They should have kept coming, hit the crabs and take back the general, or if not . . ."

If not, then make sure he's not able to talk.

Cold, but necessary.

"But we're not going to sit here with our thumbs up our butts.

236

We're going to act."

Teo felt a tremor of excitement sweep through him. "We are? How, sir?"

The CO acted like he hadn't heard the question. Instead, he turned to watch the Marines tie down the bodies on the tank for the trip back to camp.

"Did you see the bodyguard? The big woman?" he asked.

"Yes, sir."

"They executed her, pure and simple."

Probably, yes, they did.

"Bastards," the CO said before falling silent.

The man's mind was in overdrive, and Teo knew enough to stand back and let the man think.

Two minutes later, Okanjo and Gauta jogged up, and the CO became animated, waving his good arm as he spoke.

"Those bastards, they've got the general. The G2! They must be cumming in their trou about now. But they're going to pay. For the general, for them," the CO said, tilting his head toward the bodies on the truck. "Task Force is going to circle-jerk each other before they come up with something, but we're going to act, and we're going to act now."

He looked at the three Marines expectantly, as if waiting for them to jump in. Teo liked what he'd heard, but he wasn't sure what the CO had in mind.

"What are we going to do?" Lieutenant Okanjo asked.

"What are we going to do? Come on, Trace, think! Who is standing next to you right now?"

Teo's heart fell just a little as he started to figure out what the CO wanted.

"Uh . . . Sergeant Gauta?"

"Exactly, Sergeant Gauta. The Ghost. The crabs are calling him that, you know. We intercepted that."

"Sir?" Gauta asked.

"Come on. It should be clear. You, Sergeant Gauta, are going to do your thing. You're going to get inside the Heg camp. If the general is there, get him out if you can. If you can't, then you'll need to do what's best for the rest of us . . . uh, you know what I mean there, right?"

Sergeant Gauta gulped, then said, "Yes, sir. If I have to, kill him."

The CO clapped him on his shoulder and said, "I knew I could count on you."

"And if the general's not there?" Teo asked. "They've probably already gotten him on the way to their headquarters."

"If he's not there, then the sergeant gives them a lesson. Kills some of them. Maybe their commander. The crabs have to know there's a price to pay for violating the Freesome Accords. Personnel in a downed aircraft must be rescued, not executed."

Teo wasn't sure the Freesome Accords pertained to military aircraft, and certainly did not if the Marines and bodyguards fought back, but he didn't bring that up. Instead, he looked up at the sky, which had cleared even more since the medal ceremony that seemed like a month ago, but was only less than an hour past.

"I think it's supposed to be clear tonight, and Sergeant Gauta won't be able to use the rain for cover," Teo said.

The CO looked up, then back at the sergeant. "You can still get in, right?"

Sergeant Gauta hesitated, looked down and dug at the dirt with his toe before he looked up and said, "It'll be tougher, sir. Much tougher."

"But you can still do it, right?" the CO asked.

"Sir, this is asking a lot from the sergeant. The crabs will already be on the alert because of last time, and with no rain, the visibility will be much greater," Teo said.

"I'm not asking you, Captain," the CO said with disdain back into his tone.

He turned back to the sergeant and asked, "Well, Sergeant?"

"You don't have to volunteer, Sergeant," Teo said, interrupting.

"I said I'm not asking you," the CO snapped. "So, shut the fuck up.

"I'm asking you to volunteer, Sergeant, but I can order you, too, if I have to," he said, turning back to Gauta.

Teo could see the sergeant weigh his options. It was obvious that he was hesitating. He didn't look much like any crab Teo had seen, and without the cover of rain, he'd stick out like a sore thumb.

"Are you a man or a mouse, Sergeant?" the CO goaded.

Sergeant Gauta's eyes narrowed, and Teo could almost see fire shoot out. "I'm a Marine, sir. I'll do it!"

"I knew you would, Sergeant. I knew you knew your duty," the CO said. "Let's get back to your camp and work out the plan. You are going to be our avenging angel."

Teo was as angry as anyone else, and he wanted to punish the crabs, but his saner self wondered if this was the right move. By sending Gauta in again, he might not be an avenging angel so much as a sacrificial lamb.

239

Chapter 24

Paladins

Dust blew past Richter as he and three of his men ran the stretcher with their Alliance prisoner up to the ramp of a cargo aircraft where Cataphracts and Hegemony soldiers in black uniforms waited.

The VTOL bird was part of the "ash-and-trash express" that occasionally delivered supplies and personnel, but this time, the cargo bay was empty with the exception of several soldiers in matte-black jacks and several more in simple dark fatigues who wore pistols and daggers on their belts. Seeing the Crows, Hegemony intelligence operatives, was bad luck for his Syddans.

The soldiers took the handles on the stretcher and carried the prisoner into the cargo bay.

"Nice capture," said a man with a sunken shoulder and a cane as he hobbled over to the edge of the ramp. He brought the handle of his cane up in a mock salute. "That one's been on my radar for a while."

"Don't take all the credit, Utiesh. You still owe me for Badera." Richter thrust a bag with the POW's personal effects into Utiesh's chest and stomped back down the ramp.

The VTOL's engines revved up, creating a hurricane around Richter as it lifted off and vanished into the stormy sky while the rain returned to a steady drizzle.

"Bastards could've let us move off the landing pad before they blasted us." First Sergeant Molenaar thrust up a salute of two fingers in a V.

"You ever met a fly-boy that wasn't an asshole?" Richter shook rain off his poncho as they went back to the lodge.

"Insufferable pricks, every last one of them. Still, you'd think they'd show a bit of respect for the high-value prisoner we gave 'em."

"This isn't their usual flight times. We must've interrupted some quality drinking time. Or sleep."

"Speaking of," Molenaar sniffed. "Ration? This piss should keep even that ghost of theirs down."

"Ration," Richter said, pausing as a rowdy chorus rose from the main building. "Single for those off duty. Double for those on watch once they're relieved. We're pinning Szabo already?"

"Kid was rattled when you brought him back." Molenaar reached into a pocket and placed a small silver device in Richter's hand. "Don't want to let him stew on it too long. Got to scab over the wound or it'll fester."

"This Syddan custom . . . it's a good one, and it's spreading through the rest of the Army, you know about that?" Richter glanced through a window and shook his head. "Not this part of the ceremony, I mean."

"Rest of the Hegemony's fighting men will be fighting *men* when they stop grooming themselves as women." He tugged on his soaking-wet beard. "But the blood pinning goes back to Earth. Long before the Transits."

"Get the ration. I need to do my part before this gets out of hand." Richter shook his head.

"What?" Molenaar leaned over to the window. "Nothing's on fire. Yet. As you will, Major. I'll go get the ration."

"*Skol!*" thundered through the doors.

"Better hurry."

Richter pulled off his poncho and shook it to one side, then shouldered through the door to the main room of the lodge.

The entire troop was there—minus the few in the operations center or in the guard towers—all shirtless and beating fists against their bare chests in a two count. Many had blue tattoo swirls on their backs. Most had short lines of text on their right shoulders, names on their left.

"Skol!"

Szabo stood beneath Mickey, the claws of the stuffed *chayseux* looming over him, a ridiculous headdress made from a silver-wolf pelt covering the top half of his face like it was his jack helmet. His skin was the fish-belly pale of an ice-worlder and covered in a sheen of sweat as Ceban tapped a needle-tipped rod against the skin of his right shoulder.

"Skol!"

Ceban leaned back to examine his work, then took a swig from a liquor bottle and spat it all over Szabo's new tattoo.

The troop roared a cheer as Richter jumped onto the platform. Szabo reached for the headdress, but the major grabbed him by the wrist and pushed his hand back down.

"Not yet. Just stay there."

"Skol!"

"Men of Syddan," Richter said, raising a hand, and the room went silent. "A commander can have many great moments. Victory. Promotions. But this I enjoy more than any other. To blood pin a warrior is an honor like no other. Today, one of our own went out to the field of battle, killed our enemy, and returned home in glory."

"Not too hard. You might break him." Ceban pulled the needle out of his stick and tapped in a new one as the room laughed.

"Private First Class Croll Szabo," Richter said, holding up a crossed-swords pin and removing its brass fasteners, "for shedding the blood of the wicked, for defending your brother troopers and the Hegemony, I hereby award you the Combat Mark."

Richter placed the crossed-sword pin side out on his hand and turned away from Szabo with an exaggerated motion. The troopers started cheering.

The major swung his open hand around and slapped the prongs into Szabo's chest. The radioman took a half step back and the headdress fell off his face. Ceban caught it before it could hit the ground.

"Skol!"

Twin lines of blood ran down from where Szabo's skin had been pierced.

Szabo looked down at the silver swords on his chest, then back at Richter in surprise.

"Now who wants a ration?" Richter shouted and the room shook with roars of approval.

As if on cue, Molenaar came through the back door with four bottles of liquor in his hands.

"I have no idea what's going on," Szabo said.

"Shala!" Ceban shouted, holding up his tattoo pin. "Get up here, you pungent queef. You got another mark."

Richter swiped the radioman's uniform top from the floor, took Szabo by the elbow, and led him out of the main room and into his office. He motioned Szabo to a seat and went behind his desk. The hole in the wall had been patched, and there was a bare spot where the safe used to be.

Szabo looked down at his fresh tattoo, then the pin in his chest.

"You can take that out," Richter said, opening a drawer and tossing him a bundle of wrapped paper towels. "Paperwork will catch up to your dossier, but the Combat Mark is yours. Most jack troopers fix it behind their breastplate for luck."

Szabo winced slightly and pulled the pin out, then dabbed at his chest with the paper towels.

"Didn't hurt so much," Szabo said, setting the pin on a bloody napkin and glancing at the fresh tattoo on his shoulder before he put his top back on. "Just Ayutthaya and the date?"

"Not that you're going to forget your first gunfight, or what you did." Richter rolled up a sleeve to show dates that ran down almost to his elbow. "Ceban will have to get me again later . . . just need to see him before his ration kicks in."

"That's what they were so excited about." Szabo glanced back at the door. "They were sure we'd get a ration. I thought it meant better food, sir."

"One shot per man." Richter opened a drawer and pulled out a bottle of amber liquor labeled with non-Hegemony script and two small cups made of packed wood pulp. "I know why the ghost didn't take my *sang som*. This stuff is as local as it is cheap. Probably felt sorry for me when he went through my desk."

He poured a generous finger in each cup and lifted his. "None above all and greater together." He waited until Szabo had his cup, then tossed his back. It burned all the way down and lit a fire in his belly.

Szabo hacked several times before swallowing his.

"You got prison-tier ink done, blood pinned, and a drink is where you crack?" Richter smiled.

"It was—no offense, sir—God awful. What is it?"

"*Sang som*. Some manner of rum, or so I'm told. Mama-san swears by this stuff." Richter leaned back in his chair and studied Szabo. The trooper's face was long with exhaustion, his eyes nearly vacant, the pupils too dilated for the light in the office.

"I remember my first kill." Richter touched the fabric version of the Combat Mark sewn into his uniform. His bore three stars spaced between the crossed blades and hilts. "Wasn't here. Badera. Back when the war against the Alliance was going to be just a 'police action.' I was a second lieutenant with the Gudrun Rifles, good bunch of lads. We lost them all a few years ago when the Alliance destroyed their troop transport . . .

"Where was I? Badera. I was the scout platoon leader, no jacks. Squadron commander gave me the mission to neutralize an Alliance guard post by a set time, confuse the enemy as to which way we were advancing on the missile station they were guarding. We dropped out of a parabola chute into a valley on the other side of a ridgeline to the target. Badera was a dust bowl of a world. Like Mars before it was fully terraformed. I, in my infinite wisdom as a second lieutenant, chose the drop point, thinking the Alliance would be too complacent to anticipate an attack from that direction.

"Landed easy enough and that's when I realized I screwed up. The terrain maps we'd used for planning were out-of-date; the Alliance had blown out several of the mountains to strip-mine the ore deposits since our last orbital survey. We came down in the right spot, but we lost sat nav not long after and—"

"You could've still used inertial distance vectoring to . . . sorry, sir."

Richter continued.

"And I couldn't orient off the terrain, as it was all wrong. Alliance scrambled the comms with a nuke pulse. We weren't getting anything from orbit and we were out of radio range. I was the proverbial lost lieutenant within minutes of my first combat mission. Not how I wanted to start my service to the Hegemony, but there I was.

"We shot an azimuth and set out for the target. That's when we hit Switchblades. Cluster shot up and activated a couple dozen yards overhead.

Buzzers had us in the open with nothing but the occasional boulder for cover. Lost Sergeant First Class Gadalis and Specialist Yan before we could do anything. Ran Gadalis through the chest. Yan lost a leg and bled out before the medic could get to him. I still hear the buzz sometimes before I fall asleep."

Richter touched the neck of the liquor bottle, then took his hand away.

"We popped three EMP bulbs before the Switchblades could get anyone else. Couldn't take our dead with us, so I had to grab their dog tags and record the grid where we hid the body bags. Then I carried my element commander pulser in my hands and ordered my platoon to start running. Stupid. So stupid. The pulser would've fried all our systems, and the EMP wave could be triangulated easily for an air strike or rockets. There's a reason why troopers call pulsers suicide buttons. But I was angry at the Alliance for killing my troopers and at my own failure to find a better route through that mess.

"We got to a ridgeline overlooking the guard post without tripping any more Switchblades. I was exhausted from too much adrenaline and too much running on a planet a hell of a lot hotter than Ayutthayan. There was a time hack, you understand? Squadron commander wanted the attack to happen at 0432 Zulu hours—so arbitrary, but I still remember it to this day. I crept up to a boulder and got a decent survey of the Alliance position with all of seven minutes to spare.

"That's when I saw him. Right there through my carbine's scope. This . . . kid. Might've been a local conscript the Alliance dragged into their fight. He couldn't have been older than seventeen, the barest hint of a moustache. Deep tan. A necklace with small carved totems that he kept playing with. Just another soldier on his guard post. Not sure what the hell was going on, or if the Hegemony was ever going to finally launch their attack.

"I ordered my platoon to come online and call out their targets. Four-hundred-yard shot. Easy for scout platoon-qualified troopers. I aimed at the kid's chest and . . ." He mimed holding a rifle and pulling a trigger. "He went down behind a concrete barrier. Wasn't exactly sure I hit him.

"I led the charge with the assault element, and we'd almost made it to their walls when the rest of the guard post realized they were under attack and woke up to the fight. They opened up with a machine gun with me as their first target. Bullet hit in front of my left boot, next one clipped me." He rubbed where his neck met his back. "Didn't even feel it until later.

"They kept shooting and killed Otash and Mueller. Saw their icons wink out right on my HUD. Then the overwatch element hit the post with our one and only anti-armor rocket and collapsed the main building. I vaulted over the cerrocrete wall they had for a perimeter and my troopers laid into the Alliance. Quick, controlled bursts. They called out targets and took them down too fast for me to do anything but try and keep up. Gadalis trained them well. Never got the chance to thank him properly . . ."

Richter looked away for a moment.

"I did my sweep around the burning building and that's when I found him. The kid I shot. He was there on the ground, neat hole, center mass of his chest, a decent amount of blood in that gray dirt. He was dead, just looking at the spot where I shot him with this sort of dull surprise on his face, like he couldn't believe he was lying there with a round through his spine and his lungs collapsing.

"You train. You train for years. Call the patties every last name you can think up. You know the long litany of their crimes against the Hegemony that's been on the broadcasts ever since they opened fire on one of our ships. You train to shoot them. Knife them. Call in air strikes and artillery and tanks to crush them into paste. But when you're standing there over one you killed . . ."

Szabo burst into tears.

"You realize that you can train to kill, but not to be a killer." Richter went to Szabo and put a hand on his shoulder. "Tamp it down, trooper. You'll need to get good at that for a while."

Szabo stifled a sob and ran an arm over his eyes as he nodded quickly.

Richter went back to his seat.

"We rigged the guard post with Bennies soon as we were sure every Alliance there was dead, then ex-filled out for pickup. That was the last time anything went right on Badera. Over the next couple days, I struggled. I thought I should feel like some sort of conquering hero of legend for killing the enemy. Instead, everything came into question—and I grew up aboard the *Highest*, where the Hegemony is at its best.

"Let me save you all the soul-searching I had to do because I was too scared to talk to another soldier that had taken a life . . . that kid would've killed me. He would've taken out my entire platoon if given the chance. It's war, Szabo. We must kill. If we hesitate . . . the enemy will not be so kind and then your hesitation will cost you or—even worse—your fellow troopers. What went through your mind when you saw that pattie break through the door?"

"That . . . it was just instinct. I saw him and . . . he was dead. Barely registered that I fired."

"Thank your training. You did exactly what you were supposed to and it got you back to the post for Mama-san's ramen and jasmine tea. You chose to kill him so that *I* could live. Next time you're alone in the dark and that moment replays in your mind, know that if you'd done anything different, it would've been me lying there dead and you would have followed with the next pull of his trigger. It's not right. It's not fair. It's war, Szabo. Killing is our burden, but if we don't carry that burden, the consequences are worse. Worse for your fellow troopers. Worse for their families. Worse for the Hegemony."

"I would've appreciated a talk like this *before* the shooting, sir." Szabo gave him a half smile.

"You wouldn't have understood. Like someone explaining sex to a virgin."

Szabo's mouth tightened into a thin line.

"Ugh, you're from a planet of prudes, aren't you? No matter. Go. Shit, shower, shave. Show Mama-san your chest and she'll give you one of those coffee candies she doesn't sell to anyone. You have more trouble with this, come back and talk to me."

"Yes, sir. Thank you." Szabo stood and saluted.

Richter returned the salute and opened a drawer as the radioman left. From the drawer he took out a beaded necklace with small, broken charms, set it down gently on his desk, and stared at it for a long while.

Chapter 25

Marines

Teo watched silently as Sergeant Gauta hooked on a third belt of SR-94s to his combat harness. They were larger and more powerful than the 88s he took on the last mission, and even with his wide frame, they were hard to miss. This mission wouldn't be another wandering around in a towel around his waist, hoping to blend in with the crabs.

"Sergeant, you don't have to . . ." Teo started before trailing off.

"Don't have to follow orders, sir?" Gauta said. "What kind of Marine Corps is that?"

"But this is a . . ." He paused, not wanting to say "suicide mission."

"I know, Skipper," the sergeant said in a subdued voice before laughing, and with a false sense of joviality, held up one foot. "But I'm still going in barefoot!"

That's not going to be enough.

With his bulk and lack of a beard, Sergeant Gauta was going to stick out like a sore thumb, and he wouldn't have the cover of rain this time. After months of constant rain, Teo wished that it would come back again, at least for the night.

"Look," Teo started before turning around to make sure the CO hadn't returned from where he'd finally relented and was having Doc Sanaa treat his injuries. "Just get in and get out. Don't screw with finding their commander, as much as I'd love to cashier the bastard. Just set those charges and boogie."

Sergeant Gauta gave Teo a sideways glance as he clipped the last bandolier to his harness. "And our CO? What about him? You heard what he wants."

"Fuck him," Teo hissed. "You set the SR-94s, and you've accomplished your mission. And if he doesn't agree with that, it'll be on my head."

Teo had never spoken like that about a senior officer in his Marine Corps career, but there was a first time for everything. And the CO's orders were bullshit. Yes, they had to have a response to the crabs, but let them come up with one that was tactically and strategically sound, not one that sent a good Marine into an almost sure death.

Gauta had accomplished his first mission, but the crabs, assholes that they were, were not stupid. They'd have closed their gaps.

Sergeant Gauta shrugged his shoulders to seat his IFU's Protective Outer Layer, laden with his war kit. "You want to give me a check, Skipper?"

"Sure." Teo stepped closer and started tugging on Gauta's gear. The rock of a man didn't budge.

"Look, Skipper," he whispered so that the other three Marines preparing to go out couldn't hear. "I appreciate what you're trying to say. But if you got the order, what would you do?"

Teo hesitated. He wanted to tell the sergeant that he'd refuse, but he couldn't lie to him, not now.

"I'd take the order and do my best," he said miserably.

"Of course, you would, sir. Of course, any of us would. We're Alliance Marines."

Teo nodded. He shouldn't have expected anything else.

"And who knows? I'm a tough motherfucker, and I may just take down the entire crab camp, bagging their commander to boot."

Teo laughed despite the situation. "You know, if anyone could, you sure the hell would!"

Yelsik, Juarez, and Uribe looked up at Teo's laugh from where they were strapping up.

"Just like last time, Marines. Just like last time. An easy patrol out, Sergeant Gauta does his thing, and an easy patrol back. No big thing, right?"

If the ooh-rahs sounded a little bit forced, Teo wasn't going to question them.

Chapter 26

Paladins

Richter could feel the coming rain. He was outside the gym, his muscles singing with blood from the exertion and with a line of sweat down the back of his shirt. Lightning lit up an approaching storm front, the flashes like an artillery barrage just over the horizon. He looked up at a starry sky, catching a few short lines of falling orbital debris as they burned away.

A cold breeze washed over him, its scent laden with moisture. Richter felt like Ayutthaya was about to punish him with rain for appreciating the brief glimpse of the heavens.

The door opened behind him, and Vukovic leaned out, a line of white light casting across the ground as rock music floated out. Inside the meeting-center-turned-gym, troopers ran circuits between lumpy kettlebells made from cerrocrete with repurposed metal rods bent into handles to a pull-up bar bolted against once-intricate woodwork. Coffee cans filled with more cerrocrete and a bar sunk into the center served as dumbbells. Troopers "sat" with their backs against the walls, their legs at right angles and sandbags on their laps.

"Squat rack's free if you want to do more bicep curls," the trooper said.

"Say again," Richter said, half turning around.

"Oh shit, sorry, sir. Thought you were Bekim. He only works the beach muscles and—" he paused to hold out a water bottle, giving it a shake, "—pre-workout? I got the good stuff in a care package. Not that

253

Yuttie stuff that's got to be half amphetamines and half—"

"Noise and light discipline," Richter said and Vukovic shut the door.

Richter shook his head and passed a hand over his thigh, touching the holstered pistol.

He stepped away from the gym and went to the perimeter fence. The new razor-wire stacks glistened in the moonlight, the difference between them and the older—and more rusted—stacks was stark. The contrast bothered him, as adding the additional layer of security had come only *after* a Marine snuck into his base, killed a man, and got away with a distinct tactical advantage for the enemy.

Should've improved our physical security before *that happened,* he thought.

He glanced up at a guard tower, and the two troopers inside flashed a red light twice to acknowledge him. Even in the low light, his men could recognize him by his gait and silhouette.

The tink-tink-tink of bells farther down the perimeter caught his attention. He increased his pace and drew a small penlight out of a pocket. Richter pushed the tip against a cupped palm and double-checked the bulb was blue with a quick snap of the button.

He turned it on and swept the weak light over the stacks of razor wire. The distinct lack of his jack, or even a flak vest, left him feeling vulnerable. If one of the Bennies seeded into this part of the perimeter went off for whatever reason, he was at considerable risk.

Maybe a new ring around the base? Move the Bennies out farther?

He worked out the math for the logistics request to squadron and chided himself. Asking for more defensive material would make him look afraid . . . but his troopers deserved better than what they had now. So what if some rear echelon motherfucker joked about it?

The scent of pungent tea wafted over him just before Lieutenant

Kontos in flanker fatigues and armor walked up, a burning ember protruding from his lips. He had his loaded carbine slung over one shoulder.

"Thought I had the walk tonight, sir," he said.

"Mind if I join you?" Richter asked.

"As you like." Kontos tapped a thumbnail against the visor over the upper half of his face and took a drag from the cigarette in his mouth. "I've got thermals on."

The two officers strolled along the perimeter.

"That cancer stick's not throwing them off? And since when did you decide to go native and switch to Kretek?" Richter asked.

"Washes out after a second, sir. And this is a hemp smoke from back home. From the family farm no less. I can spare one; helps with the back pain from the jacks." Kontos flicked ash off the cigarette to one side.

"Hemp? I thought that was a regulated substance?"

"It's not marijuana, sir. Hemp looks like its illicit cousin, smells like it too, but it's like a glass of water next to a glass of vodka. Both will take care of a parched throat, but only one will fuck you up in the process. But this," Kontos held out the hand with the smoke clenched between his fingertips, "smells like home."

"Your family manufactures those?"

"Nah, just grow it. From there it's made into hemp milk, butter, clothes. Our house is even made with hemp-crete. Great stuff, keeps the weevils out and . . . why'd you stop, sir?"

Richter went to one knee and pushed his penlight through strands of razor wire. The mud beneath was smooth, like something had slid over it. He angled the light up to follow the wire and tapped it with a finger. The wire split; it had been cut and reset.

"Fuck." Kontos flicked the cigarette away and touched the side of his helmet.

A sudden smell of thick ozone hit his nose, and a band of electricity rose up from the generator stacks like a Jacob's ladder. The generators exploded into a cloud of fire that roared into the sky.

The blast wave slapped Richter off his feet and into the wall of a storage shed. The thin metal side buckled, absorbing most of the impact.

Richter lay facedown, his head swimming, and a high-pitched whine was all he heard. He coughed out smoke and dust and pushed against the ground to bring himself up to his knees. Blood dripped down his face, the spatter of each impact captivating him for a moment as the concussion left him dazed and confused.

He raised his eyes and saw Kontos' boots, then looked up the lieutenant's body to where it ended in a bloody ruin just above the shoulders.

Richter crawled to the carbine still attached to a D-ring on the dead lieutenant's chest, calling out to his first sergeants and his other men, but he barely heard his own voice. It was muted, like it was coming from inside a grave.

Yanking the carbine off Kontos, he chambered a round.

The main lodge building had partially collapsed. Black smoke and flames rose through gaps in the roof, and a wall fell in on itself, sending up a cloud of soot and embers.

"You still here?" Richter roared as he turned around and almost fell, his battered eardrums struggling to find any sense of balance. Out of the corner of one eye, he saw a section of the perimeter wire waver back and forth.

He stumbled forward like a drunk, the ground swimming beneath him as he got to a bungalow and leaned a shoulder against it for support. Bringing the carbine up to his shoulder, he tried to aim down the holo sights, but the red rings danced around.

There, right at the parapet where razor wire met the top of the trench, a man in Alliance IFUs and wearing a band on his wrist crept out beneath the wire.

Richter fired. The burst sprang off the razor wire, and the ghost slithered forward like a cockroach caught when the lights turned on. The major fired again, missing even worse as his concussed head and body failed to maintain any sense of balance.

The ghost slipped out of the perimeter, but a spur on the wire caught his pants leg near the ankle.

Richter squinted hard . . . and saw a Benedict mine hanging in the wire a few yards from the ghost. He switched the fire selector switch to AUTO and pulled the trigger. The magazine emptied within seconds, tracers and bullets ripping through the wire fence until one round hit home.

The mine exploded, sending out a hail of shrapnel and another blast wave that knocked Richter onto his backside. He swore and crawled forward, abandoning the empty weapon and drawing his pistol from a thigh holster.

He got to the mangled wire—no ghost.

"Son of a bitch." Richter moved through the twisted remnants of wire where the mine had gone off and crawled out the other side. He fired twice at the jungle, then put a hand to the side of his head as a splitting headache set in.

He was about to return to his burning base when he saw a slick of red on a frond. Richter charged into the jungle and saw a streak of blood on a tree trunk, then more droplets forming a trail into the undergrowth.

The ghost lay on one side, one hand over a slit stomach trying to hold in spilt intestines. The ghost was panting, his lips dry and eyes half-shut.

Richter kicked the Marine's pistol away, then nudged him onto his back with his boot.

"Wat . . . water," Gauta said, staring up into space.

"I have nothing for you." Richter fell to one knee, a vise of pain closing around his head. "It was you . . . you killed Consanio."

Gauta's lips smacked as he nodded.

"Kiss my ass, crab. Captain Alcazar . . . he's got your name. Got your number. He'll get you." He groaned and lifted up his blood-soaked hands to see them.

"I hope he does." Richter reached over and grasped the exotic-looking knife on Gauta's belt. "I really do." He ripped the dagger away.

"Give me that back!" Gauta gasped, reaching weakly for it.

Troopers crashed through the jungle and formed a half circle behind him.

"Finish that asshole," one said, raising his carbine.

"No." Richter waved at him, then leaned over to shake Gauta's shoulder. "Hey, ghost, you want the bullet or you want the cold?"

Gauta's head shook slightly as a blood bubble formed over his mouth. It popped and the Marine's eyes softened.

"Not how I wanted it . . . sorry, Skipper." A last breath rattled out of him.

"Sir, you OK?" a trooper asked. Richter's world was spinning so badly that he couldn't tell who was speaking to him.

"Need a minute." He rolled back and one of his men caught him before his head and shoulders could hit the ground.

The heavens opened, and the rain began anew.

Chapter 27

Marines

The rain poured down on the four Marines crouched outside the crab wire.

"You think he made it, Skipper?" Corporal Yelsik asked.

Teo only stared in the direction of the crab camp, hoping to see a dark shape emerge from the trees, just like he'd been doing for the last hour.

Sergeant Gauta had made it in. Teo had watched his progress on his CCD. He'd heard the explosions, the shouting, the weapons firing. A drone shot Sergeant Wymer sent him showed much more devastation inside the crab camp than he'd expected.

More pertinent, he saw Gauta's avatar go gray just as the rain started to fall. He hadn't told the other three Marines, hoping against hope that there was a glitch in the system, a false reading. It had happened before.

But not this time, he had to admit. If Gauta was somehow alive, he'd have made it out by now.

"No, Snake, I don't think so. I don't think he made it."

"Hell," Yelsik said before looking up toward the camp and saying, "*Vigil tee*, Devil Dog."

Teo keyed the CO on the P2P. "No sign of Sergeant Gauta."

"Well, we thought as much," the CO said. "Too bad. He was a good Marine. But you're sure that he leveled the Heg camp before he died?"

259

No, I'm not sure, and I'm not going to waltz in and make a survey.

"There were some big explosions. I'd have to let the Intel guys listen to the recording to know how many, but I'm pretty sure the damage has to be extensive."

And you can just ask Force to run a surveillance pass.

"Then it was a win, Captain. A win," the CO passed, sounding excited. "I'm going to let the colonel know we kicked their asses."

We? Gauta did that, and it cost him his life. You had nothing to do with it except send him to his death. There were other ways to do this.

"Dawn's coming, and I'm bringing the patrol back," Teo passed, his heart heavy.

"Very well. I'll see you when you get back. And I've got a little . . . uh, libation, that we can use to toast the victory."

I'd rather choke, you bastard.

He cut the connection, knowing if he didn't, he'd say something stupid, and he was not going to do that to Gauta. He wasn't going to sully the sergeant's actions.

"Let's move out. Uribe, you're on point."

Teo turned one last time where the dull orange of flames still lit up the rainy night sky.

"*Vigilamus pro te*, Devil Dog. *Vigilamus pro te.*"

Chapter 28

Paladins

Rain spattered against Richter's face, each cold impact stinging like a pinprick against his skin.

Iliev drew a hypo back from the major's neck and let go of the side of the jack as he stepped down.

"Sir, you're maxed out for stims and ependymal boosters," the medic said. "If I give you any more, it'll go toxic. Or your heart will pop."

"Still have work to do." Richter shook his head, the haptic pads on the back of his head and on his cheekbones whirring as thunder rolled overhead. Lightning forked across the sky and Richter shifted his weight from side to side, thankful for the rubber padding in the jack's foot soles.

He raised his gun arm and clacked the mechanical fist over his hand.

The base was in shambles, the main building collapsed into smoldering rubble, and most of the smaller buildings crumbling. The blast had weakened the mortar, and the deluge hastened the disintegration of the entire hunting lodge.

Light poles cast weak spotlights over the destruction as sheets of rain flapped through and gusts of wind shook the poles.

Troopers moved around, soaked to the bone as they loaded gear onto a half-dozen trucks idling on the landing pad.

Richter stomped away, each footfall splashing through puddles. He'd abandoned his helmet after the first hour of rescue work, the IR links nearly useless in the storm. He could see, hear, and speak better bareheaded anyway.

"Molenaar!" Richter went to a cluster of troopers near a fallen section of wall, where the remnants of the stuffed *chayseux* poked out through shattered ceiling tiles.

"Think we found him!" The first sergeant waved to Richter and jammed a length of rebar beneath a hunk of concrete. The troopers around him were tired and had shed their uniform tops, as there was no escaping the rain and soaked clothing just slowed them down.

"Alive?" Richter stepped up to the concrete hunk and looked it over.

"Can't tell." Molenaar held up a helmet. "Scan showed a void underneath, a heat source. Think this was the kitchen area. Maybe he got in a freezer or something before it all came down."

"Stand aside." Richter grabbed the edge of the slab with his jack's hand and pulled, using the hydraulics to brace against the ground, and drew the concrete back. A hunk broke away in his grasp and the slab settled back in place.

"Help!" came from beneath. "Help me!"

"He's there." Molenaar dove to the edge and shouted, "Hold on, Nemec! We'll get you out!"

"Water! I'm going to fucking drown!"

Richter looked down. He'd shifted the concrete just enough to let in a standing puddle forming around them.

"We need—" He looked back at the trucks where more troopers in jacks were loading up equipment. "Shit, we don't have time. Get them anyway!" He slapped a man on the shoulder and sidestepped over to Molenaar. He heard splashing in a deep recess just beneath the slab.

"Stuck! I'm stuck in here!" Nemec shouted up. "For fuck's sake, hurry!"

"All of you, on me." Richter grabbed the edge with his gun hand and spread his feet wide. He lifted up and the other troopers added their muscle power. The slab came up, then broke in half. Hunks fell down the hole and Nemec shouted in pain. Water sloshed into the hole and panicked cries came up.

"Hold on." Richter shoved a hunk aside, then flopped to his belly and thrust an arm into the hole. The cries stopped as more water poured in.

Richter popped to his feet and slapped the emergency release on his jack.

"I touched him. Pull me out when I give the signal." He jumped out of the frame, took a deep breath, and slithered into the hole as water came up and over his back.

"Grab him, grab him!" Molenaar got the major by one ankle and tugged backwards as the leg kicked at him. "Ugh . . . deeper," he said to the other troopers and they pushed Richter's body down.

They stopped as the water reached his knees and Richter went rigid.

"Top, I don't know about this," the trooper said.

"The boss knows what he's doing. Probably," Molenaar said just as Richter began kicking wildly.

"Up! Up!" Molenaar tried to lift Richter out, but the weight was too much. He tried again, no luck. More troopers grabbed hold, but they couldn't budge Richter.

"Move!" Briem shouted as he ran over and shoved the first sergeant away with his jack arm. He vised his gun arm down on Richter's ankle and hauled him up. Richter's muddy form came out, Nemec clenched in his arms.

Briem dropped them to the ground and Richter coughed.

Nemec lay still for a moment, then gagged. He rolled over and vomited out water.

"Top," Richter said, wiping a rather thick, dark sludge off his face, "we're a hundred percent accounted for?"

"Yes, sir, every trooper." Molenaar slapped Nemec on the back and looked the man over for injuries. "Nemec, where are your pants?"

Nemec hacked and slapped at his bare bottom.

"He was on the shitter when it went down." Richter accepted Briem's help back up to his feet. "Floor collapsed into the septic treatment hold."

"Explains the smell," Briem said. "Least you're getting a shower."

"Get the medic," Molenaar said, "and some pants for Nemec. He's indecent." A trooper took off back to the trucks.

Richter closed his eyes as sludge dribbled off his body. He resigned himself to leaving his bodyglove behind.

"We've got everything loaded up that we can," Briem said. "Szabo's got your gear in truck two, sir."

"Leave nothing behind for the enemy." Richter flapped his arms out to the side. "How many Bennies we have left?"

"Nineteen."

"Set them all." Richter made his way over to the trucks, his boots squishing with every step.

He climbed into the back of one truck, where wounded men were on stretchers or sitting against the sides. The place smelled of blood and antiseptic.

"We got everyone, sir?" a man asked, his head and one eye covered with bandages.

"Everyone. We'll leave soon. Nurses and hot chow for everyone."

"What about the ghost?" another asked.

"Dead. I left him in the jungle for the pigs." Richter touched a pocket where he had the pattie's knife tucked away.

"Don't make us laugh, sir, hurts," the one-eyed trooper said.

"Stay tough, almost there." He squeezed his hand and jumped out. Szabo was there, radio on his back and mic in hand.

"Sir! Sorry, but squadron broke through on the radio band and I couldn't—"

Richter swiped the handset away and put it to his ear. "Paladin Actual, go."

"Paladin, this is Wolfpack Actual," Colonel Toman said. "My logistics platoon leader says your recovery efforts are complete?"

"Roger. A number of casualties, but all are stable enough for a ground evacuation. All jacks and weapons accounted for. Total loss on the generator and battery rack." Richter felt something slough down his leg and he swallowed hard.

"Heard. Need you to get on a bird I've got en route to your base. Your presence is required at the Union Red Cross center in Krabi. Patties agreed to a cease-fire for all inbound transport."

"What? Wolfpack, my troop's about to return to the spaceport and they'll need quarters, a resupply of equipment. That's—"

"Well aware, Paladin. The S4's under my direct and specific orders to take good care of your men when they arrive. Your platoon leaders are capable officers, correct?"

"The two that I have left, yes." Richter felt his headache coming back.

"Bird has space for two. No weight allowance for jacks. Pickup is in twenty minutes. Wolfpack out." The earpiece clicked and Richter handed it back to Szabo.

"Where is my gear?"

"I got it loaded into truck two. Don't think I left anything in your office."

"Get me a set of fatigues, boots, and a carbine. And ping Briem to come talk to me ASAP." Richter sat down on the step of a truck cabin.

"Sir," Szabo said, then turned and ran. Richter raised his head slightly, half expecting the need to repeat the order or be more specific.

He looked out at what remained of the base. After the blast, his injuries, and the mad rush to rescue as many troopers as he could, his mind and body were flayed down to nubs.

"*Khun*-Major." Qwan peeked around the front of the truck. "Ah, there you are." She came around with a plastic sheet drawn over her head, a steaming cup in her hand. "This one's on me."

The smell of a sweet-and-sour soup hit him. He took a sip and felt human again.

"Thank you, Mama-san." Richter drank again. "Mang OK?"

"He good. He good. Just a little scared. Helped get everything packed. He's resting now." She smiled at him.

"You? This is great, by the way."

"Kitchen O-K." She winced and rubbed an ear. "Everything in my storeroom's ruined by smoke, but I can get more food. My stove and pots survived. I can stay with Paladin, yes?" A plastic bag tied to the waist string of her apron bounced against her thigh with a *tink*.

Richter frowned at the lumpy bag and bits of alabaster spikes poking out of small tears.

"What's that?" he took another sip.

She touched the bag as the plastic stretched. She gasped as fragments of a shattered statue spilled out into the mud.

"Oh no, no, no," she fell to her knees and began frantically picking pieces up and placing them gently into the fold of her apron.

Richter set his soup aside and bent over to help. He picked up most of a painted porcelain head and rubbed a thumb across the face to clean it off.

"Who is this? From the shrine in your kitchen, right?"

"*Guan Im,*" Mindy snatched the head away. "Sorry. She's the Goddess of Mercy. Protection. On Ayutthaya . . . not every family had a shrine before the war. But now we all do. We all need her to watch over us. Break the statue and Guan Im will turn her face from you. No one to save you from hell."

Richter placed shards in her upturned apron. He looked over one shoulder at the devastated base.

"Can't doubt that," he said.

"I have to give the pieces to a monk. Pay for a proper burial and buy a new one before I can reopen the kitchen," she said.

"I can contribute?"

"No," she shook her head quickly. "I'll take care of it at the big base. I can stay your mama-san?"

"Yes. Show your band to anyone who gives you trouble. I'll deal with them." Richter went back to his seat and finished the soup, then touched the zipper on his neckline. "Excuse me."

Ayutthayan culture frowned on men going bare-chested, especially around the opposite sex.

She held one hand to her chest in a half gesture of respect and walked away, the bulge in her apron clutched tight to her midsection.

Richter stripped off his top and tossed it away. Szabo arrived a moment later with a green duffel in hand and a carbine slung over his shoulder.

"Sorry, sir, thought I'd just grab everything and bring it over instead of—"

"Good work." Richter pulled clothes out of the bag as they grew wetter and wetter beneath the rain. His hand brushed past something hard and he frowned. The sheathed knife he took off the ghost came out and he turned it over, examining the intricate leatherwork for the first time.

"What's next, sir?"

"You and I are flying out," he said, stuffing the knife into a thigh pocket. "We'll catch up with the rest of the troop back at the spaceport."

"Say again?"

"Just when we thought this day couldn't get any worse, politics rears its ugly head. Just need you to smile and nod, Szabo. Don't shoot the non-government organization reps."

"NGOs? The Red Cross?"

"They're not as bad as the Alliance, but not by much." Richter held his arms out to his sides and tilted his chin up as he looked over the remnants of his base. Each raindrop hit him with the sting of failure.

Chapter 29

Marines

"Hell, bad luck to them," Lieutenant Wooster said as he read the readout Teo had handed to him.

"Yeah. Bennies, then Switchblades. Chewed them up, and did you see that last? Killed a Union citizen."

"Was it our fault?"

Teo shrugged. "Who's to say? But the convoy was out of the Safe Zone."

The XO re-read the message. "Lucky for us the crabs hit them, too, especially with the talks going on. They can't spin this against us.

"So, is the CO going?"

"Nope. To quote, 'I'm not going to a meeting with those pansy-ass Union do-gooders. You're going, Captain,'" Teo said in a reasonable imitation of Lieutenant Colonel Khan's voice.

The XO laughed and said, "Rumor has it he got his ass chewed by Colonel Gutesh-Lin for going on the rescue mission and getting his ass shot up."

Teo had it from a reliable source that, in this case, the rumor was true. He didn't blame the CO for going—Teo had gone on more missions than a commander should—and given the importance of the mission, he thought it was appropriate. But he still had to stifle a smile at the thought of the regimental commander chewing Khan's ass.

"So, this says 'two Marines' . . ." the XO said, his eyes hopeful.

"Two Marines from Kilo, representing the area combat element. There're going to be two desk-jockeys from Force there, too. But don't get your hopes up, Lyle. I need you to take over while I'm gone."

He had to stifle another smile at the XO's crestfallen face. "I know it sucks, Lyle, being the XO and losing your platoon just a month before we deployed. But you're doing a helluva job, and that's where you're needed. I promise you, I'll see what I can do to get you into something else when we get back."

"Something where I can see some action, sir."

There wasn't much where a senior first lieutenant could see action, at least as in leading troops. But there were a few, recon being the most likely option . . . if Wooster could make it through training.

But that was on him, not anyone else.

"No promises about action, but maybe."

The XO shrugged, then said, "So, who're you taking? Trace? The first sergeant?"

"No. I don't want to make it look like we're jumping at Union demands. I'd rather have a trigger-puller."

"Taylor?"

"No. I think Uribe."

"Uribe? Are you sure, sir? I mean, he's not really, uh . . ."

"He's a liberty risk? Not polished enough for polite company?"

"Well, yes, sir. There's going to be Union, Red Cross, and crabs there."

"*I'm* not polished, Lieutenant. I'm not known for my *el-o-cu-tion,*" Teo said, drawing out the word, "and posh manners. Uribe's a fighter, and if I'm going to be in the company of crabs, I want someone who can cover my six."

"I'm sorry, sir," the XO stammered. "I didn't mean—"

Teo cut him off with a wave of his hand. "I know you didn't. Do we have any ground transportation working, or am I going to have to hump it?"

"The two-ton's still down, sir. But Berens managed to get one of the golf carts working."

"Golf cart? And it has the range?"

"To the refugee camp? Yes, sir."

"OK, then. Get Uribe up here, full battle rattle. Put a damned red cross on the golf cart, one of the Union transponders, and log in my routes. I don't want some crab hunter-killer team to take a potshot at me, saying they didn't see the red cross. I want to leave in an hour."

"Roger that, sir. I'm on it."

"I better get cleaned up," Teo said. "Don't want to look like a low-life."

"Golf cart," he mused as he left for his room. "Maybe I'm kinda posh, after all."

Chapter 30

Paladins

Richter's VTOL landed, the engines blasting a thin layer of rainwater off the pad and into the darkness. The ramp lowered and a pair of Cataphracts came down, cyclers held low as they scanned the perimeter.

One held up a hand and motioned to Richter. The major tugged at his fatigue top as humidity swept through the aircraft. Another two Hegemony VTOLs were on the landing pad, along with different model aircraft with white paint and red bands around the nose and tail sections. There was a golf cart, of all things, parked at the near side of the pad.

A few lights were on in distant buildings, multistory affairs that once held thousands in the now defunct resort town.

"Sir . . . is this safe? Aren't we behind enemy lines right now?" Szabo bent down to look out of the VTOL.

"Krabi is pattie territory, but this is a Union refugee camp. Neutral territory." Richter stomped down the ramp, then looked back up at Szabo. "Drop your radio. We won't need it."

"But we're surrounded by patties, sir," Szabo said, his radio half-on and half-off. "What if . . . I mean, they might—"

"Holy shit, where'd you get this kid?" one of the Cataphracts asked.

"Hello, yes!" A man in a powder-blue jacket and trousers emerged from the darkness with both hands held high, light reflecting off round glasses. "Red Cross, no shooting if you please."

His accent was off—not Hegemony, Alliance, or Ayutthayan. A Union voice if Richter had ever heard one.

The Cataphracts shifted their feet to a firing stance, cyclers bobbing up and down as the troopers fought against their combat conditioning to target sudden movement.

"I'm looking for a Richter, Major, and a plus one." He was in his mid-thirties, with close-cropped blond hair and deep-green eyes. The major saw a tiny screen reflecting off the inside of his glasses.

"Here," Richter said.

"And there you are." He ran a fingertip down the side of the thin metal frame of his glasses. "Welcome to Supreme Union Humanitarian Refuge 94. This is a no-conflict zone enforced by treaty agreed to by all belligerent parties. Any overt hostile acts committed against those seeking protection within the established perimeter, by fault or not, will be considered hostile acts against the Supreme Union with—"

"Just tell me where to go," Richter said.

"—retribution reserved at the discretion of the Union military. Please leave any and all projectile weapons on your conveyance. I am Joaquim Sundstrom, and I am your liaison while you're within this refuge. I will also add that intelligence collection activities are forbidden."

Richter handed off his carbine and pistol to a Cataphract and held his palms up for inspection.

The Union rep frowned at the knife on Richter's belt.

"Cheers, follow me." Sundstrom leaned to one side to look around Richter as Szabo came down the ramp.

"Sir . . . you're sure about this?" Szabo asked as they followed the Union man. "Why are we trusting them?"

Sundstrom glanced back to give him a dirty look.

"The Union's serious about their refugee camps," Richter said.

"It's about the only useful thing they manage outside their borders."

The rep kept walking, not responding to Richter's jab.

"You ever heard about the Pallas Incident?" Richter asked.

"Where a Union fleet glassed some Zaibatsu planet?"

"The corporate commander from Pallas-IV raided some Union camp on some nowhere moon after the system fell to one of their 'capitol expansions.' When the branch manager refused to hand over the responsible parties to the Union—"

"And it was the last time we had to go to such lengths to enforce our policies," Sundstrom said, raising a finger. "Let's not test to see if we're still that serious, yes?"

"No worries from us," Richter said.

Szabo opened his mouth to speak, but Richter shushed him.

The Union man brought them to a warehouse whose walls bore warnings stenciled in multiple languages about violent acts and responsibilities to others.

"Wait here." Sundstrom touched a handle and a bio reader flashed down the metal. He went inside.

Szabo turned around, his arms bending and hands grasping.

"I want my weapon," he said. "I'm so used to always having it."

"I know the feeling," Richter said.

"They wouldn't . . . could this be an ambush?" The radioman touched the knife and scabbard on his belt.

"If the Union turned a blind eye to something like that, the Hegemony would revoke their charter on Ayutthaya and the Union would have to pull up stakes. What'll happen then to all the refugees here? The thousands and thousands of refugees?"

"They'd . . . the patties would have to feed them."

"And clothe and protect them after they move north to the next rebel city and pick the countryside clean like a plague of locusts. Refugees aren't rational, trooper. You get people who've lost their status quo to war or disaster, and they glom on to any sense of structure or safety like a babe to a tit. Learned helplessness sets in real quick. You throw people like that out into the cold again and things go atavistic real quick."

"Ata . . . roger, sir. So we're safe here?"

"The Alliance has a hell of a lot to lose if they take out one officer and one fidgety enlisted man on a Union camp. Still keep your head on a swivel. We can't run surveillance drones over the place, but we can pay attention to our surroundings."

The door swung wide, and Sundstrom held it open. Inside were two groups on either side of white lines painted on the floor with eight feet of space between them. Richter's heart sped up as he recognized Alliance uniforms across the room.

Szabo stifled a warning.

A tall Hegemony officer with a gray beard that stretched halfway down his chest and a hint of stubble for hair saw Richter and cocked his head to one side.

"Colonel Toman," Richter said, keeping his gaze on the Alliance across the room as he joined his commander in the group of other officers.

"Emil, you look a little banged up," Toman said.

"Bruises. It's nothing." Richter caught a glimpse of an ornate knife on one of the Alliance as he meandered through the throng on his own side.

"Sir, there's coffee," Szabo said. "Would you like—"

"No," Toman and Richter said together.

"Stand there like you're an officer. Try and look older," Richter said to him. "Cross your arms. Brood."

Szabo did his best.

"There was an . . . incident," Toman said. "Ayutthayan relief convoy coming out of the west got turned around during the storm. Ended up on Route Blaylock through the battle area instead of Sizemore like they normally take."

"Let me guess," Richter said, scratching his beard, "they hit Bennies."

"Hit them about ten miles after they made their wrong turn. From what the Union's told us, it was just the two lead vehicles that were hit, minor injuries. They probably could've recovered and kept moving, but that's when the Alliance hit them with Switchblades."

"Uh, oh." A cruel smile went across his face, but he forced it away. "Apologies. Been one of those days."

"No problem, but there is an issue as it was a Red Cross-sponsored convoy," Toman said.

"It was in the conflict zone, not their bubble. Blame the dipshit they had navigating," Richter said.

"A Union citizen was killed," Toman said evenly.

"Not the first time one of their bleeding hearts got caught in the cross fire. They summoned us here for that?"

"Things are . . . delicate right now, Emil. I'll explain later."

A door opened between the white lines and a woman in a powder-blue pants suit entered the room. Her blonde hair trended to white, and was done up in a low beehive with complex curls.

"Most gentlepersons," she said, striding into the center as the officers on both sides lined up along the white boundaries, "I am Director Svetlana Mauro, head of this refuge and senior Union representative on Ayutthaya."

Richter looked over each Alliance officer. All were lean men, battle-scarred and decorated. The pommel of one knife caught his eye—it was ornate and distinct compared to the rest. He'd seen it before…when a Marine had tried to kill him eye to eye and cut his face.

The bearer was a broad-shouldered, hook-nosed rock of a man, dark-skinned and shorter than average, but he carried himself like a street-brawler. He looked like a thug. It was him. Captain Alcazar. The ghost's commander.

And he was staring daggers at Richter.

The corner of Richter's mouth pulled into a sneer, and he snapped the safety strap off the ghost's dagger, giving it a pat to draw attention to it.

The Marine captain went pale.

Chapter 31

Marines

The crab major flicked a thumbnail against the hilt of Gauta's pahoa la'au. Teo had known that Gauta was dead, but this confirmed it. There was no way he'd ever let an enemy take that weapon if he still lived.

And that meant this major had to be Richter, his opposite commander. Teo felt a surge of adrenaline flow through him.

"Quite recently—and far too frequently—one of our aid convoys was badly damaged by combatant weapons," Mauro said as she walked between the lines of Alliance and Hegemony officers. She held her arms out to her side and still had room to spare. The Supreme Union followed the old tradition of keeping belligerents "two sword lengths and one inch" apart, and right now, that distance was the only thing keeping Teo from strangling the crab.

"These are needless deaths!" Mauro pulled her fists to her chest with cringeworthy theatrics.

The crab drew Gauta's blade a few inches out of the scabbard, leaving the tip still sheathed, and spat on it.

Teo started forward, but Uribe grabbed him by the elbow before his boot could step over the line.

"Gentlemen, is there a problem?" Mauro asked.

"Where is he!" Teo pulled his arm free and planted himself against the deck. He stared as the crab major's mouth tilted up in an insolent smile, and anger washed over him in a welcomed wave, one he embraced. His vision narrowed, the conversations around him faded, and his universe became the crab and only the crab.

"Was he one of yours?" Richter asked with a gleam in his eye. "I thought this belonged to just another Yuttie slinky-boy sent to steal food when we shot him like a dog."

The fire burned, and it took a force of will for Teo to hold back. His muscles twitched like a thoroughbred in the gates. He was vaguely aware of shouting from his fellow Marines, the Union rep bleating for calm.

"I'll take that back." Teo held his hand out, and silence returned to the room.

"No, no!" Mauro waved her hands over her head. "There will be no exchange of anything—"

"You sure this belonged to your ghost?" Richter asked. "Looks like a cheap knock-off the locals sell outside the wire."

"His name was Gauta. Sergeant Gauta Gauta."

Marines to either side of him backed away slightly, giving him room to move. He felt a change in the air from his side. The crab was going too far, truce or not.

"You know what we did with him?" Richter drew the knife and looked at it like he'd held something foul. "We left his body in the mud for the pigs to eat."

Teo's world went red, and he launched himself forward. The major's eyes widened in surprise, and he tried to bring up Sergeant Gauta's knife to defend himself, but Teo knocked the major's arm up, sending the knife flying across the room. He crashed into the major's chest, taking him off his feet.

They both landed hard, which caused the elbow Teo had aimed at the major's throat, hoping to crush his larynx, but hit just below the clavicle, sliding to the side. He spread his legs to gain stability, then punched up, missing the chin as the major struggled, but connecting against the side of his cheek, slamming the man's head back.

The room erupted into shouts, chairs crashed, and people jumped to their feet. Teo didn't care. He knew he didn't have much time, and he wanted to kill the bastard. Using his left shoulder, he leveraged the crab's right arm up, out of the way . . . and took a wicked shot to the side of his head from the major's left fist.

Shit, the bastard's strong, he thought as he dug his face into the man's throat where the blows would be more ineffectual.

The crab was much taller than him, and he bucked, freeing his legs from under Teo, who shifted back, planted both legs around the man's thighs, and squeezed, taking away some of his support. He'd immobilized the crab, but it put him into a weaker position for the kill even as hands started reaching for them.

Now or never!

He gave up the legs, pushing forward and ducking his head under the major's trapped right arm, all while the man continued to wail away with his left, hitting Teo on the back of his head and shoulder with surprisingly powerful blows.

Teo slid into position, right arm across the major's right arm and throat, and wrenched . . . but the man's trapped arm had saved his life. Without it, his neck would have snapped. Teo was going to have to strangle him. He shifted his grip, and stars burst across his eyes. In that split second, the major had craned his head back and slammed his forehead into Teo's face.

He twisted, dug his head into the crab's shoulder, and slid his right arm deeper, locking his left hand in his right. The major tried slamming his head back again, but it just grazed Teo's head. He saw the crab's right arm flail for the knife at his belt.

Teo had two choices: release his hold to stop the crab major from drawing his blade, or double down, putting all his efforts into his chokehold. With a grunt, Teo doubled down.

He hadn't counted on the arms pulling at him, the blows landing on him as more and more Hegemony and Alliance officers joined the scrum.

"Stand down! That's an order!" broke through the cacophony, and Marine Corps training coupled with years of practice took over as if the voice was connected directly to his brain. He immediately let up on the major's neck as bodies pulled the two apart.

Hegemony officers hauled Richter back, his arms held fast, but he kept struggling to get at Teo. One of the officers retrieved Gauta's blade and gave it back to him.

"You want that knife back, cocksucker?" Richter shouted, holding the knife high. "I'll fucking feed it to you!"

The door to the Hegemony's side was kicked open, and Richter was dragged out. The door slammed, and muffled curses and pounding against the walls carried over the chaos in the meeting room.

People were yelling, and accusations were flying, but what registered with Teo, his adrenaline fleeing, was a woman's voice just repeating, "Gentlepersons, gentlepersons, gentlepersons," over and over.

What the hell have I done?

Chapter 32

Paladins

Colonel Toman leaned back in his chair, one far more utilitarian in design than the one Richter had lost in the explosion, and steepled his fingers just below his chin.

The colonel's office was far from opulent but had enough decorations in it that a visitor would know that Toman was more than a typical combat commander. Broken knives taken from slain Alliance Marines were hung on the wall behind him, along with the ubiquitous photo of the *Highest* in orbit over Rentha II, where the Hegemony was first declared. Embossed award certificates—some with real ink signatures from each of the Most High—took up most of a wall.

Hegemony regiments would, on occasion, have a full colonel like Toman leading a squadron. The job was normally helmed by a lieutenant colonel, but their regiment had more support units attached—a dedicated close air support Hornet squadron, a "plussed up" of armor, and two batteries of artillery. With much of that extra combat power assigned to Toman's Wolfpack Squadron, he merited a bit more rank in the field to match the larger forces under his command.

Toman's familial connections back to the governor of Essach were unrelated, Richter was sure. The colonel was a rare confluence of ability, competence and nepotism.

"Combat losses happen, Major. Just how did that ghost of theirs get into your base? Again." Toman ran fingertips across a stack of satellite photos showing what remained of the lodge.

"No excuse, sir," Richter said. He stood at attention before the colonel's desk, another simple affair of pressboard and plastic from the Hegemony's supply chain.

"Of course there's not, but there could be an explanation. The captured bands? Negligence on the part of troopers on watch? Give me something, Richter. The rest of my commanders and our brother units want answers. If the Alliance has figured out some way to bypass our force-protection measures, then we're in more trouble than I want to admit."

"Sir . . . he must have had a band when he infiltrated the first time. I don't know if it was taken off one of our dead or—"

"Too many out there. We have to give some bands to the locals so they can run supplies for us down the few logistics routes we can keep open. Rebels would pick them off otherwise. We expect some leakage."

"Then cycle the crypto on the bands and the emplaced Benedicts more often."

Toman picked up an ink pen and clicked the end cap several times.

"That would set the emplaced Bennies to neutral, making them more dangerous to us than the enemy. Our supply situation isn't as secure here as the nets would have the people back home believe. We're one lost transport away from eating local food and fabricating our own ammo. Keep that close hold."

"Yes, sir. This ghost of theirs . . . he was cunning. Smart. He didn't take the same way in or out and he set up distractions to cover his movements. The only failing I can find is that he . . . he was just better than us."

"Then how'd you kill him?" Toman raised an eyebrow.

"His luck ran out. Such is fate on the battlefield."

"We call it *kriegsglück* on Syddan." Toman dropped the pen on his desk. "But luck is no strategy. I'll have every outpost rework their security plan. Have some surprises for the next pattie that thinks they can pull off the same thing as your ghost. Meanwhile, what happened with you and that Alliance captain?"

Richter's jaw clenched and the bruises from the pattie captain's blows burned. Some teeth still felt a little loose, but he'd been hurt worse.

"Seems I've had some back-and-forth with him and his Marines for some time," Richter said. "He's capable. Something of a hero to his side. The ghost mentioned him before dying. So, I showed my own war trophy during the meeting with the Union. Let him know the scales were moving back into balance."

"Not bad," Toman said with a smile. "As neutral as the Union pretends to be, you goaded him into embarrassing the Alliance."

"I could've killed him," Richter said as his face darkened, "if you'd let me. Why didn't we take them all out right then and there? Hostile act initiated by them. Self-defense is always authorized. Now so many of their officers made it back to—"

Toman slammed a fist to the desk and rose to his feet.

"Because we're not savages!" Toman shouted then leaned on the knuckles of both hands. "It was a flag of truce, Richter. The Hegemony won't win this war by killing the Alliance, and they won't win it just by killing us. Years of war have proven that. But it is our code, the honor at the heart of the Hegemony that will bring more systems in line with us and isolate the Alliance into the petty little failed social experiment it was meant to be. I know that's . . . the orbital view of this conflict," he said, sitting back down, "but that's the message I've been told from every officer with stars on their collar. And if they're in lockstep, then that's the message from the Most High and the *Highest*."

"Then what about my troopers, sir? We're supposed to stay out there and bleed to prove that our deaths are more virtuous than theirs? I had to bag up three more men and . . . Christ, I don't know how I can even write to their families. What do I say that they died for? Policy? That the Hegemony nobly sacrificed our sons for the greater good of Ayutthaya and a concept?"

"Careful, Emil." Toman gave him a stern look. "That's too close to sedition for many to let slip. I know you've had it worse than usual and I can ignore it. And your family name isn't doing you any favors right now, despite your father's service to the *Highest*."

"Can you . . . tell me why?"

"I would if I could, but when the Watch is involved, it's best not to pry." Toman paused for that to sink in. The Watch were the Hegemony's secret police. They worked only for the Most High and on matters that were either a direct threat to the state . . . or deeply embarrassing to the state."

"I didn't know I was of concern to the Watch."

"You must have passed inspection, or a shadow hand would've sprung up out of the ground and dragged you away to Hades. Just know that they've got the eye on you." The colonel made an OK symbol with his hand and ran it down his arm, a Syddan gesture to ward against evil. "Speaking of inspections, you're due at the regimental S6 shop for an interview."

"What does public affairs want with me?" Richter asked.

"*Front Line Heroes* is doing the rounds. You were picked as the squadron's golden child. Congrats."

"You didn't make the decision."

"Did not. When the tasking came to me, I tried to fight it and send up Major Darada from the Lancers as he's co-located on the base. Choosing you meant a logistics pain in the ass getting you to and from, and you were in and out of firefights. Besides, Darada is a hell of a lot better looking. So it's you, as I have no excuse for it not to be you. Courtesy of a Division order. Congrats again."

"Thank you. Sir."

"Go do the dog-and-pony show and link back up with your troops soon as it's done. Enjoy the break. I've got the planners working out a raid on the patties that I want you to spearhead."

Richter's eyes lit up. "Any day killing patties is a good day, sir."

Chapter 33

Marines

"So, you decided to attack one of the crab officers?" the CO asked over comms suite.

Teo wanted to explain, to tell the CO what the bastard crab commander had done, but it wasn't going to do any good, and with both CP watches there, it was just best that he take it on the chin and bow out quietly. Not before he gave a pitch for the XO to take over, however. He owed Lyle that.

"Yes, sir. That's about the right of it."

The colonel tossed his head and barked out a short laugh before looking back into the pickup. *"Well, it's about freakin time, Captain, that you showed some balls. I've been wondering all this time how the hell you got that POA of yours. Maybe I see why now."*

Teo's mouth dropped open. Whatever he'd expected from the CO, this wasn't it.

"But . . . but, sir, the Union and the Hegemony have filed grievances."

"Fuck the Union, and fuck the Hegemony! We don't bow to them!" he said, getting excited. He leaned in closer to the pickup and said, *"I spoke with Major Tillis. He said people were trying to pull you off, but you hung on like a bulldog. You would have killed the asshole if he hadn't ordered you to release him."*

His eyes sparkled with eagerness, waiting to hear Teo's response.

"I . . . yes, sir, I probably would have," Teo said, warily.

"Oh, God, if I'd known you'd run amok, I would have been there just to

watch."

Teo didn't know what to say, so he remained silent.

"Probably for the best, though, that the limp-dick Tillis was there. If you'd have killed the bastard, you'd be facing charges. Too hard to cover it up. Might have been worth it, though."

Easy for you to say.

Killing someone under truce was a crime against the Freesome Accords, and the crabs could demand he be extradited to stand trial in their court system.

"Anyway, I've got another meeting with regiment, but I just wanted to touch base with you and tell you good damned job. There may be hope for you yet. Khan, out."

Teo stared at the screen for a long moment, trying to digest what had just happened. Not only had he not been relieved of his command, but the CO had congratulated him.

He felt eyes burning into him, and he looked around at the entire CP, both port and starboard watches, who were waiting for the word. With the privacy cone, they couldn't see or hear the conversation, but they could watch Teo and see his demeanor.

He gave them a thumbs-up. "Seems like the CO thinks I did right," he said, still not believing it.

Smiles broke out, and the XO came up to shake his hand. "I'm glad you nailed the sucker, ooh-rah!"

A chorus of ooh-rahs filled the CP, and Teo finally managed to relax. Somehow, against all odds, he'd managed to dodge a bullet. He stepped away, giving Corporal Wainsett back his suite.

"Oh, sir, you got a Priority 2 from a Master Sergeant Baroca. Do you want to hear it now?"

Teo perked up. The top had come through for him. But he didn't want to hear it here, in the CP.

"No, crystalize it."

"Roger that, sir."

Wainsett leaned over his suite and recorded the message. He picked up the optiscan and held it up. Everyone in the CP knew Teo was the commander, with the power of life and death over every Marine in the company, but Corporal Wainsett was not going to hand over a Priority 2 without an optical scan. Teo leaned in, the scan confirmed his identity, and the message had officially changed hands. He slipped it into his breast pocket.

"Now, I don't know if the crabs are going to retaliate, but let's keep alert.

"Sergeant Wymer, let's see if we can't pry some more surveillance from Force. I don't want a swinging dick to be able to get within a klick of our lines without us knowing about it.

"And XO, make sure Lieutenant Popovitch is on top of things. Walk the lines with him.

"Other than that, business as usual. Any questions?"

"Do you want me to run another nanoscan?" Doc Sanaa asked.

Teo raised a finger to his nose. The bruises from the crab's headbutt had gone a deep blue, but the nanos were hard at work healing it, which depleted their energy. He wasn't too sore otherwise, even if his face was tender, so he thought the nanos were still fairly well charged.

"Not now. I want to read this message in my room. I'll let you run a scan in about an hour."

With that, Teo climbed the ladder out of the CP, wincing as his shoulder complained. He didn't even know how he'd hurt that.

His pace picked up as he headed to his room.

"Hey, Skipper, get some!" Lance Corporal White Horse yelled while Uribe did some shadowboxing.

"Hell, yeah!" someone else shouted.

"Tow here," White Horse said, using Uribe's nickname, "he told us all the skinny. You fucked up that crab but good. Would've killed the son-of-a-bitch for what he was saying 'bout Sergeant Gauta if it weren't for that major."

"Oh, you did, did you?" Teo asked Uribe. "What was that I told you about keeping it to yourself?"

"Sorry, sir, but the guys, they needed to know what you did! We all loved Sergeant Gauta."

Teo shook his head. Technically, Uribe had disobeyed a lawful order, but he hadn't been that specific on what exactly couldn't be repeated.

He looked around as more Marines were approaching with eager looks on their faces.

"I've got to go," he said, pulling out the crystal and waving it for them to see. "From Force."

"Skipper, if anyone tries to give you any crap, you tell us," White Horse said as Teo climbed the steps into the lobby and turned down toward his room.

All of the Marines in the company combined couldn't do much if the CO, or the CG, for that matter, had wanted to press charges, but still, the sentiment touched him.

God, I'm glad I command these Marines!

He stepped into his room. With a couple days of sunshine and a heavy scrubbing with an antibacterial, it didn't hit him with the smell of mold. It still wasn't much, and the company Marines had better quarters when they weren't on the line, but at least he had some privacy.

Teo sat at the foot of his rack and pulled out the crystal. It slipped easily into his CCD repeater, a hand-held terminal linked to his helmet—as a Priority 2 message, it could not be read by his pad. He had to do a retinal scan again, but a moment later, Master Sergeant Greg Baroca appeared on the screen.

"Good to see you're still kicking, Captain," the master sergeant said. "And I was able to get something for you. I hit up another master sergeant in G2, and he got me the intel."

Teo let out a sigh of relief. He'd put in an RFI through the normal channels, but those were answered based on priority, and they were often incomplete. Like almost every Marine, however, he knew how to work the back channels to get what he needed, and of all the back channels, the SNCO mafia was by far the most capable.

As a captain, and one who'd only made sergeant as an enlisted Marine, this channel would normally be closed to him, forcing him to go through the gunny or first sergeant. But Top Baroca had been his Senior Drill Instructor back at Camp Horton. The Top had ridden him hard—too hard, he'd thought at the time—but bonds were forged, and with the notoriety of his POA, the top had been more than willing to help.

The master sergeant held up a tablet with a picture of Richter in the corner. The rest of the screen was tight and utilitarian text, a military file if he'd ever seen one, even if not Alliance.

"This is embedded as an attachment. It probably goes without saying, but you didn't get this from me. Let your RFI make it through the process before you start using any of this. Given that, here's what I got on your crab."

Teo hit the pause and downloaded the file so he could follow along with the master sergeant.

"Major Emil Richter. Void-born. That's a little unusual for the crabs, as he's not from a Hegemony trading guild. Turns out he grew up on the *Highest,* the crab rulers' pleasure barge. Last we had on his father is that he was one of the senior security men for the ship, but he fell off the radar a few years back. Only real reason we have anything on this Richter is because he's adjacent to a crab scandal. You know about the great encabulator purge?"

"The what purge?" Teo muttered as he swiped through more pictures of the major.

As if he could hear the question, the master sergeant continued. "Some of the Most High got caught with their fingers in the cookie jar. Part supplier overcharged for warship encabulator parts. Faked bills of sale. Fraud all over the place. Hegemony taxpayer money went into accounts belonging to the big wigs and not to the war effort. The true believers among the Most High were *not* amused. Some of the dirty ones had sudden and fatal shuttle accidents. Couple others skipped town to the Union and took a bunch of staffers with them."

I don't care about crab gossip, Teo thought, tempted to fast-forward the message. *Let's not pretend that kickbacks never happen in the Alliance.*

"The crab's sister was tits-deep in the scandal," the master sergeant went on. "The Hegemony has several open bounties on her. She's gone to ground somewhere in the Union. We've been looking for her too . . . maybe she'd accept sanctuary in the Alliance in exchange for laying the whole scandal out for us. Good psyop against the crabs. Secret squirrel stuff."

"So, that's how I'm going to beat this crab? Insults about his sister's graft?" Teo paused the message and swiped to a picture of the sister near a Hegemony Most High member, the red trim on the man's uniform unique to that ruling body. She was blond and attractive, and he wondered if that helped her get a position so close to the Most High. Enough pretty boys and girls used their looks to worm their way into the halls of power in the Alliance.

He started the message back again.

"This Richter's been in this war since day one. He was at the first skirmish on Telast. Campaigned on Badera. Shengen's World. Dunning."

I fucking hated Dunning, Teo rubbed a thigh as an old wound suddenly ached.

"He graduated from Britannia Academy. The Hegemony claims all their officer finishing schools are equal, but some are more equal than others. Now, here's the thing. I think your boy's clean."

"He's not my 'boy," Teo growled to nobody.

"He must be on the straight and narrow to stay in command of jack troops. Crabs normally send their piss poor officers to their conscript brigades or convict press brigades if they really screwed the pooch. So, he's both competent and clean. Rare for a crab officer. Must be a true believer in the cause."

The master sergeant stretched his arms up over his head.

"That's about all I got, Captain. All surface-level intel we gleaned from collecting elsewhere on the crabs. I can keep digging, you know, like what kind of panties and what bra size he wears, but anything else might take a little time. Maybe tap the Mama-san network to see if he's into something kinky with the locals. But I start calling in favors, and then my brass will want to know why."

No, you helped me color in the lines on this guy. Teo had expected something like that. The top in the G2 would have wanted to limit his liability. He could put the meat into his pad, but that would be breaking the SNCO mafia's trust. Hopefully, most of this would be coming back to him through official channels.

But the details didn't matter. It was the overall picture of the man. Thousands of years ago, Sun Tzu had said, "If you know the enemy and know yourself, you need not fear the result of a hundred battles." That was just as true today as it was back then, and Teo was going to figure out Major Emil Richter.

"As an aside, word got out about what you did. Everybody knows. That's what made it so easy getting the intel. I didn't even have to call in favors after you beat the shit out of the asshole who took their general. The Deputy wanted your ass, but the CG said no. You're something of a hero again. I guess I made you into a good Marine," the top said with a laugh.

"Well, Captain, I've got to get down to the comms center while a certain gunny is still there so I can get this out to you. I don't know what you're going to do with it, but I hope it's to finish what you started at that Red Cross meeting.

"Baroca, out."

The screen went dark, and Teo considered what he'd heard, and what could help him. The part about his sister was interesting. Richter was what the Alliance poor called "hiso." Born into privilege, then making all the right moves, getting all the right tickets punched on his way to the top, kind of like Trace Okanjo.

But for Richter, that all ended when his sister got nabbed for corruption. He was probably at his terminal rank, if the Hegemony was anything like the Alliance. Richter didn't do anything wrong, but blood was blood, and if one sibling goes bad, then the other probably would, too.

Maybe that's why he's such an asshole. He's angry because he knows he won't go any further, and it wasn't his fault. The question is how do I make use of that?

Teo had his own problem with anger. Even before the frustration he'd experienced as an officer with being accepted, he'd had a short fuse. So he understood anger and how it affected a person. Maybe this Major Richter and he weren't that much different, both angry at their situation but trapped by duty and honor.

Honor? No way, he chastised himself. *An honorable man wouldn't take a war trophy and dishonor it like that.*

"Maybe I can get him to blow his top?" he muttered to himself.

"And not in a Red Cross meeting."

Richter had made a mistake. He'd played his cards at the meeting, probably not realizing how much Teo could be on a hair-trigger. If the crab commander had gotten Teo to go berserk on the battlefield, things could have gotten ugly.

The crab major was a tough son-of-a-bitch, strong as an ox, but Teo knew, without a shadow of a doubt, that he could take the man. But crabs fought in their jacks, and that was a different story. Teo had tangled with a jacked crab during the fight in Rawai, and he'd been lucky to get out of that in one piece. Maybe he could have still prevailed, but it would have been no sure thing.

No, with a jacked crab, better to just stand back and send a Gryphon up his ass.

Teo put his remote on the rack and just let what Top Baroca had told him sink in, to try and form a picture of Richter. As he sat there, his eyes fell on the folder sitting under his coffee mug on the scavenged stool he was using as a nightstand.

He'd glanced at it before—a letter home, some letters to relatives of fallen troopers. He should have turned them in, but for a reason he didn't quite understand, he'd kept them.

Teo leaned forward, pulled the folder free, and opened it, carefully taking out the letters. Not many people still put stylus to plastisheet these days—or real paper in this case—but Richter evidently did. Teo wondered what that meant.

Hell if I know, he thought with a shrug.

The top letter was to a next of kin. He skimmed it, then realized it was for one of the crabs killed at Rawai. Most of it could be what he might have written himself, even if more literary than he could possibly write.

That made him feel a little self-conscious, as if he wasn't up to the crab major's standards.

". . . observation post . . . larger Alliance force . . ."

Probably one of the crabs inside the hotel.

Teo skimmed through the next one. More of the same.

He picked up the third and was about to put it down when a single word jumped off the page: "bolt."

What the . . .

There was only one Marine at Rawai with a VW-9: him. The weapon he'd lost in the battle, but not before he'd killed a crab.

He dropped the other letters to the deck and brought this one up to his face to be able to read it better:

To the family of Staff Sergeant Miles Illushin Cengic,

It is with great sadness that I must inform you of a death in service to the Hegemony.

Sergeant Cengic served under my command for almost eight months. Through our pre-deployment training and every day our Paladin troop fought on Ayutthaya. His career in the Hegemony Army was years long, with battle honors from campaigns on Stygia III, the Eris Moons Action, and our ongoing efforts to preserve the rightful government of Ayuttha that has allied with our great Hegemony.

He earned the Bronze and Crimson Star with combat citation, the Order of Brotherhood for saving the life of a fellow soldier, and the Blood Tear three times for being wounded in battle. Sergeant Cengic's service and sacrifice will never be forgotten.

As his commander, I witnessed his bravery against our enemy and his bravado and comradery behind the lines. He was a master of the lyre and would play for his fellow soldiers during meals and after missions. Many were the nights when his singing brought solace to our troop after difficult days.

He will be missed, and he will not be replaced.

Cengic died in battle, with steel forward to the enemy. We were fighting in support of an armor detachment, and the Alliance used a heavy bolt pistol to defeat his Cataphract plates. Such a weapon is unusual and used only in close quarters by more senior members of the enemy force.

It took one of their best fighters to bring Cengic's service to an end. He left us quickly and with little pain.

But his absence will hurt. Every holiday without him, every time you turn around and expect to share a joke or see his smile and he's not there will hurt. Your pain is mine, even though I didn't have the honor of being with him as long as you.

The Hegemony can never repay your loss, but know that his sacrifice will be honored, that his memory will never fade from me, or from the Army.

I will do my utmost to see his personal effects returned to you. Please have patience and understanding that such a task is difficult across star systems.

If you require anything of me, do not hesitate to ask.

Yours in grief,

Major Emil Richter,
Paladin Troop, 37th Squadron, 9th Expeditionary Army
Commanding

"Staff Sergeant Miles Illushin Cengic," Teo said, reading out the crab's name again.

It hit him, and he didn't know what to think.

Teo had killed before. His reaper tally was high, higher than most Marines. The Secretary Prime had presented his POA herself, sanctifying, in a sense, the crabs he'd slaughtered to save his platoon.

But he'd never known anyone he'd killed. They were just numbers, automatons in a game.

Staff Sergeant Miles Illushin Cengic. Wounded three times. Saved a fellow trooper. Bronze and Crimson Stars, which were about the equivalent of Teo's own Silver and Bronze Swords.

And now, this staff sergeant's family would be grieving for their son? Husband? Father?

Teo suddenly felt guilty for reading the letter. It was too personal. He quickly picked up the other letters, slid this one behind them, and put them back into the folder. But Cengic's letter called to him, accusing him.

"Shit, he was just another enemy grunt. He'd have killed me if I was slower," he said, shaking his head.

How many letters had he written over the years? He'd had his own Cengics, more than a hundred of them. Letters to the families of a hundred Marines, telling them that their loved one wasn't coming home.

He stared at the folder, and his hand, acting on its own, opened it and pulled out the letter again. He didn't want to, but he read it over again. And yet one more time.

Richter hates doing this. I can read it into his words. Just like me.

"But he's not like me. We couldn't be more different!" he shouted, too loudly.

He spun the letter away, letting it fall to the deck.

Teo stared at it for a moment, then with a sigh, walked over and picked it up. Staff Sergeant Cengic might be the enemy, but even the enemy deserved respect. Teo had taken his life, and he should honor that. Soldiers might be treated like cannon fodder by the generals, but if they couldn't be honored among themselves, then who would?

He picked the letter back up and put it back in the folder, then placed the folder back on the stool. He felt a little like after his first kill, back on Dunning, not quite knowing if he should be exultant or more introspective. Cengic was just one more dead crab, in the long run.

Still, he'd been a warrior, and even with the enemy, there was a bond, tenuous as it may be.

"Rest in peace, Staff Sergeant, rest in peace."

Chapter 34

Paladins

The sky was a faint gray of thin, passing clouds, almost ready to provide a glimpse of blue sky and green sun.

Richter walked up to a solid concrete building that bore no markings but which was adorned with several cameras and surrounded by razor wire deep within Port Tarl. VTOLs took off in the distance, rumbling as they hung in the air while their engines tilted forward just before they sprang away like startled rabbits.

He pressed an arm to a reader next to a metal door with no handle and a microphone hissed with static.

"Wrong building," a voice said.

"Tell Utiesh that Major Richter's here to see him."

"There's no one here by that name."

Richter punched the door and it rattled on its hinges. A moment later, there was a buzz and snap as magnetic locks disengaged. The door swung open slowly and a slightly plump Hegemony sergeant in charcoal fatigues peered at him.

"Um . . . hi," he said, wiping crumbs off his uniform, "so we can let you in only—ah!"

Richter pulled the door open and barged past the sergeant. Inside were several workstations manned by pale, bewildered-looking soldiers. A card table against the wall was loaded down with processed carbohydrates and candy. In the middle of the floor was a corrugated metal hatch; from beneath that, dozens of data cables snaked out to the workstations.

"He really shouldn't be disturbed right now," the sergeant said as Richter lifted the hatch and descended a curved staircase made of flimsy rods and grates welded together.

Beneath was a single stool, lit with a blue ring in the floor. Utiesh sat there, his cane on the floor, several holo screens floating around him. The intelligence officer was almost serene as his eyes darted from screen to screen as they formed a slow carousel around him. Each screen was full of different data overlays—video feeds from drones and satellite photos taken in series over terrain features.

"Bullshit," Richter said, "no one can process all this."

"Yet," Utiesh said, holding up a finger from his good arm while his other lay across one thigh, twitching slightly, "I do. It takes a certain type of person to master deep mind-still mind training. Only one in a billion is a Mittring aberration—the genetic quirk to link so much data together at once. Which is why I'm afforded a number of eccentricities. How'd you find my evil lair, by the way?"

"No sign. Plenty of standard-issue cameras. You're practically admitting this place is for you secret-squirrel types."

"There goes that hypothesis. I had a sign out there that this was the STD clinic, thinking that would keep people away, but we got knocks— some very late at night. The facial recognition software I have in place did provide some rather telling data. I cross-referenced their liberty passes with the serial numbers of the bills they drew from finance and found a number of brothels in the beach towns to the south."

"That's what you're doing down here? Finding cat houses?"

"That was in my spare time." Utiesh waved his good hand at him. "But what is it that *you're* doing here, Richter? I could be collating data right now. Divining the future from the data and—Tyson! Tea and Butter

Nutters, now!"

"Sir!" came from the top of the stairwell.

"I want everything you have on this one." Richter pulled out a folded piece of paper and handed it over. Utiesh sneered as he opened it and then tossed it aside.

"One of our propaganda posters for Captain Mateo Alcazar . . . easy enough request for information."

"You mean an Ayutthayan royalist wanted poster." Richter picked up the paper.

"I said what I said," the intelligence officer snapped. He spun around on his stool and raised his good hand, tiny filaments in his skin catching the light as his fingers jumped up and down.

The data tank swirled with new screens: Alliance net articles, award certificates with the enemy's crest and raised seal on them, snippets of news articles, even what looked like a high school report card. All the data points coalesced into Alcazar's face.

Richter walked up to the image and put a hand on the knife hanging from his belt.

"He's been a bad boy," Utiesh said. "Not just because he led the Alliance victory at Rather's World, where he was awarded the People's Order of the Alliance, but the Unions wagged their finger at him for—well, you were there. Not that a sternly worded letter means much from the Union. That's how it is with them—mealy-mouthed nothings or total annihilation. Strange behavior, really."

"He was at Rather's? And he got a POA?" Richter scratched his beard. "What else?"

"Safe Harbor–born, in the megaslums. Mustang of an officer. Rare for the Alliance. What is it you really want to know?" Utiesh turned to one side as Tyson arrived with a steaming cup of tea and a plate of peanut-shaped cookies. The intelligence officer proffered the plate to Richter, who refused with a slight shake of his head.

"I want to know how to kill him," Richter said.

"Have you tried bullets?" Utiesh sipped his tea.

"Have you ever tried eating by having food shoved straight up your fourth point of contact?"

"Don't be snippy. This Alcazar's popular with the *hoi polloi*." Utiesh waggled his fingers and a picture of the Alliance general they'd captured—who turned out to be the Marines' G2—appeared out of the data. "You know this one. What traffic we gleaned from the Alliance command about his bird going down was a bit . . . schadenfreude, shall we say. Took some time for him to cooperate with us, but it happened. We have our ways of making people talk. And talk he did, at length, about this Captain Alcazar and how capable he was. Takes care of his men. Says he's a 'Marines' Marine.' Didn't share the same praise for other officers. I have a high-confidence determination that Alcazar isn't as well-liked outside the enlisted ranks."

"I killed his ghost . . . who said Alcazar would avenge him."

"Data point logged and attributed."

"What's the casualty rate for his company since he arrived on Ayutthaya?"

"Ooo, now there's some deep knowledge." Utiesh paused, and one eye drifted to the side. "Likely he was in a training billet trying to turn Yutties into decent fighters . . . then . . . twelve percent while he's been on the line. Neutral determination. The Alliance tightened up some of their data leaks a few months ago."

"Twelve percent sounds low . . ." Richter looked at Utiesh, who nodded slowly. "Which means he's good at keeping his Marines alive. And I know he's been fighting my troop. My men killed all the ones he's lost."

"Ass," Utiesh said, shaking his teacup hard enough to spill some on his pants. "You beat me to that observation."

"What kind of an Alliance officer cares more about his Marines than his fellow officers' opinions? I thought they were all ruthless ladder-climbers," Richter sniffed.

"Don't believe everything our propaganda department puts out . . . that's odd . . ." Light flashed over his eyes and he cocked his head up.

"What?"

The data collage of the Marine captain vanished, replaced with a map showing the air base to the south and stretching just north of Krabi. Over a dozen pulsing red icons moved slowly south. White lines traced across the screen, some intersecting with the icons and removing them.

"Alliance just let a satellite rake loose over our area of operations." Utiesh brought the cup to his lips but didn't drink, as if he'd forgotten how. "Cloud cover lessened just enough for their lidars to penetrate. Hmm."

On the screen, stretched rectangles snapped out from each enemy satellite, looking like butterfly wings over the map.

"A surveillance sweep. They must be planning something." Utiesh's eyes glazed over and glowed. His cup tipped to one side, spilling over the floor.

"Utiesh?" Richter reached for the man but pulled his hand back when drool trickled out of his mouth.

"No, please don't!" Tyson called from the hatch. "He gets like this when he's pulling too much. Could you just leave? Sir?"

"Are they attacking or not?" Richter shrugged his carbine sling off his shoulder.

Tyson looked over his shoulder for a second, then back down. "No. They do a sat rake up to twelve hours before an operation. Sometimes they don't do one at all. We're working out the problem, don't you worry."

Utiesh groaned and a dark spot spread through his crotch.

"Also normal!" Tyson waved to Richter. "Sir, you have an appointment at the S6 shop in ten minutes."

"How do you know that?" Richter asked, going up the stairs two at a time.

"The Sir set a reminder for me to tell you as soon as you walked in." Tyson jerked a thumb back to his workstation. "Along with a message: 'It's my business to know. Go away now.' His words, sorry." He raised his hands in surrender and backed away.

"Take care of him. I know he's got a good heart underneath all that asshole." Richter yanked the door open and stepped out into the skyrocketing humidity of the early evening.

****

"And just a bit of powder to cut down on the glare." A female soldier leaned close to Richter and gave his bald head a gentle pat with a dusty pad. Her uniform was custom-made, cut exactly to her figure to accentuate certain attributes that would've been muted in the less flattering, mass-produced fatigues issued to the rank and file.

She leaned back to examine Richter, and a slight frown creased her lips, which had been stained a decent shade of red.

"Let's accentuate a bit." She took a small compact off a table and popped it open.

He'd seen this woman before on Hegemony newscasts. Despite how easy it was to have an AI composite present the day's events, the Hegemony, in its wisdom, preferred to keep more attractive heads and shoulders involved in reading a teleprompter and segueing into positive story after positive story.

Her name was Carrigan, but his troopers had a number of other nicknames for her, none he'd dare share in polite company.

"This looks like it was painful." She ran a stylus over one eyebrow and an old scar began to ache. "The dermal sutures will tighten back up soon as the interview's done. Might itch a bit."

"I need more scars?" One cheek twitched as her tool brought back a spray of tiny tear-shaped patches of skin.

"It plays better to those deep behind the lines." She smiled at him, and Richter felt a slight flutter. There were ample Ayutthayan women around, but Carrigan reminded him of every girlfriend he'd ever had.

"Almost show time." She slipped a small disc beneath one of his pocket flaps and gave it a pat. "Just speak normally and assume this will get play aboard the *Highest*."

"This will go there?"

"Some things go viral." She shrugged and he had no choice but to find it adorable. "Come on, sir." She gave his knee a shake and he got a whiff of her perfume as she hurried away.

"Dear Lord . . . thank you for women," he muttered and followed her to a sound stage set up in the middle of a warehouse. A news desk was already assembled with lighting drones floating overhead. A pair of deactivated androids were behind the desk; neither had legs, and their torsos were built into low stools. Smiling features were frozen in place on each.

"Wait . . ." Richter stopped as he moved into the set lights. "That's Vanessa Blanco and Chad Storm from *Front Line Heroes*. They're droids?"

"It's a lot easier to load a skin onto a rapport droid than send actual flesh bags from star to star," Carrigan said. "Cheaper too." She snapped her fingers over each droid's head and they perked up with a faint whine from internal servos as they looked around, smiles still locked.

"Combat zone interview loaded," said the Vanessa droid, her lips not moving.

"Color commentary protocols loaded." Storm's head cocked up and stared at a lighting drone.

"Ugh, these older units are never ready when you get them out of mothballs." Carrigan slapped Storm on the side of his head and he straightened up, smile undeterred.

"Interviewee bio processed." Vanessa's lips pulled back, baring pearly white teeth. Carrigan tugged the droid's lips out and they settled into a pleasing smile.

"Set for recording." Carrigan touched Richter on both arms and led him to a bench. He sat as lighting shifted around him, washing out everything off the stage. "OK, sir, need you to speak to that yellow light over on the left. That's your camera. Answer as fully as you like. The censors will make sure nothing unauthorized gets out. And we're on in five ... four ..."

A shadow appeared next to Carrigan. Whoever it was didn't announce themselves.

"And welcome to another real story from *Front Line Heroes,* I'm your host, Vanessa Blanco, joined as always by Chad Storm."

"Always a pleasure to be on the front lines with you, Vanessa." Chad's smile got even wider. "And we're here on planet Ayutthaya, where the long-standing, legitimate royal government has been fighting against a terrorist faction supported by the Alliance. The Hegemony's aid efforts have been instrumental in suppressing the illegal actions of both the Alliance and their terrorist allies. Glory to the Hegemony, greater as one!" He thrust a fist into the air.

"And with us tonight is Major Emil Richter of Wolfpack Squadron, Paladin Troop. Welcome, sir. Thank you for all you do for the Hegemony,"

Vanessa said, looking over at him. The uncanny valley in her eyes caught him by surprise.

Carrigan cleared her throat.

"Thank you, Vanessa, Chad, it's great to be here with you," Richter said.

"Major, you've been fighting on Ayutthaya for almost three years. What's it like out there?"

Richter narrowed his eyes slightly.

"Security measure, we'll voice-over the time frames in post," Carrigan said. "Just keep going."

"Fighting here is hard, just as it's hard on any planet," Richter said. "Not every Hegemony trooper's familiar with a jungle environment, but we adapt, overcome, and learn to use the terrain to our advantage. My troopers are mostly from Syddan, which is more tundra, but they've taken to Ayutthaya quickly."

"And how has the Hegemony's unity principles assisted in your cross-system trade endeavors?" Chad asked.

"Chad, switch to banter mode. Sorry, sir, they're glitchy. We'll fix it in post." Carrigan began whispering to the other person with her.

Richter's mood darkened, as he suspected who it was. A Watch officer. Toman said he was being watched, but having one of their own here was a bit heavy-handed, even for the Watch. Were they giving him just enough rope to hang himself?

"And what is the best part of serving on Ayutthaya?" Vanessa asked.

Richter's jaw clenched for a moment. If this was a test of his loyalty . . . then let it be the truth.

"What is best is destroying the Hegemony's enemies. The Alliance is a cancer, and the longer they're here, the more damage they do to the

Ayutthayan people and the more Hegemony lives are lost fighting them. The Alliance has metastasized, poisoned far too much of the planet. The time for a shot of smart nanos to deal with it is gone. We, as the Hegemony, must burn them out."

"And in your experience, that's possible?" Vanessa asked.

"Only if we have the will, the determination to prosecute this war to the last man. To the last bullet. Half measures accomplish nothing but dead troopers and the continued cost in blood and treasure."

"Sounds a little pricey for my wallet!" The Chad android leaned back as far as his stool would allow and began spinning around slowly.

"Post, just keep going!" Carrigan said.

"And how have you contributed to this solution?" Vanessa asked.

"My troop and I have one hundred and sixty confirmed kills," Richter said, looking hard at the camera. "And that number's not high enough. There's one Alliance beast out there named Alcazar. He has Hegemony blood on his hands from other worlds. He's killed my troopers. I am going to hunt him down and kill him. An oath to the *Highest*, I swear it."

"And what can the Hegemony do to help?"

"Let us off the leash. No mercy, no half measures." The low sound of artillery fire thumped against the warehouse. "I hear the guns. My men need me." He plucked the microphone out from under his pocket flap and walked offstage, tossing it to Carrigan as he went toward the door. A man in a dark suit with a strong jaw who was standing behind her nodded slowly with a slight smile on his face.

"Sounds terrific, Vanessa! Let's cut to sports," Chad said as Richter slammed the door behind him.

Chapter 35

Marines

Major Korinth, the battalion operations officer, stood in front of a map of the peninsula, with the Marine camp, the town, and the crab camp prominently highlighted . . . along with a slew of designated targets.

Teo sat in silence, just as he had for the entire forty-minute operations order. A bombardment on the crab positions, a punitive mission for taking General Mullen—not that it had been spelled out that way, but Teo could read between the lines. And the battalion CO didn't think the crabs either could or would react? They'd just sit there and take their punishment like good little boys?

"I want your target list by 1400 for approval, Captain," the major said.

"Any saved rounds?" he asked, turning to the S4 and S2, who'd given their parts of the order and were now sitting around him.

They shook their heads, and the major looked into the pickup and asked, "Any questions, Captain?"

Teo looked around at first sergeant and XO, who were looking at him expectantly. He knew maybe he should bring this up in private, but the major hadn't given him much time.

"Yes, sir, I do. With all due respect, sir, whose dumb-ass idea was this?" Teo asked the major, sure that it was the CO. "An escalation during the peace talks?"

This time, Khan's gone too far. The bastard's just a battalion commander, and

310

he doesn't have the authority for something this big.

"This came from on high, Captain."

"On high?" Teo asked, surprised. "You mean Force wants this?"

The major gave his head the tiniest of shakes.

What? If not Force, then . . . oh, shit.

"The Puzzle Pal—"

The major waved him silent, and Teo belatedly snapped his mouth shut. No one knew when the folks in Department 99, the ones who could come in the dead of night and disappear citizens, were watching. At the top levels, whether this was within the Ministry of the People's Military or the civilian agencies didn't matter much. They were all the same, and they didn't appreciate disloyalty.

"The CO sent me here in person to make sure you understand the importance of this mission. We cannot allow the Hegemony to kidnap general officers and refuse to register them as POWs. They must be taught a lesson."

Teo stared at the major, trying to see if there was a hidden, unspoken message there. He couldn't tell, and frankly, it didn't matter. Maybe this was payback for General Mullens, maybe not. This was far, far above Teo's paygrade.

"OK, sir," Teo rushing to change the subject. "From looking at the order, this will take my entire combat load. Will I be getting a resupply?"

"When time and supply allow."

Which means when hell freezes over.

Not that Lieutenant Verdun had fired many of their 3.5mm RYN rockets—only twenty-four of them so far, to be exact. But they were one more tool in Teo's toolbox, and without them, he'd feel far more vulnerable—especially if this damned war was going to escalate.

"What can I get for support, sir? I mean, the RYNs aren't the galaxy's heaviest hitters."

The major's eyes flickered ever-so-slightly, and his lips tightened. "You realize that your position here is isolated."

Teo steeled himself for what he thought was coming.

Yeah. We're at the ass-end of a long Marine line, forty-five klicks from Lima Company. Stuck here out-of-the-way where the threat was supposed to be manageable. But now it seems like we're the tinder for a wildfire.

"In support of the offensive, battalion has had to relocate the battery. Out of range for you here."

Teo's mouth dropped open, and all thought of rank disappeared as he shouted, "What the fuck? No support?"

"No, Captain. You're getting support. We've got a section of Bravo Battery with the KAS-8. Eight rounds. And like I said, I'm going to need your target list by 1400."

Teo raised an eyebrow as he considered this. The "Kick-Ass" was the Corps' tactical ballistic missile. At eight meters long and 88 cm wide, it could carry any one of four warheads, each of which packed a big punch.

"Navy terminal guidance?"

"No. You need to take care of that."

As designed, terminal guidance was normally done with suborbitals. When they weren't available, a rifle company could provide terminal guidance with either the PPC-67s or even Corporal Wainsett's comms suite in a pinch. He could better the odds by having Sergeant Wymer flood the area with his drones, but after the first missile, or even when the first was detected inbound, the crabs would EMP-sweep them out of the sky. A Kick-Ass relied on a big punch, and without guidance, hitting *near* the target was considered good enough.

"Can I get MWDs?" Teo asked.

The Multiple Warhead Deployment substituted four warheads for the single one so that something could be relied upon to make it through enemy counter-measures. Teo had never been supported with Kick-Asses before, but he'd heard enough. When terminal guidance was iffy, it was better to use the MWDs.

"Your choice, Captain."

Eight rounds weren't enough, but they did go a way towards making up for not having 120s in support. Thirty-two warheads, each powerful enough to take out armor, bunkers, or a good-sized building. Or enemy artillery.

Because the crabs weren't going to just sit there and take it. They'd be counter-firing with their big guns.

"You sticking around, Major?" Teo asked.

Major Korinth was a good-enough guy, if a little standoffish, but having a major in his hip pocket could be beneficial if he needed more from battalion.

"No. I need to be back for the kick-off. You've got your mission, and you've got . . ." he said as he checked his CCD, "three hours and forty-four minutes. I'd suggest you get to work."

Teo motioned the XO and first sergeant down and followed the major out of the CP, wondering what he could ask to get more clarity. This was just an unusual mission, one that didn't make sense.

But the major didn't give him the opportunity. He waved at the civilian go-fast operator down on the beach who spun the boat around, ready to launch. The major started to say something, then stopped. He seemed to reconsider whatever he was going to say then settled on, "I know it sucks, Teo, but it is what it is. Just get your rounds downrange, and you'll do fine."

He spun around and jogged down to the shoreline and his go-fast.

This is stupid. There's no strategic value to it.

But it wasn't his call. It was up to him to make it work within his AO.

"*Officers and senior staff, to the CP, now,*" he passed on the company net. "*Squad leaders, get everyone in their fighting positions and check your overhead cover. We're going to need it!*"

Chapter 36

Paladins

BOOM!

The muzzle blast slapped rain away from the artillery piece and pelted Szabo with a sudden shower from a whole new direction, stinging his face as he carried a shell as long as his arm and as thick as his leg. The damn thing was heavy and he wished—oh, how he wished—he was in his jack.

A rocket-assist motor at the base of the just-fired shell ignited, a brief flare of light in the rain clouds like the glow of a protostar in a nebula that winked out seconds later.

Soldiers shouted terse commands and updates to each other through the din of falling rain and booms from more artillery pieces around them.

Szabo stopped near the end of one of the two trails splayed out from the weapon's breach, his heels sinking slightly in the mud.

"V-T, eight meters, deflection one-two hundred, quadrant three-seven-zero, set!" The gun sergeant turned around, shirtless and with a dark sheen on his forearms and hands, a helmet on his head. He pointed at Szabo then to a metal sled with four handles on the ground behind the breach.

Nemec was bent over the sled, panting hard. "Drop the round! Load!" the sergeant shouted at him.

Szabo nodded quickly and tried to set the shell as gently as he could. Nemec swore at him and rolled it out of his hands. It landed on the sled with a clank.

"Load, load!"

Szabo grabbed two handles and hauled it up with Nemec, then shuffled forward and slammed the edge of the shell into the bottom of the open breach. Heat wafted out and an acrid smell stung his nose.

The gun sergeant slapped a wrench-looking tool over the fuze on the tip of the shell and a green light flashed twice.

"Fuze set, ram!"

Spiteri let out a weak battle cry and hit the rear of the shell with a long rod, pushing it into the breach. An artilleryman pushed a bright-orange cylinder behind the shell and smacked Szabo on the shoulder. He and Nemec backpedaled and Szabo almost tripped in the mud.

"Set!" The other artilleryman slammed the breach shut and grabbed a lanyard on the opposite side from the sergeant.

"Ah, shit . . ." The sled slipped out of Nemec's grasp and the heavy metal slammed against Szabo's shins. His heel got stuck in the mud.

"Move!" The sergeant kicked Szabo in the back, sending him face-first into the mud.

BOOM

Szabo felt a rush of air as the breach slammed back over his head and snapped forward again. He blinked, realizing that if he hadn't been knocked into the mud, the breach would've hit him.

"Up, you dumb shit!" the sergeant shouted and pointed to a towel draped over the trail. "Clean up the sled. Don't get my breach dirty!"

Vukovic appeared out of the rain, a shell in his arms.

Nemec yanked the sled away from Szabo and wiped mud off.

"Get another round," the sergeant told Szabo. "You want to kill patties or don't you?"

Szabo shook mud off as he ran back to an ammo truck where

artillerymen were ripping packaging off pallets of shells and screwing fuzes onto the tips.

He wasn't sure how many times he'd run this circuit. The troop had been in the transition barracks, enjoying a few quiet hours and hot showers, when Lieutenant Briem and the first sergeant ran through the place like a whirlwind, demanding them into cargo trucks with nothing more than their carbines and flak vests. They were dropped off at this artillery park and given quick-and-dirty instructions on how to be artillerymen.

It wasn't too complex: carry fucking heavy shells back and forth, load them into the gun, get the hell out of the way, repeat.

That was when it started raining.

Just where the lower enlisted artillery soldiers that were normally assigned to this job were supposed to be remained an open question.

"Why . . . why can't we use Winnie?" Perko asked as he received a round and did his best to run with it.

"Because God loves the infantry," Iliev said as he adjusted the shoulder strap on his medic bag and took a shell.

"Nope, cheese-dicks," said Ceban, hefting a shell over both shoulders and walking off, his pace almost casual.

Szabo wasn't sure why Ceban—technically a civilian—was hauling shells, but he didn't mind the help.

"Gun four," said an artilleryman as he passed a shell into Szabo's arms and turned around. Gun four was at the edge of the sandbag perimeter, naturally. Was he getting the worst route because of his low rank or because he'd pissed off the sergeant? The answer wouldn't make the shell any lighter.

He breathed hard as he carried the shell, eyes locked on his destination.

BOOM BOOM BOOM

The firing put a spring in his step and a devilish smile went across his face. Wherever the shells landed would be hell, and he wanted that steel on target. No matter how bad he had it, the patties must have it worse, incoming *and* the rain.

A wall of hot air slapped him from behind and pitched him forward. He twisted as he went down, clutching the shell close to his chest as he fell on his back. The fuze struck his face, leaving a line of pain up his nascent beard.

A fireball shot up from one of the other guns and men—ablaze from the lit propellant—ran from the destroyed artillery piece.

"Drones! Drones!" someone shouted.

Szabo looked up at the storm and saw dark shapes circling overhead like vultures. He froze, the steel pressing against his chest cold to his touch. What was it about the Switchblade drones' targeting he was supposed to remember? Don't move? Move, but do it slowly . . . or was the magnetic signature of the shell he was clasping enough to bring a drone down on him?

One of the drones nosed down, and a rocket fired.

Szabo's heart froze as it came right for him.

A wave of blue light cut through the sky, but the Switchblades kept falling. Images of a girl at the rec center they had access to before they got yanked away to be gun bunnies flashed through his mind, and his arms started thrashing.

The drone struck several feet away with a wet plop, the rockets bolted to the side sputtering. A smell of spent fireworks and ozone sent him into a coughing fit.

"I'm not . . ." He tried to sit up, but the shell was too heavy. "Damn it!"

Someone leaned over him, ran their arms beneath the shell, and raised it.

"On your feet, trooper," Major Richter said. "Fire missions don't stop." He ran—ran!—the shell to the nearest artillery piece. Szabo pulled himself out of the mud with a *schlurp* and followed, giving the disabled Switchblade a wide berth.

The sergeant on the gun was dead, slumped over the trail with a hunk of shrapnel through his chest. The other artilleryman was in several pieces strewn through the mud. Nemec was on the ground, arms over his head, the breach door swaying from side to side over him. He peeked through his fingers at Richter.

"How're you still alive?" the major shouted as he slammed the round into the breach.

"I have no idea," Nemec said, handing the ramrod to Szabo.

"Get the charge. What's the angle and deflection?" Richter jumped over the trail and wiped blood off the gunner's controls.

Szabo looked over the other trail and dry-heaved. Most of the assistant gunner's torso lay in the mud, one arm cradling the charge, his pale face resting against it like a pillow, his eyes loose.

"Fuck if I know," Nemec said, reaching unsteady hands up to the trail as he tried to get to his feet.

"Deflection one-two hundred, quadrant three-seven-zero," Szabo said, pushing the ramrod back to Nemec and prying the charge out of the dead man's arm. The still-warm hand brushed over Szabo's and sent a chill through his body. He wiped mud off the charge and pushed it into the breach.

"Get on the lanyard." Richter pointed a knife hand at Szabo, then at Nemec. "Ram and secure the breach."

"You believe they had to send gun bunnies to school to learn this?"

319

Nemec fumbled with the rammer.

Szabo went over the trail again, removed a primer cartridge from a bandolier hanging off the gun, and plugged one into a small hole like he'd seen the dead assistant gunner do. The lanyard swung slowly from side to side, and he looked down the length of rope as it grew redder toward the bottom.

The assistant gunner's hand was still holding on, severed just below the wrist.

"Set. Fire!" Richter ordered.

Szabo stared at the hand, his world shrinking down to the horror in front of him.

"Fire!" Nemec punched him in the shoulder and Szabo snapped back. He grabbed the middle of the lanyard and twisted his body to one side.

BOOM

"Still have three rounds left!" Richter put a hand to one ear, his face contorting with pain from the shot. "Move, Szabo, move!"

"Sir," the trooper said, kicking the hand off the lanyard and running back to the ammo truck.

Chapter 37

Marines

"How good is the intel, sir?" Lieutenant Okanjo asked.

"Good as any we get, I guess," Teo said as he used binoculars to look over what used to be a middle school ballfield and track.

No one was going to want to play sports on the field again. It belonged to the dead now. Several trenches had long been filled in, and Teo wondered how he hadn't known about this before. It made sense, though. With the civilians trapped in place, what else could they do with their dead?

But it was the four open trenches that concerned him now, or more specifically, the nearest one. There were Ayutthayans gathering around the other three, and as he watched, a cloth-wrapped body was lowered into one, a group of about a dozen villagers, led by an orange-robed monk, accompanying it. Their wails reached the squad of Marines as they lay on their bellies and watched.

There wasn't anyone near the fourth, a shorter trench, but if the intel was accurate, Sergeant Gauta's body would be inside of it. That asshole Richter had been wrong, and Gauta hadn't been eaten by animals. Teo didn't want to think about what shape it would be in after a week in the hot, humid Ayutthayan days, but it didn't matter.

Like many in the Alliance, Gauta belonged to the Church of Fa'asamoa, and it was *fa'a* to be buried in the family's church cemetery. And the Marines made a promise to all recruits that every effort would be made to bring the dead home. Teo was not of the same religion, but he was a

Marine, and he owed it to Gauta to bring his body back.

The intel could be faulty, however, something planted to draw the Marines out. But if there was a chance that it was true, could he afford to pass the opportunity by?

"We've got movement," Corporal Nyoki, who'd taken over Third Squad after Gauta's death, said. "North end of the field."

Teo shifted his binos, an ancient optical pair that, while it didn't have the capabilities of modern devices, it was not subject to jamming and EMP bursts. A jacked crab appeared from out of the road leading away from the field. He stopped at the edge for a moment, running his scanners most likely, before he moved out. On his tail, one, then another appeared.

"Should we light them up?" Okanjo asked.

The squad had six Gryphons, and at this range, it would be an easy shot. The little missile would hit before the crab knew it was coming. But the crabs rarely sent out jacked troopers at anything less than a squad, and once the Gryphons were fired, it would be down to grenades and darts.

The ballfield was in the Safe Zone, but that hadn't stopped fighting before. Teo could claim self-defense, and no one at Force would blink an eye.

A loud, piercing wail caught his attention, and he shifted for a moment to the Ayutthayans. One older woman was being restrained by three others from jumping into the trench where her loved one had just been placed.

If a firefight did break out, more of the civilians could be caught in the crossfire, and Teo thought they'd suffered enough.

"No, hold on. Let's see what we've got first," he told the platoon commander.

He shifted back to the crabs . . . but not just crabs. A Union officer Teo somehow hadn't noticed, an electro-clipboard under his arm, rushed over to the crabs and started gesturing.

What the hell is the Union doing here?

The Union was supposedly neutral in this fight, but like all Alliance citizens, Teo was sure that the much more powerful Union ------- The Union was supposedly all about the civilians on the planet, so it might make sense that they would be present when the crabs wanted to visit a mass grave in the Safe Zone, but Teo wasn't going to bet his retirement on that.

Within a minute, the last crab entered the ballfield, making a squad. A jacked Hegemony squad versus a Marine squad. Edge to the crabs. But they could hit them hard, cause them grief, then withdraw before the crabs could mount much of a counterattack.

And if we withdraw, what about Gauta?

"Keep it calm," he told Okanjo. "We just watch for now."

Teo shifted back to the Union rep and zoomed in. The gaunt-looking man wore the light-blue collar tabs of an observer, so it was possible that he was there in an official, humanitarian capacity. He seemed to be lecturing the crab, and for a moment, Teo felt a twinge of sympathy for the crab.

For a moment.

This was the enemy, and they were in the way of his Marines recovering Sergeant Gauta.

He wondered who the crab was when the jack seemed to split open, and the trooper stepped free . . . and Teo's blood ran cold.

"It's Richter," he hissed.

"What did you say, sir?" Okanjo asked.

Teo didn't answer. He felt his anger bubble to the surface as Richter stood over the nearest trench, the one holding Gauta's body. This crab executed Gauta, left him for the animals, and now, he was going to do who knows what to the body?

323

"Not on my watch," he said, getting to his feet.

"Sir?"

Teo looked at his VP-51 for a moment, then placed it on the ground. He had his Wilder, he had his blade, he had his hands. He didn't need the rifle, and by carrying it, the crabs might cut him down before he got close.

"If something happens to me, kill them all," he ordered the lieutenant before he turned and jogged over to the mass graves.

Chapter 38

Paladins

The smell of rotting flesh was strong. It cut through the grave powder Ayutthayans spread over the trenches, scooped from tubs bearing the Union seal. Richter could've attached the face guard to the bottom half of his helmet, but admitting the stench got to him would be a moment of weakness. The powder was a ghostly gray and smelled of calcium and aluminum, too close to the deodorant issued by the Hegemony Army.

Richter fought his gag reflex as he walked between the many trenches, Szabo at his side. His jack extended his stride, and a bald Ayutthayan monk in frayed orange robes and sandals struggled to keep up. The Union rep, Sundstrom of course, kept pace, an electro-clipboard in the crook of one arm.

There were dozens of bodies in this trench, not all of them whole. Just how this refugee convoy had blundered into the bombardment zone during the Alliance's latest push was beyond Richter, but he didn't want to dwell on this situation too deeply.

There were implications he didn't want to face.

Richter scanned the bodies with his visor, taking readings and pic snaps to pass up to Colonel Toman. A return farther down the trench stopped him in his tracks.

"The Hegemony is aware that observed fires are highly encouraged by the Freesome Accords to prevent just this sort of tragedy," Sundstrom said. "Injury patterns are consistent with an air-release fragmentation weapon, which the Hegemony was—"

"Not all the bodies." Richter flipped his jack's release, and the frame popped off his body with a hydraulic hiss. He stepped out of his jack, eyes blinking beneath the harsh sunlight. The smell was even worse outside his helmet. He drew a pistol from inside the jack and mag-locked it to his thigh.

"Sir?" Szabo asked as sweat broke out across Richter's face.

"Call a pair of flankers up," Richter said, and slid into the trench.

"Stop, stop!" The monk flapped his arms in distress. "We've already said last rites. You're defiling them."

Sundstrom dropped his clipboard in shock, his jaw dangling open.

"Then say them again!" Richter stepped over powder-dusted limbs until he reached a pair of boots. He knelt, one knee sinking slightly into the ground moist with blood, and brushed off the laces to reveal a dog tag tucked into the boot.

Piotrowski. One of the snipers he'd lost in the field. The man's name, serial number, and religion were stamped into the aluminum square. Richter squeezed the corpse's ankle, the powder grinding against his bare skin.

He looked up at the monk. "More. There should be one more of my men. Where is he?"

"There." The monk covered his nose and mouth and motioned to the end of the trench. "We release all souls we find, as the Light commands."

Richter pulled Piotrowski's leg, and his body shifted the dead around him. Limbs rose up from the reeking soil, grasping at him. Richter stopped, his hands quivering, heart racing. There were faces, ashen ghosts crying out, demanding to know why they'd died.

He forced the illusion away and dragged the dead sniper to one side of the trench. The corpse was loose; there was no tension within the limbs as he moved it. There was no warmth to his touch, but the grit of the Union's powder stung his bare skin. All the equipment was gone; someone had stripped him of everything valuable before tossing him in with the dead civilians. Each time he shifted the corpses, the smell of death wafted up, and he knew the scent would stick with him. This bodyglove would end up in a burn pit; no number of times through the laundry machine would ever get the smell out.

"Sir? You need help?" Szabo asked.

Richter braced a foot against Piotrowski's and lifted the corpse onto its feet. Powder flaked off, finding its way into Richter's nose and mouth. He gagged and turned away, not wanting to come face-to-face with the dead man.

Szabo grabbed Piotrowski by the collar and hauled him up and out.

A white haze of disturbed powder surrounded Richter as he worked down the side of the trench, a forearm pressed to his nose and mouth to cover the stench.

Someone dropped in, too light to be a jack, but the uniform had the Alliance camo pattern.

The dust cleared. Captain Mateo Alcazar was standing there with him.

Richter went for his pistol, but the Alliance brought one hand up, palm out, while the other went to his own holstered weapon.

"You again," Richter sneered, the cold splash of adrenaline hitting his system as his body prepped for a fight. The details of the Marine's knife stood out in stark relief from his camo. Alcazar's face was firm, but Richter didn't see murder in his eyes. This time.

He was aware of the Union rep bleating outside the mass grave, but he didn't care what he said.

"Yours are in here," Alcazar said, moving his hand slowly off his holster. "Mine too. This pit isn't for them. Agree?"

Richter lifted his hands to his sides. "I won't let my men be buried with trash."

"Same here." Alcazar gestured at the bodies in front of him. "There's yours. Mine's behind me."

"Go." Richter went to a bald head amidst the dead Ayutthayans and found Bradford. He reached into the dust and grabbed him by the armpits. He heaved, but the dead sniper was stuck in the jumble.

"Hey," Alcazar said, "let me help."

Richter's mouth contorted with hate and he snorted dust out of his nose. "Don't you touch him."

Alcazar nodded quickly and shifted a dead Ayutthayan off the pile, and the hold on Bradford went slack. Richter got the body to the trench side for his newly arrived flankers to take out.

"Just say the word," one muttered just loud enough for him to hear.

Richter shook his head.

Alcazar was at the end of the trench, his ghost Marine propped up against the side. The Marine commander was kneeling, his head bowed, one arm on the ghost's shoulder as he quietly chanted.

Richter got his last dead Hegemony trooper out and took a helping hand to get up and over the edge. He beat at his beard to get the powder out and slapped down his uniform as flankers stuffed the dead into body bags. Szabo had his cycler in one hand, barrel oriented out to one side.

A trio of monks knelt next to the grave, praying with their arms raised to the sky.

"Sir," Szabo said, raising his chin slightly.

Richter turned around. A squad of Alliance Marines was on the other side of the trench, forming a wall between them and the place where some of their number readied Gauta's body to be moved.

Alcazar brushed himself off, his gaze locked with Richter's.

Richter touched his belt where Gauta's dagger hung and unsnapped it. He yanked the knife and scabbard away, then tossed it to Teo. The Marine caught it by the handle and gave Richter the barest nod.

"Would you all just leave, this time?" Sundstrom asked. "Please."

"No issue here," Alcazar said.

Richter pointed at the Marine. "I'm not done with you."

Alcazar touched the hilt of Gauta's blade to his brow in a mocking salute.

"They're set," one of the flankers said.

"Let's go. Our troopers deserve better than this." Richter got back into his jack and resisted the temptation to power up his cycler. As much as he hated the Alliance, one did not disturb the dead. They'd suffered enough.

As they carried the body bags away, several flankers walked backwards to keep an eye on the Marines until they slipped back into the jungle.

Chapter 39

Marines

Lance Corporal Xicale emerged from the building, pulling a struggling young woman by the arm. He saw Teo and said, "Caught me another one, Skip! Can I keep her?"

"Just put her in the bus with the rest of them," First Sergeant Lippmaa told him.

"Ah, First Sergeant, you take all the fun out of life," he said as he half-led, half-dragged the struggling girl, who was yelling out an impressive string of curses.

Slender, even thin, she was no match for Xicale. Her ratty and faded clothing had seen better days, with only a bright purple headband giving her anything that stood out.

More and more civilians formed streams, which merged into rivers of people, all getting ready to be taken away. Most were afraid, and many were angry. If looks could kill, Kilo company would be dead and buried by now.

A group of five men struggled against the restraints put on their wrists by Marines. One started to run, screaming about "imperialists," before being knocked down by a Marine and then dragged, kicking his legs, by two Marines to the processing station.

"Don't they know we're not the enemy?" the XO asked.

"Maybe we're not, but we're the ones dragging them out of their homes," the first sergeant said.

"But it's not up to us," the XO protested. "It's the Union, and their own government. Getting them out of the line of fire, you know, so . . . like . . ."

"So we don't bombard the shit out of them?" Teo asked.

"We don't know that was us. The investigation's still ongoing."

"And we'll blame the crabs, and the crabs will blame us. All those people know is that their own died, and now they're all being forcibly removed from their homes. A uniform's a uniform to them."

"But we're not the crabs. We're protecting them," he persisted.

Teo liked Lieutenant Wooster. He was a good kid: conscientious, caring, and dedicated to fixing all the wrongs in the galaxy. But life was never so black and white. Could the civilians have been killed by Marine rockets? Sure. Would the hundreds, if not thousands of civilian deaths over the last three years, have been avoided had the war not arrived? Absolutely.

And now, Kilo Company had a new mission. Krabi was no longer considered safe, so all the residents, along with the citizens in the local refugee camp, were to be evacuated to a much larger camp two hundred klicks inland. Fewer than five thousand Ayutthayans had voluntarily loaded the buses. Kilo got the mission of involuntarily loading the rest.

There was to be no one left in the city as of 1800 tonight. Teo checked the time. Four hours and fifty-seven minutes. That was all the time he had left to empty Krabi.

"Come on, let's check the loadout," Teo said. "I want to know how many have gone so far."

The three Marines walked down the main street, past now abandoned shops. He had no idea if they'd been up and running the day before, or if the closures were long-term.

This was his first time in Krabi-Town proper, but he was no longer curious. He'd been in a hundred Krabis over his still short career, and no matter what planet, they were all the same: war-ravaged and desperate.

The collection-point was in the city square. A motley selection of buses, all with large red crosses painted on the sides, were being brought in from a waiting line, three at a time, where Red Cross personnel scanned each person—refugee now, Teo realized—and then directed them onto a bus. There had to be several hundred already gathered there, waiting to be processed. Lieutenant Fuentes' First Squad stood by for security, watching the proceedings. The rest of the company was sweeping the buildings.

In ones, twos, and threes, Ayutthayans were making their way into the square, most with Marine escorts. The three company leaders passed Lance Corporal Seibbert, who was laden down with an elderly woman's possessions as she hobbled toward the square.

The Marines were not supposed to be pack animals, but Teo understood what Seibbert was doing. He still had his 51 ready for action, should the need arise, so Teo said nothing as they passed the two. Let the Red Cross decide if the old lady could bring all of that or not.

She looked up as they passed, and then called out, "You're the commander here, right?"

Not really. The Union officer's in charge.

But he didn't want to try and explain that. It was easier just to say, "Yes, ma'am."

"Come here, son. I need to tell you something."

Teo was going to ignore her, but then he decided that it wouldn't cost him to listen to her complain about whatever. He stepped to the sidewalk, now buckled under neglect, and leaned in to hear what she had to say.

With a gurgle that the old sometimes make, she spat in his face.

Teo froze; the spittle started to slide down his cheek.

"Hey, Miss Alana, you can't do that!" Seibbert shouted, dropping all her belongings and raising his weapon.

"You're the devil," the old lady hissed, venom flashing from her eyes. "All of you."

Teo slowly stood up, not wiping his face. "Lance Corporal Seibbert, lower your weapon, pick up her things, and take her to the buses."

"But, sir—"

Teo held up a hand, palm out. "Just do it. Then go back and bring in some more."

Seibbert took a moment to digest what Teo had just said, alternating between looking at him and the old woman.

"I swear, if she'd spit on me . . ." he muttered as he started picking up the luggage.

"If she spit on you, you'd still escort her to the bus, Seibbert," Teo said. "They are not the enemy."

The woman kept her eyes locked on Teo as Seibbert led her away. Finally, Teo turned back to the other two, using his sleeve to wipe the spittle away.

The first sergeant caught his eyes, then gave a slight nod of respect. The XO said nothing, and the three started walking again.

The people had a reason to be angry. The Alliance had promised them protection and freedom. And what had it gotten them? Death and destruction. A mass grave where hundreds of their loved ones were buried.

Where Sergeant Gauta had been buried, he remembered, the stench of the bodies, of Gauta's decomposed corpse, almost overwhelmed him for a moment. *And that asshole Richter!*

He'd promised to kill the man, a promise still left unfulfilled.

The three leaders of the company walked silently while Teo fumed. Things were being taken out of his control, and he didn't like the feeling at all.

"What is significant about this?" he asked the XO after a couple of minutes.

"This? You mean evacuating the civilians, sir? Well, they'll be safe, out of the line of fire."

The first sergeant grunted.

"Safe" was a relative word. The villagers had been in a Safe Zone, yet many of them had died. The super refugee camp to which they were headed might be safe for the moment, but the tides of war change, and it could be in the middle of the fighting in a week, a month, a year.

"And . . . ?" Teo prompted.

"I'm not sure what you mean, sir," the XO said in a faltering voice.

"What road are we on right now?"

"Beach Road."

"Which leads where?"

"Back to our camp, sir," the XO answered.

The first sergeant was now looking at Teo with open curiosity. He obviously didn't understand what Teo was getting at either.

"I'm not talking about our camp. What's farther up the road, past this village?"

"Oh, you mean the crab lines," he said as the three reached the edge of the square and stopped, watching the goat rope of evacuation.

"And without the civilians here? Without a Safe Zone?"

Understanding dawned on the XO, and he just said, "Oh."

The three stood there for a long pause until Teo said, "With no more Safe Zone, the road is open from us to the crabs. No restrictions."

"What are we going to do, sir?" the XO asked.

"I'm going to kill me a crab commander, that's what I'm going to do."

Chapter 40

Paladins

Richter lifted a tent flap and slipped into the squadron Tactical Operations Center where the air was dry and smelled of body odor. Soldiers, many of them with close-cropped hair, manned holo screens. The adjutant and supply sections were away from the front of the room, where a ten-foot-high map of the front lines shifted as new information came in.

He walked by very clean soldiers nursing cups of coffee, their eyes tired, their waistlines pudgy from manning a desk for too long.

Closer to a line of desks and beaten-up chairs—the "bridge" for the squadron's senior officers—were the operations and intelligence sections. Standing behind a slightly larger chair was Colonel Toman, his head shaved so well that his scalp reflected overhead lights and flashes from the holos. A small scrum of staff officers around him listened as he spoke quietly.

"Sir," Richter said, giving his commander a nod.

"Paladin." Toman smiled, the bushy beard that reached down to his sternum jerking slightly. "Welcome back from the bush. Your men situated?"

The colonel raised an eyebrow at the adjutant and supply officers, who cleared their throats nervously. Frontline troopers were the priority to Toman, and any staff officer that dragged their feet to meet their needs ended up supervising sanitation details.

"Good as can be. They're anxious to get back in the fight," Richter said.

"The system has your troop green across the board, yes? Good." Toman turned and adjusted a control band that ran down the length of his left hand. He twisted an unseen knob, and the battle map shifted to Krabi. Icons of intelligence reports and satellite pictures popped up like a pox.

"The Union's moving the refugee camp out of Krabi. Neither we nor the patties screwed the pooch—we didn't harm anyone in the Safe Zone—but too many Yutties are getting killed in the crossfire," Toman said.

"This is a war zone. The locals know we've got mines and the patties have drones out there," the intelligence officer said. "It's a mystery how any of them think it's a good idea to be moving around."

"Almost like they live here or something," Richter said.

"Which presents an opportunity." Toman flicked at the air, and maneuver graphics appeared on the map: a regimental attack on the city of several squadrons of troops, armor support, and aircraft. "Previous to this, taking the city meant an infantry focus so as not to have any collateral damage to the camp. Casualty projections were too high for my blood and the big brass. But now we can be a bit more indiscriminate with our fire support."

"And we've got a better picture of the enemy's force disposition thanks to that POW you nabbed for us," the operations officer said to Richter.

"We're going to put a hurt on them." A slight smile spread across Richter's face and the knife scar beneath his beard itched.

"That we are." Toman nodded. "I'll put Crusader troop as the lead element and have Paladin as the reserve to—"

"Sir," Richter said, holding up a fist, "send me. My troop wants this. Let us be the tip of the spear."

Toman raised an eyebrow and glanced at the operations officer, who shrugged.

"You've got the manpower?" Toman asked.

"Enough to get stuck in and grind the enemy into paste."

"Make it so." The colonel flicked a hand at the operations officer, who ducked back to his section. "Understand this, Richter: planetary command is angling for a cease-fire, but one that's advantageous to the royalists. We take back Krabi-Town, which was one of the first places the rebels ravaged, and it'll give negotiations a boost."

"'Cease-fire . . .'" Richter said the words like they tasted bitter going over his tongue.

"Hard to believe. Not the first time we've heard that. Might not be the last," Toman said. "Bleed them white, Paladin. That's what I need you to do. Convince the enemy that holding the city's not worth it anymore."

"Roger, sir. They'll bleed."

Chapter 41

Marines

Should I really do this?

Teo stared out over the turquoise water, the draw for millions of tourists over the years, but it didn't register with him. To him, the Tradewinds was not a resort—it was just one more camp in his career of fighting for the Alliance.

There was more on his mind at the moment. He had to decide, and decide now.

It wasn't that he had any doubts as to what was going to happen, only when. Neither did anyone else up the chain. The full platoon of five Badgers that had just arrived by barge along with a Forward Air Controller and a full resupply of ammo and drones were evidence enough that with the peace talks faltering and the crabs' refusal to admit that they had General Mullens, the brass was sure renewed fighting was about to break out.

Kilo—and the rest of the battalion—was ready for a fight. The operations order had been given, and every Marine knew his mission. Intel said that the crabs were scrambling.

For most of history, the battle went to the bold, not to the ones who sat on their asses waiting to see what was happening. If the battle was inevitable, then why wait for the crabs to get ready?

But was the battle inevitable? There was a last push for peace going on right now, and Teo's orders were to stand by and wait until how that played out, only fighting if fired upon.

Teo didn't know what he feared more—going into battle . . . or not going in. If a fight broke out, Teo would lose Marines, Marines who counted on him to get them back home safely. Even with the tanks, the balance of power probably still tilted to the crabs, at least in firepower.

But not going in? If peace truly arrived? Then Major Richter would live, and that was almost unbearable. Teo had vowed to make sure that didn't happen.

"Not if I can help it," he muttered.

"Sir, did you say something?" Corporal Wainsett asked.

"Nothing."

"Sir, are we getting into the shit?" the corporal asked.

"I don't know. We're ready if we do, though."

"We'll kick their sorry asses, sir."

Teo laughed and clapped the corporal on the shoulder. "You've got that right. The crabs don't stand a chance."

"Ooh-rah, sir!"

Teo turned away from the ocean and faced inland, toward the enemy. Two of the Badgers were waiting at the resort gate, main guns pointed outbound. Teo was not a huge fan of armor, but this time, he was glad they were there. The crabs' jacks were formidable, but the tanks could mess them up. Teo wasn't sure how survivable the Badgers were in the jungle, but he'd be happy to make use of their firepower.

But the Marines' primary weapon was, and always would be, the well-trained, well-motivated, individual Marine.

"Wait here for me," he told Wainsett as he left and passed through the grounds of First Platoon's assembly area by the rear pool's pumphouse. The Marines were in small groups, chatting, sharpening blades, and doing weapons maintenance. Lieutenant Fuentes spotted him and came rushing up.

"Any word, sir?" he asked with the eagerness of youth.

Well, maybe not just youth. Teo had the same eagerness. Closing with and destroying the enemy was their entire raison d'être, after all.

"Nothing yet, Razor," Teo said.

"What do you think, though?"

Teo hesitated, about to spout the standard "We hope the diplomats find peace" answer, but the young lieutenant deserved a straight answer.

"I don't know. I'd put the chances of a peaceful settlement pretty low, though. So, if I had to bet, we'll be kicking this thing off."

"They need to let us end this thing. It'll save more lives in the end instead of all these piddly-ass minor engagements. The Marines and the crabs. Just let us go at each other and see who comes out on top."

Teo nodded. The lieutenant had a point, the very same point Teo had been considering.

"It may very well come to that, Razor."

He looked over the Marines in the platoon. Most had their eyes on him, even as they kept up whatever they'd been doing as he walked up.

"I'm going to go talk to some of the men," he said, then when the lieutenant started to follow him, "No, you get back to your prep. I don't need you to babysit me."

The first group of Marines got to their feet as Teo approached.

"How are you all doing?"

"Ooh-rah, ready to make the grass grow, sir!" PFC Apok shouted.

Corporal Motta rolled his eyes and said, "Doc just taught him that saying, sir."

"Well, Corporal, blood *does* make the grass grow," Teo said, "so I hope you're all ready to grow some!"

"Ooh-rah," they shouted as other Marines nearby joined them. In a moment, the entire platoon was shouting, then Third Platoon, assembling in the courtyard, heard and answered back. Within moments, ooh-rahs were echoing around the camp, even from Second Platoon's Marines who were manning the lines at the moment.

Teo beamed with pride as he listened. If he'd wondered what his Marines wanted to do, that was answer enough. He made his way through the platoon, stopping to chat, taking their pulse. Their bright eyes, their excited manner—these Marines were ready to go.

Some of them, perhaps many of them, would die if the Marines and the crabs fought. And Teo really didn't have a say in that. He was sure the clash was coming. But he did have a say when. And if he took the initiative and hit the crabs now, fewer of these eager young Marines would die, and more would make it home in one piece.

It took twenty minutes, but Teo addressed each and every one of them. He owed them that. Finally, he was ready to leave, but the platoon started another ooh-rah chorus that was picked up and echoed by the rest of the company.

Teo waited for it to die down before shouting out, "*Vigilamus pro te!*"

He turned and left, stopping short of the lobby where he left Wainsett. He knew what he had to do, but he needed to make sure.

"*Major, do you have a moment?*" Teo asked the S3 over the P2P.

He'd just been on a command call with the Three not an hour ago, but this was something different.

"*I'm up to my ass in alligators, Captain. What do you think?*"

"*I . . . I just had a question, sir.*"

"*Yeah, ask it, but make it quick.*"

"*The talks. Where are they? Are you getting any kind of progress reports?*"

The comms went silent, and Teo wondered if the major was going to answer.

"Bottom line, Captain, is that you be ready to move out, and as soon as tomorrow noon."

That was new . . . and specific.

"Are we expecting something then?"

"I can't say."

Can't because you don't know, or can't because you've been told not to?

"That sounds like the talks are breaking down for good."

"I didn't say that, Captain Alcazar."

You didn't have to, Teo told himself.

"Roger that, sir. I understand," he said.

"Hey, Teo," the major said before he cut off the connection. *"You just be ready. I've got full confidence in you and Kilo. I know you and the CO . . . uh . . . I mean to say, you're a good commander and a good Marine."*

"Thank you, sir," Teo said, but the channel was already dead.

Teo stood there, a statue.

There's no turning back if I do. There's no victory if I don't, and Richter lives.

Teo pulled up OP1 on the company net. *"Anything out there?"*

"We thought we heard something, but maybe not. All quiet," Lance Corporal Uribe said.

Teo's heart started pounding, and he thought it would burst from his chest.

"Roger that. Probably a cackla," he said.

Fuck. I've done it.

"Roger. We'll keep our eyes peeled," Uribe said.

Teo felt lightheaded. He'd just pulled the trigger. First, he'd put Uribe and Xicale together and given them an OP. The two were not even in the same platoon, much less fire team, but he trusted them to do what he wanted and then keep their mouths shut. Second, he'd given them a

342

captured crab cycler, but after removing the control module, making it a simple mechanical weapon.

Teo checked the time, then contacted each of the remaining four OPs scattered across the company frontage, checking in. There was no sign of crabs—not that he expected any. The bulk of the crabs was still back at their new camp, preparing for the clash.

He reached the lobby and sat down beside Corporal Wainsett. "I guess now we wait," he said, checking the time.

Exactly eleven minutes and thirty seconds after he contacted Uribe and Xicale, just as he'd planned, the *tot-tot-tot* of a cycler reached him from the jungle, followed by a string of 51 fire in reply.

"Contact, contact! We're taking fire!" Uribe passed over the company net. *"Returning fire now!"*

"Commanders, marshal your Marines. We cross the LOD in ten mikes. This is it!" Teo passed over the command net.

There was no time for recriminations, for second-guessing. For better or worse, Teo had just kicked off the final battle for this forgotten arm of this forgotten war.

Chapter 42

Paladins

The floor of the Ontos heavy transport rumbled beneath Richter's jack-shod feet as the grind of tracks whined through the heavy metal walls. He gripped a handle on the roof. The troop compartment was mostly silent but for the noise of the bus-sized vehicle. Ten of his Cataphracts were in there with him, all hooked up to a trickle line of power and internal comms.

Szabo stood directly across from him, the radioman's head tilted forward. His mouth guard was off and his visor flipped up.

Richter checked his HUD; they were still several minutes from the release point.

"Szabo," he said, "you good?"

"Huh? What?" Szabo lifted his head. "Tight beam to squadron linked. Tied into the other transports with minimal—"

"Not what I asked," Richter said.

"Good, sir. Jack's green across the board."

"And the trooper inside the jack?"

Szabo shifted, rolling his shoulders back and forth.

"On our way to a major dustup with the patties . . . and all I can think about is that mass grave. Back in training, we shot nothing but Alliance holo targets. Got all the briefings about their crimes during the war. You know, to be a Marine, they have to have killed a Hegemony citizen? Civilian or military doesn't matter. At least . . . that's what we were told. Now I'm out here and not once but twice I've got close enough to them to see what they really look like. Don't know if I like it."

"It's easier to see them down your sights and do as you were trained," Richter said. "Lot simpler."

"Why didn't they try and take us out at the mass grave? I keep asking myself that . . . just don't like the answer I come up with."

"That they respect their dead like us?" Richter asked evenly.

Szabo nodded slowly.

"The Alliance have always been . . . decent in some ways. Not many. What do you think's going to happen when we hit Krabi?"

Szabo lifted his cycler slightly.

"They won't hold back, son. Don't think for one second they're on par with the Hegemony. They will kill you. They will kill me. They will kill all our troopers. That's the only thing you need to know about them."

"But they didn't, sir. Back at that trench, they could've tried, but they didn't, and I—sorry, sir. Spoke out of turn," Szabo said.

"Don't judge them only for that. The only good pattie's a dead pattie."

"Then why'd you give that blade back to the pattie?"

Richter paused for a moment before answering. "We may be killing each other . . . that doesn't mean we can't give respect where it's due."

The carrier squealed to a halt and the Cataphracts stirred into action.

"Paladins!" Richter called out. "Steel forward."

"Steel forward!" the men called out and the rear ramp dropped open, hitting the road with a thunderous clang.

Richter ducked and ran out, his cycler charging up. Hornet fighters roared overhead as he stomped around the side, more and more Cataphracts flooding out to join him as he moved forward at a steady jog.

Krabi-Town appeared over the jungle, buildings smoking from

impacts, the sky red from low, thin clouds. A line of tanks advanced slowly, coax machine guns chattering and main guns booming.

Enemy shots cracked through the air, striking tree trunks and sending splinters of pale-white wood through the air.

"Hot damn, now this is a proper fight," Briem said through the IR.

"Watch your spacing." Richter slowed his pace to match the Mammoth tank several meters ahead of him. "Ready, phalanx."

His troopers beat fists against their cyclers and hooted their approval as he picked out several buildings as targets and assigned them to platoons. He tested the feed line, shifting a round in and out of the breach.

"Paladins, walking fire!"

His cycler opened up, and a steady cacophony erupted from his troop as they raked bullets across the upper stories of the closest buildings. The facades shattered beneath the impacts, sending glass and cerrocrete dust plumes into the air.

Times like this, he had to agree with the long-dead General Lee. It was good that war was so terrible, lest he might grow too fond of it.

His jack rumbled as his cycler put in the work, the barrel glowing hot as the magazine in his back went empty and internal servos moved the next mag into place. The spent mag dropped off him and he put a shoulder against a stopped Mammoth tank.

Szabo unsnapped a full mag from the back of the tank and slapped it into Richter's armor.

"I'll take this over the artillery any day," the radioman chuckled.

"Remember you said that." Richter reloaded Szabo's jack then peeked quickly around the tank, capturing a brief bit of video. The city was wrecked. The road was choked with debris and fresh bullet wounds smoldered in the walls.

Fresh graphics came through from the squadron commander,

identifying a warehouse that he and his troop were to seize. Richter stifled a curse. The target was several blocks deeper into the city than their original objective. It may not have been far on a map, but in a city fight, every next block meant blood spilled and lives lost.

He adjusted his platoons' routes and sent the new orders out.

"Ha, ha," Frakes said mirthlessly, "look where we have to go now. That's not happy."

"Original target's our new rally point," Richter said. "Advance with the armor." He punched the back of the tank twice with his servo-assisted fist, and it rolled forward. His troop flankers appeared on his HUD, well behind the forward line.

Richter sidestepped and swept his sensors over nearby buildings. The din of battle fell away until there was only the sound of the treads crushing fallen masonry and the low whine of the turret as it slewed back and forth.

"Movement." Szabo painted a target on a roof line.

"Don't be shy with ammo," Richter said. "We're not sneaking around."

A dark shape flew up from the roof and broke apart. Cylinders spun out, then arced through the air as rocket engines flared to life.

"Switchblades!" Richter opened fire and took cover against the tank as the kill drones burned right for him.

Not enough time for an EMP. His only hope was for a lucky strike from his cycler or for the drone's targeting systems to fail in their attempt to lock onto him so soon after being activated.

One Switchblade broke apart midair, and one just ahead flared as its terminal vector rocket fired. Richter rolled to one side, and the Switchblade clipped his shoulder and bounced into the tank's treads. It exploded and blew shrapnel and masonry fragments over Richter and

Szabo.

His jack rattled as it was peppered, but nothing broke through his ballistics plates. His HUD lit up with two casualty reports. One Cataphract dead.

The tank lurched forward, and there was a thick snap as it turned in place. One tread broke off and trailed behind the road wheels like a shed snake skin.

"Flanker element, provide overwatch while they make repairs. Jacks advance." Richter shook dust off his cycler and jogged toward a downed streetlight lying half over a crushed ground car.

Alliance rifle fire sprang off the pole and ricocheted off his helmet. He shook the impact off and hopped forward, bracing his feet against the road as he opened fire, stitching a line of fire across windows and then down to the double doors of a dead tour guide's office.

The bottom floor exploded with a *ka-rumpf*, and Richter ceased fire.

"This is Paladin Actual," he sent through the IR. "Patties have booby traps in place. Watch easy access points."

Shadows raced across the street in the dust fog.

"Follow me," he said and took off at a run, Szabo lagging behind. Richter saw a door sway open on a building and ran to the wall. Bringing his cycler up, he rammed it through the glass and opened fire. His HUD fritzed out as it tried to take readings over the muzzle flash. He spun around as he swept his weapon out and shouldered through the door.

A pair of Marines lay dead on the ground, while a third dragged himself away, a trail of blood leaking from perforated legs.

Richter shot a burst up the Marine's back, and he pitched forward. Still.

"Bulldog!" came through the roof and a foot stomped. "Bulldog, you OK?!"

Richter swung his cycler up and shuffled to the wall, opening fire at the same time the Marines one floor above had the same idea. Rounds crisscrossed and the ceiling splintered. Rounds whacked against his chest plate like hammer blows and he went to one knee in pain.

As the firing stopped, the ceiling buckled. Then, with a low groan, it collapsed in a deluge of tiles and aluminum scaffolding.

Two Marines lay dazed in the rubble. Richter stomped forward, planted one foot in the mess, and kicked a Marine in the helmet so hard, his skull snapped back on a severed spine, his throat tearing open.

The other still had a hold on his rifle and pulled the trigger, but the weapon seized up. The mag rings were dented in the fall, and the Marine looked at it, helpless.

Richter swung his cycler across and knocked the rifle out of his hands. He brought the cycler up and stabbed it at the Marine's chest. The other man caught it and tried to push the muzzle away from his body.

"No, wait! Wait!"

Richter wished the pattie could see his smile as he fired and sent the Marine bucking under the impacts. The Marine's outer armor layer went stiff as the first bullets struck, then it buckled as more cycler rounds struck and bullets punched into flesh. Blood bubbled up from ruined lungs and the Marine's hands fell away.

"Sir?" Szabo burst into the room.

"Too slow this time." Richter stomped the other dead Marine's VP-51, shattering it.

"Enemy's counterattacking and—"

A Switchblade burst through the wall and skipped between them as it flashed out the opposite side.

"I fucking hate those things," Szabo said, looking around for cover.

"Same here." Richter kicked down the remnants of a glass door and entered a narrow street. Cataphracts from Blue and White platoons were online. A firefight raged to Richter's left.

The dull pop of more Switchblades sounded through the city.

"Signal hard cover, company EMP going off." Richter leveled a knife hand at Szabo and retreated back into the building. He unsnapped a coil off his lower back and bashed the base against his thigh plate twice.

"Wait, sir, I haven't passed that up to squadron yet, and I—"

Richter tossed the EMP up along with his cycler ever so slightly. He caught the carry handle of the cycler with his un-augmented hand and the EMP with the servo-assisted hand and arm. He stepped into the road and used the boosted strength of his jack to throw the EMP above the highest floor of the surrounding buildings.

He ducked back in as a blue corona flashed through the sky. Switchblade drones crashed to the ground moments later.

"So, I've lost comms with squadron," Szabo said, "but their last transmission went something along the lines of 'Don't you fucking dare set off that EMP, Richter,' sir."

"Just forced the patties to come out of their holes to fight," Richter said.

"Oh . . . good." Szabo double-checked that his ammo line was still connected to his cycler.

Richter studied his HUD.

"White, move into an overwatch at that soccer field. Blue, escort the mortar section to that school, building number seven-seven-two." Richter stepped back into the road and immediately took fire. Bullets sprang off his leg plates and something tugged at his outer thigh.

A tank main gun boomed and the incoming stopped.

Cyclers fired up and down the street as he charged through a chain-link fence and into the remnants of a two-story primary school, the walls adorned with paintings of sunrises, fluffy chayseux cats, and smiling children. Bullet pockmarks marred the fading art.

He took cover next to a low water fountain and Szabo fell in beside him.

"Quiet." Richter cocked his head, and the sound bafflers on his ears turned up the ambient volume. He heard boots—different from his sabatons—shuffling against a sidewalk. He reached back and plucked the Benedict mine off Szabo's back.

He looked through an abandoned classroom, desks askew and chairs scattered about, and out a window on the other side to the soccer field where he'd sent White platoon. Richter pressed a trigger three times on the side of the smart mine, then knocked out the window glass with his shoulder. Shouts of alarm went up and he threw the mine out the other window.

It landed on the road and deployed, spider legs flat against the asphalt. Richter pulled Szabo to the ground.

"Ha!" a Marine shouted. "We're good. Go, go—!" They fired through the walls, and darts punched over their heads.

The Benedict exploded, the blast wave annihilating all the remaining windows and sending papers swirling around them.

A crayon drawing of an Ayutthayan man at the prow of a boat full of lighter-skinned and blond-haired figures settled in front of Richter's face. MY DADDY was scrawled in uneven letters across the bottom.

"The hell?" Szabo reached back to where the mine should've been.

"Set it to motion detection," Richter said. "Didn't matter that they had bands." He hauled Szabo up and they ran down the hallway and to the other side, where Cataphracts and flankers were approaching.

"But it would've popped on us too," Szabo said.

"I was going to tell you." Richter shrugged. "Drop a relay. This is our rally point."

"Roger." Szabo pried a handle off his thigh and looked around. He twisted the handle and tiny spikes popped out of it. He threw the device at the upper edge of the wall where it hit and stuck in place. "Will be a couple minutes before the atmo clears."

The pain in Richter's leg grew worse and he touched the ballistic plate. A hunk was missing, and his fingers came back stained with blood.

"Spiteri!" Richter directed the mortar man to a small playground, the rubberized mat on the ground torn up, soil exposed beneath. A pair of jacks dropped a base plate where Spiteri directed, while another swung a tube off his back and plugged it into the plate.

"Rounds!" Spiteri shrugged a pack of cylinders off his back and leveled the bubbles on the mortar system. Flankers appeared out of the woodwork and dropped more mortar rounds into a pile.

"Paladins, consolidate." Richter activated the camo in his ballistics plates and stuck a small metal stylus into the bullet hole on his thigh. There was a hiss of cold and the pain subsided.

"You good, sir?" Szabo asked.

"Bleeding stopped. It's nothing. Now we wait for the tanks to push again . . . hold what we've got." Richter felt the adrenaline fading away and the pain in his leg growing stronger.

It didn't matter. That Marine Alcazar was out there, and Richter was going to end this fight with him, even if it meant he'd leave the city feetfirst.

Behind them, tanks rumbled.

Chapter 43

Marines

"Trace, shift a squad to the west side of Route Meadowlark," Teo passed, along with an overlay. "We don't want any of the Mammoths flanking us and running up our line."

Teo had planned on getting through the town and engaging the crabs either inside or as they emerged from their camp. That was the reason he'd kicked off the attack on his terms. The crabs failed to cooperate, however, getting underway and rushing to meet the Marines inside Krabi-Town. His planned offensive assault had fizzled into a defense with the Marines digging in.

The crabs' platoons were heavier units than the Marines, relying on bulk and power while the Marines, like the crab flankers, relied on speed and ferocity of action. So, if the Marines didn't achieve surprise, then this might have been the next best thing. Confined MOUT operations tended to diminish the advantages of power, leveling the playing field.

Teo studied his order of battle. When the crab's lead element had engaged First Platoon, Teo had consolidated the company's position along Robin, which had been designated Phase Line Robin during their advance. Ratchadapisek Road, the local name for Robin, had been a major tourist thoroughfare, with nine blocks being closed off as a walking street, covered with tourist stalls and bordered by restaurants and bars. The stalls were long gone, and the open area made a natural kill zone, one Teo had covered by direct fire, indirect fire, his tanks, and deployable Switchblades. First Platoon was still in contact, holding the line so that the rest of the company could move into the defense.

Teo's advance had kicked off fighting all along the front, and for a moment, Teo had worried that the crabs would be called away, leaving Kilo facing ghosts. But even with their lead element stopped, Richter wasn't faltering. More and more of his troopers were advancing into the city. This wasn't going to end until one side or the other prevailed.

Teo was going to make sure it was the Marines.

A flurry of explosions rocked the area by the church, a couple of blocks beyond Robin. Two of First Platoon's avatars turned light blue.

"You holding up, Razor?"

"Getting hot, Skipper. I don't know how much longer we can hold."

"Wait one."

He checked the company's positions. Second wasn't ready.

"Sam, where are your alternate positions?" he passed.

"I haven't gotten to them yet. I'm trying to—"

"I don't care what you're trying to do! I told you primary and alternate positions, and now! We're in the shit, not setting up for an exercise back at Officer Basic School. If the crabs push forward, you have to have a place to displace to, or you'll lose control over the platoon. Think, Lieutenant!"

"Aye-aye, sir. I'll get right on it."

"You do that, Popovitch," Teo muttered after cutting the connection.

"Sir?" Sergeant Zuno asked.

"Nothing, just talking to myself."

Second Lieutenant Popovitch was proving to have potential, but he was still inexperienced. Teo knew he couldn't count on Staff Sergeant O'Neil, as good as he was, to take care of all the second lieutenant training. Teo had to keep his hand in as well. He had to command!

Which he wasn't going to be able to do back behind the lines with the rest of the Alpha Command. Except that he could. He could fight the battle from a thousand clicks away with his CCD. But he wasn't *in* the fight. He wasn't taking a personal risk.

The sound of the battle raised to a crescendo, and almost simultaneously, two more Marines, Lance Corporal Gabon and PFC Roberts, went gray.

"That's it, Razor. Pull back and fall into your positions," he ordered. *"Second and Third, start covering First."*

He'd barely gotten out the words when fire sprang up from the two platoons as eager Marines finally joined the fight they'd been listening to. The time for their hasty preparation was over.

First Platoon retreated in good order, one squad covering the other two in a bounding overwatch before switching up. Using the building interiors gave them additional cover and slowed the crabs, who might not have realized First Platoon was displacing until too late.

There was the distinctive sound of Switchblades deploying and the subsequent detonations. Another, deeper, but equally distinctive report of an SR-88 echoed down the streets. Teo smiled. If the crabs thought they could just run up First Platoon's asses without paying the price, well, he thought they knew now.

He had to get closer, where he could see with his own eyes what was happening.

"Sergeant Zuno, up! We're going forward," he told Rios' replacement as company supply sergeant.

Corporal Wainsett got to his feet as well, but Teo waved him down. He couldn't risk his comms chief.

"Stay here unless things get too hot."

"But, Skipper, I can face the crabs," he protested, his voice almost rising to a screech. "You need me!"

"I need you safe and communicating with Battalion."

"I'm not a coward, sir!"

"I know you're not. But I need you here," he said.

The disappointed corporal sat back down, but he was angry, Teo knew. But Wainsett, and Lance Corporal Tellu with the XO and the Bravo Command, might be the two most important Marines in the battle. They were the most capable link with higher headquarters.

Corporal Winchester stood up as Teo walked out the door, but he waved the team leader down as well. "You say here and keep Wainsett safe."

Teo, with Zuno on his ass, kept along the walls of the buildings as he rushed forward to the sound of battle. A round hit a building on the other side of the street and forward from where Teo was, collapsing what was left of a wall, but he didn't falter.

"Dookie, what's the status on our air?" Teo asked Captain Leo Morales, the Forward Air Controller.

"Still in process," "Dookie," passed, using his callsign like all the pilots did. *"We kinda left early, before the squadron had planned to be airborne."*

"They attacked, we left," Teo said, only slightly wincing at the lie. *"We need that air, and we need it now."*

"Roger that. I'm pushing it."

Why have a FAC if he can't get air?

"Over this way, and keep your head down. We can be spotted from here on out," he told Zuno, who just spit to the side, not looking concerned at all.

"Passing through your lines, Second Platoon," Teo said, not wanting to get shot by an amped Marine.

"There!" he told Zuno, pointing to a mostly intact three-story building just ahead. "That one. We've got a fire team on the ground floor."

He started the last dash, but Sergeant Zuno grabbed him by his dead-man's handle and pulled him back. The sergeant gave Teo a dirty look before he dashed ahead, weapon scanning for a target.

OK, point taken.

"Coming in!" Zuno shouted, kicking in the side door. A moment later, he stuck his head out and motioned for Teo.

Rounds hit high on the adjacent building as he crossed the street and darted inside the building. Four Marines glanced up at him before they turned back to their front.

The outside of the building looked better than the inside. Teo couldn't even tell what it was. Maybe a restaurant a long time ago.

The two Marines stumbled to the stairwell in the back.

"Jackson says they cleared the decks above us," Zuno said, and Teo waved a hand, giving him honors.

Corporal Jackson may have said he cleared it, but when one's life was at stake, it was a little different. Zuno and Teo covered each other as they climbed, ready for anything. Someone from above could just drop a grenade and wipe the two of them out.

But there was nobody, and the two made it to the top floor.

A large hole, about two meters across, highlighted the front wall, but the rest seemed intact, and whatever had made the hole didn't do too much damage inside the large, open office space. None of the windows still had plastiglass, and Teo crept low to one of the openings, then raised his head, opening the overlay over his display as he looked out. The last of the First Platoon Marines were crossing Robin and falling into position. The crabs, slowed down by Switchblades and booby traps, were not in sight.

But they were there, he knew.

Come on, you bastard, Richter. Just try and engage us. Beat yourself up. Have at us . . . and we will crush you.

Chapter 44

Paladins

Richter laid down fire through a window as a group of Alliance Marines darted across a side street. He was in a second-story classroom of which half the walls were gone, and he had line of sight to the mortar team and Szabo on the ground level.

"Fire mission, building two-two-seven, infantry in cover." Richter sidestepped as return fire snapped past his helmet and smacked against the window frame.

"Low on explosive shells," Nemec shouted from his mortar tube. He dropped a round inside, ducked as it launched, and dropped another one. Spiteri ripped open another four-pack of shells and threw the plastic tubes into a corner where a pile of packaging material had built up.

"Top, where's our resupply?" Richter asked into the company channel.

"Moving. Got a bottleneck on the main route into the city. Switchblade hit an ammo transport . . . unexploded ordnance all over the place . . . some of it's cooking off," Molenaar sent back. *"Sent ahead . . . could . . .—nd bye."* The transmission dissolved into static.

"Damn it," Richter said and dropped the ammo-count filter over his HUD. Most of his Cataphracts were down to their last internal magazine. All his flankers were getting dangerously low on rounds as well.

His company had held the line for what felt like days but were only mere hours by the mission clock. The attack deeper into the city hadn't materialized as the companies on his flanks had yet to advance to their assault positions. They were still moving through the surrounding jungle, but at a snail's pace. The squadron's plan was to attack with his troop at the fore, with the rest of the squadron ready to exploit any gaps in the enemy lines that his reconnaissance by fire discovered. His Paladins would have to advance carefully, or they'd be overextended and exposed.

"Comms, get me squadron." Richter took a quick look through a different window as Nemec's shells landed on and around the target building. One exploded in the street with little effect, but the other pierced the roof and blew out the second story. Walls crumbled inwards and Richter fired on Marines as they escaped.

"Shit!" Spiteri swung his carbine up to the rear as a shadow emerged behind them. Winnie came trotting around a corner, his frame loaded down with magazines and supply cases in each hand.

The upper edge of the robot's head was chipped from a bullet strike.

"Unit arrived at designated location," Winnie said, stopping a few yards from the mortar tube. Everything it carried fell to the ground in a jumble.

"Winnie," Richter said, double-checking his ammo reserves compared to the rest of the company, "eight millimeter, drum." He held out a hand and the robot tossed it to him. "Winnie, deliver eight-millimeter ammo to Blue Platoon."

"Confirmed." The robot attached a half-dozen boxes back onto its frame and took off at a trot. A sniper bullet hit its shoulder, upsetting its gait but not slowing the robot down.

"Got twenty carbine mags at my location," Richter said into the company net and locked his fresh magazine to his lower back plate. "Send runners."

"For fuck's sake," Spiteri said, ripping open a newly delivered mortar package, "they sent us dazzler shells. We need explosives."

"Bet you won't bitch about them if more Switchblades show up." Nemec slapped a wrench on the nose cone of the new rounds to set the fuzes.

"Got a relay, go for squadron!" Szabo called out.

"Wolfpack X-Ray, this is Paladin Actual. We're amber on munitions trending black, request emergency resupply, over," he said.

"Paladin," Colonel Toman came on the line, *"that's going to be a negative for a drone drop. Enemy has too many EMP assets in place and I can't afford to lose that asset."*

"Contact! Enemy tank on sensors!" Lieutenant Briem shouted and his warning was repeated up and down the line of Richter's company. "At least . . . I think. Definite electric motor detection."

"I don't have the combat power to advance nor can I hold this position without resupply," Richter growled. "Permission to . . . fall back to rally point delta."

"Wait one," the colonel said.

"Which route's the tank coming from?" Richter asked over the company net. He could hear the engine's echo off the buildings, but it was too discordant to pin down. No answer. "Cataphracts, ready your shoulder rockets. Platoon leaders have release authority for flanker anti-armor teams."

Richter felt gravel in his stomach giving that order. The flankers were vulnerable enough in an urban environment, but sending out kill teams armed with shaped-charge grenades to try for a hit on the Alliance Badgers came with a great deal of risk. His men would almost certainly die if enemy Marines were in close support of their tanks.

"Think they're coming down white-one," Frakes said over the IR. "Anti-

armor weapons set." A grainy video feed appeared on Richter's HUD of a road. Alliance screen grenades went off, sending up a cloud of jaundice-colored smoke.

"Action front, action front!" Szabo called out. More smoke grenades went off on the road leading straight to the school.

"Hold fire," Richter ordered as more reports of smoke came in. "They're . . . they're trying to confuse us on which avenue the attack's coming from."

"Guess it's working!" Nemec shrugged, a mortar round in each hand.

"Blue-two," Briem announced and the HUD video snapped to a different road. Through the smoke screen, a low shadow emerged. A commercial forklift with some sort of speaker jury-rigged on the side rolled through and bounced off a curb.

"What the hell?" Richter asked, his brow scrunched in confusion.

There was a sharp crack and a muffled explosion from Briem's position.

Another crack and another explosion from where Frakes had bunkered down.

"Lost Rebane," Briem sent. *"Sniper hit his 99. Blast took his fucking head and shoulders clean off."*

"They suckered our anti-armor weapons out into the open." Richter punched the wall then paused. He could still hear armor road wheels and tracks. "Szabo, tell squadron we're falling back to—"

A tank shell hit the ground floor of the school, and the floor collapsed beneath Richter. He hit the ground hard as bricks pelted him, his armor taking most of the damage as he choked on fine dust. He still had his cycler in hand, but in the darkness of the rubble, he wasn't even sure which way he was facing.

Shouts and heavy machine-gun fire pounded through the rubble.

"Szabo . . . anybody . . ." He coughed and shifted against the grip the destroyed city had on him. He felt the rumble of an approaching tank, and the thought of being crushed beneath the wheels forced him to struggle harder. He pushed down with his gun arm, the servos catching with the strain. He lifted up, and broken bricks slid off his back as a wave of dust fell down his visor.

Richter pulled a hand free and wiped his optics clear. His troop was falling back, the Cataphracts laying down fire as the flankers ran south.

His earpieces clicked back to life, and he heard the pop of tank wheels crushing broken bricks and masonry. Richter got a knee up and shook his cycler clear of dust as he craned his neck around.

A Badger tank was a dozen yards away, the turret pointed at Briem's position. The main gun fired, and the bleachers on one side of the soccer field exploded, aluminum stands fluttering through the air like feathers from a dove hit by a shotgun.

"Major!" he heard from behind as the turret turned toward him. He struggled to get his other leg free, but it was pinched by two wall sections.

"Not today, fuckers!" Nemec ran past him, an anti-armor grenade in hand. He hurled it forward and pitched to the ground, his legs tucked in, his arms covering his head.

The grenade went off a few feet from the tank, and a lance of molten copper cut into the forward armor and the driver's compartment. The Alliance tank came to a sudden halt, a line of dancing flames around a gash where the grenade had struck. Smoke rose out of the seams around the top hatch.

"Ha!" Nemec clapped dust off his hands. "Take that, you pattie mother—"

Machine-gun fire erupted from the turret and Nemec jerked with the impacts as bullets punched through his flak armor and sprang against the rubble next to Richter. Nemec fell on his face, his feet twitching.

The machine gun fired again, a long burst that cut through the air next to Richter, tracers ricocheting off the ground and soaring up. The burst was long and uncontrolled as more smoke billowed out of the turret.

Richter realized the gunner must've died at the trigger; his last act was to take Nemec with him.

The major wrenched his leg free and turned around. Szabo and Spiteri manned the mortar. Spiteri had the tube almost perpendicular, feeding shells into the weapon as fast as he could and not bothering to level the bubbles between each shot.

"Sir!" Szabo waved at him. "Squadron approved our—"

"Just get moving!" Richter lurched forward, the servos on one jack leg damaged and offsetting his stride.

"Tank!" Spiteri glanced over his shoulder and dropped another shell. "Almost rounds complete!"

Richter fired his cycler at a group of Marines charging out of a building. Another Badger came around a corner just as one of Spiteri's rounds went off. Red smoke billowed around the tank and more smoke rounds fired overhead, sending a bloody-colored cloud floating down.

"Last one!" Spiteri raised a shell, and a sniper round hit him in the armpit. The bullet exited under his neck and he grabbed the top of the mortar tube as his balance failed. He dropped the shell in and fell backwards, dragging the tube down with him. The shell ripped fingers off and slapped his head to one side before it hit somewhere in the red haze.

He fell to the ground, dead.

"Medic!" Szabo shoved the tube to one side. "Medic!"

"He's gone," Richter said, grabbing Szabo by the carry strap and pulling him away from the trooper. The smoke fell around them, turning the city into a hellscape of red sky and burning buildings.

Richter hobbled forward, his bad leg servos getting even worse.

Rifle fire broke out, stitching a line of craters across the road in front of them. Szabo pushed Richter ahead and laid down covering fire. A grenade bounced down the road and burst into a fireball, the blast wave sending Richter tumbling into the remnants of a play park.

Bullets hit the ballistics plate on his left arm, and a round struck his helmet, the impact denting the metal and carrying into his skull.

Richter collapsed, his world swimming.

Up. Up, you bastard. Your men need you. He wasn't sure where the words came from, but he recognized his own voice.

Cycler fire carried through the ringing in his ears and Cataphract sabatons passed through his field of vision. He flipped over to see the bloody sky and he felt his heels dragging against the street.

Winnie was there, the light on his cranial unit lit up in a smiley face.

"Casualty evacuation underway," the robot said.

Richter struggled, but his jack had powered off to keep him from lashing out in his wounded state.

"Comms," Richter groaned. "Get Szabo. Someone get Szabo!"

Chapter 45

Marines

Teo covered his head with his arms as the explosion rocked him. Dust filled the air, and his IFU's PCL whined as it put more power to his filters. He looked around—the office in which he'd taken cover was now open to the air, half of the ceiling and the entire east wall were gone. He didn't even know what kind of weapon had done that.

Random round or targeting me?

"You OK, Zuno?" Teo asked.

He didn't need to—Sergeant Zuno's avatar was a steady blue, but sometimes it was just good to make that connection. He wasn't hurt enough for his bios to alert to injury, but they showed that his pulse was 126, and his adrenaline was spiking.

His police sergeant raised a shaking thumb up in the air.

Zuno's avatar might be blue, but there were too many gray and light-blue avatars. Twenty-one KIA so far, and another nine WIA. The blood price for this attack was high, and would only get higher.

And all because I initiated this goat-rope.

He knew that wasn't true. The fighting would have broken out anyway, and this way, he'd been able to get Kilo Company positioned in the city, making the crabs come to him. At least, that was what he told himself.

He edged over to where the wall was gone and peered out over the city. Firing echoed between the buildings, or what was left of them. The battle had broken down into a series of small skirmishes, fire team against fire team, as Marines and Hegemony troops met amidst the rubble.

Gunny Walters' idea of rigging an old forklift with a speaker and letting it drive into the crabs had been genius. Sounding something like a Badger, it had caused the crabs anti-armor troopers to react, making one of them an easy target for Yelsik. He'd hit the crab's missile, which resulted in a most satisfying explosion.

Teo turned to where Yelsik and Juarez had situated themselves above the main market, but there was nothing to see. He didn't know how effective Yelsik was going to be with the fight breaking down into small, personal fights, but hopefully, he could keep picking off as many crabs as he could.

Two blocks away, four Marines dashed across the road, disappearing into the next building. Teo automatically checked: Corporal Tanny's fire team from First Platoon's Second Squad.

The platoon had a line inclusive of the town square and over to the Ayutthayan Credit Union, and they'd taken some heavy crab pressure, but they'd held firm. Teo wasn't sure why Tanny would be displacing and moving, but he wasn't going to get that far down in the weeds and question Lieutenant Fuentes.

"Skipper, I think we've got an R/O," Lieutenant Popovitch passed on the P2P.

A crab radio operator? That could be good, real good.

"Prisoner or dead?" Teo asked as he pulled up his Second Platoon commander's position. Building 2016, just three blocks away.

"Prisoner, but I don't know for how long. He looks bad."

"Where's Doc Sukiyama?"

"Doc Suki's with James, trying to stabilize him."

"Hold on. I'm sending over Doc Sanaa, and I'm on my way."

Let's go, Zuno!" Teo said as he dashed for the stairs.

An R/O was a big catch, if it was true, and Teo needed to find out. He ordered Doc Sanaa, as his senior and most experienced corpsman, to meet him at the building, then with Zuno on his ass, they ran to meet up with Popovitch, taking as much cover as they could. Rounds stitched the top of a wall just above his head as he darted across the second street, but there was no follow-up.

Building 2016 might have been a shop once, but there wasn't much left of it. Popovitch and Sergeant Orion were standing over a face-down crab, with Corporal Ndebele's team providing security. In his jack, he looked like a lobster tail, jointed armor pads covering his body within the jack frame.

"You sure he's an R/O" Teo asked as he approached.

"He's got the module," Popovitch said, pointing at the small attachment on the top of the crab's helmet and the cable leading to a slight hump on the back of the jack.

Teo couldn't see much of the crab, but it was obvious that he was in bad shape. His jack was dented and ripped, and blood seeped out around the armor pads to pool on the rubble-strewn floor. One leg was twisted in a way it wasn't ever meant to be, and he wasn't moving.

"Wainsett, we've got what we think is an R/O here. If he's down, what does that do to the crabs' overall comms?" he passed.

"Decreases the effectiveness. The crabs' company-level comms suite has much better encryption and counter-jamming, so it will be a blow, but all of their nets will automatically shift to other transmitters."

Which was about what Teo expected. The same thing happened with his own company comms. This R/O was a blow, but not a game-ender.

But . . . what the R/O knew could be very valuable to him.

"Let's get him out of there," Teo said.

367

"Uh, sir? How do I do that?" Popovitch asked, looking at the crab.

"Hell, what did they teach you at OBS?" Teo asked, leaning over the crab and pulling on the emergency release on the back of the armor.

The helmet popped free, and the armor unfolded off the motionless body.

"Is he already dead?" Sergeant Orion asked.

"Let's just get him out. Gently."

The body inside the armor looked even worse than Teo had imagined. He slid an arm under the left shoulder of the crab, and with Popovitch on the right, they both lifted . . . and the crab came to and screamed out in pain.

"His leg, Skipper!" Orion said.

Teo looked down at the twisted leg, which now looked to be separating from the rest of the crab, who was whimpering, eyes closed.

"Shit. Sorry," Teo said automatically. "Orion, when we lift again, you take his leg. OK, on three." Teo positioned his arms again. "One . . . two . . . three!"

They pulled the crab free, and again he screamed out before they could lay him on the ground, face up.

Popovitch went white. Teo blanched a little himself. This crab was in bad, bad shape. Besides the leg, his left hand . . . well, is wasn't a hand anymore. Half of his chest was crushed, and there seemed to be a part missing from the side of his head. Teo didn't know how much Doc Sanaa could do.

To his surprise, the crab suddenly opened his eyes and stared at him.

"Major, I've lost our nets..." Szabo trailed off.

"It's either head trauma or shock," Teo said to Popovitch.

The crab gave a vacant smile, just as Lance Corporal Adonis' avatar

368

grayed out.

Damn it! He looked out the opening in the building, wanting to get back to where he could observe what was going on. But still, this crab could be worth the effort. He didn't need everyone here, though. Zuno was enough.

"I've got this, Sam. You go fight your platoon," he told the lieutenant.

"Roger that, Skipper," Popovitch said, motioning to his Marines to follow him out.

The crab's eyes narrowed at hearing Popovitch, his eyes came into focus, and he asked, "Are you the pattie commander, sir?"

Popovitch had just screwed up with a security breach, and Teo shouldn't say anything, but this crab wasn't going to be around long.

"Yeah. Captain Alcazar."

The crab gave him a long look, then said, "My major's going to kill you."

Teo's anger didn't even stir. He gave a slight smile and asked, "What's your name, son?'

The crab's eyebrows scrunched together, barely noticeable in the blood, but evidently, he understood just as well as Teo did that it didn't matter. "Szabo. Essach-born."

"Well, Szabo, I'll tell you this. Your Major Richter may very well want to kill me, but that's easier said than done."

"He will, you know. Sir," he added almost as an afterthought. "And when he—"

Whatever else he was going to say erupted into a fit of coughing, blood splattering Teo, covering his helmet's faceshield, before he collapsed into unconsciousness.

Teo wiped it off just as Doc Sanaa entered the ruined building.

"Can you at least stabilize him?" Teo asked. "He's an Intel's wet dream."

The doc leaned over the crab—Szabo—Teo told himself, not just a crab. The doc leaned over Szabo and ran the triagescan over him.

He took a moment to read the display, then turned to Teo. "He shouldn't be alive now. I just don't think his brain knows he's already dead."

"Major!" Szabo yelled out, arching his back, his right arm grasping at the air.

"It's OK, son, I'm here," Teo said, grabbing the flailing hand and holding it tight.

Szabo squeezed hard for a few seconds before his body relaxed. He gave a small smile, his eyes unfocused, and let out a large breath of air. He didn't breathe in again.

"Well, shit. Intel would have loved to get their hands on him," he said, letting go of the hand.

He started to leave when a thought hit him.

"Hey, Doc, can a retinal scan work after the person dies?"

"You mean like him, sir?"

"Yeah."

"Well, after ischemia—"

"In Standard, please!"

"Oh, yeah. Sure, sir. After blood is cut off from the eye, the cornea's OK, but the retinas deteriorate quickly."

"How quickly?"

"Something on the order of fifty percent dead in thirty minutes."

"So, a scan now should still work?" Teo asked.

"I don't see why not. I mean, I'm not an expert on scanning, though, sir. If the scan is triggering a retinal reaction, then sure. Heck, if it works like a fingerprint, I'd say you can probably go, I don't know, maybe in the day's timeframe—"

Teo cut him off. "But it should work now?"

"Sure. I think."

"*Corporal Wainsett, do you know how to work a crab comms suite?*" he asked over the net.

"*Is the R/O cooperating? His comms suite needs a retinal scan.*"

"*He's dead, but I think we can get past that.*"

There was silence, then, "*It's pretty easy. At least, that's what they taught us in Comms School. There're two interfaces. One is optical, but you would have needed the R/O for that. The other is the back-up, a manual control in case the crabs aren't in their helmets.*"

Teo looked over the dead crab. There was a small pouch on his hip, thankfully still looking in one piece. He pulled it out. There was a tracker, a display, and a scanner.

"*And how do I connect with this thing?*"

"*I . . . I don't remember that, sir.*"

Teo took a closer look. There wasn't much to it, which could be a good thing. It might be intuitive.

First things first, however.

"Sorry about this, Szabo," he said, taking hold of the crab's beard and pulling him up.

"Now, open his right eye," he told Doc.

Doc Sanaa raised his eyebrows, but he didn't say anything. He reached around the ruined left eye and pulled open the eyelid.

Teo didn't know if there was any procedure, so he just pointed the scan lens and held it in front of the crab's eye. A moment later, there was a beep, and the control lit up. Teo lowered Szabo back down and looked at the display.

"It worked," he muttered.

The control was more than intuitive. On the right side of the display, there was a list of contacts, and the third from the top said "Commander." Teo touched the word to see what would happen.

Within two seconds, a familiar voice came out of the control. *"Szabo? Status report. Where the hell are you?"*

Anger started to build again, embracing him like an old friend. It took an effort of will not to let it take over him.

"Szabo is dead, Major Richter," he said.

There was a pause, then *"Alcazar."*

"Yeah. Alcazar."

"What've you done to him?"

Teo laughed, but there was no humor in it. *"Actually, I tried to save his life. Had my senior corpsman try. Not like what you did with Sergeant Gauta. You remember him?"*

"Yeah. I remember that one. Died like a dog."

"Un-fucking-real, Richter. Un-fucking real. Shows the difference between the Alliance and the Heg. We follow the Freesome Accords, and we medically treat our prisoners. We don't execute them."

"You assholes are real saints, aren't you? Know how many carved-up Hegemony bodies I've recovered after a battle?"

Teo knew Richter was right, but he wasn't going to cede the point. Not every Alliance commander kept as strict a hand on their Marines as he did.

"Did he suffer?" Richter asked, his voice suddenly more subdued. *"Szabo was just a kid."*

"We did what we could."

"Haven't found any of yours still breathing. Keep looking in the ruins. Plenty of Marines getting cold in the rubble. That why you got on my net? Need help with clean-

up?"

"Just to pass you a message. I started this little dust-up for one reason, and one reason only. And that's to kill you. I'm coming to finish off what I started at the Red Cross meeting."

There was a wild laugh on the other side of the connection. "Won't go the same way, pattie. I didn't think even a savage like you would break a Union truce line. That second time wasn't a charm. Third won't go any better for you."

What?

"The second time? I'd never met you before that meeting."

"Oh, yes we did. In Rawai. After your tank was destroyed."

Teo's mind raced. He'd killed that one crab, Cengic, then . . .

"That was you?"

"Sure was. I recognized your toy knife with the knock-off handle."

Anger surged again.

This asshole got away from me twice?

"My men are from Syddan, and they've got their ways. You're a vaettir, the unmourned dead that howls in the forest," Richter said.

"But, the thing is, I'm not dead."

"Oh, yes, you are. You just don't know it," Richter said with surety of conviction.

Something tickled the back of his mind.

Why does he sound so damned sure of himself?

He pulled up his battle display, but nothing was popping up to show he was personally in any specific and direct danger.

"So, Alcazar, I do have to thank you for using Szabo's radio transmitter," Richter said. The line stayed open, and Teo heard muffled sounds in the background, then a Hegemony-accented voice say four words.

"Impact in ten, over."

What's he doing? It's like he's trying to—

"Out! Now!" he shouted at Doc and Zuno, throwing the comms remote side and rushing outside.

Seven seconds later, the building exploded as crab mortar shells landed. Szabo's comm system broadcast had provided the target.

Chapter 46

Paladins

Richter took his hand down from the side of his helmet as the last of the mortar section's shells launched.

"Rounds complete," said a flanker, making an X with his forearms at Richter.

The major nodded and sank against a wall.

Szabo was gone. Another letter to write. Another face to haunt his dreams.

He smashed a fist against a crumbling brick.

That Marine was still out there, he could feel it. A couple mortar rounds wouldn't be enough to finish him off. He'd proven too lucky and too capable to die from a simple mistake like a traceable radio signal.

How? How had he lost Szabo out there? He was responsible for the life of that man . . . for all the men under his command.

Richter looked up at the battered and bloody troopers around him. They were quiet as they cleaned weapons, loaded full magazines into their armor, or did what they could to rest. He felt the same battle-frayed nerves, the constant "on" of fight or flight that war demanded.

His Paladins were close to breaking, and the attack into the city had been more of a fight than he'd anticipated. He opened a comms menu and highlighted Colonel Toman. If he sent up a report with enough details on casualties and their dwindling supplies, the squadron would likely pull them off the bleeding edge of battle for a fresher unit.

One call and all of this would end . . . and Alcazar would still live. Fragments of death letters played through his mind. Glimpses of faces of the dead and gone. Memories of ashen faces moments before they were enclosed into body bags, never to be seen again.

Alcazar was responsible for too many of those lost. There was blood between them, and Richter wasn't ready to let that debt go.

"I'll find you," Richter said to no one. "I'll find you, and I'll end this once and for all."

Chapter 47

Marines

"I think they're consolidating at the middle school," Trace Okanjo passed.

Teo studied his CCD. It made sense. Kilo had blunted the crab assault, making them pay. And if they were trying to consolidate, now was the time to hit them, and hit them hard, before they could get situated or reinforcements could arrive.

The tiniest flicker of concern ticked the back of his mind. What if this was a feint, an attempt to lure Kilo into a kill zone.

What was it that quote Gauta liked to repeat? "He who will not risk, cannot win." I'm going for it.

"Trace, get your platoon ready. You're the assault element, and we're going to crush them, once and for all. I'll send you the orders in five."

"Ooh-rah, Skipper! We're ready!" he said, his excitement palpable.

Teo wanted to remind him that this wasn't a game, that he needed a calm mind, but he didn't. He understood the young lieutenant—he was feeling much the same. He just hoped that Okanjo would not try to be the hero, looking for his moment of glory that would follow him throughout this career.

You're one to speak. You've got your POA, and you're still itching to fight, he admonished himself.

With quick, broad strokes, he drew his frag order. Third, which had taken the fewest casualties, was going to assault through the school. Second was the support element, setting up a base of fire, while First was the security element, to hold off any crab reaction. Weapons, with twelve HE and three EMP rounds remaining, was going to lay them on the school, then displace forward as infantry. One of the three remaining tanks would join Second and support the assault.

"Dookie? Where's the air?"

"Forty minutes," the FAC answered.

Teo had given up on the air. He had what he had, and that was going to have to do.

The frag wasn't pretty. It wasn't sophisticated, but it would do. He sent the order forward to the lieutenants, the first sergeant, and the gunny.

"Let's move up," he told Zuno.

The sergeant had taken a shard of something that had pierced his POL and upper arm, and the blood was dripping inside, reappearing on his fingers. He said he was fine, and his bios reflected that. Modern nanos were a miracle.

"Shit, Yelsik!" he said as he remembered his Scout/Sniper team.

With the company moving forward, Yelsik wouldn't be able to help. He sent the frag to him and told the sniper team to advance to where they could be effective. Not that there were many good spots. More and more of the higher buildings were down, and Yelsik needed long, clear fields of fire if he was going to contribute.

Teo and Zuno continued to push forward, dodging from one side of the alley to the other, making best use of the cover. It was almost surreal, just the two of them, where just a few blocks away, there could be any number of crabs. Two different universes.

His CCD display gave out the warning beep, and the figures froze.

Not now!

The comms had been surprisingly good, and they'd allowed Teo to react to the crab advance and block it. He blinked the reset, but nothing had changed.

"Razor, do you read me?" he asked on the P2P.

"Affirmative."

"The battle link's down, but at least we've got the QCs. What's your status?"

"Moving into position now. Taking light fire."

"Roger that. I'm three blocks behind you, coming up the alley between Bluebird and Nuthatch."

"Do I need to wait for you?" he asked uncertainly.

"Negative. As soon as Harris lays his rounds, that's your go."

Teo looked at his timer. Just over eleven-and-a-half minutes.

"What about the Badger? I don't have comms with him."

"He's pulling up now."

"Roger that." He paused for a moment. *"Razor, we need this, but don't waste your men. If it's too untenable, pull back, and we'll figure something else out."*

"Third's got it, Skipper. We can handle it."

Which shows me you're missing the point.

He let it go and checked with the other commanders. They were slotting into position.

Teo was not feeling a warm and fuzzy, though. Without his CCD working, he felt blind, and Okanjo's last comment was weighing on him.

"Come on, Zuno. I need to get closer. Double-time."

The two took off together, running down the alley, not pausing as they hit the next cross-street, darting to the other side.

Teo's CCD flickered, giving him a brief update, and a big surge of hope, before it froze again. The crabs had been employing their EMP bursts during the fight, but Teo didn't know if that was the cause. He only cared that his most valuable tool as a commander was on the fritz again.

As they ran down to the next crossroad, a burst of fire from a building they were passing cut Zuno down, sending him face-first onto the ground. Teo juked to the side and spun around just as a jacked crab emerged from a loading bay, his right leg frame twisted and damaged. His cycler wasn't damaged, though, and he swung it to Teo, rounds spewing like water from a hose. Teo dived to the ground and stitched the crab with his 51, but it didn't bring the crab down. The trooper stumbled, lowering his cycler as he tried to step forward, but something in his frame was twisted, and it was more of a lurch.

Wishing he still had his VW-9, which he'd lost in Rawai, he abandoned his 51 and drew his Wilder. The heavy, jacketed slug didn't have the penetrating power of his old anti-piracy crossbow, but it was enough. Teo double-tapped, and the rounds easily penetrated the applique armor just as the crab was bringing his cycler to bear again. The trooper fell first to his knees, then toppled face-down on the alleyway, bright crimson blood quickly starting to spread out beneath him.

"Zuno!" he yelled, turning back to his police sergeant.

Zuno was struggling to sit up, and Teo grabbed him by the shoulders to steady him. With his CCD down, he didn't know how badly the sergeant was hurt.

"That sure smarts," Zuno said.

"Are you OK?"

"Feels like I got kicked by a mule. But I guess my POL held."

Not completely. There was a hole down low, above Zuno's hip. Teo reached for it, probing, and he felt warm wetness. His hand came away covered in blood.

The Marine's armor could withstand one or maybe two rounds from a cycler, the POL firming up as the rounds hit. But there was a rebound effect, and as the STF armor "relaxed," even a smaller-caliber round could penetrate.

"You're hit."

Zuno looked down, ran a finger over the hole, then said, "Shit. I guess you're right, sir."

"You take a seat. I'll send back one of the corpsmen."

Zuno stood, then poked at the hole again. "I can keep going. It still hurts like a motherfucker, but I don't think anything important is messed up. And the nanos are kicking in."

Teo looked at the sergeant with concern. A cycler round was a big one, 8 mm, and there was no exit wound. That thing was still inside him, and it probably tore up his guts bouncing around in there. Zuno could very well be mortally wounded, for all he knew.

But Teo had to get up to the assault, and he didn't know if moving him would do any more harm. It was only a block-and-a-half.

"OK, if you can keep up, let's go."

Teo slowed down, but they were still able to reach Third Platoon and Corporal Nyoki before Weapons Platoon's incoming RYN rockets. Teo asked where the lieutenant was, and Private Fausten led the two to where Okanjo was in the rubble of a building with Corporal Adoud. Adoud might have been busted for the hooker escapade, but he was still the best Marine to run his squad.

Teo wanted to know what Okanjo had planned, and the lieutenant had more to do than satisfy him, but he couldn't hold back.

"How're you approaching them?" he asked, looking across the school parking lot then ducking back down when a crab decided to take a shot at him.

"My best bet is to circle to the side, then advance under the barrage. That's the shortest distance to the building, and there're fewer windows on that side."

Teo scooted over to the side then popped up again, snapping a shot with his CCD, ducking back an instant before the crab could shift his aim and fire again.

Thank God the camera on this thing still works.

He pulled up the image. There were two buildings, one up front, another a hundred meters or so behind it.

Two schools? Primary and middle?

There had already been one fight at a primary school, where they'd lost two of the Badgers, but a city this size had to have more than one of them.

They were in front of the first school with maybe thirty meters of parking between them. Two destroyed vehicles were there and the shattered trunks of two trees, but nothing else. A natural kill zone. To the right was the main parking lot, and behind was the playground and sports fields. To the left, where Okanjo wanted to advance, was a line of shops, then the street and a sidewalk before reaching the side of the school building.

It was the right decision, but . . .

"That's a little close to Sam's supporting fire, isn't it?"

"I sent a runner to let him know. I trust them not to shoot us in the ass."

Teo frowned, but unless he moved Second Platoon, he didn't know what could be a better choice. And with the scheduled rocket bombardment, there wasn't time for that.

He checked the time. Four minutes, twenty-three seconds.

"You better start getting into position. The barrage is only going to last thirty seconds.

Enough time to cross the road, but not enough if Third isn't ready.

Okanjo checked the time, then scurried back to where he could stand, and shouted, "Move out, now!"

The platoon sprang into action, using the buildings for cover as they sprinted around the block. Teo switched his 51 to grenade mode and edged up to the remaining wall. There was nothing to say he couldn't provide a little covering fire himself.

"Hey, Sergeant Zuno, come up . . . oh, fuck! I didn't get Doc Moss to take a look at you!"

"No problem, Skip. I'm still kicking. Doc can check me out after they've kicked some ass."

More blood had seeped out, and his POL's active camo was having issues with the dark red stain. But he seemed alert, and his nanos would be working full-time to stabilize him.

"Well, then, get your ass up here and provide some supporting fire."

Zuno joined him. Teo pulled the sergeant close and looked through his visor. He was a little pale, but he was breathing smoothly. Zuno winked at him.

"You tough bastard. Let's kill us some crabs."

"Ooh-rah, sir."

Firing sounded in the distance, then an explosion. Teo wondered who that was. Almost all of Kilo was right there in the heart of the city. Razor and First wouldn't have gone off that far.

He didn't have time for that now, however. In forty seconds, the EMP rounds would hit, then the HE.

"This shit's about to get real, Zuno."

Zuno laughed, then broke into coughing. "I think it already got real for me, Skipper."

The EMP warheads would knock out his comms, except for the QC repeaters, which worked on the strange magic that was quantum mechanics. But it should also knock out the damned Bennies, and since he didn't have comms anyway, there was no real loss, only gain.

And there they were. Blue light flashed that seemed to burn into his bones, his hair standing on end. His helmet was shielded, as was his powerpack, so he still had the basics, but everything else was fried. Not just his, but for Third Platoon as well.

The next rockets whistled in, singing of the death they were dealing. The first four hit the center of the school, penetrating what was left of the roof and detonating. Teo jumped up, leveled his 51 on the top of the rubble, and fired three grenades, all linked to delayed detonation. Two of the three punched through the wall—one detonated on the outside, causing minimal damage.

The tank with Second opened up, the first round hitting close to where Teo had hit. The brick wall might as well have been plastisheet for all it did to the 90mm shell. Bricks tumbled outward as the round wreaked havoc inside.

Immediately, the crabs started firing back, but haphazardly, and with a battle cry, Third Platoon rose up and started to flood across the street . . . until something exploded under the road, and five Marines were shredded into pieces.

What the . . .

The EMPs should have knocked out the Bennies. Did they rig up some sort of pressure plate?

The remaining Marines dove for whatever cover they could find as a barrage of fire, not the haphazard fire of before, pouted out of the windows and openings, raking them even as the last of Weapons' rockets hit.

"Trace, get your Marines back. I'm bringing up the tank," he passed.

"I've got it," Okanjo shouted into his mic. *"I'm going in!"*

"Stop! That's an order!"

Okanjo stood, turned to his men, and screamed, "For the glory!" before turning back and rushing forward into the fusillade.

"Trace!"

He made three steps, screaming his war cry, when a missile shot out of the school. It probably was too close to arm, but it didn't matter. It hit Okanjo in the chest, cutting him in two.

First Lieutenant Trace Okanjo, OBS Honor grad, general's son, and golden boy, was dead, cut down in the street.

Teo stood and started forward, shouting for the Marines in Third Platoon to pull back, but too many had followed their lieutenant, and more were falling.

A round hit Teo in the chin of his helmet, breaking it free of his POL collar, and smashing it into his face. He stumbled to the ground, blood splashing the inside of the visor. Dazed, he flipped the visor up and screamed at the Marines, whose charge had faltered, to take cover.

"Sam, get that tank and your platoon forward," he passed.

Nothing.

"Sam, do you read me?"

Nothing.

"Fuck!" he screamed, blood and spit flying.

Whatever had hit his helmet had knocked out his QC. Hands grabbed him, and he let himself be pulled down and into cover.

"Shit, sir, you trying to get yourself killed too?" Zuno asked him.

"I've got to get to Second," Teo said, standing on unsteady legs that gave out on him.

"I'll go. What should I tell him?"

"You're more messed up than I am. I'm OK, just a little dazed."

He wiped the blood from his face, wincing as his hand brushed his broken nose, and stood up at a crouch.

The tank blasted again, this time sounding closer. Teo looked around as more of the side of the school disappeared. The incoming fire slackened slightly.

A loud, undulating war cry of more than thirty Marines echoed within the buildings, immediately joined by the Third Platoon Marines still alive.

The incoming fire faltered more as the tank rolled into view. It fired just as the missile reached out, clanging on the top of the turret before ricocheting off into the air.

Too close to arm, stupid shit!

Beside the tank, Sam Popovitch, the boot lieutenant, was running, shouting out orders. The wall of fire—the tank's 90mm main gun and 20mm coax, along with everything Second Platoon could muster, withered the crab defense.

Teo tottered out to join, but Popovitch didn't need his help. His Marines swept up what was left of Third as he led, in the truest sense of the word, the attack. Within seconds, Marines had reached the wall of the school and were tossing in grenades, firing their weapons.

Popovitch was directing the battle like a maestro, but his Marines knew what they were doing. In fire teams, they entered, and Teo could hear the fighting.

He shook his head to clear it, then said, "Hell, Zuno, we're not doing any good out here. Let's go join Second Platoon."

There was no answer, so he turned to repeat himself louder to be heard over the din of battle, but Zuno was beyond hearing. He'd managed to take off his helmet and was sitting with it in his lap, his eyes vacant, a smile on his face. He hadn't been hit again—the round in his belly had taken its time, but it had been a mortal wound after all.

"Ah, shit, Zuno," Teo said quietly.

With a sigh, he left his police sergeant and ran across the street and into the school.

Chapter 48

Paladins

Richter looked down at his hands, one bare and seeping blood from lacerations, the other clad with his jack frame, the knuckles twitching slightly. He was aware of Ceban working on one knee servo, the man's face hidden behind a welding shield.

The world was muted. The shock of losing Szabo and so many of his men was somehow outside himself, that press of emotion held back by the physical pain and the burning core of hatred in his heart.

The hate kept him warm, kept everything he didn't need away from his mind.

"Sir?" Iliev asked, the question orbiting Richter's consciousness as he kept studying his hands. "Sir, I shouldn't do this, but I'm giving you another hit of hydro-ceph."

He felt a press against his neck and the world snapped back into focus.

"Doc?" Richter felt a pinch in his sinuses like an ice-cream headache was forming. He was in the back of an Ontos transport. What was left of his company milled around logistics points as they resupplied ammo and got a few bites of hot food.

"Hey, you're back, sir." Iliev held up Richter's helmet and touched a deep dent on the forehead. "Lowest bidder came through on the quality-control check. But I think this gear's compromised. That right, Ceban?"

"It's fine. Don't get shot in the head again." The armorer lifted his face shield and rapped the back of his welding torch against Richter's knee servo. "Got a new unit in there. Go walk around so your jack can recalibrate."

Richter grunted and shuffled out of the Ontos. He shook the new knee joint out and limped over to an ammo supply point where Lieutenant Briem stood with his helmet in his hands, staring down at a holo projection within.

"What's the butcher's bill?" Richter raised his arms out to a T pose and a pair of Winnie robots loaded his jack with fresh magazines and battery packs.

"Easier to say who's left than who we lost." Briem frowned. "I've got the company reorganized in seven squads. Frakes is getting an ouchy boo taken care of. Docs are pretty sure it's just a flesh wound, but they're pumping him full of all the good pain killers and anti-infection meds."

"Squadron?" Richter cycled a line of rounds out from the back of his jack and into his cycler. The pads against his body hummed with energy as the power cells charged to full.

"Every swinging dick that can get online gets online." Briem shrugged and put on his helmet. "Division's ordered another push. Toman's just passing on the order. Looks like we're getting some fly-boy support. Two times in a month. It's a miracle."

"Put the runt platoon under Vukovic. You're the lead element," Richter said.

"Roger. Moving." Briem nodded and left.

Richter cupped his helmet, both hands shaking as he slipped it over his head, and snapped it into place. His HUD fizzled and came in cloudy. He wasn't sure if his eyesight was off or if the unit had been that badly damaged, but when he fiddled with the settings, it became clear enough to read.

"Paladin, what's your status?" Colonel Toman asked through the radio band.

"Good to go," Richter said as graphics for the next phase of the operation played out over his HUD. Advance online and mark enemy strongpoints for destruction by air assets. Nothing too complicated.

His troop, what was left of it, filled up a hasty trench line dug out by engineer robots several blocks away from the strongpoint they'd abandoned at the school. Richter went down a set of wide steps made for jacks, his metal-shod feet squishing against mud-soaked sandbags making up the ground.

"I know you took some hits—to you and your command. Stay in the fight, Richter. The Hegemony rewards the faithful," Toman said.

"Heard. Paladin troop set and ready for the attack," Richter said, and the transmission ended.

Richter went to the nearest jack and put a hand on the man's shoulder. He went down the line, looking each man in the eye.

"Arben, how many did you kill out there?" he asked a flanker.

"Only three or four, sir," the trooper said, "I'll get more."

"Savon, your battery pack's leaking." He rapped his knuckles against the back of a Cataphract where fluid dribbled out of the seams of his ballistics plates, bubbling.

"Ah hell, Winnie! Hot swap!" Savon gave a nod to his commander.

First Sergeant Molenaar slapped a fresh magazine into his carbine and jumped up and down slightly, testing the rig on his flak armor.

"I'm going with, sir," he said. "Problem?"

"None, so long as you can keep up, old man," Richter said.

Molenaar spat *khat* juice, then plugged the wad from his jawline and flicked it away.

"See you on the high ground, sir," Molenaar grunted.

"Steel forward," Richter said, taking a deep breath, the smell of unwashed bodies and gun oil strong in the trench. A thin red haze still hung in the air, a pall over the battlefield.

A face crossed his mind. Teo Alcazar. Was he still alive? Still out there? Given the hurt the Alliance just put on his troop, he wouldn't be surprised if the Marine captain was responsible. Still there . . .

A warmth grew in his heart, an aggressive urge that pulled his mouth open to bare teeth. He ran a hand across his face, the pull to battle feeling stronger with each breath.

Soon. He could shed more Alliance blood soon. Balance the scales for Szabo, Nemec . . . all the rest.

"Paladins," Richter said, hefting his cycler's muzzle to the sky, "what is the spirit of steel?"

"Kill! Kill without mercy!" his men intoned.

"Paladins, what makes the green grass grow?"

"Blood! Blood! Bright-red blood!"

His Cataphracts beat fists against their plates, faster and faster as the flankers fixed bayonets to their carbines.

"The only good pattie is a dead pattie." Richter punched his cycler up and down. "I only want good patties left as we clear this city of their filth. That understood, Paladins?"

Men cheered and tugged at their beards for luck.

Overhead, Hornet gunships dived out of the cloud cover and came to a stop in midair, several hundred meters over the trench line. Rockets fanned out from pods, filling the sky with black lines of smoke as explosions rippled through the city.

"Follow me!" Richter pulled himself out of the trench and ran into the city, his men charging with a battle cry that drowned out the rocket strikes.

The bombardment went down in waves, blasting out a swath of the urban terrain before them, then marching forward a few more blocks to decimate what little of the city remained.

A high-rise hotel buckled at its base and collapsed on itself, the rumble sending quakes through the earth as a fresh cloud of pulverized concrete and glass mushroomed through surrounding blocks.

Richter set the pace as his men fanned out over three blocks, Cataphracts at the fore, moving steady with their cyclers leveled and ready. Flankers bounded from cover to cover, watching for snipers.

The major didn't even look at the school where he'd lost so many good troopers. He kept his gaze forward as the last of the airborne rockets struck home. The Hornet gunships turned on a dime and flew south.

"That what I think it is?" Briem jerked his chin up and to the right. A slow-moving cargo drone with a long cylinder carried in its pinchers drifted ahead of them.

"Lock down, lock down," Richter sent over the radio. He set his jack's system to minimal computer assist and severed his antenna connections. The drone exploded into an expanding blue ring as an EMP pulse rolled through the sky. Richter felt static electricity through his beard and St. Elmo's fire crept up his legs.

The EMP distortion would last for hours, crippling any Alliance drones and degrading their communication systems.

The Hegemony would suffer the same disadvantages, but it didn't slow Richter.

Short bursts from cyclers to his right drew him over and into a blasted warehouse where the roof had collapsed and flames danced around rocket impact craters. He kicked down a metal door and swept his cycler across, stopping on a group of Marine bodies.

He kicked one in the flank to make sure he was dead, and then he stopped. There in the pile were two of his flankers—Mishrak and Donal. One's uniform was soaked through with blood, his throat slit. The other had an Alliance pressure bandage over a leg wound, a pistol gripped in a dead hand.

The Marines had all been shot, though two had been treated by a medic from the look of the dressings over both the stump of a lost hand and a long gash across one abdomen. Richter rolled one of the Marines over with the toe of his boot. A corpsman.

Richter took dog tags off his men, hesitating as he tried to piece together what had happened. Had they been taken prisoner and tried to kill their way to freedom? Had they both been injured and the Marines tried to render first aid . . . and then?

No matter what it was, they were all dead. Joined together in their last moments of fear and pain.

The ghost . . . he'd offered him the bullet or the cold. That man's final moments had been with those that hated him, those eager to see him die. How had his men passed?

Richter shook his head and turned away. Not the time. Not the place.

He moved back to the leading edge of his company's advance, their pace growing slower as they went deeper into enemy territory. Fires crackled in the distance, the grumble of failing walls adding to the low symphony of destruction.

"It's quiet," a Cataphract muttered. "Too quiet."

"Shut your mouth, Hendricks," Briem said. "Stay frosty."

A shot rang out and Hendricks' legs buckled. His jack slumped backwards, his legs pinned in a way that would pain a living man.

"Open fire!" Richter's cycler churned out rounds and he broke a line out of a nearby building and perforated a car. A Marine dropped out of a side window, and Richter hit him before he could escape around a corner.

"Overwatch," Richter said, running into the building and to a window close to where the Marine had fallen against the outer wall. He punched through the glass, reached down, grabbed the wounded man by the belt, and threw him to the floor.

The Marine still had his 51 clutched in his hands. Richter stomped on it, crushing the breach and a pair of fingers in the process. The Marine stared up and a gout of blood came up with a wet cough.

One lung was shot through, and a wound to his inner thigh oozed bright-red blood with each fading heartbeat. The man was dying and no field medic could change that.

"Alcazar." Richter grabbed the Marine by the collar and shook him. "Mateo Alcazar. He alive? Where is he?"

The Marine's head lolled to one side and a wet gurgle escaped his lips. Richter turned the man to one side to see a stamp with a K above a 2/6 on his shoulder. Alcazar's unit.

He was close. So close now.

"Got eyes on an enemy strongpoint," Briem said over the IR. *"Either consolidating after the bombardment or they're massing for a counterattack."*

Richter tried a squadron channel to call in an air strike but got nothing but static. There were no mortars. No artillery available. All he and his troop had were the things they carried and their fighting spirit.

"Form a firing line and get flankers in overwatch, moving to your location," Richter said into the IR and stepped through a set of large doors.

A bust of rifle fire exploded the wall around his head. He ducked behind the paldron on one arm and let loose with his cycler, letting the recoil lift the muzzle and fan fire across the lobby of the building. Two Marines went down.

Richter's foot caught on the doorjamb, and he jerked his leg forward, almost stumbling into the large reception desk.

On the other side of the desk, an Alliance Marine was halfway up a metal staircase, limping on a bloody leg and wheezing with each breath. He fumbled and dropped his rifle. It clattered down the steps and skidded to a halt at Richter's feet. The Marine looked back, one bloody hand over a bandage pressed to his chest.

Richter aimed his cycler and hesitated. The Marine slipped back and sat down hard at the top of the stairs, his eyes swimming and mouth struggling to form words.

Richter kicked the rifle into debris against the wall and made his way toward the Marine.

"Your buddy tried to draw us away from you," he said. "Didn't get far. You're not going to last much longer, are you?"

The Marine coughed and started teetering.

Richter reached him just as he pitched forward. He caught him by the collar and hauled him back to look the Marine in the half-open eyes. The wounded man's breathing was quick and shallow.

Is this how Szabo died? His final moments spent with the enemy so close? Blood seeped out through the dressing as the Marine's hold on it slipped. Richter put his own hand over the Marine's, feeling the warmth of the man's life force seeping onto his skin.

The Marine grabbed Richter's arm and rested his head against the thin armor plate over Richter's forearm. A weak sob escaped from the dying man.

Richter pulled back slightly, and an almost alien emotion brushed past his heart.

Sympathy.

Here was an enemy that just tried to shoot him down, and Richter felt sorrow as the man's final moments played out. He was just another man, fallen in war. Like Szabo. Like too many others.

"I'm sorry," Richter lifted the man's face up, and the moment of empathy passed, replaced by the cold comfort of hate. "I'm sorry . . . but I need you to stay alive just a little bit longer." He moved his hand around to grab the Marine by collar. Richter dragged him to the next floor and to an open office door.

The Marine struggled, but could barely manage to kick his heels against the floor.

"Flankers have eyes on the enemy," Lieutenant Briem's voice came through the IR comms. *"Major, fall back to the rest of—"*

"Negative," Richter said. "They're coming for this building. Prep a hasty attack. I'll tell you when to execute. Hammer and anvil. Tell your troopers to save the pattie officers for me."

Chapter 49

Marines

"*This is it*," Teo passed to Popovitch, Wooster, and Fuentes as the crab gunships opened up, rockets slammed into already broken and burning buildings to his company's rear. "They're trying to soften us up for a counterattack. You know what to do, so let's crush them."

At least his QC was working again. For how long, he wouldn't hazard a guess. And he didn't have comms with each unit. With Trace gone, Staff Sergeant Weiss had taken over Third Platoon, but he didn't have a QC. And there had been nothing from the XO over the last seven minutes.

Teo didn't think there were crabs at his Bravo Command's last position, but he couldn't be sure of that. If the crabs were flanking him . . . well, that would suck big time. More likely, the Bravo Command had eaten a mortar round.

A finger of white smoke reached out from the next block as a Dragon lanced up, hitting the far-right VTOL. The bird didn't explode in a satisfying burst of fire, but it wheeled away, trailing much darker smoke.

Most of the VTOL rounds were hitting behind the Marines, which said to Teo that the crabs weren't sure of their positions and didn't realize how far and fast the Marines had pushed forward.

Not that he was a hundred percent sure of his positions either. He pulled up the battle map and tried to envision exactly where his Marines were. After clearing the school, Second Platoon had continued to push forward. Popovitch had somehow lost only five Marines taking the school, which was almost unbelievable. A fire team was missing after going into a warehouse, but with comms gone, they could still be fine. The platoon's mission was to advance until they met the lead crab element, then fix them in place with fire.

First Platoon was down nine Marines, still a potent force. Along with the other remaining Badger, Fuentes had maneuvered along the eastern edge of the city and pivoted. They were now poised to be the hammer on Second Platoon's anvil, running up the crabs' flank and crushing them, while Weapons did the same from the western side. It was a simple plan that didn't need comms to work . . . as long as the crabs advanced as expected, as long as the Marines remembered the control measures and kept from killing each other with friendly fire, as long as more crab units didn't come in to reinforce Richter's troop, as long as . . .

There were too many "as long as's." A thousand things could go wrong, but just as many could go right. Who would have thought that the boot louie, Sam Popovitch, would have saved the day at the school?

An avatar flickered on his display in the middle of a building two blocks ahead, about where Second Platoon should be setting in to meet the expected crab attack. The icon was intermittent, and it never resolved into a specific Marine, and all of that gnawed at him, a tickle of worry through the adrenaline dump of combat.

Had he lost someone there? Was a Marine in there dying, praying for his brothers to come and help him before it was too late?

"*Sam, do you have anyone in two-two-four, the bank?*" he asked his Second Platoon commander.

"*There could be a fire team refusing the flank there, Skipper. Corporal Ishtar. But that's his call on whether to go inside or not.*"

Teo was about to snap back asking why the hell he didn't know when he remembered that only the QCs worked. Popovitch would be as blind as he was.

"I'm with what's left of Third now, moving forward. I'll find out," he passed.

"You saw that, too?" the first sergeant passed.

So, it wasn't just me.

"What do you think?" Teo asked.

"Probably just a blip. The entire system's fucked up."

"Yeah, maybe."

But Teo wasn't sure. The avatar had flashed light blue, for a WIA. Had the Marine's battle system managed to break through for just a second?

The plan for the hasty defense against the crab attack was already motion, but now there was a problem. A persistent itch against what he knew was the right tactical choice and his duty as an officer of Marines. He couldn't leave a wounded man out there. It wasn't his job to go off to try and find a potential wounded Marine, but if he was going into the building anyway...

He stuck his head out of the destroyed door and shouted at the Marine on his belly at the front of the building. "Get me Staff Sergeant Weiss."

The Marine scrambled to his feet and said, "Roger, that, Skip!"

"Uribe, is that you?"

The Marine turned and flipped up his visor. "Sure is."

"Shit, still alive, I see."

"And planning to stay that way," he yelled as he dashed off.

It hadn't been a given. There were only eleven of the platoon still left in the fight, and two of them were walking wounded. Teo had tried to block off the loss of life so far, but the knowledge of the dead hovered around his consciousness, trying to catch his attention. Teo cared about all of his Marines, but still, he was relieved to see that Uribe was still around.

"Sir?" the staff sergeant asked, sticking his head in the door, then diving to join Teo on the deck as something exploded above them. Pieces of ceiling fell on them, and dust filled the air.

Teo waited a moment, then raised himself onto his elbows. Weiss raised his dust-covered helmet as well and gave him a thumbs-up. Teo didn't know what had hit them, and frankly, he didn't care. They'd all had enough close calls during the battle that all that mattered was they were still in the fight.

The building didn't look like it was going to collapse, and Teo stood up. He had to advance forward, first to hook up with Second Platoon, and second, there was that nagging flicker on his helmet display. If that was a wounded Marine, he had to find out.

"We're moving ahead to link up with Second. There may be friendlies in the building, maybe wounded, so heads up. Get your platoon up and guide on me."

It seemed odd to call eleven Marines a platoon, but he'd been in that position twice before, so it was nothing new.

Teo stepped out of the building, and to the north, the remaining VTOLs were all turning away, their ordnance spent.

One less thing to worry about.

Around him, Marines formed up in a modified squad wedge, one four-man team already forward and across the street, the other two teams back flanking him. Teo was just about to motion the lead team forward when the sky flashed with an almost invisible blue, and if Teo's hair had stood on end before, this time, it jumped to a position of attention, and his molars ached, if that was even possible. He checked if that ghost ping was still there, but his display had gone transparent.

"Razor? Sam? Can you read me? Harris?"

Silence.

"*Wainsett*," he tried again, but he hadn't had comms with him for twenty minutes.

The crabs had deployed one of their big EMP drones; that was obvious. But that shouldn't have any effect on the QMs. Completely different physics, almost in the supernatural range.

He stepped away from the building, out in the open, trying to get a connection. He slammed the side of his helmet several times, trying to force the comms to work.

"*Any station this net, can you read me?*" he asked.

Nothing. Teo didn't know how the crabs did it, but he was cut off.

"Skipper!" Adoud shouted.

Teo looked over, saw him motioning him down, then realized what he was doing. Huge rookie mistake, losing tactical clarity. He'd been fixating on comms, and in doing so, he'd wandered out into the open.

He rushed back to a more protected position and flopped onto his belly. Had anyone spotted him? He felt exposed, as if he was walking into a trap.

Get your head on straight, Mateo!

He shook off his apprehension. On either side of him, Third Platoon Marines were lifting their visors. Teo wanted to tell them to keep them down—the visors provided some degree of protection—but then he thought screw it. He could feel his IFU shutting down, and each one only carried twenty minutes of emergency air. Besides, an unpowered visor didn't give the same immediacy as naked eyes did. Teo unsealed his and flipped it up as well, then gave his hand-and-arm signal and direction for the lead team to step off.

Moving in an unpowered IFU took a bit more effort. The tiny joint assists were evidently fried. At least the armor in the POL was reactive and didn't require power.

Heavy firing sounded from ahead and to his left. Second was in contact, sooner than Teo had expected. There was no way Third was close enough to launch their assault.

"Adoud!" Teo yelled, giving him the arm pump for double time. The corporal nodded and broke out into a trot. Together, the eleven Marines, covering a city block, surged forward.

Something big whooshed over their heads, but whatever it was, it kept going to detonate somewhere to the south. It wasn't hitting them, so the Marines ignored it.

Bounding through the rubble of a leveled building, Teo started panting. He was heating up, and sweat dripped into his eyes. The damned cooling system was out, the cooling fluid—which didn't need power—was not circulating.

Teo was damned if the Marines and he were going to get knocked out by heatstroke. He called out to Adoud again to slow it down just a notch or two. The corporal turned to acknowledge when the tot-tot-tot of a crab cycler opened up, and his pelvis disappeared in a pink mist, the top of his body, a surprised look frozen on his face, toppling over to the ground. The other two Marines were scythed down before they could move.

Teo fell to the ground an instant before the stream of fire reached him, the snap of the big 8mm rounds hurting his ears. All around him, rubble was being reduced into smaller bits of cerrocrete as the crab raked them.

Marines were firing back, but the cycler fire kept up. As the stream of fire passed over Teo, he popped up to spot the crab . . . but it was two, both jacked and standing shoulder to shoulder in the intact doorway in the next block like old-time gunfighters.

Stupid assholes. Thinking those cyclers would keep them safe.

But those "stupid assholes" had killed at least three of his Marines.

Teo still had his grenade mod attached from the fight at the school. There was a tiny pause in the incoming, and Teo popped up again, acquiring, sighting in, and firing in less than a second-and-a-half. It wasn't until he ducked back down that he realized what he had seen: one crab had dropped his cycler and was staggering back. At least some of his Marines had hit flesh.

It didn't really register before his grenade hit an instant later. Teo chambered his last grenade and popped up again, but withheld his fire. His target had taken a direct hit, and was now a smoking pile of twisted jack. The second crab was on his back, half inside the building.

Four Marines rushed past Teo, weapons trained on the two crabs. They barely paused at Teo's target. One Marine stood on the second one's cycler, another pulled the crab's emergency release before putting three rounds into the cavity that opened.

"Inside!" Teo yelled when they looked back. "Clear it!"

Teo couldn't pull up his map, but if he remembered correctly, this building, which covered a full block, was on line where Second was setting in. The flurry of firing to his left was a pretty good indication that he was right.

"Check them," he shouted at Weiss and the other two Marines, pointing at Adoud's team. Adoud was gone, but the other three could still be alive.

Teo ran over the rubble, across the street, and into the door, hopping over the dead crabs. Four Marines—one of them was Uribe, he could see now—were busy clearing the lobby of what looked to be a bank. Something had detonated inside, blowing apart desks and customer interview offices, but the room was basically sound.

Teo moved to the front, looking out the large window. It had pockmarks, but it was still in place. Made sense for a bank window. But he couldn't see much. No wounded Marine calling out for help on the ground floor, but it was a big building, with many floors. He had to get higher.

Staff Sergeant Weiss came in the back. He caught Teo's eyes and shook his head.

Teo had been gut-punched too many times today with losses, and his emotions were numb. He'd mourn later, but he couldn't afford to do it now.

"Send a runner to try and connect with Second Platoon," he said a moment before the building shook with a blast, the big front window rattling with hits.

Teo looked out, and the next building was collapsing in on itself while smoke and dust rolled toward him until his vision was blocked.

Staff Sergeant Weiss hesitated, and Teo said, "Now! Use the smoke as screening."

"Uribe! You heard him. Go!" the staff sergeant said.

"Catch you all on the rebound!" Uribe said as he bolted out the back.

"Secure this floor. I'm going to try and get higher," Teo told Weiss.

"Just this place or the rest of the building too?"

Teo had assumed the bank took up the entire building, but looking around, he realized it took up half, maybe less of the ground floor. The upper floors could even be other businesses.

Weiss had five other Marines, not enough to secure an entire block. Their job was to face the oncoming crabs, not go off chasing a ghost avatar. He needed them right here. But he needed to get a better picture of the area, and if that meant finding a wounded Marine at the same time, then all the better.

"No. Just here on this deck. I'm going to get a little higher and try and see what's going on. Wait until I get back down."

"Hikok, go with the skipper—" Weiss started before Teo cut him off.

"I'm fine. Just make sure no one who isn't a Marine comes in."

The side of the bank lobby opened up to a central security or information desk and the main entrance. Signs alongside the desk looked like it once was a directory of floors, six of them. Someone had taken out their rage on it, emptying a clip at it, from the looks of it, and destroying the electrostatic field that held up the letters—which were now in a scattered pile on the deck. Beyond the desk, opposite of the bank, was the main building lobby with the remnants of a coffee stand, some couches, and restrooms in the back corner.

A tall statue of an Ayutthayan goddess carved in faux-ivory with slight curves beneath silk robes stood perched between two clear elevator shafts. The statue was cracked, the remnants of a bouquet held in the right hand, left hand across the waist with the palm up. Her face looked down over the main lobby, a serene expression on the face. The desiccated remnants of devotional flowers and dead candles crowded around the plinth. At almost five meters tall, it dominated the open space between the upper floors. The Goddess of Mercy, he recognized from his pre-deployment Ayutthayan cultural appreciation lectures.

Rather ironic, here in the middle of a war zone. No mercy here that I can see.

It was only then that he spotted what looked to be some bodies beyond the statue. Teo brought his 51 up and shifted his position to get a better view, but it was obvious that they were crabs, and they were dead. He slowly scanned the 40-meter length of the lobby considered going to check them out, but he didn't see a Marine body there, and going a floor up would give him not only the high ground, but better lines of sight.

Behind and to the right of the information desk were three air lifts. Without power, the air wouldn't be running. Teo stuck his head inside the ornamental barrier, but there was no way for him to climb it.

I guess I take the stairs.

The door to the emergency stairs was half-open, and Teo slipped inside. For all the high-tech, tourist-oriented air lifts, the stairs were basic metal. He stepped to the bottom stair and raised his Wilder. He slowed his breathing as his heartbeat thundered in his ears, watching and listening for a hint that any crabs were waiting on the upper levels. Stairwells were not the place for a firefight for anyone who wanted to see tomorrow. Carefully, he crept up, attention laser-focused forward. Each step sounded too loud as his feet hit, even with the rumble of the battle outside.

Drying blood spotted the steps. Someone had come up here while they were freshly wounded. Crab or Marine? His heart beat faster realizing that he might be closing in on whatever, or whoever, set off the avatar display.

He still wasn't sure why that single flicker weighed on him so much. Kilo had lost at least sixty Marines so far this morning, probably more, and his job wasn't to track down individuals.

Maybe it was a culmination of the losses finally breaking through the command wall he'd tried to erect. Maybe he just couldn't ignore the death and destruction of the men who counted on him anymore.

The bottom floor was double-height, and by the time Teo reached the top, he was dripping with sweat.

Screw this.

With a quick twist, he detached his helmet, dropping it on the ground, and unsealed the first ten centimeters of the POL, exposing his neck. He grabbed the edges of the seal and pulled out, fanning them to get air inside. It didn't do much, but anything was better than nothing.

He bent to pick up his helmet but then hesitated. His CCD was dead, but the helmet shell still offered some ballistic protection. Teo hated wearing it, however. He always had. It made him feel somewhat detached, which was not a good state to be in combat.

He left it on the ground and looked around. There was no more blood on the floor, which was surprising. At the moment, he was above the security desk. To his right, he could see through a plastiglass wall down and into the bank lobby. Staff Sergeant Weiss was gesturing to someone just out of his sight. To his left, the building lobby below was open, and on this floor, an open hallway stretched along its length with a handful of doors. Behind him, a more typical, enclosed hallway stretched, small plaques indicating offices.

Teo had a little better view from this floor, but he couldn't see any sign of First Platoon coming in from the east yet. Another explosion rocked the building, making the plastiglass shake in its frame like a tympanic membrane. Two blocks away to the west, flames licked out of another half-destroyed building.

How close are we to Second?

Teo started down the open hallway above the building lobby. The plastiglass making up the far wall stretched up another two floors, and that should give him some pretty good observation.

He started down the hallway, the open lobby and goddess statue over the rail on his right side, a lawyer's office suite, the door slightly ajar, then a couple of generic offices on his left. The smell of death, of blood and bodily fluids filled the air. As he reached midway down the open hallway, he leaned over to look at the crab bodies.

There were three of them. One was sitting up against the far window, head slumped to his chest, stained red bandages covering his neck. Two more crabs were crumpled next to the blasted remnants of some potted plants. The window was pockmarked, and the overturned coffee stand and surrounding walls were perforated by small arms fire . . .

Hell!

It wasn't just the three crabs. Two . . . no, three Marines, were scattered between the coffee stand and one of the shredded couches. One was on his back, eyes open as if confused.

"Corporal Ishtar!" Teo shouted, hoping against hope that the NCO was still alive. "Are you with me?"

The dull eyes never flicked, and from the massive wound in his pelvis, they never would.

Teo thought he'd heard something, and he spun around, his 51 seeking a target. But the lobby was as silent as death.

Stupid for me to yell out like that. What a rookie mistake.

Teo tried to picture what happened. Second Platoon might have engaged the crabs as they ducked inside for cover . . . or the crabs had come after Corporal Ishtar's team, and there had been a fight here. But Ishtar would have had three more Marines, unless one of them had already been killed.

That meant, there could be another Marine, someone wounded, but trying to seek cover until the rest of the company arrived.

Or there could be crabs here, in the building.

Stop overanalyzing and focus. If the crabs got this far, who knows what surprises they might've left behind.

He glanced at the Bennie band on his wrist and took some comfort in the protection.

Teo leaned over and looked back through the double glass walls into the bank. He couldn't see Weiss, and for a moment, he thought about going back and getting what was left of the platoon to clear the rest of the building. But even with them, the building was too big. No, they were better left in the more defensible bank. He'd do a quick check, then join them.

Teo continued on, slowing down as he neared the windows. The wall of plastiglass might be strong, and it might still be basically intact, but it couldn't stand up to a direct hit of anything heavy, and Teo wouldn't want to be there when it was hit and transformed into thousands of shards of sharp knives that would flay him to the bone.

Teo reached the end and looked down. Across the street, he spotted Uribe talking with Corporal Winchester in the wreck of a building. Somehow, without a working CCD and going from memory, Teo had managed to slide into position right alongside Second's flank.

It looked like Second had to fight its way into position, which made sense with the six bodies below him. And outside, across the street, another crab flanker lay face-first not five meters from the two Marines, a deep red pool staining the ground beneath the body.

As he watched, fire opened up, and Winchester spun and went down. Uribe grabbed him by the dead-man's strap and dragged the corporal to the side while the other Marines in the team returned fire.

Teo put his hands up on the window, trying to figure out where the rounds were coming from, before he realized how exposed he was, standing in front of what was essentially a five-story-tall picture window. He backed up a couple of steps, weighing his options, trying to figure out where he could best fight the battle.

He had no comms. He was out of touch.

"They didn't have comms two thousand years ago, Mateo. And you can still fight!" he said aloud. And it was true. He had his 51 and his Wilder. He knew how to kill.

He turned around to rejoin Staff Sergeant Weiss and had taken half a dozen steps when a muffled voice cried out, "Fucking crabs! Die!" followed by the sounds of a 51 firing.

Teo froze. The shouts were from close by, as in inside the building.

Another burst of fire, just down the hallway, and more screaming.

Uribe hadn't hooked up with Second's flank. There were more Marines in the building.

The lawyers' suite, the door slightly opened, caught his eye, and Teo broke into a dash. There was another burst of 51 fire as Teo stopped outside the door.

"Marines! Coming in left!"

He ducked low and dashed into the receptionist's outer office. On the deck was a Marine, face down. Teo cursed himself for not switching the 51 module back to darts, and he pulled out his Wilder again, freezing and listening for any sign of crabs. On complete alert he sidled up to the Marine and reached with one hand to feel for a pulse.

And he frowned. The Marine was already cooling to the touch. He risked a quick look down. Something was wrong, very wrong. He turned the body over. It was PFC Lazaro, from Ishtar's fire team. Lazaro's chest was sticky with blood, but there was no splatter, no pooling. Just one small smear of dark-brown blood on the receptionist's desk, as if the body had been dumped here after he had been killed.

And no 51.

Who the hell fired? he wondered as he stood up, his instincts, trained by too many battles, screaming for attention. He stepped to the side of the door overlooking the foyer, keeping his exposure to a minimum.

As he tried to spot movement, a section of the wall to his left shattered, splinters flying, and a jacked foot appeared, then was drawn back. Another kick, and most of the wall was destroyed, a cycler emerging as the crab fought through.

Teo snapped off a shot with his Wilder as he started to retreat, the round ricocheting off the side of the jack's breast plate.

The crab clutched at his side where Teo'd hit him, then looked up at the Marine. The optics line on the half-helmet flashed red like a demon's eye.

"Alcazar," a smile spread across Richter's mouth. "I'm glad you could make it. I knew that beacon would draw you out."

Teo reacted, more on muscle memory than anything else. He spun back and darted through the door again. With one final kick, Richter was through the wall.

Humans were humans, even the crabs, and Teo bet his life on Richter's reactions. Armed soldiers expected others to run from them, and even if being charged, they fired high, aiming for the head and torso.

Teo wasn't running, and as Richter brought his cycler to bear, Teo went down low, using his left hand and legs to propel him forward as he drew his tecpatl with his right. He covered the intervening distance just as Richter fired high, just as Teo had predicted . . . but not high enough. One round clipped the side of his head, and fire exploded in his left ear. He didn't care, he was so focused.

Teo got under the outstretched weapon, and with one slice, severed the trigger feed to the cycler. The stream of rounds cut off. Teo bent his elbow, trying to redirect his blade to puncture the seal where helmet met collar, but the blade tip hit higher than he expected and skittered up the side of Richter's protected face. The tip caught against the optic line. Teo pressed home, and the visor cracked but didn't buckle. Richter twisted his head to one side, and momentum carried Teo into the major as his blade twisted free.

With an inarticulate roar, Richter swung around, flinging Teo to the side, near the broken wall. He leveled the cycler and tried to fire, not realizing it was inoperable. Teo gathered his feet under him again and lunged forward, blade ready to cut. But while the cycler couldn't fire, it was still a heavy hunk of metal. Using the full power of his jack, Richter swung it like a war club. It would smash Teo's skull like a grape if it landed.

Teo managed to dodge, but not far enough. The cycler grazed his back, feeling like a mule kick, and knocked him face-first onto the ground. He struggled to get to his feet, knowing the next blow was coming, but swinging the cycler around had knocked Richter off balance.

He stumbled near the entrance, putting one hand up the doorsill to steady himself.

With his tecpatl in one hand, he drew his Wilder and double-tapped two rounds as he got back up and charged, launching himself feet first and hitting Richter in the helmet.

In his jack, Richter far out-massed the smaller Marine, but he'd hit with enough force to stagger the crab backward, sending him up against the low wall that served as a rail over the lobby below.

Richter caught his balance, turned to Teo, and said, "Come on!"

Teo fired his Wilder again and charged. Richter reacted, raising the big plate on his non-augmented arm, watching Teo over the top of the plate. But Teo didn't go high. Like a rugger second row, he lowered his center of gravity, got up under the upraised arm, and pushed.

Richter's legs were against the low wall, and they had nowhere to go. He toppled over, but not before he was able to grab Teo and pull him over too.

Teo struggled to kip around and get his feet under him, but the two hit the side of the Goddess of Mercy statue as they fell, and that spun him around. He hit hard and almost lost consciousness. His body armor stiffening up was the only thing that saved him.

He landed hard, gasping for air and struggling to catch his wits, hoping against hope that the fall had killed the crab commander. The statue had shattered into a fog of choking dust. He turned his head, and there were his Marines.

Ishtar lay five meters away, his dulled eyes still staring up, looking for answers that were not there. He knew the name behind each and every pair of dead eyes. Ishtar, Hwang, Reslin. Lazaro up stairs. Still-fresh blood mingled with the dust from the desecrated Goddess of Mercy, giving the tang of copper to each breath he still drew.

The dust settled over dead Marines and troopers alike, and for a moment he was back at the mass grave where he'd found Gauta . . . but this time there'd be no truce with the crab.

Richter's legs just a couple meters away, pieces of broken sculpture all around him.

"We're not done." Teo spat out thick spit, tinged with blood that could have come from him, could have come from his slain Marines.

Teo had somehow managed to keep hold of his blade, and he pushed himself forward on hands and knees to give the stunned Richter his coup de grâce, but as he pulled on the helmet, there was no resistance. The jack was empty.

Still stunned, Teo looked at the jack stupidly. There was a swish, and Teo barely had time to react. The blow hit him over the back where his armor could protect him and not the head, but still, he was slammed back to the deck. He rolled away just at the next blow hit, gouging a hole in the expensive stone floor.

Richter was out of the jack, a meter-long hunk of the goddess in his hand, and he was in a rage. Fire burned behind his eyes, and his shoulders heaved with each breath. One side of his beard was matted with blood and dust, an open gash up one side of his face.

Teo scrambled back on his hands and knees, trying to get out of the crab's reach, absorbing too many blows. Without his armor, he'd have been beaten to death. Even so, he was taking a pounding.

"I've had enough of you!" Richter shouted at the top of his lungs.

The crab slammed the improvised club against Teo's side, and pain almost overcame him.

"That's for Szabo." Richter struck across Teo's back, and the Marine went face down into the dust. He tried to get up, drops of blood falling on the floor, splattering over fragments of the Goddess of Mercy.

Richter tossed aside the shards of his disintegrating club.

"Your ghost died with more dignity," Richter said.

Teo twisted and scrambled forward to give himself a little space, and he spotted the Wilder just a few meters away where it had bounced after the fall. But he needed time, even if for an instant. He heard a snap of pieces of statue being crushed, and he kicked out, hitting the trooper in the ankle and knocking Richter's feet out from under him.

Teo lurched forward but came short of reaching his Wilder when Richter grabbed him by the ankle. Reacting on instinct, Teo spun around and threw his tecpatl at him.

The blade was never designed for throwing, hitting Richter in the chest with a flat blade, but it had accomplished what Teo had wanted. Richter flinched and lost his grip on Teo's ankle.

It was enough.

Teo dived for his Wilder, bringing it up in one smooth motion. Richter had picked up Teo's tecpatl, still intent on finishing him. Teo pulled the trigger twice, but there was only one round left in the mag. It was enough. The heavy slug hit Richter in the gut, carrying through to shoot out his back.

Richter huffed and looked down in surprise. Teo's blade fell from his hands to clatter onto the floor, and as if deflating, his legs collapsed under him until he was sitting. He looked up at Teo, then back at his gut, reaching with one hand to touch it. As if opening a floodgate, bright blood spread out over his belly.

413

It was a liver shot, severing the celiac artery. Richter was a dead man.

But he wasn't dead yet. One hand pressed to his gut, he drew his sidearm with the other and pointed it at Teo. The barrel was surprisingly steady, and Teo stared at it in almost fascination for a moment.

Is this how it ends? With both of us dead? Fitting.

Teo took a step forward, turning his chest to Richter, as if presenting himself. He tossed the empty Wilder aside as a surprising sense of calm flooded through him. He'd been through too much in his career, seen too much death. Most of Kilo was gone, he knew, and maybe it was time for him to join them. Maybe it was time to end the pain.

Richter hacked, blood spat out of his nose and mouth, and the pistol wavered ever so slightly.

"What're you waiting for?" Teo asked, raising his arms slightly, giving the major a better target.

Richter pressed his hand against the wound tighter, and blood seeped through his fingers. The major glanced around, looking at the dead men all around them.

"This . . . this what we want?" Richter asked. "I finally . . ." He groaned and looked to the side, his eyes scrunched in pain, then he snapped back at Teo. "I finally get to see you dead."

Teo's battered face couldn't hide the slight smile that appeared, as he waited for the shot that would end him. Richter's browed furrowed, but Teo didn't know if that was from the pain or in surprise at his smile.

"I can't stop you from killing me," Teo said. "I can't stop you from dying, either."

Richter seemed to consider that. "Then we both . . . ahh . . . both end up in the same grave, won't we? Besides…besides all our dead. Look around…we're already there."

The building shook as artillery landed nearby. Cycler and 51 shots echoed through the city. Comms warbled from Richter's empty jack.

Teo considered what Richter had just said. Suddenly, he didn't want to die. He could charge Richter, but he'd be dead meat. He took a quick glance around. Outside, he could see Uribe and Lance Corporal Tines pointing at him, then starting to run around the building. In the bank, Weiss might have heard the firing and could be reacting. And for what? So more could die?

"We would." Teo nodded. "And maybe that's fitting. But if you do it, then that's the last of us. No one will tell our men to stop fighting. The killing will go on and on. That's the price we'll pay to die together. Is that what you want?"

"Lost too many," Richter said.

"Same here. Too many." He paused a moment, then asked, "Did you recognize the statue here? The Goddess of Mercy?"

Richter started to say yes, and that set off a series of coughs, blood trickling out the corner of his mouth.

"I thought her being here was ironic, but maybe she was a sign. You can still kill me, but I need to do this," Teo said.

He hesitated, then raised his closed fist to Uribe and Tines, stopping them. He gave the hand-and-arm signal to cease fire, then the sign for passing the word.

"Our comms are out, but I'm stopping this, at least here, for our two companies. It isn't going to make any difference in the long run, but maybe some of our men can live to see their families again."

Richter nodded, which started him coughing again. He took a hand off his stomach and let the blood flow into a growing red apron over his thighs as he touched an earpiece.

"Paladins . . . withdraw to squadron." His words came out slurred as shock set in. "I'll hold the line. Don't wait for me. Richter out."

The major looked at his blood-soaked palm, then lowered his pistol. His face went pale, and he struggled to keep his eyes open.

"Another time. Another place . . . and maybe we could've been friends," Teo said.

"We'll never know." Richter slowly tipped over to his side. "Send me back . . . back to Eliseabeta."

He moved his face against the dust and rubble and tried to speak again, but nothing came out. Richter went limp, and his eyes faded away to stare at nothing as he died.

Chapter 50

Paladins

"I see them." Lieutenant Briem leaned back from the edge of a broken wall. Both hands gripped his cycler tight, and his jaw worked from side to side as distant fire echoed through the war-torn city.

"White flag?" Frakes touched the side of his helmet as pics from Briem spread through Paladin Troop. Those that were left.

"Yeah, they got the flag." Briem glanced at the ammo line running into his cycler. Rounds stopped halfway through, barely enough for three short bursts. "Doesn't mean they surrender, just means they want to talk."

"Squadron's going to lose their shit if they hear about this. But if we do tell them, then maybe they won't call in an artillery strike. Or some fly-boy sees us as a giant target." Farkas scratched his beard.

"You want to leave the major out there? You want his spirit on us because we left him behind? We owe it to him." Briem drew the ammo line off his cycler and slapped a magazine into the bottom. "Last mag."

"We don't know that they have him. Richter's too smart, too tough to—"

"They called us on the major's comms. They read off the serial number off his cycler. I'll go out there, so it's my ass if this is a trap. I get killed, you're troop commander. Congrats." Briem did a combat peek around the corner, then took a long, steady breath.

He swung around the wall and stood in the open, waiting a few moments for a bullet to end his life and prove he was an idiot for trusting

417

Alliance Marines. Briem walked toward a two-story building. The bottom floor used to be a restaurant, and a pale-yellow sign in several different languages dangled partially over the doors.

A Marine—holding his rifle by the barrel to one side—waved to Briem from a shattered glass wall.

Briem paused, his every instinct to open fire and keep killing. He almost had to pry his hand away from his trigger as he stepped through jagged glass at the bottom of the wall.

A round table was in the middle of the restaurant, flanked by two Marines. Major Richter was there, a black body bag zipped up to his chest.

A corpsman treated a Marine sitting on a bench against the far wall, his face battered with welts and ugly bruises.

"Thank you for coming," Captain Alcazar said, struggling through a swollen jaw. "There's your commander."

Briem went to the major and closed the eyes staring into nothing.

"I brought four men like you said over the radio," Briem said. "I'll call them up, but if this is some sort of trap, I swear we'll come down on you—"

"You haven't heard? Armistice. Cease-fire."

"What?" Briem's jaw clenched.

"Not just here. Everywhere." Alcazar winced as he stood up and limped toward Richter. "He might have been the last one to fall. Maybe if word had come just a bit sooner, who knows? We could have parted as . . . well, as brothers-in-arms."

"To hell with you," Briem said. "He wanted you dead."

"Not at the end." Alcazar shook his head. "I was there with him. He beat the hate."

Three more Cataphracts entered and the Marines backed off to form a guard around Alcazar.

"Just got a radio message," Farkas said quietly. "There's—"

"Save it." Briem gripped the corner of the body bag, then beat a hand against his chest in salute to the Marine captain.

"Is there someone…someone I can send my regards to? To let them know what happened?" Alcazar asked.

"No. You've done enough. Don't push it." Briem and the three others slid Richter off the table and carried him away.

Briem glanced over his shoulder many times until there were a few blocks between them and the Marines.

"Forgive us, sir," Briem said to Richter. "We should have been with you. Let your spirit rest."

Epilogue

Eliseabeta Richter heard a chirp from her slate in the next room. A drone buzzed past the window, and she felt a familiar sense of dread. Every delivery was another chance for the Hegemony's intelligence directorate to track her down.

She brushed dyed-black hair off her face and glanced at a drawer where she kept a snub pistol. Using a weapon from the Hegemony always struck her as ironic. Most people on a Union world like Denton used a locally manufactured firearm for home defense. But if she needed to use the weapon, that meant the Hegemony was damn sure who she was, no matter how many times she'd changed her name or her appearance since she'd fled.

Touching her fingers to a sensor on a window frame, the glass slid up. The whoosh of stacked lines of air cars roaring assaulted her. The space between nearby archology towers that disappeared in the cloud layers was always busy. It was always rush hour in this part of Denton.

Delivery drones buzzed between floors and up ant lines on the glass façade of her apartment complex, ferrying food and most anything else her neighbors ordered.

A small package was in the delivery cage. Even this high up, porch pirates using hacked drones were still a problem.

The slick plastic around the package shimmered as she picked it up. The name Genevieve Delacroix flashed at her touch and her heart skipped a beat. That wasn't the fake name she'd been using; it was the name her

Hegemony contact used.

She shut the window and sat down on her couch as she ripped open the package. Inside were three data crystals and a single thumb drive. She held up the drive and frowned at it. The device was almost archaic and rarely used. The only messages she ever got on drives like this came from her father . . . and she hadn't heard from him in years.

One crystal went into a slate and she skimmed over news headlines about the war against the Alliance. She muttered curses and popped the crystal out. The war had been over for months. Old data.

The next crystal had letters from her brother, the oldest nearly a year out-of-date from when he first arrived at a new assignment.

"Ayutthaya?" A chill went through her heart. The fighting there had been bitter and the casualty rate so high that it even made the Union news. She scanned over the dates of the letters from her brother, all sent at two-week intervals until the last one dated right around the time of the cease-fire.

But nothing after that.

She looked at the thumb drive and gnawed at her bottom lip.

"Damn it." She snapped the drive into the bottom of the slate and a letter popped up.

The Most High regret to inform you that Major Emil—

Hurling the slate into the wall, she broke down sobbing, falling to her knees in front of the couch and pounding the floor.

Her brother was gone. Taken by a Hegemony that didn't care about him, that sacrificed him on the altar of service.

Eliseabeta took a deep breath and forced her emotions down. Emil Richter was dead. The one thing that had to be protected in her life was gone. The Hegemony's corruption had sent her into exile, sidelined her father after a lifetime of loyal service . . . and now there was no reason to hide that corruption from the Hegemony or anyone else.

She went to the wall where the slate had fallen, pushed a cabinet to one side, and removed a single-use quantum phone. She pressed a thumb against the reader and an icon filled up. She steeled herself. The device had cost most of the funds she'd managed to escape with.

"Eliseabeta?" a woman's voice asked.

"I'm ready," she said. "There's no . . . I need to tell the truth about the Hegemony. I have all the evidence. Everything."

"That's . . . quite a step to take. You know there's no going back if you do this."

"I've lost . . . I lost the last thing that mattered to me. The Hegemony's taken it all. My brother's gone. Let's burn it all down. Bring me back into the rebellion. No more waiting."

"We didn't win the war against the Alliance . . . the fire's rising throughout the Hegemony. I've got a trace and I'll send a car for you. Bring everything you have." The phone snapped off and smoke hissed out from the seams.

Eliseabeta stood and picked up a framed picture sitting on top of the dresser: herself and her father and brother, the same photo Richter had in his office. She touched the glass over her brother, then smashed it against a corner. A crystal wafer fell out amongst the shards.

She picked it up and smiled.

****

"Welcome to Nouveau Niue, gentleperson. What is your destination?"

Teo slipped into the cab's seat. "Saint Damien Square, please,"

"That will be thirty-six unis, forty-three cents. Given present road conditions, we should arrive in approximately forty-three minutes. If that is acceptable, please look into the scanner."

Teo leaned forward, got scanned, and with a gentle acceleration, the cab merged into traffic.

"Would you prefer conversation during your ride?"

"Silence is fine."

"Very well. If you need anything, please voice your desires."

Teo grunted. The cab was high-end, not like the basic cabs on Safe Harbor where the AIs only communicated with a few basic sentences. If Teo closed his eyes, he could imagine that he had a human driver.

Which was to be expected. This was Nouveau Niue, after all. From the moment the shuttle landed at the spaceport, it was obvious that the planet was light-years ahead of his home planet. It was so . . . clean.

This was Teo's second trip to one of the Alliance's Prime Worlds, the eleven that founded the Alliance. The first was when he was presented with his People's Order of the Alliance, on Cakobau, but he'd been escorted everywhere at a rush, and he'd barely had time to catch his breath. Now he was content to watch out the window, taking in the sights.

"Can I see the Atu along the way?" Teo suddenly asked.

"That will add one-uni, twenty-one cents, and will add approximately five minutes to the trip."

"Do it."

The cab diverted off the highway and into a section of residential high rises, then merged on a tree-lined parkway that curved along the waterfront. They passed several marinas full of pleasure boats, a true reflection of the citizens' affluence.

Teo saw the head of the Atu first, towering over the hotels and conference center.

"Do you wish to stop?" the cab asked.

"No, just drive by."

Teo might be an Alliance citizen, but he wasn't from the Pasifiki Federation. He didn't have any cultural affinity for the people. The giant statue was a famous landmark, however, so it was just curiosity on his part.

As the cab rounded the end of the harbor, the statue came into full view, and Teo couldn't help being impressed. The giant man was over 120 meters tall, an ancient Samoan seaman, the first to leave Samoa to settle other islands. The statue gazed out over the water, as if looking for new, unknown destinations.

Teo turned to look back as the cab continued on its way. Safe Harbor had no such landmark, and that was telling. Safers were more concerned with scrabbling out a living, while Pasifikins could afford to look back and embrace their histories. That was why they were so tied up with their traditions . . . and that was why Teo was here.

He looked down at the package he was carrying and clutched it tighter.

Teo settled back into his seat as the cab merged back onto the highway. Downtown turned to the suburbs, and suburbs to countryside, and his mind started drifting, back to Ayutthaya, back to the war. As always, he started on the what-ifs. What if he hadn't let Sergeant Gauta go alone into the crab camp? What if the general hadn't been shot down? What if the mass bombardment hadn't taken place, and the civilians hadn't been evacuated?

What if he hadn't kicked off the final battle?

Teo had received an Order of the Palm, First Class for his part in the fight. It had been touch and go for him there for a while after the battle, as far as Teo had known. He could have been court-martialed—first, for kicking off the battle with a lie, if that had ever gotten out, and then second, for losing so many Marines and corpsmen. He'd gone into the fight with 168 men, both Kilo and attachments, and came out with 29 unscathed.

Another 33 were WIA. The rest were lost.

But the top brass didn't care. He'd "won" the battle . . . which was utter BS. Richter ordered his troops to withdraw to save lives in a needless war. Kilo company had just consolidated its lines to protect itself should another crab unit attack, one not under Major Richter's command, but to the Marine command, that sure looked like a win to them.

Teo had given a full account during his debrief . . . almost. He didn't tell anyone that he'd had Uribe and Xicale fake the initial "attack." But he'd been pretty thorough in the rest. Yet between the acting battalion commander, Major del Mora—Lieutenant Colonel Khan had been killed in combat fighting with India and Lima Companies—and Force, the fact that it was Richter who had ordered his troopers to stand down had been conveniently deleted from the official record.

The Marines, and the Alliance, had needed the win. Fighting had broken out all along the front, with Hegemony and Alliance forces both taking and losing ground. When all was said and done, almost nothing had changed . . . except to the loved ones of all those lost on both sides.

The need for the win was undoubtedly the reason there had been the shower of awards. Customarily parsimonious with awards, this time they were given out like candy. Lieutenant Okanjo and Lieutenant Colonel Khan were both awarded the POA posthumously. Second Lieutenant Popovitch was also awarded the Order of the Palm, First Class along with HM3 Sukiyama. Two Order of the Palms, Second Class. Six Gold Swords, twelve Silver Swords, and every other survivor a Bronze Sword at the minimum—and that was only within the company.

Teo had accepted his OP1, then slipped it into his seabag, vowing to never bring it out again.

And all for what? Four days after the battle, this branch of the bigger conflict ended. The peace treaty was signed. Within a week, the

Hegemony and Alliance forces started a staggered withdrawal, with numbers overseen by the Union observers.

The peace treaty did not extend to the Ayutthayans. They had signed on with regard to foreign forces, but no determination was made as to the initial conflict that started it all. When it was finally Third Battalion's turn to withdraw and leave the planet, a newly reformed militia appeared and took over the camp and anything that was being left behind.

Teo never even knew which side they represented.

After almost three million Ayutthayans dead, that evidently wasn't enough for them.

Teo had been the last one to get on the bird, stopping for a moment to look at the almost too-bright turquoise water gently lapping at the beach. A warm breeze kissed his face, and he could understand that with peace, this place could be a paradise.

Too bad that wasn't going to happen.

It had been a busy few months back at Camp Lesta. The battalion had lost too many Marines, and it had reverted to cadre status. Teo was bumped up to be the acting Operations Officer. Popovitch, as the only other surviving officer in the company, became the Kilo commander. It had taken him several months developing the training syllabus to bring the battalion back to combat-ready as replacements reported in, but finally, four months after leaving Ayutthaya, Teo had time to take leave and travel to Nouveau Niue.

"Gentleperson, you have arrived at your destination."

Teo started and looked around. He'd been lost in his thoughts too often lately, losing track of the here and now. Not a good habit for a combat Marine.

The door lifted, and Teo stepped out.

St. Damien was understated, as were most churches within the

Pasifiki Federation. For all their wealth, the Pasifikins evidently thought that flaunting it from a religious standpoint was not in keeping with their core beliefs.

The cab had brought him to the front of the church. It looked like it was built with lava rock, as was their tradition, but Teo knew that was only an affectation. The church might look old, but it was as modern as all the buildings he'd seen downtown. He started up the steps to announce his arrival, then stopped. He didn't need anyone, and it wasn't the inside of the church that brought him here.

Without saying a word, he turned to go around the church, to the back. An elderly man, his face wizened with age, looked up from where he was planting a row of flowers along the church wall. Teo could see the questions in the man's eyes, but he didn't voice them. Teo nodded and kept walking.

He reached the back and stopped for a moment, taking in the view. The builders had chosen the spot well. The promontory was at least a hundred meters above the ocean, and from the back of the church, there was at least a 270-degree view. Waves crashed on the rocks below, each crash creating a short-lived rainbow as the late-afternoon sun's rays hit the droplets.

Between the church and the dropoff were more than a hundred gravestones, the grass between them closely manicured, and a single flower in front of each one. Teo turned to look back at the old man, who had stopped to watch him. He gave the man a small, non-military salute. The man smiled with pride and nodded, then went back to his planting.

It didn't take him long. He found it at the end of the third row. About a meter high, the stone still had the polished shine of being new, un-weathered by the sea air.

Teo stood in front of the grave in silence. He thought he should feel an emotional surge—sadness, grief, something. But he was just empty. And that made him . . . sad. He should feel something.

Too many Marines had died, Marines who he sent into the fight. Rios. Okanjo. Wainsett. Wooster. Sanaa. Rose-Wilcox. Win. Fuentes. Seibbert. Xicale.

Cengic.

Richter.

The last two came up unbidden, and he guiltily tried to force the names from his thoughts, but then he relaxed.

Why the hell not? What did Richter say? We'll both end up in the same grave? It might take me a bit longer, but I'll be buried soon enough too.

With a sigh, Teo slowly unwrapped the package he'd carried from Camp Lesta. He stared at the object for a long moment, running his hands along its length, almost getting lost in his thoughts once more.

But he'd come here on a mission, and it was time to finish it. He stepped up to the gravestone and laid Gauta's pahoa la'au, still in its sheath, on top of it. Maybe someone would retrieve the blade and give it to Gauta's family, maybe not. Teo had brought it home, and that was all he could do.

"*Vigilamus pro te,* Sergeant."

He stood there another minute, just drinking in the view, cementing it in his mind. He knew he wasn't ever coming back, but he wanted to remember it forever.

Teo patted the blade one last time and turned to leave.

He had to get back to Camp Lest and train up the battalion. There would be more battles, that was a certainty, and it was up to him to make sure they were up to the task.

THE END

From Richard Fox

Hello, Dear and Gentle Reader,

Thank you for reading Hell's Horizon. Jon and I had a blast writing this story and bringing a tale of war that we—as veterans—wanted to tell.

A generation of fighting men and women have had a lifetime of war, and for good or for ill, we've learned lessons that we never thought were out there.

Jon and I are glad you got a glimpse at what warriors go through.

Please be so kind as to leave an honest review wherever fine books are sold.

--Richard Fox
Las Vegas, 2020

From Jonathan Brazee

Thank you for reading *Hell's Horizon*. It was a fun write with Richard, and I hope you enjoyed it. It was a different way to write a book, but I think the end result was worth the effort.

I started this book in Las Vegas where Richard still is, but as I write this, I am looking out of the window at a September snow while hummingbirds squabble over the sugar water I put out for them. It was 96 degrees two days ago. With the move and caring for my twin baby girls, that swing in temperature pretty much mirrors my life lately, and that has affected by writing output. Writing *Hell's Horizon* with Richard forced me back into my writing routine, for which I am grateful.

Now, it's time to get back to the keyboard. I've got a lot of stories to tell.

--Jonathan Brazee
Colorado Springs, 2020

CPSIA information can be obtained
at www.ICGtesting.com
Printed in the USA
BVHW040834251020
591772BV00032B/910

9 780991 442959